David Wolstencroft was born in
but now lives in Los Angeles. He is the creator of *Spooks*, the
BAFTA award-winning spy drama, produced by Kudos for BBC
ONE. *Good News, Bad News* is his first novel.

You can contact David via his website at
www.davidwolstencroft.com

'A sinuous, addictive read' *Time Out*

'With echoes of Le Carré and Graham Greene – and a hipness
all of its own – *Good News, Bad News* revitalizes the espionage
novel and dishes up a breakneck plot, dizzying twists and two
of the most memorable characters in recent suspense fiction.
This book is a pure delight!'
Jeffery Deaver, author of *Garden of Beasts*

'Sharp and funny . . . brilliant . . . exciting . . . A dazzling
performance, full of surprises, and the only doubt it leaves is
what will this most promising author ever do for an encore.'
Chicago Tribune

'An exuberant and satisfying debut' Mark Lawson, *Guardian*

'Races and twists like a rollercoaster. A brave and triumphant
reimagining of the espionage genre.' Boris Starling, author of
Messiah

David Wolstencroft

Good News, Bad News

HODDER

Copyright © 2005 by David Wolstencroft

First published in Great Britain in 2005 by Hodder and Stoughton
A division of Hodder Headline

This edition published 2005 by Hodder and Stoughton

The right of David Wolstencroft to be identified as the Author
of the Work has been asserted by him in accordance with the
Copyright, Designs and Patents Act 1988

A Hodder paperback

1 3 5 7 9 10 8 6 4 2

A CIP catalogue record for this title is
available from the British Library

ISBN 0340 83163 4

Typeset in Fairfield by Hewer Text Ltd, Edinburgh
Printed and bound by Clays Ltd, St Ives plc

Hodder Headline's policy is to use papers that are natural, renewable
and recyclable products and made from wood grown in sustainable
forests. The logging and manufacturing processes are expected to
conform to the environmental regulations of the country of origin

Hodder and Stoughton Ltd
A division of Hodder Headline
338 Euston Road
London NW1 3BH

To Mum and Dad, for everything.

Eating chocolate may be a good way to keep the heart healthy, say researchers.

A study, presented to the European Society of Cardiology suggests that polyphenols – which occur naturally in cocoa – may help to maintain cardiovascular health.

– BBC News

Most chocolate bars contain high levels of saturated fats and sugar that contribute to high cholesterol levels, obesity and coronary heart disease.

– BBC News

1

Heads, tails, heads, tails.

It was an ordinary coin. Worth ten ordinary British pence. Enough for half a phone call. Enough for a penny chew or two, a finger of fudge.

The two men watching it spin through the air knew better than this. The value of this particular monetary unit was more than anyone at the Royal Mint could have imagined. The difference between heads and tails . . . well, it was a lot.

The first man flipped the coin expertly onto his right wrist, burying it under a sweaty left hand. A passer-by, hearing the audible *click* of metal against wedding ring, shot them a glance over her glasses and was gone.

She had been to Tesco Metro, the men noticed. The bulge in the side of her carrier bag suggested she had bought a baguette. The takeaway coffee she was holding was from a different chain store altogether, however – and this led them both to deduce that she was a very picky consumer who was prepared to shop around.

The two men regarded each other for a second. Behind them, London's rush-hour ritual evolved. Buses belched past, motors churning, exhausts disgorging into the chill evening air. Commuters sighed back into stations. Collars were up and mouths blew vapour trails, the cold draining all colour from their faces.

All of them unaware of the coin.

All uninformed of its import.

All unconcerned that whatever the result, heads or tails, one of these men was going to die.

All that mattered now was *who*.

'Good luck,' said the first man.

'And you,' replied the second, who wasn't wearing a ring. But a closer look would have shown a faint scar on the finger that could have worn one.

The men smiled briefly and turned their eyes downwards. Queen Elizabeth the Second flicked a sidelong glance back up at them. Scarfinger nodded and unconsciously began cracking his knuckles.

'Right then,' he muttered, venturing a thin smile. But when he tried to swallow he found his throat was dry.

'Sorry,' said Wedding Ring.

Scarfinger shrugged, feigning the diffidence of a Parisian waiter. *Don't worry about it*, he seemed to be saying. *People die every day*.

The phone booth was innocuous enough. Dirty, rusting, sulking in the centre of a deserted square. As he lifted the receiver and began dialling the number that would change everything, Wedding Ring found himself having a thought; an unconnected conceit that had shoved its way to the front of his brain and demanded to be dealt with.

You enjoyed that thriller, the thought was saying to him, *the one you read recently. It was really good*.

He kept dialling the number, but the thought would not go away.

Strangely reassuring, the thought continued. *Because despite all the unknowables, all the twists and turns, all the while there was always the absolute certainty that you could skip ahead a few pages just to see how everything turned out.*

The number connected. A small conversation ensued, nothing fancy, a functional exchange, a curt verbal handshake. A voice told him to stay on the line. So he did.

Another noise soon distracted him. A Yamaha motorcycle roared out of a nearby alleyway. Two seconds later its wheels were smoking in a half-turn. A second after that it hoved broadsides alongside the booth. At that point, the thought, which had previously left the building, was back.

Very different to now, it went. *Because now, anything is possible, this is real life, and when you're dangling from the cliff there's no skipping ahead. The only way you'll know how it all turns out is by going through it alone, one second at a time.*

The motorcyclist pulled the portable rocket launcher from his side bag, shouldering it quickly in one smooth move.

What a tragedy, went the thought in finale, *to feel there's a final twist needed in your life. And it never comes.*

The rocket grenade hisssssssssssssed angrily from the gaping mouth of the barrel, the impact flashing white hot and hellfire, incinerating the booth, smelting the coin slots, liquefying the pavement down to the sewage pipes and mushrooming a plume of flame and smoke high into the London sky.

By the time the dust had settled, there was nothing on the street but rubble. Tears. The distant sound of sirens.

2

Two days earlier

The cold seeped in through the window, through the gaps in the panes and the holes in the sill. It crept over the carpets, threadbare and beer-stained. Past the discarded socks, up over the unwashed duvet and onto the exposed shoulder blade that lay there gently twitching. Then, slowly, it eased the man awake.

Charlie rubbed his feet together. Counting to five he made a dash for the electric fire. An autopilot *flick* and he was back under the covers. The smell of burned dust filled his nostrils. The grey bars of the fire turning slowly orange in the grate. In ten minutes the room would be fit for human habitation. In five minutes it would be warm enough for a Scotsman.

Charlie rose six minutes later and dressed in a balletic frenzy, keeping as close as possible to the heat as common sense would allow. Soon he was looking at himself in the mirror and attempting to put in his contacts. At least that was the plus side of living in a bedsit. Everything was so close at hand.

His shirt was chafing his neck again and he reasoned it was only a matter of time before people presumed he slept in a noose.

Then it was out into the frost, down the stairwell, to slot into the condemned as they trudged towards the Underground in a scene that always reminded him of *Invasion of the Body Snatchers*. Charlie pulled his tatty overcoat around him and tried not to look at the pavement. He looked at the rooftops instead, squinting up at the chimneys and the birds keeping watch. He'd learned this from a homeless man who'd bumped into him on one such morning. 'Watch where you're going,' Charlie had snapped, before feeling guilty. The homeless man had fixed him with a smile.

'I was,' he'd said, 'I was.'

After that, Charlie had always tried to look up as much as he could. Particularly as so much of his life was down. And sometimes, up there, up, way up, for a fleeting moment, he could see the sun.

Today it resembled a small saucer of grey.

Charlie descended into the Jubilee Line and sought out a space at the far end of the last carriage. Three Japanese men in beige suits were sitting in a row, staring up at the adverts in silence. Each of them sported a small laminated clip-on tag on the breast pocket of their jacket. The tag said simply, 'VISITOR'.

No-one on the Tube carriage looked at him. No-one even really noticed he was there at all. Charlie had that effect on people. And he liked it that way.

He arrived on time, of course.

Charlie always did.

Always had done.

Ever since.

It was a soulless place to work, full of paper cuts, clingfilm, the faint whiff of ozone. When people passed, they looked in with the same piteous expression. It went: *rather them than me*.

Charlie worked in a photo-developing 'station'. Technically it was a booth, but the company that he and his colleague George both grafted for liked to call it a 'station' in their corporate literature and so 'station' it was. The fact that they were already *in* a station seemed to be lost on their senior management. Ten yards above them, London buses swerved suicidally around Oxford Circus on their way down Regent Street. Down here, in the ticket hall of the Underground, a cupboard near Exit Six served a double function as their place-of-work and place-of-arguments. Still, people waited around at stations and Charlie and George did a whole bunch of waiting around at theirs too.

There wasn't really much of a point in having two people working down here. For one, the actual job – taking people's films and developing them in a large dual-capacity machine – was an increasingly obsolete endeavour that could be done by a trained monkey. And for two, the place was so elbow-foldingly small that even a trained monkey would put in for a transfer after a month.

George and Charlie had been there just over a month.

'I'm putting in for a transfer,' George said again. He was facing the escalators, but Charlie presumed the statement was aimed at him. Particularly as George had now said it four times in the past ten minutes.

'Too stressful, all this,' continued George, with a vague hand gesture towards the ticket hall. 'It's too much.'

Charlie turned slowly to face him.

'I mean, my cousin dropped dead last week,' continued George, making a face that suggested he was waiting for some form of sympathetic noise from Charlie's direction.

Charlie did not oblige, but George sallied on nonetheless. 'Quite a shock. Heart of a lion.'

Charlie blinked a couple of times and returned to his paper.

'Aorta of a gnat, unfortunately, as it turned out,' continued George. 'Had a bit of a valve *issue*. You know.'

He was walking over to the counter where he plucked a biro from the brim of a stolen Starbucks mug. 'When they opened him up the doctor said his arteries resembled the inside of a calzone. Which I thought was particularly insensitive seeing as how he loved Italian food.'

Charlie wasn't sure whether George had meant him to laugh at this or not. He decided not. He reasoned George's endless and near-psychotic amiability might just draw the line at jokes about the deaths of close family members. Then again.

He turned away to the photographs that had been troubling him. Charlie sat in silence for a minute, leafing through them one by one, thumbprints greasy in the corners, hoping that now, at last, the conversation was at an end.

He was mistaken.

'New one for you,' ventured George. 'A man is found dead in the bath. He's been stabbed. The water is still warm. The only footprints the police can find are the victim's. And the bolt lock of the bathroom is pulled across the door from the inside. How did the murderer get away with it?'

Charlie escaped to a part of his brain he kept aside for moments like these, when pain and frustration meant there was no place to go but *in*.

George was still looking at him expectantly. 'Any ideas?'

'Suicide.'

'Nope.' George was enjoying this now. 'Book's called *The Postage Stamp Murders* by the way. That's not a clue, I'm just, you know, telling you.'

'I don't care. Is that the answer?'

George shook his head. 'The killer,' he smiled, 'committed the murder wearing the victim's shoes. He then walked backwards to the door and used a powerful magnet to bolt the door from the outside.'

'George?'

'Yes.'

'I still don't care.'

George's locked-room anecdotes had been part of life down here ever since Charlie began the job. For some reason George had committed nearly all of Robert Adey's *Locked Room Murders* to memory. Almost the first words George had ever uttered to Charlie were to inform him of the ingenious remote-control arson of a fishmonger's shop in *Flashpoint*, a novel by Hugo Blayn. Not 'nice to meet you'; not 'what part of town do you live in then'. Instead, a cup of cold tea and a five-minute monologue on the ingenuity of leaving a block of frozen nitroglycerin for the fishmonger's hammer—

Charlie felt himself leave the reverie as

—clackclackclack—

Three film canisters appeared in a neat row on the counter.

And there she was.

There are many beautiful people in London. Some of them come out during daylight hours but very few use the Tube. The London Underground is mostly a troglodyte empire, beauty doesn't last long down there, and that's why beauty is usually taking a hackney carriage somewhere along Old Brompton Road.

But the woman now standing in front of Charlie was of a different breed. And the fact that she was here, below ground, in the land of the ugly people – it somehow added to her mythology. She was practically a unicorn.

She stood slightly taller than George, five-eight, a sheen of hair spilling down over her Donna Karan. Charlie, being nearer six foot one, could see that her roots were perfect. Either she used a cotton swab to apply her peroxide or she was a natural blonde. Her hands, clasped in front of her, revealed a life of moisturised bliss. A holiday tan. And a ring. Not a wedding band, not an engagement rock. Somewhere in the middle. A mystery to Charlie but also a glint in the darkness.

The woman locked eyes with Charlie. That was another thing. The eyes. They had a certain irony about them, a sparkle of pure and mischievous intelligence that Charlie found utterly irresistible.

'I need these by tomorrow morning,' she said.

'No problem, madam.'

Charlie moved a small distance to a pile of A4 sheets assembled with more or less no thought under a stapler. But as he turned back he saw that George had already usurped his spot, form in hand, leaning over the counter with a smile.

'If we could just have your name and address there,' he syruped, indicating the bottom of the sheet. He removed a biro from his top pocket and presented it to the woman. Gripping it as close to the nib as possible, she wrote her name.

'I'll be back first thing,' she smiled.

And then she was walking away.

But George was still talking – mouth curled in a gently expectant half-smile.

'Absolutely no problem whatsoever.'

She didn't turn back as she left.

If she had, this is what she would have seen: a man in his late twenties and a man in his late forties staring silently back at her. Their faces pallid, frozen in ill-disguised awe. Charlie, the younger man, had short cropped hair that was beginning to recede, albeit tastefully. His arms were a little longer than seemed comfortable, anglepoise and mozzarella-white, ending in bony fingers and guitarist's fingernails on the left hand. One of the fingers sported a Band-Aid. Next to him slouched a baked potato of a man with flint eyes that glistened amiably under a haphazard sweep of hair. George's jowl was dotted with curls of untended beard, less a conscious effort at style than a complete unwillingness to shave. His purple fleece was from a surfing company despite the overwhelming visual evidence that he would surely scupper any ocean-going surface he stood on.

Their silent meditations lasted till the final strands of hair had disappeared into the sea of scarves and umbrellas teeming up the stairs to the outside world.

It was Charlie who broke the moment.

'She is,' he said.

'She is *not*,' sighed George.

For the next four hours, neither man said another word.

The impasse continued through lunch. Charlie had retired to an inner recess of the booth, away from prying eyes. George had moved to the counter to read the paper.

Despite the distance, however, George knew exactly what

Charlie was looking at and he knew what was coming. The facts were these. Every fortnight or so, the beautiful woman known to them both as Carrie Watson would pitch in front of them, bronzed, glowing and weather-beaten. And every fortnight she would have three or more rolls of extremely boring photos to be developed. At which point Charlie would corner George with said photographs – and his theory.

'Here we go again. See?' said Charlie, triumphant.

It was a long-distance shot of landscape. A closer inspection revealed some hills and a tree.

'I do see. I see a tree.'

'And again.'

Another picture. This time, deep snow, an urban *banlieue*, bleak and grey. Some squat buildings. A road sign in Cyrillic.

'Very pretty,' said George, trying to prise his paper out from underneath Charlie's hand – which was now pressing hard on the print.

More images followed in quick succession. Blighted beaches, uniform countryside, rotting urban centres, all with one thing in common. They were all very dull indeed.

'So where d'you think that is, then?' Charlie was pointing to the latest print, a parched shot of scrubland, slightly out of focus.

'Vietnam?'

'Mosque in the background.'

George looked. It was true. Actually, it was the only thing in focus.

'Indonesia?'

'A Gulf emirate, I'd say.'

'You would, Charlie. You're the most likely person I know to say that.'

Charlie smiled despite himself, briefly and accidentally

11

flattered by the comment. He held up another photo. Concrete office blocks and not much else.

'Croydon?'

'China. Look in the distance.'

Again, George peered. A red flag fluttering on a distant hilltop. 'So?'

'So,' sighed Charlie, 'quite a trip she's had. Again.' He was clearing up now.

'Lucky woman.'

'Egypt, Korea, China, Cuba, Saudi Arabia. Travel on that scale. To those countries. All the bloody time.'

George took a pen from the mug and chewed.

Charlie kept talking, 'And she's not in *one single picture*.'

George stopped and looked again.

All of the photos were long shots, wide, some telephoto. But it was true. Not only was Carrie not in any of the prints, none of them actually had any definable people in sight whatsoever. George cleared his throat.

'She's—'

'A spy, George. She's a secret fucking agent.' Charlie took a triumphant step back, narrating as he flicked slowly back through the prints to make his point. 'She's in Egypt. Do I see the pyramids? No I do not. I see a small civic building. Hanoi. Another small civic building. Beijing. A slightly larger building, function unknown, taken at considerable distance, at night. Government facility, is it? Chemical plant? Do you know what an Aunt Minnie is? It's a photograph just like this. An ordinary scene, usually with a person in the foreground, but the real target's the background. It's a spy term. A *spy* term.'

'So how come you know it?'

'It's in my *Dictionary of Espionage*. And about every single spy novel I've ever read.'

George was facing something he hadn't considered before. Charlie had an argument. But it irked him. He sighed.

'If you were a spy, Charlie – and I mean *really, actually, a spy* – would you get your covert photographs developed in a shithole like this?'

Charlie glanced at a stain of mayonnaise still glistening on George's purple fleece. Reaching into his pocket, he handed him a tissue. George dabbed at the offending mark, nodding in thanks. 'Maybe,' said Charlie, 'if I liked the customer service. Or I fancied the good-looking young guy who worked there . . .'

George flashed him a sarcastic look and cleared his throat. 'Okay, then. Supplementary question. If you were planning a secret mission, a secret *spy mission*, Charlie, let's say to China, why would you choose the tallest, sexiest, most beautiful blonde woman you could find?'

Charlie went quiet. 'So she can attract other agents,' he said after a few seconds, 'and then sleep with them to get information.'

'Charlie, how many tall blonde women are there in China?'

Charlie shrugged. He thought of a facetious answer but stopped himself. George was looking too serious.

'The answer,' said George, 'is *one*. Her. Whenever she's there. And she'll stick out like a priest with an erection whenever she goes.'

Charlie, defeated, gathered up the offending prints and began mucking in. Despite losing the argument he was vaguely lifted by the idea that the day was almost over. The two began to shut up shop, a rare ceremony of co-operation for both of them.

13

'Maybe Carrie has to be pretty.' Charlie was musing for his own benefit now. 'For cover.'

And suddenly George was in his face. The smell of stale coffee on his breath and a bloodshot tremble in his eyes that suggested this was the last he was going to say on the matter.

'Haven't you ever read le Carré? Deighton? Robert bloody Ludlum? Spies are nobodies, all right? Ordinary crappy people in ordinary crappy jobs.'

Charlie took in his frustration. The dust, the fluorescent glare from above, the time sheets, till receipts, the grubby smell of shared proximity.

A thought occurred to him. 'We're in crappy jobs.'

George folded his arms silently. 'Yeah, Charlie. Well spotted.'

Outside, the rush home had started.

3

The wind tore into Charlie as soon as he hit the top of the stairs. He determined, as he often did, to find a pub and get monumentally drunk. Replaying the argument with George, he convinced himself his theory was still correct. Spies might be nobodies in books, but as far as he was concerned, Carrie had 'secret agent' written through her like a stick of rock. And one day he was going to prove it.

A gale ripped down Regent Street. He plunged his hands in his pockets. As he did so, a thought struck him hard. A lack. Specifically, a lack of keys.

He turned around and headed back downwind towards the Tube entrance. He cursed his short-term memory. He'd have to open up the shop again. Things just weren't going his way.

Things weren't getting any better for him as he rounded the corner.

He wasn't exactly sure why his gaze had been drawn to look at the man in the suit. He wasn't a very appealing sight – short, sweaty, a halo of ginger hair and a cheap novelty tie. Behind him stood a bewildered pensioner. To her right, five ladies from sales. Three City boys. A media trendy.

Charlie was being led somewhere by his brain.

A trail of stepping stones to what his subconscious already knew – there's something even more interesting over there – no, there – there –

There.

In the northeastern corner of the ticket hall through the barriers and towards the escalators, past the throng of passengers. Over there, a small and intimate conversation was taking place. From the body language, both parties knew each other well and were downloading a great deal of information in a very short space of time.

One of these people was Carrie.

The other was George.

There was something different about the way George was standing. Gone was the slouch. Gone, even, was the jowl, as his improved posture had smoothed it out almost to the point of invisibility. His mouth, normally curled gently upwards in a gesture of amiability, was set solid in a purposeful frown that seemed to mean business. The transformation was almost preternatural in its intensity.

Charlie was still trying to process this information when George turned and shot a furtive glance in his general direction. Charlie ducked behind a pillar, brain whirring, pulse racing. Peering back over the heads of the crowd he could see that George had turned back – and the intimate conversation was continuing as they both descended slowly out of sight towards the Victoria Line platforms.

Charlie counted out twenty elephants before following.

He passed ginger suit, powered through the ticket barriers, and set off down the escalators in pursuit.

Charlie hit the bottom of the escalator at a trot. He scanned the bobbing heads and spotted them again, twenty or thirty yards ahead.

The shock of this second sighting hit Charlie with considerable force. Here was George, talking to a woman he claimed he didn't know. *Why the lies, George?*

They were headed for the second set of escalators that would take them to the Tube platforms. At the centre of both escalators stood a man playing 'Stairway to Heaven' on a mandolin.

Charlie waited until George and Carrie were three-quarters of the way down the second escalator before climbing on, ducking behind two London Transport Police and their favourably large helmets. Charlie glanced down to note that his quarry had turned onto the southbound platform.

He reached the bottom out of breath and clammy from nerves. He needed a better view. Edging past a Cadbury's chocolate dispenser he made his way to the yellow danger zone at the platform's edge. Moving past it he craned his neck out into the void of the line itself. The French-curve sweep of the platform edge offered him a glimpse of faces in profile. Charlie scanned carefully, bobbing out then ducking in, working his way through the throng. As he eased himself out a third time the howl of an approaching train stirred up a breeze that smelled of warm rubber. But Charlie was too distracted to care. He had lost them.

The sign on the platform now read:

NEXT TRAIN APPROACHING

Charlie tried a final time. The noise was deafening. At last, amongst the profiled noses, he saw them. Still engaged in heavy discussion. But as Charlie tried to duck back in a large suit stepped in his way. Losing his balance, Charlie realised too late that he was falling. He thought of Becky, quite suddenly just thought of her, as gravity dragged him down towards the electrified rail. The train erupted with a shriek from the tunnel darkness and Charlie's ears popped. A sweaty palm shot out from the crowd, gripping Charlie's overcoat and dragging him roughly back from the brink as the train became a blur in front of him. He could see through the flitflitflitting windows to a poster on the station wall on the other side of the carriages. He could make out the words: 'NOW – MORE THAN EVER'. He wondered what it meant.

'Silly cunt,' murmured two teenage kids Charlie had seen upstairs. One of them had a ring through each eyebrow. Both eyed Charlie sarcastically.

Several other commuters were equally unimpressed. He turned to thank his rescuer and was surprised and guilty to see it was the ginger businessman. But Charlie was too stressed to smile, heart pounding harsh on his chest, his intestines in a clove hitch and double bow of pain.

Everything was starting to fall into place.

4

'The victim,' George was saying, 'committed suicide but wanted to frame his enemy. He knew he had a heart condition. So he carried his accomplice, the dwarf, on his shoulders and ran into the middle of a snow-covered field, whereupon he died. The dwarf then took a pair of shoes belonging to the victim's enemy and walked backwards from the scene of the crime, thus framing him for the death.'

Charlie was trying very hard to appear normal. But as any resident of a psychiatric ward will tell you, acting normal is a hell of a challenge if you're not feeling up to it. Charlie had opted for the silent treatment, but the lack of sleep and surging arrhythmia of his breakfast espresso was making it almost impossible.

George had been late, of course, and had arrived smelling vaguely of focaccia. He appeared to find it almost impossible to forgo his morning treat of grilled mushroom paninis ('the breakfast of champignons'). His prolonged tardiness had given Charlie a usefully long period to get wound up.

It was as if yesterday evening never happened. George was George again, complete with jowl and body odour. The upturned lips that hinted a quip was not too far away.

'You're not very forthcoming today,' George was muttering as he walked out of the booth.

'Hangover,' managed Charlie. And this was partly true. Unable to sleep, he had chased four pints of Guinness down with four more pints of Guinness. Clinging to the bed through 'Sailing By' on the radio. Burrowing under the pillows and praying for the morning.

Charlie's eyes began to sting and he realised that George had left without telling him where he was going.

Looking around the booth there was no sign of any custom. The machine was busy. Charlie took a decision and stepped out into the ticket hall. He eyed the concourse. No sign. But a glance in the fish-eye security mirror showed an overweight middle-aged man in the adjoining corridor.

George.

Charlie eased himself around the edge of the booth and looked. George was heading towards the exit. Charlie glanced at the booth.

By the time he turned back, George was staring right at him. Charlie froze and realised there was nothing he could do but smile. George said nothing. He just pointed to the small doorway to his right.

'Loo,' said George.

Charlie nodded. And gave the thumbs up.

Turning back to the booth, there was someone standing by the counter. It was Carrie.

She seemed agitated. Peering over into the booth, as if for some strange reason she'd find someone hiding behind the till.

'Hi,' managed Charlie as he walked over. She whirled around and met his gaze. Giving nothing away she placed her receipt on the counter.

'Just be a sec,' said Charlie, attempting a grin.

He pushed three envelopes back over to her. She responded with the exact money and was gone.

Two minutes later, George was back. Charlie was still clutching her receipt.

'She's been, then, has she?' said George.

Charlie nodded. George frowned, clutching his stomach. Rubbing it gently he sat down on a stool. It was Charlie's turn to visit the gents. By the time he returned, George's frowning had turned sour. He was wincing, clearly in considerable discomfort.

'I really don't feel too good, mate,' he said.

'What is it?'

'Dunno.' Another twinge. 'I think I'm going to have to go home. See a doctor.'

'Seriously?'

George nodded, breathing deep, still clutching his midriff.

'Where does it hurt?'

George stared at Charlie witheringly. 'Where d'you think?'

'I mean specifically. Is it across the top, is it your guts, where?'

'Since when were you a doctor?'

'I'm not a doctor,' sighed Charlie, 'I'm a hypochondriac. With broadband Internet access. So I know my stuff.'

'If it's all the same to you,' groaned George, 'I'll go get a second opinion.'

Within minutes he was zipping up his fleece and walking out of the door. He turned back for a moment – suddenly guilty. 'Sure you don't mind?'

'If you don't feel well,' said Charlie, 'you don't feel well. I can call you a cab if you want—'

'No, honestly. I'll grab one upstairs. Thanks.'

21

And he was gone.

'Feel better,' shouted Charlie, as an afterthought. He wondered if it sounded sincere. It had been.

A thought hit him hard.

George had been fine until he'd seen Carrie's receipt. He had not eaten anything since he arrived – a major achievement in the day for George. Charlie looked at his watch. Thirty seconds had passed. He scribbled a note, 'Back in ten', and closed the security grille. He took the stairs two at a time.

Lunchtime crowds had swelled the numbers. Charlie scanned the flow of human traffic up the pavements.

George, at his lumbering pace, had not gone far. He was headed north, towards All Souls Church. A taxi with its light on passed close by. George didn't even make a move. Didn't even glance at it.

Charlie took a deep breath and began to walk. Quickly at first, dodging between shoppers and slow-witted tourists. He needed to make up some distance, to anticipate any sudden moves, yet be far enough away to blend with the crowds should George decide to glance behind him.

But the man seemed preoccupied. He was speeding up too. Charlie matched him stride for stride, some thirty yards behind him now.

Just to be sure, Charlie shrugged off his reversible jacket. And reversed it.

Two more taxis chugged past George, and by the time George crossed the access road to BBC Broadcasting House it was clear to Charlie that this man was not interested in going home at all. Charlie was nearly run over by a cyclist on the same road. Luckily the sound of construction at an office building nearby masked the torrent of abuse coming his way.

Crowds were thinning considerably as George continued north, past the Royal Institute of British Architects. Charlie was suddenly aware that he was isolated. If George turned round now he would be in plain view, with nowhere to hide but the railings or the doorways to his right. Charlie realised that the road was wide enough to allow him a clear view of George even from the opposite pavement. He crossed quickly, dodging in front of a bus whose brakes squeaked in irritation. Reaching the other side, through the bus windows as it passed, Charlie could see it had been a wise decision. George had stopped to light a cigarette – Charlie hadn't even realised he smoked – and had glanced back as he did so. Charlie maintained his gaze on George until he reached the Marylebone Road.

George trotted across just as the lights changed to green. Charlie tried to move fast but the flow of cars and buses was too quick off the mark. He caught glimpses of George's purple fleece as it continued east along the other side of the road and then north once again, towards Regent's Park.

Charlie rounded the corner. Ahead, some fifty metres away, the south gate of the park. Despite the chill, business was brisk, both in and out. George was entering right now.

As he did so he dropped a packet of cigarettes into the rubbish bin by the gate.

Charlie covered the ground with long strides, keeping close to the railings in case George wheeled around and walked out again. Chancing it, Charlie peered down the gravel entrance and into the park. Even from here he could see George walking towards a set of benches at the far end of the flower garden, now barren and deserted.

Charlie's overwhelming curiosity got the better of him and he reached inside the bin. Passers-by glanced at him and

23

walked on. Charlie turned his nose up at the smell. It wasn't long before he had retrieved the packet of smokes – empty. He chucked it back in and edged around the corner to check on George.

And caught his breath.

Carrie was now sitting next to him on a bench. They were talking again. Close.

This was all Charlie needed. His chest was hurting from the efforts of his heart inside. He turned round at speed, keen to get back to the booth.

As he moved off he heard a small thud. Looking down he had knocked into a small child. A boy. His parents wore identical windcheaters and zip-up polo necks. On their feet, snow-white sneakers and matching socks. They were American.

Their child, standing up, took in the situation. In his parents' eyes, concern. In the stranger's eyes, anguish. Evaluating the factors for and against, the kid decided to breathe in deep and holler.

'What the hell are you doing?' screamed the father.

The mother glared at her husband to do more than shout. She turned down to her tearful bairn. 'Kyle, sweetie, it's okay, it's okay . . .'

'I'm really sorry,' ventured Charlie, aware that the noise and the growing scene around him were attracting unwanted attention.

'Anything the matter?' asked a passing couple.

'Yeah, I'd say so. This idiot just kicked my son to the ground,' yelled the American.

'I didn't *kick* him . . .' argued Charlie, realising this was not a clever approach to take.

'Do you want me to call the police?' asked another spectator.

24

'Look, it was a mistake, all right?' snapped Charlie. The boy, whose cries had receded, started up again, a wail of despair.

'He hit me,' he was singing, 'he hit me he hit me . . .'

Charlie glanced around him. A crowd had gathered and out of the corner of his eye he could see George and Carrie parting company. Carrie, to the eastern gate of the park. George, right back this way.

He had to think of something quickly.

He couldn't think of anything.

And felt himself starting to cry.

The child, who had thought he had the goddamn exclusive on tears here, was momentarily distracted.

'I'm sorry,' said Charlie. 'I've just been diagnosed with a serious illness. And I just wasn't watching where I was going. I really am sorry, though.'

Mom and Dad were suddenly respectful. Mom even took her boy a little step back. Just in case, Charlie mused, it was contagious.

'Well, that's terrible,' said Dad.

'I'm not in the habit of hurting small children,' added Charlie.

'Glad to hear it,' muttered Mom.

Charlie bent down and spoke to the boy directly. 'I'm sorry I hurt you. Can we be friends?'

He extended his hand. The boy eyed him sceptically but realised his bluff had been called. A show of mercy here would almost certainly guarantee him a treat of some description.

He nodded, snotty and red-eyed. And took Charlie's hand.

As Charlie rose he saw that George was rounding the gate. Dad patted him on the shoulder.

'Sorry to shout,' he said. 'We've just gotten off a plane.'

'I understand,' smiled Charlie through the tears.

George had just exited the park. Charlie turned away, his back hunched, twisting down in one movement to the ground as if to tie his shoelace. Between the legs of the dispersing onlookers he could see George's ambling gait proceeding south again, towards Marylebone Road.

With a final apologetic look of self-pity, Charlie walked into the park. Turning back to watch the departing George it suddenly occurred to him that the big man was heading back to work.

Charlie waited until George had disappeared across the road – then broke into a run.

He jinked left, down Bolsover Street, as George retraced his steps on a parallel route down Great Portland Street. Delivery vans clogged the pavement at several points. Charlie's lungs began to scream for mercy as he sprinted round, behind, under, over any obstacle in his path. Crossing Oxford Street a motorcycle courier missed his kneecaps by inches. He danced past the *Evening Standard* vendor and bounded down the entrance to the Tube. Hands trembling, he unlocked the grille and threw open the booth once more, pocketing the errant note and wiping his sweat on his sleeve. He had swallowed most of his hyperventilation when George appeared several minutes later.

Charlie pretended not to notice him. Then jumped.

'I thought you'd gone home,' he ventured. He thought he saw George glance at his sweat-matted hair.

'Fresh air seemed to clear it,' replied George.

'Fair enough,' mumbled Charlie.

But George just stood there, staring at him.

'I know what you're thinking,' he said. Charlie looked up

at his colleague, a frown of bemusement crinkling on his face.

'I've been acting strangely and now I'm going to tell you why.'

Charlie braced himself. Damn his curiosity. His need to know had brought him too close to the flame. And now he was going to pay. He closed his eyes and took a deep breath.

'Thing is,' said George, 'it's my birthday.'

5

Charlie was in the corner of his bedsit by the sink. He gazed at his reflection and reflected. The day had taken its toll on his skin and now it was abandoning ship in large mournful flakes. He felt like a tree in November. He should take better care of himself.

The sink had an innovative design. It was a corner unit with taps fixed flush against the cheap ceramics, and had been devised for one of seven people, all of whom lived with Snow White. It was almost impossible to bend down and drink from either tap. Charlie had a small red mark on his forehead from where his drunken attempts to suck hydration from the silver teat had usually met with the equal and opposite force of the wall.

He rubbed some E45 between his eyes and decided to change before he left.

The rain was still pounding the pavement when Charlie stepped out into the world once more. Two taxis and a bus passed by. But he would walk. He liked the rain at night. He liked being in it. It gave him a sense of his role as a leading man in the urban jungle. The tragic hero on a solitary path. Charlie found he needed fictions like these to keep his life meaningful. He wondered whether before too long there'd be no fact left at all.

George, it turned out, lived only a half mile or so away from him, in the same neighbourhood in fact. A typical London coincidence. Two lonely lives that happen to take place round the corner from each other. A person could be born, grow old and die in this city never knowing that their soul mate was living just around the corner. A city full of near misses and might-have-beens.

Charlie had had his share of those.

He forced a memory away.

George. Birthday.

When George had invited him to his party his immediate reaction had, of course, been to decline. But the opportunity for further scrutiny had been too good to pass up, and after a suitable period of time he invented some previous fantasy engagement that he then made a fictional effort to reschedule for another day. George had been delighted. He'd even stopped talking for a while.

Charlie pitied George, even if he was still unsure about him. Getting older was tough. Throwing a party, in your own flat, that's stressful enough as it is. And if Charlie was invited then God only knows, George must be in serious need of some friends.

Charlie passed the boarded-up windows of a corner shop and turned onto a slate grey street of mouldering Victorian conversions. The streetlights here had something of No Man's Land about them, blazing a harsh bleached white that forced itself on all-comers, rendering their shadows short and brutish. In that kind of light, everyone looked guilty.

Glancing at the address on his hand, Charlie glanced up

to see an old woman staring forlornly from a front-room window. Two doors on he found a cracked and soggy stoop and the number 73.

On the first floor, lights glowed through net curtains. Charlie began to feel queasy. As he neared the front door he began to realise why. Someone inside was playing Kenny G.

He rang the bell. George yanked open the door as if he'd been standing there all evening. He was wearing a small purple party-hat and a badge that read, 'Birthday Boy'. Charlie proffered his gift of alcohol and was ushered inside.

Charlie tried to say something about the house.

All he could manage was, 'oh.'

It was a shambles. A rainbow of stains on the carpet. Boxes and packing materials, newspapers and magazines teetering together in a 'must deal with it' kind of a way in the corridor. Ahead, a kitchen, wet with condensation. It made Charlie's place look like a coffee advert.

George chatted animatedly to Charlie and opened the living-room door. Two overweight, fleece-wearing men, identical to George, grinned back, slowly munching on a Ritz Cracker buffet. A Dixons-branded mini hi-fi was the objectionable source of the soprano saxophone. And that was pretty much it.

'Drink?' asked George.

Charlie nodded. George beckoned him past the staircase to the kitchen. Glancing up, Charlie could see two door-ways.

The kitchen was in a worse state than the hallway. The sink was full of dishes. Cupboard doors yawned off their hinges. Glasses lay half-full and abandoned next to mildew-ridden dishcloths. Charlie secretly congratulated himself on bringing a six-pack, and tucked into his own stash with relish.

More guests came. Before too long the cracker buffet had been decimated, a wine box consumed and cheap Scotch was flowing. Charlie chastised himself for saying so, but he was actually having a pretty good time. George was good company. He could hold a room. Despite his slouch, his eyes danced with humour. Charlie, too, could tell a joke. It took a while for everyone to mesh with his anhydrous wit but once they were there, they connected. Charlie had forgotten how much he liked going to parties and made a mental note to attend more in the future.

'So, your transfer,' Charlie was saying. George was polishing off a bag of crisps, munching thoughtfully. He made a small circular motion with his finger to communicate that he'd be picking up on that very point just as soon as these crisps were swallowed.

'Yeah,' he said finally, with a smile. 'I was thinking about somewhere closer to home.'

'Where's that, then?'

'Newcastle. But I might just pack it in. Thinking of going back to college. Teaching or something. Then head off to Africa.'

'Good for you.'

Yet more people. Music blared. Drunken dancing shook the foundations. Even George took to the floor, what was left of it, and Charlie smiled as he watched. George took his dancing seriously, even if no-one else did.

Perhaps Charlie had been mistaken after all. The poor guy just wanted to be liked. It explained his ingratiating manner. It explained his need to talk. And every now and then Charlie saw his expression and posture change when listening – almost to the positions they had been in when he'd seen him with Carrie. Even while dancing, the man looked different.

A whoop went up as the opening bars of 'YMCA' filled the dance floor. George took off his fleece and whirled it around his head. Charlie drained his drink and climbed the stairs.

The upper landing was tiny, lit only by the glow from below. Two doors. The first, a bathroom. The second, undeclared, was slightly ajar.

Downstairs, the song was explaining how it was possible, under specific circumstances, to spend time with a large variety of males.

George's wheezing baritone rose above all the other voices. Charlie smiled and pushed the door gently. It responded, creaking in protest – but he persisted. The gap could now accommodate a slim man edging sideways and that's exactly what Charlie was doing.

Inside; dark. Curtains drawn. Streetlight picked out looming shadows of furniture. Charlie's hand fumbled for his Maglite keychain and a gentle whisper of unease caressed the back of his neck.

What if, thought Charlie.

What if George really *was*.

What if this party, this collection of fleeces downstairs – organised at the last minute, Charlie now remembered – was all for him.

To throw him off the scent.

Charlie turned on his Maglite and, for a brief moment, stopped breathing.

The song continued, developing its theme of how enjoyable it was to reside at a certain temporary housing and recreation facility.

The room was immaculate. It wasn't just organised. It had the kind of soulless, ordered perfection you can only find in show homes or interior-design magazines. The bed was made with hospital corners. A sweater was folded dead centre of an otherwise barren dresser.

Something in the far corner caught Charlie's eye.

Past a long clothing rail of starched and regimented garments was a small door. Next to it, on the wall, half-hidden by a curtain, a keypad. A little smaller than a burglar alarm. Charlie crept softly over to it. A tiny red light flashed with ominous regularity on the display. Charlie tried the handle. It was solid and unforgiving.

Stepping back, he cast his eyes over George's clothing rail. All were hung with the utmost care and attention to detail. They were arranged in order from bottom to top. Trousers, shirts, jackets.

Charlie noticed something between the jackets.

He took a closer look. They were jerkins of some sort. Vests, probably. Closer still. Yes, that was confirmed now. They were very special vests.

Bulletproof vests, in fact. Three of them.

The main light came on. Charlie whipped around.

George stood in the doorway, a plastic cup in his hand, a gentle smile on his face. His cheeks were flushed hot but the eyes were cold. Downstairs the song was still in full swing. 'Everything all right?' he asked.

'Yes, fine. You?'

George pursed his lips for a moment. Shook his head and sighed. 'Not really.'

The men regarded each other across the room.

'I'm sorry to hear that,' said Charlie.

'I just take offence when I find people rooting around uninvited in my bedroom, I guess,' continued George in a tone that unsettled Charlie.

'I didn't mean to.'

'Yes you did.'

George sighed again. Rubbed his eyes and began to walk over to Charlie who back-pedalled in time with his strides. Soon there was nowhere left for him to go, he was against the clothes-rail.

'Can I ask you a personal question?' asked Charlie. George nodded. Charlie unhooked a vest and held it out at George. 'Who do you work for?'

George paused. Then burst out laughing.

'Are you a spy?' shouted Charlie.

George smothered his giggles in his drink.

'Aren't you supposed to flash a light in my eyes or something?' Charlie pocketed his Maglite and stared back in silence. George's eyes twinkled. 'You're not serious.'

'Carrie. You said you didn't know her. I saw you with her. You lied.'

'Oh, you mean on the Tube. You really want to know?' Charlie nodded, trembling slightly.

'Okay. Well. She came back for her prints after you left,' George explained, rolling his eyes skywards. 'She wanted to know if they'd be ready early. And as you'd taken the trouble of doing them that morning, I was able to tell her yes.'

'Okay. And then you left with her.'

'We were talking. She noticed my book of *Locked Room Murders* on the counter. She asked me about them. It turns out she's a fan of that genre. Quite a collector, in fact.'

'And then you left with her.'

'She was heading north on the Tube. So was I. Are you sure you're feeling all right?'

'Why were you heading north? You live west. Why?'

'Is this really that important?'

'Very.'

So George explained it all. Carrie was staying at the Langham Hilton. It was in the same direction as George's friend Paul. They had shared a Tube ride and discussed their book tips. George's cousin, the one who had recently died, had been an aid worker. He sometimes stayed with George before he went to Heathrow and on to Points Dangerous. He kept a few work clothes around just in case. Including, as it happened, bulletproof vests.

Charlie stared at George. He seemed comfortable defending himself like this. Almost, thought Charlie, too comfortable. But George could see the glint forming in his eye and began to chuckle.

'You've got a bloody nerve, Charlie, I'll tell you that.'

'Me?'

'You're the one who's been following people all over the place. You're the one who's been rooting around in my bloody bedroom on my birthday – Jesus, if anyone's the spy here, Charlie, it's you.'

Charlie was starting to blush. A rush of reality slapped him in the face. 'I'm sorry, mate.'

'Don't worry about it. Go downstairs and enjoy yourself.'

Charlie nodded. And turned to go. And saw it. A fragment of time that threw everything into reverse.

Passing George on his way out he caught something in his peripheral vision. George's eyes. In this private second, away from scrutiny, all warmth had gone. In its place a surreal neutral gear. Take a photograph of that expression, thought Charlie, and you'd be looking at a mask. As this realisation crept across Charlie's face, George turned back to him and the hearty glow returned in a heartbeat.

Charlie summoned a smile.

'Happy birthday, mate.'

'Cheers.'

Downstairs, Charlie charged another Stella. His last one. He drank it down in one and left two minutes later. He had something to do.

6

The top deck of the Routemaster was almost deserted. It smelled of curry. In the very front sat a man fresh from late-night shopping. At the back, asleep, a drunken estate-agent whose head bobbed forward with every touch of the brake. At his feet, a polystyrene box in a bag, leaking marsala sauce. Charlie sat in the middle, his favourite place. He rested his forehead on the glass and stared out as the diesel engine sent juddering vibrations through the floor. It made his cheeks wobble. Through the glass, misted by condensation, Charlie surveyed weekday London revellers. It was still mid-evening for most people. Charlie's embarrassment had already curtailed his entertainment.

But not his curiosity.

The Langham Hilton glowed expensively over the BBC Headquarters on Portland Place. Charlie's shoes squeaked like trainers on the marble as he approached the front desk. When he spoke, he did so with the confidence of a six-pack of Stella. He didn't exactly know what he was going to do, or why he was going to do it. But he was here now and that was that.

The concierge smiled up at him, his hair bleached and receding.

'Carrie Watson,' Charlie heard himself say.

'Who shall I say is calling?'

Charlie thought for the briefest moment, and smiled back.

'George,' said Charlie.

The concierge nodded and picked up the phone. Out of the corner of his eye, Charlie saw him dial a number. A brief calculation told him it was 748. Charlie avoided his gaze as the phone rang and rang. The concierge replaced the receiver.

'There's no answer I'm afraid. Would you like to leave a message?'

'It's okay,' smiled Charlie, calmly placing some hotel stationery into his pocket. 'I'll wait.'

Charlie took a detour around the lobby and located the bar. It was full of muted colours, lazy armchairs and whispered conversations of private intrigue. Outside, rain had begun to fall. Pools of sulphurous light illuminated the dark green leather of the barstools. Charlie took a seat on a corner and shovelled some sweet Chinese crackers into his mouth with a *crunch*.

The barman approached him as he might have approached a small pile of unwashed clothes.

'Just tap water, thanks,' smiled Charlie.

The barman raised a laconic eyebrow and pointed to the jug and glasses in front of him. *Help yourself*, he seemed to be saying. *Cos I won't*.

Charlie drank down a couple of glasses in quick succession. Nerves jangling, he realised his bladder needed emptying too. He began to prise himself from the stool when the barman approached again, placing a tall glass in front of him that looked suspiciously full of gin and tonic.

'From the young lady,' whispered the mystified barman. Charlie followed his gaze to the far corner of the bar.

There sat Carrie. Drinking alone. She smiled and toasted him. It was a gesture that said: come. The slice of lemon bobbed and spun. The tonic fizzed and popped. Charlie obeyed.

Carrie's voice was like cashmere. The overall effect on Charlie was hypnotic. 'So what do you think of my hotel?' she smiled. 'Does it meet with your approval?'

'Very nice,' managed Charlie, taking another slug of gin. There was something so clean, so freshly scrubbed about her that Charlie felt grubby in her presence. He couldn't help but sit forward in his armchair, perched on the edge. Carrie didn't seem to mind. But her air of total calm was driving him to distraction. Her smallest movements caught his attention. The shape of her mouth as she formed her words. The crinkle of her eyes as she smiled. The small, revealing slit in her skirt that displayed a lower thigh so smooth you could, Charlie's brain mused, go curling on it.

In front of her was a selection of three Polish vodkas poured into conical glasses. The glasses themselves were suspended in crushed ice. Charlie thought he saw a rose petal floating in one of them. She'd been pleased to see him. She'd enjoyed the quality of the prints they'd provided for her. She mentioned George from time to time, asking questions about the business.

Taking the opportunity, Charlie casually asked what business *she* was in. She was happy to tell him. Urban planning. Renewal projects around the world. Not the most exciting camerawork you'll ever see but important for her job. Charlie smiled and speculated she must have photo guys in every port. Carrie smiled back and said *no-one like you*. Charlie allowed himself to bask in the compliment. He hadn't felt this relaxed in front of a beautiful woman for . . . well, a long time.

'What are the rooms like here, then?' he asked, finishing his drink.

Carrie's face didn't so much as flicker. 'Quite spacious. Would you like to see?'

Rain was hammering on the great windows of the bar now. Outside, people were running for cover, the pavements getting slick. Carrie drained an entire cone of rose petal in a slow, deliberate sip.

'Sure,' said Charlie.

They entered the lift and Charlie had to stop himself pressing '7'. By sheer coincidence, the only other passenger was a dead ringer for Charlie's mother.

The woman stared at the odd couple before her. Charlie smiled back, immediately horrified by the resemblance. His bladder was making life very uncomfortable now, but he was damned if he was going to let that spoil things.

Carrie led the way across the herringboned carpet, through a maze of room numbers and arrows. Soon they stood outside 748. Charlie mentally patted himself on the back.

As she pushed the door open, she trailed her hand behind her and caught hold of Charlie. The force of her grip and feel of her warmth was enough to flood Charlie's loins. It was like she had pulled the ripcord on a life raft. Charlie was grateful for the darkness of the room.

She turned to him and pushed herself close. Her lips moved closer. She guided her mouth to his ear and blew gently. A whisper as the door clicked shut behind them –

'Now,' she said.

Charlie kissed her.

She responded and curled her leg up to his hip. Locking her mouth to his, her tongue gently sought out his and they coiled together against the minibar.

He broke off and stared at her. His eyes became used to the light and in the half-glow she was becoming less mortal by the second. Shrugging off her jacket her nipples were unambiguous and button-hard. As she began to undo her blouse, Charlie found he couldn't help himself any more. It was, after all, a hugely pertinent question.

'Why—?' he asked.

She moved to him, soft. 'Ssh.'

She led him to the middle of the room, pushed him gently down on the bed and straddled him. Charlie winced. His bladder was near breaking point. Carrie whispered in his ear.

'I don't – have any – you know.'

'Me neither,' admitted Charlie. He'd stopped carrying condoms in his wallet when the sight of them had become ironic.

'I think there's a machine – somewhere,' she smiled.

Charlie nodded, holding her and kissing her once more as he tried to rise from the bed. But she pushed him back down again.

'Don't worry your pretty little head,' she teased. 'You'll only get lost. Leave the lights off. I'll be back in a second.'

Charlie nodded numbly as Carrie whisked her jacket on and made for the door. She left it on the latch.

Charlie lay back for a moment. Slowly, his horniness was replaced by a creeping paranoia. Realising a window of opportunity was at hand, he took a deep breath – and went to work. Taking care not to leave fingerprints he began to open drawers. Cupboards. He needed evidence. Paperwork. Any scrap of detail that would shed some light on this woman. Because if there was one thing Charlie was sure of, Carrie Watson sure as shit wasn't Carrie Watson.

His nervous breaths whistled softly through his nostrils. He didn't see the shadow in the bathroom door.

It was a large shadow. Bulky, even. And utterly silent.

The shadow moved across the bedroom floor in a single, noiseless movement. From here it could see Charlie muttering to himself as he rifled through the clothes hung behind the sliding cupboard opposite the door.

The shadow lifted up its hand. Held there, lightly but firmly, was a Sig Sauer 9mm silenced weapon. The bullet inside the chamber would, if it travelled in a straight line, go straight through Charlie's brain. The shadow began to gently, quietly, apply pressure on the trigger.

At this point in Charlie's life everything began happening very fast. Above the rhythm of the blood in his head, a new noise. The unmistakeable *thlupp* of a bullet leaving a silenced gun. The gunpowder had created a high-pressure pulse of hot gas which had propelled the bullet down the barrel. But the expanding gas, which would normally explode out of the end of the gun to noisy effect, instead expanded into the larger area provided by the silencer and the bullet emerged with barely a whisper.

The bullet then made its way towards its intended target. The next noise Charlie heard was of a man falling to the ground. Charlie wheeled round to get a better view.

There on the floor lay a man clad in black. The contents of his head – blood, brains, plasma, fragments of skull – spilling out across the Wilmington shag, gun still cradled in his lifeless hand. Milliseconds later Charlie's brain had calculated that the shot that did this terrible damage would have come from the doorway.

He looked at the doorway. Framed there, a man.

In a purple fleece.

His name was George.

In his right hand, a .22 calibre silenced pistol.

In one balletic movement Charlie dived to the ground next to the still-bleeding corpse beside him. At the moment of impact he twisted his torso clockwise, rolling into a crouched position by the assassin's right hand.

In the same fluid movement he reached out, grabbed the gun, pointed it at George, and fired.

George, utterly unprepared for this, had no time to react.

Charlie's aim was true – the bullet just missed George's shoulder and entered the left nostril of the woman who had crept quietly up behind him. A blonde woman in a Donna Karan suit, known to both men as Carrie.

Once inside her nose, the bullet ruptured the cartilage and proceeded to the bone that separated her nasal passages from her sinuses. Here it began to cause real trouble, shattering everything in its path. In its wake, extensive subdural haemorrhaging, ripping linear fractures through the bumpy insides of her skull that extended down to the neck. The consequential shock wave then brought about a major tissue trauma, and as bone particles reached the brain the woman's nervous system shuddered to an instant halt, causing her blood pressure to drop like a stone and her left hand to drop the steak knife, the serrated edge of which had, until a half-second ago, been poised to slash across George's carotid artery.

The doppler of a fire engine filtered up from the street

below. As blood seeped slowly under the feet of the two men. Charlie stared at the bloodied mess of Carrie's body. He could still smell her on him.

In a single leap he was in the bathroom. Lights flicked on, off. Shower curtain pulled away. Just in case.

Back in the lounge, George stared at the carnage as Charlie ran to the window. His face set in grim determination he began to heave it up. It stuck halfway. George finally dragged his eyes back to Charlie.

'Can I have a word with you please?' said George.

'In a minute,' said Charlie. He was pulling his shirt over his hand so his fingertips would leave no trace. His jaw strained with the effort but the window was not budging.

'Um, now, actually . . . if you don't mind—'

'Help me with this—' hissed Charlie. 'And shut the bloody door!'

The window loosened and slid up without further protest. George ran to the corridor and dragged the messy corpse of Carrie inside, streaking more blood on the carpet. He returned to find Charlie climbing out of the window and onto the small ledge outside. The rain was still strong, insistent.

He beckoned George to follow. A scream from the corridor hastened his decision. George clambered out with difficulty and joined Charlie outside.

Below them, some seven floors as the crow falls, concrete. Iron railings. And death.

George stifled a burp and stood up.

The two men sidestepped carefully towards the northern corner of the hotel exterior, lashed by rain, wind, fear. Easing themselves around the corner, a lucky break – a fire-escape, dropping down to an alleyway. Charlie leaped onto the ladder and climbed not down, but up. George, sighing, followed.

On the roof, Charlie extended a hand. A little unsure but unwilling to try it alone, George took it. Charlie yanked him up to safety.

More sirens from below. Reflected in the BBC buildings, blue and red lights flashed. The wind, if anything, stronger up here. George's split-ends danced and waved ludicrously above his forehead like kelp in a typhoon.

Past the far edge of the roof, a gap of twelve floors to the ground. Past that, an escape route – to the roof of an adjoining building. There was no other option. Without a glance at George, Charlie began to run.

George followed, shouted after him—

'Need a bump!'

Charlie whipped round – a what?

George cupped his hands. A plaintive look on his face.

Charlie nodded – understood. He reached the edge of the building and kneeled down. His hands cupped in readiness as George lumbered forward at surprising speed. George's foot met Charlie's hands, his ample thighs hiding tremendous explosive power. And in an instant he was catapulted over the gap and onto the gravel roof beyond. Charlie shook the pain away, backed up and leaped after him, landing dead weight on top of the winded George. Both men sucked in the pain as they rolled over and over each other like a human tumbleweed and came to rest beside a darkened roof-access doorway.

Their faces inches from each other. Grazed, bloodied, peppered with gravel. George was the first to speak.

'We really need to have a chat,' he said.

7

Black Hush Puppies scudded on the cement. The football, green and slightly deflated, had been pummelled high and long from the goalmouth by Davy Ross, headed down by Neil Mackay and was now trundling close to the byline. An empty packet of Salt 'n' Shake crisps slowed its progress and clung to it for dear life.

Charlie's foot caught the ball just in time, scooping it away from the brink and keeping it, back under control, near the fencing by the Art Department. But the shouts of his friends and the rumbling of the earth beneath him also told Charlie that Andrew Crombie was bearing down on him full pelt. Crusher Crombie was someone you did not want bearing down on you at any kind of pelt whatsoever. Charlie jinked left, but Andrew's wildly swinging shin caught his knee and corkscrewed him painfully to the cold hard playground.

It was starting to drizzle. For a second, Charlie watched the droplets descend. They seemed curiously elongated to him. The sky was grey. The sky was always grey in Edinburgh. A shout from further down the pitch told him that Crombie had scored. Charlie tried to lift his shoulders from the concrete. The big lug was doing a victory lap. Charlie scraped himself up and got to his feet. His head was ringing. So was the school bell.

Walking back towards the classroom, Neil caught up with him and whacked him on the right arm. 'BCG!' he shouted. Even through his blazer a harpoon of pain juddered down Charlie's spine and into his tailbone. The school had all recently had their combined immunity jabs and no-one was safe. Charlie smiled, grabbed Neil and returned the favour. At eleven years old in Scotland, this is what passed for friendship.

'How's the head?' grinned Neil. He always grinned. Years later, when he managed a small sandwich franchise in London, he'd still have it. Neil popped a dab of what would become an illegal confectionery product into his mouth. His eyes lit up as it fizzed malevolently on his tongue.

Charlie shrugged. 'All right,' he lied.

'So, you want the good news or the bad news?'

'Good news.'

'Pongo's not taking us for science today.'

'That's not good, that's brilliant.'

'Aye, well. Bad news is, it's RatFace.'

It was one of those trends that seemed to sweep school from time to time. For a while it had been humming en masse in assembly. Then there had been singing the rhyming words of hymns in a broad Geordie accent. Several years previously there had been a highly amusing bout of whistling your 's's in every ssssingle sssyllable you sssaid. But Good News, Bad News was a relatively recent phenomenon and highly addictive. Unbeknownst to Charlie and his schoolpals it was becoming a popular pastime up and down the country.

'Good news is . . .' someone would shout at your face, '. . . You're on a plane. You're going to Jamaica. Bad news is, the engine's fucked.'

'Good news is, I've got a parachute.'

'Bad news is, there's a hole in it.'

'Good news is, there's a reserve chute.'

'Bad news is, it's still on the plane when you jump out.'

In many ways it was a form of Socratic dialogue. The game was simple. In any given situation there were positive outcomes and negative outcomes. The aim of Good News, Bad News was to end up alive and in one piece, a logical cul-de-sac, before you both got bored or the teacher found you talking at the back of class.

Charlie was very good at the game. Neil had tried this Jamaican gambit on him one morning as they got cream buns and frothy coffee at break. They'd become friends when they both spotted each other in a high-street 'poster' store trying to buy the same pop-art monstrosity in a red frame. They were both buying the picture less for its masterful depiction of a triple-decker cheeseburger and more for the important reason that they had both heard Karen Holmwood once mention she *quite liked it*. They had never talked of the meeting, or the picture, again. This was to be Charlie and Neil's first successful secret together. There would be many more.

'Good news is,' Charlie had said, 'I hit the ground and walk away.'

'You can't do that!'

'I can. Cos the plane never left the ground.'

'Aye it did.'

'You said it was going to Jamaica,' Charlie jabbed Neil's shoulder with his finger. 'You never said it was in the air.'

'Bollocks.'

When they left school Charlie knew Neil hadn't given the game another moment's thought. For Charlie, on many occasions, it had helped save his life. They'd kept in touch since then. Once a month became twice a year. But they still talked and still had the occasional pint and picked up exactly where they'd left off. The way old friends always do.

Ninety-three minutes had passed since Charlie and George had tumbled ungracefully together on a gravel-strewn London roof. George was now staring at the burnished gold liquid sloshing around in his glass.

'The only problem with whisky are the whisky bores . . . I just hate them. Don't you?'

George slouched in a leather armchair, vaguely Buddha-like, with his glass now balanced on the folds of his stomach. A fire crackled amiably in the grate. Across a small trestle table a half-finished bottle of cheap Scotch and another heavy crystal tumbler. Charlie was opposite him, listening intently, the alcohol hardly even denting his adrenalin rush as George continued.

'It's just so – well, I'm going to say it – pretentious. I used to know this bloke at university. He only drank single malt Lowland whisky that was aged in someone's peaty grandmother for a hundred years. I mean, that's just stupid. Nothing wrong with generic scotch. Cheap Scotch on the rocks. Does the job. Lovely.'

He drained his glass and smiled at Charlie. His eyes glittered like wet stones. 'Good news,' he said. 'I've decided to take the pressure off this little stand off.' George locked his eyes back onto an area just to the left of Charlie's nose.

'Thing is,' he whispered, 'I'm a spy.'

And the words just hung there, in the air.

Charlie kept his eyes on George but in his peripheral vision took a brief visual audit of the snug hotel bar they had hunted down an hour earlier. A late-night haunt of bankers, lawyers, diners and hookers. Self-consciously high class, it achieved almost the opposite effect. It was stuffy to the point of nonsense. But reassuringly discreet. There were wood panels. There were drawings of beagles. The walls had soaked up centuries of drunken conversations and if they could talk, it is almost certain that they would slur. A couple of younger male pinstripes were chuckling soullessly by the bar. Both of their legs were bouncing almost imperceptibly up and down on the legs of the barstools, a tiny oscillation that Charlie reasoned was either boredom or the physical manifestation of a sub-conscious and highly repressed attraction.

'Me too,' said Charlie.

George chuckled softly. 'Our side?'

'Sure,' said Charlie. 'Domestic stuff.'

'How long?'

'Five years. You?'

'Coming up to twenty.'

Charlie nodded. 'Wow.' He sipped his drink. 'Just one thing, George.'

'What?'

'Why do you believe me?'

George stayed silent, unblinking.

'I mean,' Charlie was smiling now, a thin and well-rehearsed noncommittal sort of smile that was designed to put the recipient slightly on edge, 'I appreciate your candour. But there's nothing to say that all of this isn't just steaming coil of cow dung on my part. Pardon my Flemish. I mean, I know we both just shot people, with weapons, and that was a horrible business – murder, in fact, if you think about it, from a legal standpoint – but that shouldn't qualify as a lie-detection device. Should it?'

'Just say it, Charlie.'

'We can promise and assure all we like. But there's absolutely no way you can truly, one hundred per cent, believe me. Is there?' Charlie sat back and let his diatribe settle.

George shrugged. 'Well, there sort of is a way, actually.'

'And what's that?'

'Do you know what VEX is?'

Charlie nodded.

'Well, I just put some in your whisky.'

Charlie's eyes widened in horror. The two pinstripes glanced back briefly at them as he rubbed his temples vigorously. A new and potent step forward from the likes of thiopental sodium, VEX, as it was known, was the fastest and most wholly effective truth drug in the business. The letters were a slang acronym – Verbal Expectorant – and it had a chemical formula so long it was best not mentioning. A fast-acting, inhibition-loosening, information-freebasing and altogether odious little barbiturate. Charlie felt his pulse slowing. A leaden feeling in his stomach. The classic signs that the stuff was taking effect. His face flushed red.

'You put truth drug in my whisky?'

George was shrugging again. 'No.'

Charlie rubbed his eyes with his fist.

'I lied,' explained George. Charlie's eyes were watering now. 'But from your reaction just there,' continued George, 'I'd have to wager you were telling the truth. You looked like someone who'd just been found out.'

Charlie had been telling the truth. It was the most truthful he'd allowed himself to be for sixteen months, four weeks, and eleven days.

'Well maybe you'd be so kind as to be truthful back. Who do you work for?' whispered Charlie.

'A well-known British espionage outlet,' smiled George. 'A total-solution provider for domestic and worldwide intelligence product.' He poured and consumed another full glass of Scotch with alarming ease. 'Just like you.'

Charlie and George smiled at each other.

Both men knew the young pinstripes had glanced over at them a total of four times during the last sensitive minutes. At this distance there was a one in twelve chance that some of the more sensitive words of their conversation would have travelled across the wine-darkened carpeting and made their way into their ears. For all its cosiness, the interior of a hotel bar was no place for chats like this.

Charlie was the first to stand. 'Not here.'

8

The Georgian mews led back onto St James's, where Charlie and George now walked, two feet apart, eyes on the pavement, awareness stretching, feeling, all around, just as the years of training had drummed into them.

It was late now, the residual morass of humanity had been chucked out of the boozers and grabbed the last Tubes. The air was bitterly cold and provided, for both men, a welcome slap in the face.

'Floor Seven, Euston Buildings,' Charlie was saying.

'Who's your point man there?'

'Bill Skelton.'

'Never heard of him.'

'You?'

'T15, Thames-side,' said George.

'Well, that's why, then,' Charlie glanced at George briefly as if suddenly noticing him for the first time, 'if you're up there. No wonder I've never seen you around.'

'You thinking what I'm thinking?'

'It's got to be.'

Both men smiled ruefully. There could only really be one explanation for the current chaos.

'Logistics,' they said, together.

They were walking past hotels now, some modern and ugly, some old. And ugly. Between-job male models glared back from behind frosted glass in the lobbies. Private gossips floated in dark taxis between women in furry hats. London, in its dark places, held more secrets and told more lies than any number of feral intelligence officers. The two men turned around and headed back towards Piccadilly.

Charlie and George were certain now. Not only had they been posted to the same cover story – the photolab – but no-one in the organisation had realised the mistake.

No-one at all.

A spectacular, and in other circumstances theoretically amusing, balls-up of the first order.

George was the first to offer up the truth. His last operation had been liaison work in Russia, he explained. Carrie's face had not been familiar to him but her regular visits to the photobooth had put him on the defensive. He reasoned she was a honey trap of some sort, a favourite ploy of the SVR, trying to lure him to the hotel. The lurking man with the gun had been a Russian assassin – it was he who had tried to kill George in Moscow last year. George had met 'Carrie' a couple of times, as Charlie had witnessed, but always in the open. She had made her feelings plain, using the photos to give their interactions the flavour of espionage and their interest in books as a lever to get them together. Then she had invited him over to her hotel. When Charlie had turned up before him, George reasoned, she had decided to deal with him before George arrived. 'She probably thought you'd see her sooner or later. So you became part of the problem,' he explained, allowing himself a chuckle. He coughed as the sharp London air crept too far down his throat. 'You and those photos, Charlie. "She's a spy, George, definitely . . ."'

Charlie smiled. 'Double bluff. The least likely thing a spy's going to do is talk about espionage in broad daylight.' An ambulance keened past towards the dark expanses of Hyde Park, narrowly missing a cyclist. 'You realise,' continued Charlie in a curious tone, 'we'll have to compile a report. A long one.'

George eyed him, aware of the tone in Charlie's voice. The tone was . . . not completely committal. A lure dangling at the end of the line.

'True,' said George to the pavement in front of him. 'I guess we will. Have to.'

'They'll just start us over again of course. New legends, new prep.'

'That's procedure for you.'

They walked in silence for an entire minute. On the sixty-first second: a look between them. A look that said: *unless* . . .

'But quite frankly . . . fuck that,' muttered George, 'for a game of, you know, "soldiers".'

Charlie nodded, a shy smile creeping slowly across his face.

A couple emerged from a communal doorway nearby. The doors were fancy and led to mansion flats. He seemed much older than her and she was laughing. It may have been the first time she had been back to his place and from the looks of the stubble-burn on her delicate chin, and his self-satisfied smirk, they were only very recently post-coital. He was leading her to a taxi and the look between them suggested she'd love to stay, she really would, but she can't, she couldn't, she shouldn't, not tonight. As the taxi pulled away the man blew her a kiss and across his face drifted a pall of the most profound sadness. Perhaps there was something about this young girl that reminded the man, very abruptly, that someday, much sooner than her, his life would be over.

Charlie and George were across the street. And a look passed between them, too, at that moment. A look that could have told anyone with an eye for these things a very simple fact.

Somewhere, slowly, a friendship was beginning.

Charlie stood in the doorway of his mouldering bedsit and listened to the taxi's engine gurgle away into the night. He shuffled in, shut the door and, as the exhaustion took over, stubbed his toe on the corner of the bed. Protesting would take too much effort. He'd wanted to run a bath; now he didn't have the energy. He closed his brown curtains. They retained a frustrating gap in the middle that no amount of tugging would close. He gave up, choosing instead to let gravity do its work, and he collapsed on top of the covers. He was asleep before his face hit the mattress.

And as Charlie slept his dreams, as ever, sought out Becky. The scene was familiar to him. He would emerge from the arrivals door at an airport. At first the faces would be blank, uniform, featureless. Eventually he would see her, and she would wave with a smile, sidelong and mysterious. As he walked closer she would take his hand and kiss his knuckles.

'I want to woo you,' she would say. 'I think it's only right I do some wooing.'

He would smile back and reach to touch her hair. She would take his baggage trolley and push it ahead of him. He would follow, jetlagged, bleary, ecstatic, and admiring of her legs as she strode on. The doors would slide apart and she would reach the kerb. A murmuration of tourists, luggage valets and taxi hawkers would congregate around her. In his bubble of exhaustion, Charlie's attention would be distracted. And when he looked for her, she would be gone and the pale eyeless faces would return and he would be screaming, crying, keening into his pillow, sucking in gulps of stale air and shuddering out the agony that lay festering inside him.

George lay dreaming too. His dreams were smooth and white, like the surface of an egg. His eyes never roved under his lids. He kept his dreaming straight ahead, arms folded like a Pharoah, feet together, window open to the sounds and glow of the city night.

In the morning, Charlie awoke and realised he couldn't feel his left arm. He was about to put it down to pins and needles when he realised his right arm was much the same. As was his left leg. His right leg. And his neck.

He lay there for a few moments, eyes twitching from the pillow to the clock. He half-wished George had been there to witness it, because despite his predicament Charlie was aware that this was, if viewed from another angle, actually quite funny. But there was only one audience member in here. Himself. And there was no doubt about it: he could not move. This had happened once before, on a piece of Service business. The need to get out of bed then had been far more pressing than this. But whatever the situation it was far from pleasant. Charlie knew from experience that this was something he simply had to ride out. For some reason he remembered the pinstripes from the hotel bar. The oscillating legs. The physical tip of a subconscious iceberg. He wondered how long it would take those men to realise they were gay.

A car alarm sprung to life outside. Charlie zenned his way through the ring cycle as he had done every night since he moved in.

Slowly, sensations slithered their way back through Charlie's body. His fingers twitched. His toes wiggled. And carefully, but carefully, he dragged himself out of bed.

The fall, he reasoned. That had been a hell of a fall.

The Underground was packed and he found himself wedged into a corner. He closed his eyes. Carrie's blood-spattered face came to him suddenly. He felt a lurch of nausea.

George was already behind the counter when Charlie showed up. Also behind the counter was a steaming cup of coffee, freshly brewed and welcoming. It was keeping a Danish pastry company.

'I didn't know how you take it,' smiled George. 'So I just told them to put everything in.'

Charlie took a long, deep sip and realised that George hadn't been kidding. His heart began to thunder. And he smiled in thanks.

That morning, local news had reported the deaths of a man and a woman at the Langham. Despite two security cameras and a number of witnesses who said they were sure the lady who died left the bar with someone else, there were no concrete leads. If the heat got to be any stronger, George and Charlie agreed to report the situation. But for the moment, as with many instances of sudden and necessary action, it was all over bar the paperwork. They would keep the incident quiet.

George sipped his cappuccino. It left a thin crescent of chocolate powder on his lip. He looked down at Charlie's left hand – the Band-Aid had slipped from the fourth finger. George only glanced for a moment but even in the low light his sharp little eyes were able to pick up evidence of a small scar where a wedding ring might once have been.

9

They'd been reminiscing all morning. With no customers to speak of, they'd managed to cover a lot of ground. The atmosphere was bright, warm, chatty. It had been raining outside and lunchtime travellers shook their umbrellas out as they struggled to the ticket machines.

'So who was in charge of your training?'

'Man called Forbes,' said George.

Charlie's eyes flashed bright with the memory.

'Mackinnon?'

'The very same.'

'Shit. He did my intake as well.'

Both men grinned.

'Future . . .' said George.

'Outcomes . . .' returned Charlie, imitating a very particular Scottish accent. George and Charlie collapsed into infantile laughter.

Mackinnon was something of a legend in British espionage circles. Over time the wave of sandy fringe had speckled with grey; the mad eyebrows had evolved into something altogether more lunatic; the paunch more voluminous and solid; his voice an octave deeper. Scowling over his spectacles, he instilled in the new recruits to the Service much more than requisite cryptography standards, acronyms, paperflow guidelines and bureaucracy procedures. He bestowed upon them an entirely new way of thinking.

'*Future outcomes,*' he would sing in a nasal tenor to the back of the lecture hall on the third floor, '*can be predicted, generally speaking. Given enough time with any scenario, general probability vectors can be plotted and action taken to prepare. The world is an uncertain place, random, unknown. Every situation offers up possibles.*' He always used the word over 'possibilities'. The way he pronounced it made his students giggle. '*A good officer knows to look for that which is least likely in any given situation. And move it to the centre of his planning.*'

Forbes would catch a female recruit's eye and smile. '*Or her planning,*' he would add, creepily. And continue: '*That, gentlemen — and ladies — should be the lynchpin of your thinking.*'

When Charlie heard those words, on his first day, he smiled. He knew he had made the right decision in signing the Official Secrets Act. Because what Forbes was positing was nothing more than a gigantic, careerwide game of Good News, Bad News. And no-one — but no-one — was better than Charlie at that game. Just ask Neil Mackay.

'Funny . . .' said George.

'What is?'

'The same people telling us how to do our job. Giving the same lecture, year after year. You'd think they'd have found something else to do with their time.'

'People get entrenched in things,' mused Charlie. 'There's a huge institutionalisation problem with that place. The rut gets so deep it's a tough place to leave. You get stuck in the mud. After a while.'

George stared at the crowds outside for a second. That mask was back. Not a flicker of emotion, anywhere. A waxwork.

'D'you reckon?' he said.

Lunch hour was soon upon them. And, for the first time, Charlie and George agreed to play truant. They closed up the photolab and made for a local café refreshingly rude enough to dissuade the Starbucks crowd from frequenting its greasy tables. No-one here would dare to ask for chocolate powder on their cappuccino. And anyone foolhardy enough to request soya milk would be hauled over the counter and stabbed to death with a cheese slice.

George wasn't really from Newcastle, he explained to Charlie. Charlie nodded. And told George he wasn't really from Swindon. Charlie told him about his childhood in Edinburgh, his love of football and movies. And the many playground hours playing Good News, Bad News.

George was especially tickled about that.

The two men then lapsed into silence, a little uncomfortable. This was like going from first date to honeymoon in a single leap, and it suddenly showed in their eyes. Men unused to sharing even the most trivial of details were doing the Service equivalent of French kissing in public.

The coffee grinder powered into motion with such startling ferocity that all conversation in its vicinity had to stop.

Charlie and George walked back to the shop in silence. There was a spot of work to do on the developing machine. It was relatively new and streamlined. Rather than mixing chemicals, fixer, bleach and so on, there were four individual canisters, interchangeable, designed for a monkey. A trained monkey, but a monkey nonetheless. Charlie knew it was his turn to unscrew the feeds and prep four new canisters for the afternoon's processing duties. George had suddenly gone quiet, which previously would have led Charlie to worry that a locked-room anecdote was somewhere on the horizon. But now, in the flush of their new bond, he just found the silence extremely pleasant. Until the moment George slowly approached Charlie. A trusting glow in his cheeks. The warm sincerity of a friend. He turned to Charlie as they walked.

'Can I ask you a question?'

'Sure,' said Charlie.

'When did you start hating it?'

10

Lecture Hall 11, Curzon Street Offices

'The coding methods of the slaves on the plantations were not
that different to the methods used by the ancient Egyptians.
Ciphers and cryptography have been the fulcrum of history's
successes and failures . . . depending on which side you talk to.

'But I want to talk to you not about the cryptographic
intricacies of composing secret messages, but the more mundane and practical communication modes with which you will
be conversing, sometimes at considerable distance and with
some urgency, with field agents in your case-officer rotations,
and in your field postings, when case officers are assigned to
you.'

Forbes was already in full flow. His Scottish vowels echoing
off the walls and into the ears of two men, Charlie and George,
separated in space by three metres; in time by fifteen years. For
the record, Charlie had been dressed in khakis, George in
stonewashed jeans.

'Coding protocol four is our focus today. You will see the
small roll of fillum in front of me. This fillum is your Bible. If
you find yourself out in the field, that is to say, on an operation,
and a courier delivers such fillum to you, take it immediately to
a developer. It will not be urgent – we have other ways of
communicating such messages that will make themselves

known to you via these lectures in the very near future. But treat the fillum with respect. The contents will almost certainly involve your tasking information and will be important.

'Our protocols dictate that any pertinent information will be recorded via the frames of this fillum. Slide one.

'Frame One is for contextual microdots. The shape or form of a circle or a circular object prominent within the image will denote the existence of a dot in one of the four corners. Find the respective negative and decode using the appropriate equipment.'

The sounds of scribbling pencils.

'Frames Two, Three and Four are requests for differing levels of observation in human, automotive or static targets. Should Two contain an image such as a house or exterior flat, this will denote a recent shot of the domestic situation; ditto number Three, which should, if Two is analysed properly, contain a photograph or other such image of the target. The proceeding frame should finally contain a microdot containing pertinent information.'

Forbes whined on. And the pencils kept scribbling. Until he came to the thirteenth frame.

And then the scribbling stopped.

11

Hate. Such a strong word. So very full of itself. Charlie resisted using anything of that intensity unless he genuinely meant it. It was a behavioural hangover, an ingrained habit from happier times.

But even Charlie had his limits. George's fish-hook had finally snagged a nerve. As they approached the Underground entrance again after lunch, he finally gave in.

'Okay, fine,' he said, 'what can I say. I'm young, the job seemed interesting. I didn't know what I wanted to do with myself at university. I knew what I *didn't* want, though. Banking. Marketing. Retail. Milk round. I wanted to at least make a show of trying to do something different – there's the irony. Did I ever get it. But hate it? No. Ups and downs, sure, same as anything else. You could shag swimsuit models for a living, you'd still have off-colour days, wouldn't you?'

George shrugged. 'I'm not entirely sure you don't feel exactly the same as I do.'

Charlie tried to work around the double negative – or whatever the hell it was that made George talk like that sometimes.

'I mean, sure, there's an impact on your private life, but what job doesn't have that? Apart from unemployment. And even then, you're unemployed, and that makes a difference too.' Charlie shrugged. 'Being a spy means you can't have a girlfriend. It's really as simple as that.'

George sniffed imperiously. 'Really? Why?'

'Well. You know. Secrets. And stuff.'

George screwed up his nose. Discarded the thought he was about to launch into. And sighed. 'Yes, well, whatever excuse makes you happy, it's fine by me.'

Charlie looked at the ground. His lace was undone. 'It's not an excuse,' he said.

'Nothing to be ashamed of—'

'I'm not—'

'Whatever you need as a crutch, you go right ahead.'

Charlie turned volte-face and headed off in a huff towards a record shop as George hurried down to the lab.

The reason George was heading back was twofold. Firstly, because he was annoyed at the way Charlie was sublimating his evident hatred of the Service – something George had cultivated for many years and frankly could do with sounding off about.

His second reason for heading back was because, as they had departed for lunch, he had noticed a small lump of chewing gum on the Underground map closest to their exit. It was centred on Chancery Lane.

In the modern world of espionage, mused George with some degree of sadness, information technology had supplanted invisible ink. But the thrill of the pen still remained in George; his early missions had been a low-tech fairyland . . . dead-letter drops, lemon juice, plant pots in the window, classified ads and even *poste restante*, the once essential travellers' tool now displaced by email. The old-school tricks of treachery were to him notes well-bowed on a Stradivarius, procedures to delight in, to celebrate and pass on in hushed voices to future minds. As the years had rolled by, technology had removed some of the last vestiges of fun from the cut and thrust of workaday missions. Part of the reason George had agreed to this rather dull posting was in order to receive orders old-style. Thus the chewing gum of Chancery Lane made his heart sing. Because that meant that his orders were about to arrive.

The arrangement for issuing commands and allotting projects could vary from job to job. If a more low-tech approach was being mooted, as in this case, the following strategy would commonly be employed. The same approach that Forbes had prepared them for so many years ago. A courier – these days resembling anyone from an unwitting shop assistant to a well-meaning pensioner – would drop off a single canister of film to be developed. The kicker would be in the address. 73c Kavanaugh Gardens, SW3. There is no such street in that part of London. And therefore no such flat. According to the drill, once delivered, the recipient would open the canister and process the contents. As soon as was convenient, the operative would consult the pictures and, if needed, remove appropriate negatives containing microdots for further analysis. George often imagined number 73c Kavanaugh Gardens in his mind's eye while waiting. First-floor balcony, blue curtains. A small Chagall reprint on the wall. A vast cream sofa, immaculate, housing two very spoiled Persian greys.

George was still imagining the furnishings when the courier met his eye. *Pretty fucking unsubtle about it*, thought George as he approached the counter and opened up again. The young woman was wearing a sweatshirt with big red words on the front. The words read: 'It Wasn't Even My Sandwich'.

He fingered the film canister nervously – and decided to wait until Charlie arrived.

At that moment, Charlie was wandering the brightly lit alleyways of HMV Records. When he was twelve he had heard Janice Long's Radio One show, spread out on a blanket in the summer sun after a long afternoon spent kicking a ball against a wall. Quite out of the clear blue ether came the most beautiful tune he had ever heard. But as much as Charlie listened on, there was no mention of the artist, nor the title of the track. Since that day he had been searching for the band. Humming down the phone, humming in record shops, humming to anyone who'd listen and several who wouldn't.

The spotty kid in an HMV T-shirt shook his head and Charlie jogged back to work. He'd seen a chalk mark on the pavement that anyone else would presume was the telephone company marking out the site of their next botched digging adventure. But Charlie knew better.

The film canister was waiting for him. He found it in the 'to do' pile when he got back.

The two men got to work in pregnant silence. Negatives were coaxed in the darkness from their fetal positions and the minilabs began whirring and churning quietly to themselves, heating and mixing and bleaching and fixing deep within the grey bowels of their cabinetry. Once underway, both George and Charlie tried to busy themselves on paperwork: Charlie on his overdraft, George on the curious case of 'The Three Widows', a short story involving the death by poisoning of a man in his sickbed. As the rough-cut series of prints was flopping out into the dispenser, George was nodding in admiration as the doctor's thermometer was revealed to contain a poisoned tip. He wondered if any

Markhov-haters had read this tale some time in 1978 when Charlie tapped him on the shoulder. George gathered up the photos and the two men, together, began flipping through them:

Ground.

Ground.

Ground.

Ground. Ground. Wall.

Wall.

Wall.

Another bit of wall.

Wall.

No creativity in these messengers any more, thought George. *When I was on courier elective I'd give them the best collection of buttocks they'd ever seen.*

Charlie was feeling the same. His collection of photos was an equally dull affair. Usually when the orders came like this the more exciting outcome you could hope for was a document delivery. Maybe even some breaking and entering. But even those were glamorous options at the moment.

Wall. Ground. George flipped again.

Wall.

Frame number twelve was equally dull.

Number thirteen wasn't.

In both cases, it was blank.

Both men looked at each other.

'Ah.'

'My thoughts,' said George, 'exactly.'

12

'The thirteenth frame', said Forbes, 'denotes one specific act. In my seven years of working in the "field", as it is in my humble estimation rather ironically known – hardly ever being anywhere with greenery – I was called upon to exact this order only once. And even then, in extremis. With the world in such chaos, all rules have changed. In the past our Cold War bipolarity had about it a sort of rule of law, a sense that there was a game to be played, a brutal game that nevertheless had certain rules and codes that were to be followed, and transgressed, with care.

'But the new world order has fragmented these codes and as officers of Her Majesty there might be cause, at certain points, to find oneself receiving a blank thirteen.

'A blank thirteen means you have been instructed to kill.

'Upsetting, of course. But not as bad as the frame to come. Because the fourteenth frame will contain a picture of the human being whose life it is suddenly imperative that you curtail. And no matter how many kills you have on your CV, this first face-to-face with target always has an impact. I should know. The first time it happened to me, I contracted a form of shell-shock at that stage unknown to medical science.

'My problem was that I could not believe that this person,

this stranger staring up at me from the photograph, could have done anything wrong. And so I balked, I called my supervisor, I made the mistake of thinking too much and acting too little.

'And he told me what I shall tell you. Frames thirteen and fourteen are not entered into lightly. Frames thirteen and fourteen are never known to be wrong.'

13

Some of the greatest changes occur in the most mundane of circumstances. History has many grand gestures and heroic feats that have heralded the dawning of new eras. Caesar crossing the Rubicon, the falls of Troy, Constantinople, Paris. Columbus 'discovering' the New World. But the flow of human history is mostly predicated upon smaller events, timeless human moments, and new futures are decided more on telegrams than wars, handshakes than murders, insults than famines. These are the true building-blocks of life, myriad and minute, and they rise up like coral from the sea bed, birthing tidal pools that wash the future clean. The hole in the condom. The turning of a card. The keeping of a promise.

The viewing of a picture.

There was a growing hubbub from the ticket hall. Someone, it seemed, was trying to pay for a single to Tottenham Court Road with a supermarket loyalty card. Behind them, twenty-five foreign-language students with bright rucksacks were loitering on the other side of the ticket barriers, looking around in innocent wonder at the station interior. At odds with the way everyone else reacted to their environment, the students gazed in awe at this London Underground Paradise to which they were suddenly and joyously privy. A logjam of commuters built behind and in front of them and as the numbers swelled they began to broil with impatience.

Charlie looked at George.

George looked at Charlie.

Silently, the two men exchanged their prints.

Each man now looking at a photograph of himself.

14

Movement. Yes. Charlie was sure of it. George was moving. The physical evidence of it was so tiny, so impossible to judge if indeed it was a move at all, that nothing came of it. But Charlie knew that George was in motion. He'd been the first to break the frozen posture of awe that both men had been struck with when they saw the pictures in their hands. Which suggested to Charlie one of two things. George was getting ready to run. Or, he was getting ready to strike. Charlie's heart, previously plodding along at around 73 beats per minute, rose on a steep ascent to nearer 130. Adrenalin now pumping in his muscles made his reactions sharper, quicker.

George was certainly moving. In his mind he was already at the second-bottom drawer of the stationery cupboard. He didn't want envelopes. He wanted something else in there.

It took a great deal of concentration not to give in to the instinct and make an ungainly leap for it.

This was madness, of course, both men knew it was, and yet everything in their training forced them to conclude that it was precisely because it was madness that they had to act – now.

The bustle of the ticket hall was building. Commuters

were angry, they wanted to get home. The language students, blissfully unaware of any impending crisis, were finding new and exciting things to point to and chatter about. Look, said one, a barrier. Amazing. And over there, a map, look, you, a map of the whole Underground. Soon, they were thinking, we will go to Rock Circus.

Charlie tried to recall if George had anything on his person that might constitute a weapon. A penknife? Not that he had seen. A keychain? He couldn't quite remember how many keys he'd seen, enough for a brass-knuckled fist perhaps. With a lack of anything else to go on, the two men simply stared at each other. Charlie tried to time his blinks with George. If needed this would give him a 150 millisecond advantage – as long as the brain would take to reprocess a new image.

'It's a mistake,' said Charlie.

'Clearly,' said George.

George still moving microscopically backwards towards the cabinet . . .

'Logistics. Come on. They've already messed up—'

'Undoubtedly,' said George.

'So . . . we should talk about it.'

George smiled, disarmingly. 'I'd like that.' His bodyweight shifting imperceptibly . . .

'So you should stop acting so strange,' said Charlie.

'I'm not acting strange.'

'Yes you are,' hissed Charlie, 'you're being strange.'

'Well, you're looking at me funny. That's why I'm acting strange.'

'You just contradicted yourself.'

'Precisely, it's all this pressure you're putting me under. A man can't think straight.'

Charlie computed the time it would take George to open the cabinet and remove an object and try to kill him with it. Needless to say, the time would also depend on what the object was. Knowing the real George as short a time as he had, Charlie reasoned he was the sort of spy who could kill someone with a tortilla chip if he really wanted to. 'Where's your gun?' he asked.

'What gun?' George was sweating now too. He tried to remember what Charlie kept in his pockets. He knew he had no gun but he also knew that Charlie had marginally better acceleration than he did, and could, if required, take him down before he reached the stairs. That said, George had a longer stride length and would pull away over a longer distance.

'The gun,' said Charlie, 'you shot someone with recently.'

'Oh, *that* gun.'

'Where is it?'

George sighed. 'I don't bring a gun to work unless it's bring-your-gun-to-work day. And even then, I'd think twice.'

'You had a gun in the hotel.'

'I followed you from home.'

George had stopped moving and it was now Charlie's turn to ease himself into a more beneficial position.

'This is a mistake,' Charlie repeated, almost to himself. 'There's been a really bad mistake here.'

'There's a lot of it about.'

'We can't seriously go through with it.'

'It's orders, Charlie.'

'It's bullshit, George, come on. I think we should make a phone call.'

'You think we should call them? On the *telephone*? Our allocations got mixed up, Charlie. That's all. Where we are right now doesn't matter. The orders are clear.'

77

'Think for a second. I'm betting there's some other legend base, some other photolab somewhere else in London with two other pictures, the two people we're supposed to target, which by the way is a real bloody liberty to ask of a loyal employee who wants to move on to new challenges.'

'You're planning to leave?'

Shit, thought Charlie. *Too much going out here, not enough staying in*. 'You said *you* were leaving.'

'The way you said it implied—'

'Never mind what you think it meant, what I meant was that you're leaving and it's an insane thing we have here – *please stop doing that, George*.'

George froze his hand, where it was quietly proceeding behind him to the developing machine.

'Doing what?' he asked.

'Your hands. Put them where I can see them.'

'And you.'

'My hands are here, look. Right here.'

Ticket hall was now at DefCon One. Security had been called as someone in a suit, possibly the ginger man again although it was too hard to tell, someone businessy at any rate, was pushing a fifteen-year-old Belgian boy out of the way, causing his girlfriend – who unbeknownst to anyone in the ticket hall had been thinking up ways to break up with him that night – to hit the suit with her backpack. She screamed, loud and shrill enough to make Charlie's eyes flick instinctively over to her. The light entered his cornea, impacted on the retina, whereupon his brain allotted some time and space to reprocess this information as electricity, and in the time it took his brain to register all this and instruct the eye to move back to the Imminent Danger, the developer tank was already in and out of George's hand and hurtling through the air towards Charlie's head.

Ducking away from the fluid at the moment of impact he still saw George leaping towards the second-bottom drawer of the stationery cupboard, and even as the stinging sensation hit his eyes Charlie reasoned it was time to use his legs in a rapid running motion.

He ran straight at George. Charlie slid feet first, an ankle-high roundhouse kicking away George's feet and flooring him as he loaded a clip into his recently retrieved .22. The fall was hard. George's head smashed on the photolab. Charlie, semi-blind, leaped over the counter and pulled down the grille behind him. The kids were quiet now. They stared at him in admiration from the ticket hall and Charlie ran around the corner, beckoning them, shouting 'ici, ici' . . .. And, lemming-like, they followed, surging towards him and blocking the passageway as Charlie chose not to run up the stairs to the sunlight but instead took a detour into the toilet.

Not the gents, but the ladies – where he ran past the stalls and up to the sanitary-towel dispenser. Just underneath the box he located a loose tile. Inside of this, a plastic bag. Inside of that, a Glock 9mm with a full clip.

'Module One,' said George as he kicked the door open. 'Evasive tactics. Locate your weapons stash within easy reach of camp.' He said these words into the toilet area from the doorway. They echoed harshly against a background of tiled walls and the sound of running water. 'Well done, nice work, great job, A-plus, full marks, where the hell are you?'

In his defence, Forbes had presented it far more eloquently when he had introduced his fresh-faced new intake to the world of fieldwork. *'Evasive tactics,'* he annually explained, *'apply as much to the urban environment as to the intensely rural. One of the main first lessons you must learn in executing evasive maneouvres is not movement but planning. If you plan ahead, your survival is disposed to succeed, even against overwhelming odds.'*

When Charlie heard the door he whipped around in a 180-degree turn and, grabbing the underside of the nearest cubicle, slid himself along underneath four of the six like a rat under wheels until he came to rest near a pair of square-heeled Manolos. A woman was here, on the toilet, reading *Marie Claire*, her thick black glasses slung between her legs in the hammock of her underwear. In one swift movement, one that fighter pilots might call an Immelmann Turn because it was part loop and part roll, Charlie was squatting on the toilet seat just behind her, his hand over her mouth, his gun at her head and his voice soft and reassuring into her ear – *'Sorry, sorry, many apologies, won't be a second . . .'*

George chose wrong and kicked the door of the next cubicle down, during which Charlie launched himself over the top of the adjoining wall. He grabbed George's ears. Wrenched with all his strength and sent his head *slamming* into a patch of graffiti that read 'Lick My Clit'. Using the wall as further purchase, Charlie jackknifed over the edge and fell with his full weight on top of George.

'Module Two,' growled Charlie, a millimetre from George's face. 'Use your environment.'

In fact, Forbes had spoken about the applications of environment as a thread throughout the Evasive Tactics seminars but had introduced the concept very simplistically in the early training stages: *'Many officers fail to appreciate the benefits of utilising their surroundings first rather than bringing other variables into play such as weapons or other tools. The things at your fingertips matter most when time is most compressed. Therefore, make sure your decisions are based with what you have now, rather than with what you'd like to have in a second's time.'*

The woman next door had climbed up onto her toilet seat to stare at the two men's struggle. The automatic flush, a relatively new addition from American lavatory suppliers, was having a field day as Charlie and George hoved in and out of its range. The woman caught Charlie's eye as he was being wrestled to the ground. 'You can make noise now if you like,' he said.

She signed at him furiously. She was deaf. The sign said 'What the fuck are you doing?' Either she had a sore throat or she was quite enjoying the spectacle. Perhaps she hadn't seen the guns. *Perhaps she was blind*, thought Charlie; *blind, deaf, dumb, or maybe plain stupid – just like me—*

George's elbow came out of nowhere. Charlie couldn't understand where he would have found the space for any backswing but the impact was strong enough to wind him. In the enclosed rectangle of space there was hardly any room to aim a gun and both men's hands were attempting to do exactly that.

'I thought you liked me,' said Charlie.

'I do like you. But this is how it is.'

Charlie knew that George's hand was close to achieving a clear shot at him and he realised *this was not the story of his life*, that of all the places he was going to die, the floor of the ladies' toilets in Oxford Circus Underground Station was not one of them.

An anger welled in him. A flash of memory from a

darkened bedroom. His father's voice, drunken and cruel. His mother's quiet sobs. Just the two of them now.

He blistered with anger. More at the potential obituary than the fear of death. Would anyone come to the funeral? Not likely. That would be a one-woman show, all right.

'You made my eyes hurt, you bastard.'

And George could only watch as his wrist was bent back into a position that defied, for a brief moment, every chapter of *Gray's Anatomy*.

George reasoned it was an advanced jujitsu hold. But as his hand bent even further over, he identified it more correctly as a component more derivative of joonbong. Charlie was straining a little. There should have been a snapping sound by now. At the very least, intense pain . . .

'Double-jointed,' murmured George, before his knee sallied forth towards Charlie's groin. But Charlie and George were classmates separated only by time and where George thrust, Charlie parried. Punch and counter-punch, strike and block, for each man it was like fighting with himself. In a rare moment of clarity, Charlie's knee impacted with the space between George's upper lip and his nose, a theoretical 'pressure point' on the central meridian. George concertinaed to the ground. Charlie concealed his gun in his jeans and sprinted out of the toilets. Scudding across the ticket hall he pushed in with the crowd of language students now filtering through the barriers. He leaped ahead with one of them, slipping through without a ticket and down the stairs as a still-smarting George powered through from the other side of the hall.

The platforms for the Victoria Line didn't interest Charlie this time. He was headed straight for the big red bullet-train, the Central Line. He knew the crowds would be greatest there. Forbes's words bubbled from memory as he ran:

'In this module we shall discuss another field tool. Use of cover in a built-up area. We might suggest here that the urban jungle provides as many hides, false trails and undergrowth as the greener variety. And needless to say, both forms of terrain offer deadly and accessible means of ambush and surprise. In terms of concealment, urban evasion offers the hunted a greater latitude of movement and a smaller requirement to maintain silence. It is, however, a corollary to state that this also means the hunter will be able to approach far closer to the prey should the extraneous noise be too great.'

Charlie arrived on the busy platform. His hair blew back. A train was just arriving. Through the surging front row of suits, Charlie danced and excuse-me'd to the front of the train. Concealing himself behind two pinstripes by the far door, Charlie had his hide. The doors beeped, and then shut.

He was safe.

'Whoever's playing silly buggers with the doors on the last carriage,' went the driver's near-suicidal whine, 'stop it. There's another one behind this one.'

At the very last carriage, George, the silly bugger, wasn't listening. He was trying to pull his foot through the ankle-sized gap between the rubber edges of the doors. He gave up, kicked off his shoe and pulled his stockinged foot through instead. The doors then opened for a second. George leaned out, grabbed the shoe and sidled back into the wall of wool-clad sweaty flesh that had been squeezed and shaped into the inside of the Tube carriage like so much stressed-out gelatin in a mould. A commuter terrine, thought George randomly as he sucked in his stomach.

Charlie, hearing the announcement, presumed the worst. He always did. It was the job. The bad news is always coming round the mountain.

The train moved off and so did George. It was nearly impossible to breathe inside the cattle-truck atmosphere but somehow George was managing to make progress. The crowd were uniformly silent in their protests, apart from one woman who improvised something under her breath along the lines of 'the Youth of Today'.

The train arrived at Bond Street just as George reached the last sliding door of the carriage. He pushed his way off and on again, using the time to survey the carriage ahead. Was Charlie on or off? George held the doors. A sudden rush of wind announced the arrival of the eastbound train, only a short run across the platform. The doors of both trains stood open.

Then he saw him – sprinting across for the eastbound train. Doubling back. Very clever. Way ahead of you, Charlie.

George jumped out and powered to the second train, diving into the crowds just before the doors slammed shut. Now George was at the front and Charlie was at the back. No matter. He began to move again.

George repeated the same process at every single stop. With each station, one carriage closer. On some occasions he managed to get to the connecting door in time through the slowly thinning wall of flesh that still filled the train.

Oxford Circus again. Tottenham Court Road. Holborn. Chancery Lane.

Charlie, on his part, looked for George. But he wasn't looking to catch his eye. He needed George to be uncertain.

Slowly but surely, Charlie knew it was time to get off.

People draining from the Tube now, a collective unconscious release. Human beings cannot take proximity for too long. So many personal spaces, so many border incursions.

Everyone walking at a fast but panicked clip, yearning for the escalator, the exit, the glimpse of sky. Charlie's blood reflooding with cortisol now, his bones preparing themselves for more pain and punishment. And as St Paul's arrived, Charlie had an idea. The platform was packed. Lawyers on their way home, negotiating their way to Liverpool Street.

Charlie merged into their masses, walking backwards, sideways, any way but turn his back, crouching as low as he could, to the black grille across an old accessway, padlocked. His Glock's silencer dampened the sound of the broken lock and as the train pulled away Charlie pushed the grille quietly open and disappeared into the stench and darkness of a stairwell.

George, of course, had seen him.

He powered along the platform and into the gloom – just as Charlie heaved the heavy grille with all his might. The bars impacted with George's forehead and he flipped backwards onto the platform, landing on his tailbone. His gun skittered out from the back of his jeans and under the path of the departing train. He glanced up at the security cameras and decided not to retrieve it.

He leaped up and, vision clearing from the blow, ran into the tunnel.

Charlie had always been fast. His school sports days were usually awash with medals and trophies. His best distance was the 400 metres. Not quite a sprint, but close enough to hurt. He thanked his talents again as his furious strides took him along the narrow passage that curved off at the bottom of the stairs.

Behind him, chunky legs powering like pistons, came a determined George. Frustration and anger on his face as he shouted after Charlie, red-faced but gaining.

Charlie was frantically trying to work out a strategy but the only order that really made any sense at the moment was: Keep running.

'Charlie, look,' growled George, 'you might have a point.'

'So stop chasing me!'

'I'm not chasing you, you're running away.'

George suddenly struggled to catch his breath. A slightly asthmatic wheeze crept into his heaving chest. Charlie listened as he ran, a little concerned.

'You should get that checked up.'

'I know.'

'It really doesn't sound very good.' Charlie swung himself around another corner. He caught a second wind and accelerated. He could hear George slip and regain his step.

He almost didn't see the lift shaft.

Charlie's hand flailed out into nowhere but a merciful collection of pipes allowed him to grab hold and stop his fall. But the gun in his hand clattered against all four walls before clanging to its death far below. George's footsteps slowed as he realised that Charlie's had stopped entirely.

Charlie pressed himself against the filthy darkness of the passageway, using another defunct pipe as semi-cover. From somewhere, the bells of St Paul's Cathedral echoed in the squid-ink blackness.

'It tolls for thee,' panted George. 'That's who the bell tolls for.'

'Whom,' sighed Charlie.

'Your gun, I believe, has gone.'

Charlie turned to face George as his eyes adjusted to the dark. George sighed and adopted an old-school karate pose. Charlie kept his eyes on the older man's hands.

'And so has yours . . .' teased Charlie.

Forbes had final words to say about final standoffs. 'The number one rule of combat must be, don't. Never get into a fight you don't think you can win. Of course, we cannot always pick our moments. So if, given all your resources and efforts, the enemy has you within its grasp and you are forced to fight for your life, then use whatever means there is at your disposal to survive. Surrender, plead, cajole, distract, promise. All of this is talk and keeps your heart beating until you can find a way of improving your situation.'

George lunged like a cobra, a furious snap of his hip that hissed in perfect form towards Charlie's chest. His foot caught Charlie below the rib. Worryingly close, Charlie thought, as the pain seared up to his brain and down to his perineum, to a one-touch kill. Charlie then caught and twisted George's foot and shifted his weight till George's momentum carried him towards the lift shaft. But George knew this would happen, he had anticipated the move and it was suddenly Charlie who found himself once again on the edge of what could have passed for the rubbish chute to Hell.

'Tai chi,' smiled George. 'An extreme form.'

'I think I missed that day,' smiled Charlie, and headbutted him.

In the bloody pain of the impact, George saw that Charlie's headbutt had also set him off balance. But the pain was too great to move and Charlie was on the edge of the end, arms now haymaking to keep him from falling. A small slip sent him over – an arm shooting out to the edge now – and suddenly Charlie could feel the cold air of a long drop breezing up through his trouser legs.

Charlie watched George's Hush Puppies approach. His fingers were starting to slip from the slimy edge of the lift-shaft floor. He noticed that one of George's laces was undone.

George stopped a foot from the precipice. 'You're really very good,' he said. 'I mean . . . at your job.'

'Thanks,' said Charlie.

George stared down at Charlie as if wrestling with an unvocalised dilemma in his head. Charlie, sensing his finger muscles straining with every passing second, attempted to engage him. 'We should call someone,' he said.

'Who?'

'Control, Despatch, someone – I mean, look at us, this is ridiculous, this can't be right.'

'I know what you mean, Charlie. I do. What a mess.' George sighed, crossed his arms, slouching momentarily into a flash of 'old' George. 'I'm going to level with you,' he continued. 'And I want you to level with me.'

'Sure thing.' Charlie was gritting his teeth, trying to will himself up, but the fibres weren't twitching hard enough. Charlie's trips to the gym had focused more on his biceps than his finger muscles.

'I'm retiring,' said George. 'There, I've said it. I'm leaving the Service. I think you should know that.'

'Well, thanks for being honest.'

Nails in concrete now . . .

'And I want to hazard a guess. I think you are too.'

'Retiring?'

'Leaving. Getting out.'

Charlie tried a final time to pull himself up. He failed. 'Bingo,' he shouted up. 'Bull's-eye. Affirmative.'

George nodded, leaned down and offered his hand. Then drew it back.

'It would seem to me,' he leaned in so Charlie could hear

him, 'that our shared goal has something to do with our current predicament.'

'My current predicament, George, to be fair.'

'That's true.' George kneeled down now. 'All this running around has got me thinking. And what I've been thinking is – I'm quite keen to find out just exactly how all this came about.'

Sweat poured off Charlie's face as his last remnants of strength ebbed away.

'George . . .'

'And it strikes me that two heads are better than one. I'd quite appreciate your help. We're not really going to hurt each other. Are we?'

Charlie shook his head as George's hand edged forward again.

'Are you in?'

'In. Yes. Help. Now.'

George smiled and leaned over. 'No pulling me down now.'

Charlie's feet, flailing in the darkness, suddenly found a ledge, an uneven piece of brickwork that gave him balance and purchase. He realised he could indeed pull George down if he wanted. He could tug George down and complete his mission – his stupid, ill-thought-out, surely-a-mistake mission – when George's skull surely split open fifty metres below. But George had offered him his hand. He could test out this new phenomenon called trust.

'Okay. I promise. No letting go either.'

'Agreed.'

Hands were gripped tight.

And for the first time since either of them could remember, promises were kept.

15

It was the end of another work day and the pub was packed. Which was just as well. In the light of current events both Charlie and George needed cover, retreat, human bodies and human noise. They needed to bathe in anonymity.

Because they were attempting the most difficult feat a spy can accomplish. They were telling each other the truth. It was this: they were both getting out of the game.

George had decided early on that he would not abandon a world he found, at least to begin with, addictively complex. But as the years wore on, the job wore him like an old jumper and his very fabric began to fray. Errors, like this current situation, were occurring too often. Lives were being lost. Now was the time, he said, to jump before it was too late.

Charlie had found himself on a different trajectory. He had entered this world out of something akin to intellectual curiosity. George had wanted idealistic victories for freedom. Charlie had wanted a good and interesting job that wasn't graduate accountancy trainee for a marketing firm. He knew there was a secret side to the way he would have to conduct his life, and in his relationships he knew there would be elements of his existence that would be hermetically sealed.

But quickly he had found that no matter how satisfying this is in theory, in practice it can rip your insides to shreds. Because the women that Charlie wanted to be with weren't theories at all but actual women, amazingly enough, real people, and they needed more. They needed to feel not just part of his life, but entwined with it. And where they moved towards, he pulled away. Not through desire but through necessity. Dates were broken. Phone calls unreturned. All because of work. And work became the other woman. Small print, he had called it. They tell you what to look out for, but not how to cope with it.

Two men. Leaving their jobs. Suddenly marked for murder. Charlie had to admit, it didn't look good.

'So where,' said George, after the two men had shared an uncomfortable silence, 'does this leave us?'

'Confused,' said Charlie.

'Life,' sighed George. 'It does this sometimes.'

Charlie nodded as George stood up and zipped up his fleece like a man with a plan.

'Whatever the truth here, we need to test the water,' said George. 'Buy some time.'

'How would we do that?' asked Charlie.

Faking a death, in the long term, is almost impossible. Particularly if the people who ordered the wet work want the evidence. Teeth can be pulled, of course, and placed in fresh jaws. There are ways and ways of *delaying* the inevitable. But the inevitable always comes.

Faking a death in the short term, however, is worryingly easy. It just requires a phone call to convey the simple message. 'He's dead.' But even phone calls can be tricky.

Charlie spent ninety minutes following George on a

whistle-stop tour of local electrical suppliers before they closed for the day. Both men were careful to avoid high streets and chain stores with integrated security cameras. Instead, they found themselves in George's immaculate yet crippled Ford Escort, rescued from underneath a dusting of pigeon droppings. They toured backstreets in an eclectic range of local neighbourhoods. In each shop, George was careful to buy only one item, only ever speaking when spoken to, only ever using cash. Crocodile clips in Hampstead. A cheap telephone handset in Islington. Wire-strippers in Southwark. After each purchase, Charlie noticed, George would be careful to wash his hands. Charlie began to realise that the real George, far from being a slob, was actually intensely anal.

With these odd purchases safely stored, both men retired to another pub for another very strong drink. They needed it. Because even the shortest-term employee of Her Majesty's Espionage Providers has instilled into them a strong sense of inhibition. There are lines drawn out that are *verboten* to cross – moral, ethical, even procedural boundaries. Some, it is known, are breachable. Others are boldened, double-yellowed and unassailably set. And calling in a false job report was one of the boldest and yellowest there was. If the Service had a bible, it ranked as a single-figure commandment.

'We call in,' George had explained.

'How?'

'Just as we're supposed to. One of us has done the job. We call it in and see if anyone cares.'

'Why?'

'Because unless they're expecting us to enter into some bizarre suicide pact,' George was whispering now, 'it's the most likely thing that would have happened. Had we not found out. Remember. It made sense because whoever despatched these orders had no idea we'd be in the same bloody station when we got them.'

'So one of us dies, and one of us calls in.'

'Exactly.'

'So who gets killed?'

George removed a ten-pence piece from his pocket and the two men stepped outside into the road rage and gridlock of the evening rush hour.

'Winner makes call,' he said. And tried to smile.

It was an ordinary coin. Worth ten ordinary British pence. Enough for twelve seconds of parking in Central London. Enough to cool the lids on the smiling corpse of a one-eyed man.

George and Charlie watched the silver disc as it was caught in the yellow glow of a streetlight. For a moment it seemed to defy gravity, soaring higher and hanging longer than might reasonably be expected. To Charlie, it looked like a silver hummingbird, phasing in and out of solidity in a gravity-defying hover. To George, it looked like a coin.

A woman passed them with her shopping as George caught and buried the piece of metal under his palm.

'Good luck,' said George.

'And you,' replied Charlie.

They took George's car along Pall Mall, alongside the procession of empty cabs flowing back into town after depositing night owls to their beds. George parked in a 24-hour underground facility and the two men made their final approach on foot.

They were headed towards a phonebooth.

John le Carré had a lot to answer for in the Service. Since his novels exploded into the world of publishing they had impacted on the very way the Service had conducted its own business. The Watchers, the Circus, all the fictional mythologies concocted in his head had been appropriated by the real world as miniature trophies to their own importance. So it was with the administrators of casework within field operations, or ACFO/5. They had decided long ago this was a boring thing to have on your business card and instead, after too much coming in from too much cold, they decided to call themselves something a little sexier.

They called themselves 'Controllers'.

As with all calls to Controllers, a public payphone had been allotted to each field officer to ensure legitimacy. The Controller manning the line would only accept calls from certain officers on certain numbers. George's 'comms node', as it was called, was in Chinatown. The two men walked the arterial routes up to and surrounding the payphone four times, doubling back on their steps and surveying the surrounding buildings before quietly shaking hands for luck. It was coming up to three-thirty a.m.

The Gerrard Street end of Chinatown is neon-soaked, even in the early hours of the morning. Slick cobblestones mix with discarded chopsticks, padlocked grocery stores, piles of rubbish and detritus from the thousands of meals cooked, served and consumed along this strip every evening. The carcasses of ducks, chickens and piglets protrude from clear plastic bin-liners.

Late-night revellers still meander through the giant Pagoda Gates, the airlock to Shaftesbury Avenue. In high windows and low basements, shadows and murmurs, illicit gambling and solitary dishwashing. Around the benches and litter of Gerrard Place, a moment's peace. Here, dirty as sin and oddly pathetic, stands a phonebox rendered in an almost entirely insulting mock-Shanxi Province pagoda style. What with the bird droppings and the chewing gum it almost looks like it has been deep-fried.

George had been watching the silence for twenty minutes. The street cleaners had been and gone, the last bar closed up and locked, the last bloodshed tussled over and exacted on the cold walls and still-damp pavement. Charlie was less involved with the action, or lack of it, in the square. He was more concerned with the routes leading in, and the coverage of the oh-so-subtle police closed-circuit cameras that monitored the main drag. From the shadows, by a vehicle access gate, Charlie watched the third taxi chug past and admired, for a moment, the empty roads of London. He gave the signal to George, and George, suddenly forgetting the context, began to relish the prospect of what was, for him, a routine piece of criminality.

He had located the manhole cover in the street with ease. It lay some thirty metres or so from the phonebooth, close to a corner – presumably, George thought, to ensure the maximum visibility for anyone about to attempt what he was doing. Inside, just a few feet below the pavement, lay the Holy Grail of phreakers everywhere, the local CAB exchange. The phonebooth, like all local lines residential and commercial, was connected here before proceeding in an orderly fashion towards the main trunk lines of the UK telecommunications grid. Here, in the centre of London, there were no telegraph poles to clamber up. Patching into the local lines for free required a little more effort than that.

George strode quickly to the manhole and wrenched it up with stubby fingers, cold and trembling from nervous excitement. Leaning down, he pulled a hex wrench from his pocket and heaved open the front panel. He looked up to Charlie, who was still watching both exits to the square and still as a corpse. The signal was 'all clear'.

Pulling a length of wire from his pocket George elongated the connections that he knew, through experience, provided the point of contact for the payphone. He placed two crocodile clips on the red and black ends of the exchange housing and, like the diligent telecoms engineer he was pretending to be, dialled a service code on his handset to test the connection. It was good. He patched in to the payphone contacts and, with a signal to Charlie, began to unwind the hundred metres of wiring in his pocket, checking right and left for any signs of life. In the darkness and drizzle, the wire was practically invisible against the tarmac and cobbles. Charlie joined him moments later, his hair flattened against his forehead from the rain. Without a word, both men withdrew to a narrow alleyway behind a recycling bin. The alley was open to a small passage that led, eventually, to St Martin's Lane. The bin was surrounded by refuse from the restaurant next door, and Charlie thought for several minutes that he would puke.

George cleared a small space in the rubbish to gain a view of the street. Charlie watched him with ill-disguised dread. 'Wouldn't it be easier just to pay the 20p?' he whispered.

George glared at him for a moment before lifting the receiver. The dial tone purred. Dawn would be here in a few hours and from the feeling deep in George's bones both he and Charlie would be lucky to see another one.

'This way,' said George, 'we're sending a message. If they are watching this box, they'll know we mean business.'

'Perhaps we could make the call from somewhere that doesn't reek quite so much of vomit?'

'Cab box,' replied George, as if Charlie should have

known. 'You can only do this sort of malarkey from the local exchange node.'

Charlie just nodded.

'And anyway,' said George. 'You lost the toss. You're the one who's dead.'

George dialled the numbers. The payphone was making a call with no-one inside it. At the receiving end, the caller-ID verified to the operator on the end that this was, indeed, the correct point of contact reaching out. This payphone was slap bang in the centre of at least twelve eyelines from differing properties on all sides, and if things were as bad as George felt they might be, it really would be a good idea to make the call from somewhere a little less . . . visible. Such as right here.

Somewhere, either deep in the bowels of an air-conditioned basement near the Thames, or in any number of unseen booths or bunkers in the subterranean London that no Saturday shopper has conceived of underneath their Muji-laden steps, a phone was picked up. The Control (née ACFO/5) operator on the other end. She sounded like she was in the middle of her second cigar and answered with a rasp.

'Yes.'

'Hello, it's Paul. I've done your shopping.' *Keeping to the code*.

A pause and crackle on the line. George worried for a panicted second the crocodile clips were slipping, but the noise soon stopped.

'Thank you.'

Silence. Then:

'Stay on the line.'

Thank you was normal. *Stay on the line* was not. *Stay on the line* was categorically quite a long fucking air-conditioned coach ride away from normal, in fact. George made sure his voice wasn't too nervous when he spoke again. He tried to suffuse it with a *soupçon* of barely concealed irritation:

'What for?'

'Just stay on the line, please.'

George's heart rate was starting to climb. *Please?*

'All right but hurry up, it bloody stinks in here.'

George let himself be momentarily pleased with his subterfuge. A small dab of local colour to bolster up the lie. He pressed mute and turned to Charlie, who was squatting beside him, hands over his nose.

'What's happening?'

'Shut up.'

Charlie shut up. Until George nudged him.

'Can you hear that?'

'Hear what?' said Charlie.

A grumbling sound floated on the air. The roar of an engine. A motorbike.

'That,' said George.

It was a Yamaha, in fact, rapidly switching gear and screaming around the corner – George and Charlie turning now to watch as the voice came back.

'Are you still there?'

'Yes.'

'Stay,' went the voice, 'on the line . . .'

In the darkness, through the panes of the phonebooth, it was impossible to tell if someone was inside or not. By the time the bike was alongside the phonebooth, George and Charlie were turning to run. By the time the grenade impacted, they were at full sprint.

They reached the car in under a minute. George was hyperventilating. Charlie was barely breaking sweat, his face an ice storm of fear and frantic thought. It was as if every second breath, every second moment, was somehow misplaced, mislaid – a confusing disjunction, a swirl of heartbeats and breathing. A gap into which some clear and logical thinking was needed, in the breach, right now.

As George turned the key, there it was, in a hidden cortex – one synapse embraced another in a flash of knowing that he took pains to hide well away from Charlie. A tidal wave of sadness burst through his mind. Deeply bitter now, deeply glad he had someone, at least, he could still vaguely trust.

No skipping ahead here . . .

One second at a time . . .

George floored the accelerator and the car squealed up up up the onramp in concentric circles, emerging into a dust storm, a strange and curious metallic cloud that was blowing from a nearby street. Police already cordoning off the area. An explosion of some kind, bystanders were saying. A group of Swedish clubbers trudging home after a hard night's partying clamoured around the policeman in a yellow jacket. Charlie could lip-read the tourist's bad English: 'All closed here please?' The policeman replying: 'The road is closed, Madam.' In the rear-view as they drove away: 'There's been a small incident.'

Small, thought Charlie. *Like Hiroshima*. George stared at him briefly. Charlie had said it out loud.

George ground the gears and reduced his speed. Scrutiny now would surely mean a swift and deadly net. There was only one place to head now. His face turned green as if in sympathy with the traffic light. Several hundred yards ahead, he turned into a quiet side street, opened the door, and vomited.

Charlie rummaged in the glove compartment and found an old take-out flyer from an Indian restaurant. He folded it in half and sought out a pen. Fingers trembling, he balanced his feet up on the dashboard, laid the blank over his knees, and began to write a list. It was a list of certainties in his life and it was entitled 'Things I Know'. For a horrible second, Charlie couldn't think of anything. Then it came:

THINGS I KNOW

- *My name is Charles Lachlan Millar.*
- *I am 27 years old.*
- *My mother's name is Jane.*
- *My star sign is Capricorn.*
- *I am an employee of a division of the British Security Service.*

Charlie sucked the nib of the pen and tried to think of something to add. He couldn't. Then could.

- *I have signed the Official Secrets Act.*
- *My favourite meal is baked beans on toast.*
- *I enjoy the music of Orbital and Groove Armada.*
- *My employer wants me to be dead.*

George wiped his mouth and shut the door. The two men stared at each other, slowly realising a fact that made both of them, quite unconsciously, bite their bottom lip. *The only certainty you have, right now, is each other*.

'I have a good relationship with my department,' said Charlie softly, offering George a mint.

'*You* might. *They* might not. I don't know if you've noticed at all, but someone somewhere doesn't like us.'

'Not us, George, you,' said Charlie.

George shook his head. 'They only killed me cos they thought you were already dead. My guess is, if you'd made the call you would have ended up in the same pile of ash. You're forgetting we both ended up on a Frame Thirteen.'

The hurt in Charlie's eyes looked so innocent it made George want to heave up all over again.

'They don't kill everyone who leaves.'

'And how do you know that?'

'Because,' said Charlie, 'I've always been honest with them. And they've always been straight with me.'

George drove on for nearly a minute in an uncomfortable and angry silence. Then he began to laugh. A bitter, shrill laugh that showed his eye teeth. His tone unforgiving as sandpaper:

'When,' sneered George, 'in your entire career as a spy, has anything anyone has ever told you ever turned out to be on the level?' Before Charlie could answer: 'When, Charlie, during an operation, has anyone ever told you the truth? When . . . what was it you said? When has a piece of *good news* ever been unaccompanied by a piece *of bad news*? Let me answer that for you – never. There is no such thing as a free lunch and no such thing as a piece of good news. Trust me, to coin a phrase. I've done a little audit of our current situation and from the look of my data, this unholy buggeration is only just beginning.'

Charlie's mind now took some time out, filtering through recent experience with a mental sieve in the vain hope of finding something solid. George was talking. Some of his words made sense to Charlie. Need some headspace to work this out, George was saying, need to sort through this. And finally George was pawing his shoulder, meeting his eyes and insisting:

'We're going back to my place.'

16

Morton was upset. His breakfast, his most favourite of all meals in a busy day, had been ruined by a telephone call. He understood it was important, of course, and normally he would spoil any meal, any activity, for the person on the other end.

But it was breakfast, for God's sake. It was *pancakes*. A little early, even for Morton, but when the sun rose enough for first light to show, Morton liked to be doing pull-ups in his doorway, looking out at the buildings on the horizon, carbohydrates in his belly fuelling the glycogen in his muscles.

He'd seen a few horizons in his time. Belfast skyline, Liberian foothills, Indonesian skyscrapers. Wherever the military had sent him, he'd ensure he woke every morning with one eye on the furthest point he could find. He would call it his vanishing point. To stare at the horizon was somehow to ensure his ultimate departure. To book his mental return-journey. To remind himself that there were other places – that not all of you was here.

This was said a lot about Morton. Wherever he was, he was usually not all there. The people who usually said this, however, were generally whispering, out of eavesdrop range. Morton did not take kindly to criticism.

His foul mood took him to the weight bench in the corner. A few sets of dumbbell flys took the edge off the rage. He had no cause to lash out now unless commanded.

He shrugged on a T-shirt over the long-sleeve top he was wearing. Pulling on a small woollen hat, he was already jogging when he hit the stairs.

The Yamaha was still sinking slowly into the mud at the bottom of Camden Canal. He would take the Suzuki. An altogether more anonymous kind of bike.

Morton roared through the empty roads and occasional street sweepers, hardly noticing a small birdshit-covered Ford Escort taking its time on the Harrow Road.

17

George parked his Escort just around the corner from his house, opposite a newsagent's. It was some seventy metres along the terraces to his doorway. The harsh Eastern Bloc-inspired light still streamed from the streetlamps as the first light coaxed its way into the visible spectrum. Charlie had suggested a long route to get here, a standard procedure to thwart any tail. Evasive driving was difficult, as Forbes had once pointed out in Module Seven. Paranoid driving, on the other hand, was relatively easy. George had been happy to oblige. Immersing themselves in spycraft, however briefly, gave them both a small bubble of calm in which to breathe.

'If we are working under the assumption that this situation is bona fide and true,' said George, 'then we must also assume that they will be working on our domestics.'

George knew a concerted steam-clean of any asset's domestic arrangements was usually the first thing on a case officer's 'to-do' list in these sorts of circumstances. It felt strange to be on the receiving end. Charlie stared at him intently. This was where George was good at his job. He could keep it together and think straight.

But the cleaners might perhaps delay until a full audit of the phone site was completed. George felt sure they would be meticulous with that. No reason to suspect the caller of reporting a spurious operation. They presumed he'd been in the booth, and would presume he had killed his target and smelled no rat. The administrative fuck-up of posting them both to the same cover had saved both of their lives. That would not have been planned. So. They at least had some time on their side. He had Charlie, for the moment. And George needed Charlie to help him with something very badly.

Something inside the dark recesses of his musty little house.

From here Charlie could just about make out the front of the building, the outside stairs, the light on across the street. The noises from further down into the neighbourhood, to the dark children's playparks where the crack addicts – and, indeed, crack novitiates – played on the swings.

A car full of teenagers swung by, pausing to navigate the speed bumps in the road. A party ending, or a party beginning, it was hard to tell. Their music and attentions elsewhere. A solitary dog-walker pulled his woolly hat over his ears and stayed near the light.

'The corner of the bedroom,' George was saying. 'The door is operated on a security lock. The keypad you saw. It's basically an alarm system. You'll need the combination.'

'What is it?'

'You'll need to write it down.'

'No, I'll remember it.'

'Fine. The code is 1–2 . . .'

'Yep . . .'

'. . . 3–4.'

Charlie blinked slowly a couple of times.

'That's it?'

George looked at him blankly.

So Charlie asked again. 'That's the code?'

George nodded. Charlie's face prompted a reply. 'What's wrong with that?'

'It's the stupidest thing I've ever heard in my life.'

'Wrong. What's the most likely assumption when you approach a lock? That the person who has installed the lock has an interest in keeping you out. He or she will therefore have chosen a very rare and personal number in order to prevent your entry. The least likely outcome would be that this person would just choose the first four numbers on the number line. So simple, it's brilliant.'

'So simple it's stupid.' Charlie put his hand on the door and paused. 'Wait. Why am *I* going in there?'

'They'd be expecting *me*. They know *me*. They won't be expecting *you* and so *you* are going in there. And hurry up. By the time they pick through the wreckage of that phonebooth . . .'

'Fine,' said Charlie.

They both agreed a rendezvous point in twenty minutes' time. With that, Charlie got out of the car.

As he walked towards the front of the house, he replayed the furious argument that had raged in the car on the way there. George's point was simple, and annoying. He needed what was inside the secure room. That was clear. He had made that point. He would not tell Charlie what it was in the bag, nor indeed the attaché case inside it, only that the contents could help them, that he had to have it if they were to continue looking out for each other in this time of need. Charlie explained that George could, as many people do, simply walk up to his house and turn the key in the front door. But for George this was too dangerous. If there was any watch put on the dwelling, he argued, and they had to assume now that there was, this would be a fool's gambit. Better for Charlie to pose as a burglar and break in unnoticed.

Charlie had understood the reasoning behind this. But it hadn't made it any easier to agree. George had a way about him that suggested that any opinion other than his own wasn't worth the air it was hung upon. He'd been pleasant about it, of course; George always was. But now Pleasant George was sitting in the relative warmth of a red Ford Escort. And good old reliable Charlie was freezing his nads off here on the street. About to commit what an eighteenth-century hanging judge would have termed *Theft with Malice from a Dwelling-House*.

He was nearing the doorway itself when he noticed a light in a top-floor window. Not of George's house, but, worry-ingly, the one across the street. *A handy eagle's nest*, thought Charlie. *Where Eagles' Nests Have Dared*, he mused, his active mind fizzing with thought under stress. *The Eagle's Nest Has Landed*.

Calmly turning round, he swiftly counted the houses up to George's stoop and retraced his steps around the corner. Cutting back around the row of terraces Charlie could see the decrepit line of back gardens and washing lines glowing in the grey predawn. He had two choices. Either hurdle the garden walls, cutting cross-country as it were, to George's back garden, or enter the house that immediately backed onto George's. In the first case he was trespassing six times. In the second, once. A garden can contain dogs. So can a house.

Charlie grew tired of thinking and hurdled the wall. The voice of Forbes Mackinnon was loud in Charlie's head as he crouched in the bushes.

'The likely scenario would suggest that the house is being watched,' whined the voice in Charlie's head. 'They will be expecting you to behave like you're scaling the Berlin Wall circa 1972. Therefore, the opposite approach may well pay more dividends.'

A dog barked nearby. From the sound of it, it was angry but lived on another street. Licking the chilled sweat off his top lip, Charlie crept quietly but efficiently through the back lots, avoiding impalement on fences, walls and plastic children's playgrounds, until finally he tucked his toe into a gap in George's fence and vaulted his way into the weed-infested jungle beyond.

A workaday sentry would keep it simple. They would presume that the errant individual would seek to gain access to the house via the roof. The front door would be too visible from the street. Charlie decided to triangulate these theories with a third option. The back door.

He looked at the sky. The clouds were darker than the night surrounding them. A storm front approaching. Once, Charlie's eyes had seen a similar cloud. He had seen it through torrential tears and a dark, winding road. The headlights of a fast-moving car probing the hedgerows on the turns.

He forced the memory away.

Work to do. Work to do.

He held his breath and lifted a small garden gnome, dirt underneath grinding slightly as a small key was revealed under his feet. He had found it a little strange that someone as clearly paranoid as George would keep his house keys under a gnome. Then again, strange meant unlikely and unlikely is exactly what he wanted. Quietly, Charlie unlocked the door. He pushed it open an inch. A frosty thought slapped him.

Was this all a ploy?

To kill a man in Frame 13 means you are not supposed to make it known. Or get caught doing it. George may not have wanted to kill him in the Tube station. Or indeed in the car. Where would Charlie have elected to end George? Not in public, for sure.

He would have waited, thought Charlie.

He would have bided his bloody time.

A tingling on the back of his neck made Charlie whip around but the breeze was the only culprit, lonely and cold on his face.

Charlie turned back, mind racing again. He would have bided his time and chosen a moment where there would be no witnesses.

Like now.

Expect the unexpected, Charlie reminded himself. *Live with the paranoia. Use it to stay alive. Use it because that's your job*.

Do your job.

Another inch. Inside, the front windows cast strange shadows on the carpet. The kitchen immediately ahead of him was quiet like a mausoleum. He squeezed himself inside, closing the door behind him with a muted click. Heart thudding now inside his head. *It should really be in my chest. But let's not split hairs right now*.

Counters to the left and right. Breadcrumbs and fugitive shards of dry pasta stirring unwanted noise underfoot. As his eyes adjusted to the dark, Charlie froze.

A figure was standing in the hallway.

It seemingly hadn't heard him. It had its back to him and was quite, quite still. Stepping to the side, Charlie avoided what he felt was a potential eye-line. Soon, as no new noise came from the hallway, long-forgotten courage returned. He peeped around again. The figure was still there.

It was wearing a fleece.

The fridge *buzzed* suddenly to life behind him and Charlie sucked in breath – the figure must surely have heard. But it didn't make a move. This didn't make sense. Charlie stepped forward, ready for anything.

Only one more step was needed. This was indeed a fleece, but an unoccupied one, hanging in shadow on the banister. Charlie shook his head and kept his guard.

Jumpy is as jumpy does.

Charlie cleared the downstairs rooms in a series of swift, silent movements, and began to climb the stairs. If they thought for a moment the two of them were still alive, thought Charlie, they would be crawling all over this place.

Charlie's footsteps began to fall more heavily. Muscles relaxed. There was no-one here.

He walked in the centre of the stairs now, his weight creaking the floorboards and, seemingly, the entire house. He reached the top and turned towards George's bedroom.

He was halfway along the upper landing when the knife slid under his chin.

'Keep quiet and nothing's going to happen to you.'

Charlie cursed his lack of foresight and took in what he could. The voice was male, deep, slightly tremulous. Not George. No way. Unless he was a genius at impressions. The blade was real enough. Smooth, non-combat. The arm was strong and lean. From what he could smell, the aftershave was not cheap. When no-one else ran to confront him, Charlie made a deduction and stuck by it.

'Get on the fucking floor,' hissed the voice.

Charlie let the words hang in the air for a sarcastic moment.

'Now!' The voice was panicking.

'Look,' sighed Charlie. 'I don't live here.'

'Didn't you hear what I said?'

The knife edged closer to the tougher flesh located near to Charlie's oesophagus. Charlie tried to convey to his unseen conversation partner that his eyes were rolling at him.

'I did hear you, yes. But you didn't hear me. And what I said was: I don't live here. As in, you don't live here, and neither do I. Can you guess what that makes both of us?'

'You're off your tits. On the ground!'

'Look. Mate. You're burgling the wrong house at the wrong time, that's all I want to say.'

'One more peep out of you—'

It was, in fact, the last thing Kieran said that evening. He had seen the house lie in darkness all night and decided he could swell his coffers with the minimum of risk come early morning. He'd once scored a television just by walking in behind some posh lads who were moving their stuff into a rental house-share. The area was becoming like that. Pushed out of the truly expensive areas around Notting Hill they migrated here with their flat-screen tellies and Nakamichi hi-fis and black-rimmed glasses and mussed up hundred-quid hairdos. They'd been so gobsmacked by his front – just walking in, picking it up, fucking off, thanks very much – that they didn't say a word as he left. Polite, you see. That's posh schooling for you. It's what's made this country great.

Charlie's weight shifted so subtly that Kieran had no idea what was coming next – a lightning strike that broke his right foot and right elbow almost simultaneously, followed swiftly by the snapping of his right wrist, a sound reminiscent,

Charlie realised, of the crack of a sniper's bullet. Kieran's screams faded to unconscious whimpers via a blow to the head.

Gathering himself together, Charlie continued along the corridor towards the bedroom. *Life*, he was thinking, *has been doing this to me for too long*.

The bedroom was a shambles – thanks, in part, to Kieran's amateurville attempts at finding anything of value. The boy, he had decided, was not there on official Service business. If the powers-that-be had decided to burgle George's house after his 'death', they would have sent professionals. It was actually quite hard to make a room look as amateurish as this one. They could employ the kid to do aftermath makeovers, thought Charlie, as he strode across the chaos to the keypad.

And stopped.

That thought arrived again.

That horrible, paranoid rumination.

Things were occurring, spiralling things, and he needed to talk to someone. He sat on the bed. A loose spring boinged in protest underneath him, spreading rumourous murmurs throughout the rest of the mattress. He rubbed his temples.

His Mum, well, she wouldn't understand. 'I just want you to be happy.' That's what she'd say. A noble sentiment, and comforting. But not a priority right now. No, Charlie needed to run something by a man who knew his mind. Someone who could shed some objective light on his situation. He was alone and George was out of earshot. It was, in fact, the perfect time.

He located the *Yellow Pages* and found the category marked 'Sandwich Bars'. Dialling the number, he realised it was pointlessly early. But there might be an answering machine, there might be some way he could tell him where they could meet, talk, chat–

'Hullo?'

The voice had not changed in seven years. No reason why it would. It was still chirpy, full of latent enthusiasm and no small amount of dry irony. And still ever so fucking loud.

Ever so Neil Mackay.

'Neil?'

'Speaking.'

'It's Charlie. Charlie Millar.'

'Fuck a duck, how the devil are you?'

'Neil, listen—'

'Hey, can I call you back on another line? Right away?'

Charlie gave him the number. And Neil rang off. Charlie stole a glance at the hallway. Kieran was starting to stir. Nothing to worry about. Not yet. The phone startled Charlie and he snatched it so hard the receiver flew out of his hand and for a few moments he was juggling with it. When it finally slotted against his ear –

'Sorry about that. So. My God.'

'What are you doing in so early?'

'What are you doing *calling* so early? Jesus, I don't speak to you for yonks and then you ring me out of the blue —'

'I'm sorry.'

'I just happened to come in to meet a new cleaner. You're a very lucky man. So how goes the rambling life you fucking wastrel layabout gypsy bastard?'

Charlie had always come across to Neil as someone who still hadn't really settled on what they wanted to do. Un-surprising, as Charlie's cover stories required him to change jobs every few months.

'Neil, you have to help me.'

113

'Name it.'

'I need you to play the game with me.'

'Play the game?'

'Good News, Bad News.'

'Erm . . . been a while, like.'

'Come on. Good news, you're a spy. Bad—'

'Wait, wait, Charlie, hud up a sec, you serious?'

'Yes. Just play along, you remember.'

The phone went silent for a second.

'Are you on the bevvy, Charlie? Is that it?'

'Neil . . .'

'Or on drugs? Oh, don't let it be drugs, you'd be an idiot to get all mixed up in that business—'

'Neil, *please* . . .'

The stress in Charlie's voice sent the phone quiet again. Finally:

'All right. Go on.'

'You're a spy, okay? A spy . . .'

'I don't want to be a spy. Living a lie, Queen and Country, all that bollocks—'

'Just *play*, Neil—'

Neil sighed. Bloody hell. *It's been a while, pal* . . . 'Fine. I'm a spy . . .'

'. . . Bad news is . . .'

And Charlie laid out his problem to Neil. No BCG this time, no playground bell. Just two old friends in the dark shadows of a damp-afflicted hallway and the fluorescent shine on the plastic floor-tile of a sandwich shop. Neil, of course, was still bloody good at the game. And as Charlie predicted, the options open to him at the moment were not good. Neil had outlined them in stark detail:

'Good news, they think you're dead,' Charlie had offered.

'Bad news, they're going to find out sooner or later,' said Neil.

'Good news, you have time to do something; get away.'

'Bad news, after that I don't know who I can trust.'

There was silence between them.

'I think that's it, Charlie. I think it's bad news on that one.'

Neil cleared his throat politely. 'Charlie?' he said softly. 'I have a friend, a psychiatrist, and I think that maybe you should have a wee chat with him—'

Kieran was on top of Charlie before he could reply – a massive Hail Mary punch that Charlie only saw in his peripheral vision at the last minute. He drew back enough, however, for the blow to clip his shoulder and not his chin. Charlie waited for the follow-through to unbalance Kieran and then floored him again with a sharp jab of the telephone. As Kieran fell to the floor, Charlie checked the line was still clear.

It was. And so was Charlie's mind.

There was no time to chat.

'I have to go, Neil—'

Charlie hung up. A noise downstairs startled him. He ran to the door in the bedroom. Still plenty of time to make the rendezvous.

George hadn't been kidding. 1–2–3–4. A green light. And he was in. Or rather, he was able to open the door.

The space behind the door was a cupboard. Hardly deep enough to hang a shirt. On one side, a filing cabinet. On the other, a fireproof safe. Charlie opened the filing cabinet. In the bottom drawer was a small coffee tin. Unscrewing the tin, Charlie found a matchbox in the bottom. Inside the matchbox, another small key. He took the key and opened the safe. Inside the safe, another key. He moved to the back of the cupboard where, under a piece of masking tape, he found another keyhole, at knee level. He unlocked the door, his forehead now bathed in sweat.

Quite security conscious, then, our George.

The door opened into another void space, a crawl space really, but George had wanted only one thing, and that thing was sitting forlornly in the middle of the doorway.

The holdall had a squeaky shoulder strap, and made a hell of a racket, and it made Charlie even more nervous about what Forbes would have called The Egress. All that was needed to complete the picture were a hooped jumper and small white letters across the black plastic reading: SWAG.

Charlie was careful not to move across any portion of the interior that was visible to the upper floors of the house across the street. He checked the still-unconscious form of Kieran and placed his body in the recovery position. There was definitely a person downstairs. Charlie peered over but couldn't make out any features. Charlie realised that the window was his only option. *Need to stop making this a habit*, he thought to himself as he shinned down the drainpipe and into the garden. Retracing his steps was easier than he thought, and as he reached the rendezvous point with a minute's grace he allowed himself the smallest rush of pride in a job well done. It was quickly followed by a pinch of bitterness. He may have loved his job, but the job sure didn't love him.

Bitterness morphed into rage as the minutes ticked by. Each second seeing lights flick on in house after house. A postman's trolley squeaking across the uneven pavement on an unseen but nearby street. They'd had no time to dryclean the area to ensure their total safety. And now the tidy quiet was unravelling. Soon there would be witnesses, gossips, suspicious and territorial neighbours . . .

Charlie was facing a brutal truth.

No doubt about it.

George had gone.

18

The lift had broken down and so Latham was forced to take the stairs. He didn't really mind but the heating in this particular building seemed permanently set to tropical, even at this hour. By the time the sign for the sixth floor swung around, the charcoal-grey jacket had blooming stains of sweat under the arms and down the centre of the back. This didn't really bother Latham. What really bothered him was the time.

Latham did not like to be late.

The staff weren't even in for early morning checks. In fact, Latham had counted out the midnight cleaning staff meticulously, sitting quietly in the fragrant leather atmosphere of his silver BMW coupé, picking his fingernails clean with a toothpick.

There were problems, it was abundantly clear, and in addition to lateness, Latham did not like problems. There were potential solution-providers out there who could help. The *Bordeaux-on-the-chaise-longue* was that no official eyes should be aware that these individuals were embarking on any problem-solving. Because as far as official eyes went – as well as official ears and official minds and, most importantly of all, official guts – there was no problem.

He had been operating like this for some considerable time and had come to realise the advantages of independent thought, even in an organisation that so valued, along with certain religious cults, more lemming-like behaviour. The advantages, of course, only applied if the organisation had no idea whatsoever about such independent thoughts – and, more importantly, the independent actions that flowed from them. Always important, in any covert endeavour, to have a bodyguard. Bodyguard, after all, protected the Normandy location of the Allied invasion of Europe in World War II. Churchill had called the operation by that name as 'all truth should, in war, be accompanied by a bodyguard of lies.'

Opening the door to the conference room, Latham stopped abruptly. Morton was already there. He stared back at him unblinkingly for an uncomfortably long time. A talented weapons expert and ex-IRA informer, Morton had rejected alcohol and embraced physical fitness in a disturbingly evangelical way. Still, the sense of balance and poise it gave him had its uses. The studious application of rocketry from the seat of a motorcycle, for example.

He had been trained in some of the country's most feared and respected Special Forces contingents. His story was like all the others that Latham found uses for. Those that discovered themselves under-promoted or over-scrutinised when the drugs, the weird sex, the corruption, the booze, or any combination/permutation took hold. They had all spiralled in a downward direction. They had all taken heavy hits and had careers poisoned by colleagues, by circumstance, by both. Latham was drawn to the vibrations these situations caused and to the people who were contaminated by them ever after. Drawn to them because they were desperate, because they were needy. And Latham particularly valued

dependants who could . . . be both dependent and depended upon. Seeking them out in their personal and
professional gutters, Latham would cajole them, nurse
them, train them in the ways of expediency, of indepen-
dence and fortitude. After a while they would feel – if not
human again, then as good an approximation of the state as
was practicable. Along with a sturdier pair of legs, and the
bootstraps they'd used to pull themselves up, came another
addition to their new arsenal. Loyalty. Not to the State, the
Monarch, the Job or the Law. Not to any of the sleeping
policemen that interfered with them or tripped them up in
their previous incarnations. This loyalty was to one person,
and it was unswerving, far-reaching, and wide-ranging.

As freelancers, or 'stringers', they now lent their not-
inconsiderable services to Latham. Free of charge. And
when the call came, they answered.

Just as Morton had done tonight.

Latham's entrance had the usual result. He had a well-
practised and long-revered air of authority – which quickly
motivated Morton to stand. A good sign, he felt, under any
circumstance.

There was a large brown leather chair at the head of the
oval table. Latham moved to it and sat down as a distant glow
promised another day on the horizon.

Latham stared and spoke. Every word measured and
weighed like the diamonds of Hatton Garden. It wasn't
entirely clear if Morton was fully awake.

Latham explained that a situation had arisen, one that
required immediate attention. Morton spoke at last, eager to
please as ever. Latham leaned back and listened. A new
thought, cold and grey, forming even now in his mind.

19

Charlie waited only another charitable minute before he abandoned the rendezvous point. He was too nervous about the residential street. People were getting up, brushing teeth, persuading children into breakfast. He moved to a busier thoroughfare, aware of the risk he was taking. Yet doubly aware of how hard he would punch George on the nose should he ever see him again. One minute late is excusable. Ten minutes, by and large, is usually fatal.

And Charlie knew all about that.

Ever since.

Ever since.

Focus. No time for that now.

Charlie had been stood up. He had been stood up twice before in his entire life. Both of those events had involved Becky.

Their first date had been an unmitigated disaster from start to finish. He had asked her out at a bus stop after a mutual friend had introduced them. He had timed the question as his bus came up the hill to take him home. Becky had, rather sweetly, walked him there and felt his nervousness; allowing him to ask her if she wanted a drink next Friday, kiss her goodbye and jump on the bus like a conquering hero, all within twenty seconds.

There had been considerable scepticism amongst his schoolfriends. She was a year older than him and was already training to be a chartered surveyor. They had met in what both referred to as a 'George Michael moment'. The reference took on new associations as time went on, but for them the reasoning was the song, 'A Different Corner'. Becky and Charlie had literally bumped into each other. He, at fault, carrying books. She, also at fault, carrying a large 'poke' of chips. The books never rid themselves of the stain of brown sauce. Charlie never rid himself of the marks Becky left.

The time of their date had been eight o'clock; the place, a robust bar on the Mound that was conveniently down the road from a cheap Italian restaurant that had waiters savvy enough to make teenagers in love feel like grown-ups.

Charlie, for reasons best known to himself, had decided to wear a suit. It was his first time in a suit and it was clear from his demeanour that he wasn't comfortable. Rather than waiting for her in the bar, like a sane person, Charlie had decided to loiter outside and present her with a flower as she walked in from her bus. Charlie knew she would catch the number 23. He knew which bus stop. He knew everything about everything.

Apart from the fact that she had interpreted 'next Friday' as 'next Friday'. And not 'this Friday'.

So there he had stood for an hour and a half, surveying through half-tears the majesty of Edinburgh before him, the sweep of Princes Street from east to west, the most picture-perfect high street in the country, the world even, and all of it laughing at him.

The second time she'd kept him waiting was the day they got married. And when the half an hour mark zipped by, the priest was looking just about as nervous as Charlie. In fact, the car really had broken down on the lane that approached the church and Becky had been forced to sprint the remaining fifty yards to the altar across a field. There were grass stains on her dress. No-one cared. Everyone cried.

Both events had led Charlie to believe that expecting the unexpected was usually the sanest course of action in any given set of circumstances.

Such as the ones before him right now.

He searched his mind for a solution to his problems. Suddenly realising his enormous folly, he glanced for the first time at the holdall. He unzipped it. Inside, a purple fleece. Camouflage. Of sorts. Underneath, two items. The first, an attaché case with a small numerical lock. The second, a brown Jiffy Bag envelope.

He removed the case. Four numbers beckoned. He saw no reason to suspect George of originality and so entered 1-2-3-4 with nimble fingers. The case refused to click. He tried 4-3-2-1. No joy.

He replaced the case and pulled out the envelope. He ran his nose quickly along the seams. No whiff of anything explosive. And no real nerves about it anyway. The way things were going, Charlie was starting to consider his own demise as a welcome relief from the hassles of staying alive.

Still, his heart thudded in his ears as he eased the envelope open. Timidly at first, but once the realisation he was still alive took hold, he tore at the seal. Inside he could see the beginnings of what appeared to be over ten thousand pounds in fifty-pound notes.

Charlie replaced the Jiffy Bag in the holdall. A police siren whined over the rooftops from a nearby access road. Charlie pulled instinctively back from the kerb but was drawn to the car at the lights in front of him. It was a white Daihatsu hatchback, uniformly ugly and in dire need of a clean. It did, however, have a small sign in the back window:

FOR SALE *Bargain @ £850 ono*

And below, in smaller writing:

Ideal First Car!

Charlie walked along the pavement to get a better look at the driver. A harrowed-looking man in his early twenties was hunched over the steering wheel, tapping his finger in rhythm to some Speed Garage. He was lanky like Charlie, with a small cap pulled down tight over his head.

Charlie glanced at the lights. They would turn green any second. He thought about the envelope. He thought about the money. The lights were still red. He looked hard at the sign on the car. There was no phone number on the sign. He gripped the holdall tight and waved to the driver. He didn't respond, so Charlie made a leap for the door – and got in.

Before the man could speak:

'I want to buy your car,' said Charlie.

Horns blared sharply behind. But the man wasn't moving off.

'Can't you use the phone like any normal person?'

'And do what?' hissed Charlie. 'Throw it at you?'

The man stared at him, mouth open. He wondered why anyone would want to lob a phone at him. Charlie tried to elucidate:

'There's no number on your sign!'

The man's name was Craig, and he now suddenly realised

124

why, despite a competitive price and front-seat airbags, his car remained unsold. He removed his cap, rubbed his head and put it back on.

'Well I can't talk about it now—'

'What's wrong with now?'

'I have to drive somewhere. Call me.'

'I can't bloody call you unless you tell me your number! What's your number?'

And Craig told him. Charlie didn't need to write it down. More horns from behind and in the side mirrors Charlie realised the horns were coming from a red Ford Escort.

'Talk later,' shouted Charlie and leaped out of the car, dragging the holdall with him.

George pulled up by the kerb, around the corner, away from the irate eyes of the traffic queued behind. Charlie saw George staring curiously at him. He looked again. It wasn't curiously. It was furiously. Charlie walked calmly to the window. George unspooled it in haste.

'Where the hell were you?'

'About to ask you', spat George, 'the same question.'

'You were late. So I figured I'd go buy a newspaper. Go up West. See a show.'

'Yeah. Well. I wasn't around because as soon as you left a police car came cruising. I had to move off.' He dabbed at sweat on his brow. Hair was sticking to it.

'For half an hour?'

'Correct. Then I got stuck in traffic. Look, get in.'

'If I get in, I drive.'

'We can talk about this later—'

'I drive or we talk right here, right now.'

George glanced at the bag and the shopkeeper four doors down who was putting out the morning papers but who looked nosey enough that, if interrogated by the right kind of people, would be able to tell them the colour and make of the car they were driving.

Charlie drove aggressively for a few minutes. George clutched the holdall to his stomach.

'We need a friendly face,' said George.

A police car keened past. Charlie immediately turned onto a side street to avoid a numberplate check.

'First things first,' said Charlie. 'We need to ditch this heap of shit.'

'This is not a heap of shit.'

'It's filthy.'

'It's only *filthy*', spat George, 'because you're bringing mud into it.'

'I just clambered over your bloody garden. For you. So if you even so much as mention dirty feet to me again—'

'All right, I'm sorry. Think, think. We should hit the Angel Brothers.' George was staring out of the window now, mind clicking over, over, over . . . 'They've done things for me before.'

'We're not getting a paint job, George, we're getting rid of it altogether.'

'Not just a paint job, Charlie, a change of plates.'

Charlie sighed as loud as he could. 'What would you do in this situation?'

George's left eye was trembling slightly. 'What do you mean, what would I do? I'd do that.'

'Exactly,' said Charlie. 'And what do you think *they* will be expecting us to do?'

'They think we're both dead.'

'*For now*. What happens when we turn up to any of the paint shops we know? Or even ones we don't? Those nitpickers in Euston Road or Thames-side would root us out in no time.'

George sighed. 'They would indeed.'

'If we're going to stay alive long enough to sort this out, we're going to have to do more than second-guess.'

George bit his lip and played what Charlie would have called a quick game of Good News, Bad News in his head. The good news was easy. The bad news hurt a lot. George didn't think this mode of thought was helping much at the moment.

'What's in the bag?' asked Charlie.

'Not now.'

'Apart from the cash.'

George blinked, not looking at him. 'You looked.'

'You were late.'

'Not very trustworthy of you.'

'Neither is abandoning me on the street after I broke into your own bloody house.'

'Presumably you've looked in the case as well?'

'I chose not to.'

'Or couldn't break the code.'

'I *chose* not to open it. All right?'

'Fine. So what do we do now?'

Charlie was grinding his jaw for a second. And stopped. 'I know what,' he said.

And he did. He had brains. Those brains were going to get them out of trouble. Those brains would work their wonders. After all, he reflected, he was the first boy from Lauriston Secondary School to be recruited into the intelligence services. Which must count for something. But not for the first time, Charlie was mistaken.

*   *   *

Neil spent several minutes staring at the phone after hanging up. He spent several minutes leaning on the sandwich counter, and several more minutes pressing his forehead to the cold glass, cooling his eyebrows and gazing out of the front window of the sandwich shop at the slow build of traffic into rush hour. Soon the Embassy staff in the building next door would be at their desks, and soon his own operations, which went on in a small room underneath the sandwich shop, would be underway.

Charlie was indeed not the first boy from Lauriston to be recruited. In fact, he was the second.

Neil checked the window for the signal. The bay window of the second-floor flat that overlooked the sandwich shop had one curtain open. All was well.

Charlie Millar.

He tried saying this out loud a few times to make it appear more normal. It didn't work.

Charlie bloody Millar.

His oldest friend from school working for the Service, just like him. No real surprise, of course, considering it was Neil who had recommended him for recruitment in the first place. But there's a difference between rationalising something in your head and having it call you on the telephone.

It was the first time he'd actually spoken to him – in an official capacity, that is. The two had never met at work. Again, no real surprise. Neil knew friends at big law firms who bumped into old flames after three years in the same place. And it wasn't exactly in the nature of espionage professionals to network. Until they literally collided with each other in the lifts or the coffee station. It wasn't the sort of thing you could bring up in polite conversation. For all

Neil knew, the minute Charlie had been recruited they'd turned around and sacked him.

Neil had actually been working there much longer than Charlie. He himself had been approached by his uncle's buddy, Forbes Mackinnon, who had asked to be made aware of nimble minds and solid characters. Neil hadn't wanted an ivory-tower university experience. He'd been desperate to get on, to work, to be involved, and to earn some cash in an interesting way. Travel. Meet interesting people. And lie to them.

Neil soon found himself in a junior analyst position in a halfway house – an international security firm with ties to the Service. After a couple of years of immersion in close-protection logistics, language courses and report after report after report after report after report, Neil was invited to work in the Analysis Department. After six months he was also seconded to Information Gathering.

He had shops like this one throughout London. They were listening stations, mostly, and his administration of them was part of a gradual responsibility creep that his bosses were entrusting to him. He was glad of it, as he knew other colleagues weren't getting on too well with the job. They were calling it the Seven Year Itch.

With this in mind, then, the tone of Charlie's call – and the time of it, of course – made Neil concerned. The guy had sounded a bit panicked. That was generally enough of an excuse to start rooting around, in Neil's experience. He resolved to let his deputies deal with the mundane jobs of the day and mosey into Euston Buildings for a little innocent exploration of the personnel files.

20

The meeting had only lasted twelve minutes in total. Enough had been said by both parties to make the future absolutely clear in their minds. There were things that needed to be done.

In an abandoned car park some five hundred metres away, Morton walked silently towards the silver Volvo S40 sitting in the corner of the lot. He was mildly resenting the need for immediate departure, as well as the cold, the car, and the lack of breakfast. Morton wrenched his thoughts back to the job in hand. Latham had not wanted him to retain ID photos of the targets. That had been strange.

'Wasn't my fault he wasn't there,' he said to no-one in particular. His breath formed mist in an irritated sigh.

Back in the building, Latham climbed the remaining floors to the top of the grotesque Sixties office block. A chain-link fence was set up in the middle, some old tarpaulins breathing in and out like grimy blue lungs.

Latham gazed out in a northeastward direction towards the waste ground in the centre of the factory yard. In the distance, empty gasworks framed the night sky.

Down in the car park, Morton had the key in the ignition. He sat for a moment, strangely drawn to the interior. Here he was, thirty-five, another bleary morning, another strange car. It smelled of leather. It was a diesel. Morton wondered why he'd been given a diesel. They were, in his experience, pretty noisy fucking cars. If he—

But Morton couldn't finish the thought.

It was all to do with the key.

The key had turned in the keyslot. This had in turn triggered the starter of the car. But the action had also triggered an electrical pulse which travelled down to a small detonator that was itself attached to a slab of plastic explosive known as C4. The chemical bonds between the slab's atoms, once broken, released their pent-up energy that took the form of extreme heat and expanded with ferocious speed, a shockwave travelling at 26,400 feet per second. Thus, before his heart could pump its last thimble of blood, Morton, the car, and everything in it, were all suddenly consumed in a fireball that sent the rats scurrying on the Jubilee Line some half a mile below.

Latham watched the flash and heard the bang milliseconds later. Latham knew he had done the right thing. Morton knew these men. He had also failed to achieve the planned closure with the motorbike not so many hours before. And so Latham had decided it was time for the Volvo. There had been another car with no C4, of course. But Latham was a Volvo kind of guy. Reliable under stress. If you really want a job doing, you're always best doing it yourself.

The brief, after all, was to cauterise the weeping wounds of the Project. To fumigate. To sanitise. Not a job for emotional empaths. Not a job for someone volunteering for the soup kitchen or the midnight helpline. The problem was minuscule. Molecular, in fact. It was a fragment of a microdot, a shard of a dust particle of truth that had somehow floated onto the lapel of a small number of desperately unlucky individuals. These people – most of them, at any rate – knew not a sausage of what they were carrying. But tainted by it they were, and Latham, more than anyone (except Rose Willetts, perhaps), knew how virulent this vector was. It was a hantavirus. It was espionage Ebola. And everyone knows that in such extreme cases, when the very organism itself is faced with a potentially mortal hae-morrhage of information, extreme measures need to be taken to prevent the spread to the wider population.

Thus, fumigation.

Before anyone else came down with it.

This would be a procedure that required a surgeon of the service who would not get salty-eyed at the sight of blood. A person of a cold and acute separateness.

A person like Latham.

The Project. Rose hadn't set out to label it so dramatically. It had really sprung out of a rather mundane realisation. There were times when Rose wished she'd labelled her box-file 'Misc.', or 'Odds & Sods'.

Being a powerless bystander when a man's life's at stake was not easy. And yet that is what Rose had felt, increas-ingly, in the years her Security tenure had lasted. There were committees and memos, steering groups and think-tanks. A level of managerese that swelled the ranks but not the rank and file. And it was only in the engine room that things actually got done.

On several occasions, Rose became aware of networks and sources who were seriously, sometimes fatally, compro-mised because an equipment acquisition form, a blue piece of paper labelled AF/35, had been delayed. A delay in the

AF/35 had delayed another piece of paper, a memo acknowledging receipt of said acquisition. The result of this lack of communication was almost always the non-delivery of an item. On some occasions, a paperclip. On others, the only thing standing between a field agent and a certain, grisly death.

Rose Willetts stepped into this breach with that most dangerous of management tools – independent thinking. Thus the Project was, and was still, simple. To get things done. With or without an AF/35.

The shockwave from the explosion sped away from Latham's feet. Several miles underground it shuddered along, through pipes and tunnels and corpses and Roman pottery, the wave reaching effortlessly across London in a way that the Mayor's Transport Policy Committee could only dream about. Within a couple of seconds it had reached a lanky man in a cap. He was sitting nearly five miles away, in a cramped plastic booth at a fast-food chain, and his name was Craig.

Craig had been drinking coffee and the microscopic ripple in his cup went unnoticed. He was two bites into his breakfast roll when his mobile phone rang. He was a little suspicious as no-one wants to buy a car this early in the morning, but quite frankly dosh was dosh and Craig knew for sure he could do with some of that.

He arranged to meet the man with the money by a row of lock-ups near the estate, half because he didn't want to see his mum looking out when he sold her car without her permission, and half because he knew some genuinely violent people in the immediate area should negotiations get knotty.

He turned up late, as he often did, because he liked the

idea of his presence being required. To his chagrin he was the first to arrive. He tugged his jeans a little lower and did up the top button on his sweatshirt. He experimented with his cap turned backwards but thought he might put off his prospective buyer if he looked too much like a player. He experimented with leaning on the bonnet of his car, one leg hitched up on the bumper, but he thought he might look like a ponce. Craig was not a person who was comfortable in any position for any length of time. He was always on the move.

The road surface was in a bad state of disrepair and stretched ahead some two hundred metres, cracked and potholed, scattered with gravel and dirt. On one side, garage doors. On the other, a wall and a nest of barbed wire keeping citizens safe from a High Voltage substation.

Craig looked at his mobile again. No messages. He always wondered why everyone else in the world got so many calls. He heard the crunch of tyres on gravel and looking up saw the red Escort turn slowly and stop at the far end of the road. Craig waited for something to happen. It didn't. Craig began to get worried and tried to remember which speed-dial Big Simon was under. He had a spider's-web tattoo on his neck.

'Oi, mister.'

Craig turned around to see a small lean teenager in a hooded top. He didn't seem to be leaving, either.

'Fuck off.'

'I've come about the car.'

Craig looked at the boy again. He'd seen him around the estate once or twice.

'Look, fuck off back to Borstal, all right?'

'Is this it? Oosh. What a pile of pants.'

The kid was now checking out the tyres, the lights.

'I told you—'

'I work for them, all right?' The kid was pointing at the car in the distance. Craig glanced over. The lights flashed once. 'They just want me to check out the car and give you the dosh, s'all. I'm an associate. Cool your jets.'

Craig stood back as the boy made a cursory inspection of the vehicle.

'It's not the Ferrari pit at Monza, shitface, get on with it.'

The boy turned to the Escort at the end of the road and gave thumbs up. The lights flashed again and the boy turned to Craig.

'Wait here a sec.'

And he ran off in the direction of the Escort. Craig looked around, hoping no-one was witnessing this. 'We got a deal or what?' he shouted. But no-one replied. The boy got to the Escort and George wound down the window.

'Seems all right,' said the boy.

'Good work.' George handed him an envelope. 'Money's in there, bonus is here when you come back with the keys.'

The boy nodded and ran back towards Craig. Charlie stared at George for a moment.

'Was this really necessary?'

'Twenty years in the spy game, Charlie, you learn one thing. Never do anything yourself if you can help it.'

'He could have scarpered with that money.'

'But he hasn't.'

They looked ahead to see the transaction taking place. Craig kept peering over at them but they were too far away for any facial recognition. He counted the money and, with another look in their direction, departed. The boy turned back to George, who flashed his lights and turned the key in the ignition for the last time.

A dry cough from the engine.

No problems from the Daihatsu at the other end of the road, however, as the kid jumped in, engine roaring to life—

'Oh – shit—'

George pumped the accelerator and tried again. Nothing doing as the boy spun the Daihatsu in a roaring wheelspin turn. Third time lucky on the Escort – and George and Charlie found themselves pursuing the joyrider in the car they had just bought as it disappeared around the corner.

They squealed around the bend to find the car, neatly parked. And the boy outside it, laughing himself silly.

'Sorry. Couldn't help myself.'

George held Charlie back and handed over the money. The boy ran off, grinning from ear to ear. George got out of the car.

'Where are you going?'

'Final check,' said George as he opened the bonnet of the car. Charlie hated mechanics. It was one of the many means his dad had used against him to prove his worthlessness. So he'd made himself get good at it. Whenever Dad came back from his stints on the oil rigs, he'd quietly demonstrate further expertise, which would drive the man up the wall. Despite these small victories, Charlie still hated it. He left George to grease-monkey tinkerings.

A few cursory glances and he was back.

'Get on a motorway,' said Charlie.

'Why?'

'You can drive fast on them.'

The wheels spun again in the gravel.

A few hours later a call was placed to a local police station. An abandoned car was causing an obstruction. A daisy-chain of telephone communications eventually caused a large tow truck to be despatched from the depot. The offending car was a Ford Escort, a red one. It was covered in bird droppings. The car was then towed to a small garage in South London. It was there, an hour or so later, that Latham arrived, placed rubber gloves on his hands and opened the passenger door.

Latham produced a small pocket switchblade and tore a small wound in the far edge of the front-seat carpeting. Underneath the padding and crude engineering he revealed a hollow area. Taped to the side of it was a small grey box.

Rose Willetts, who Latham worked for, had ordered the comprehensive surveillance audit of all the Service's K-list personnel six months previously and Latham thought this was informed paranoia at its very best. The more you know about the people who work for you, the more you can trust them implicitly. She had, for example, divined what George Shaw was up to long before he had tendered his resignation. These were the actions of a woman in total charge of total secrecy. It made Latham feel reassured.

In a stuffy room in a long-forgotten wing of Thames-side Buildings, a small tape-recorder was removed from the grey box. The tape played back every conversation that had taken place in the vehicle in the previous two weeks. Somewhere, fifty metres above this fluorescent coffin, the river Thames glugged and sloshed. There was a maze of rooms and corridors that connected the Service with several less-well-known state agencies under the river. The Thames held secrets in the sludge and the mud, and it seemed only natural that the Service kept their own down here too.

Normally the tapes were long-playing enough to last the fortnight. A slower recording process had been developed since the last time this particular unit had been used, in

Gerry Adams' car during the Northern Irish Peace Process talks in Stormont.

Eventually the tape wound forward in the semi-darkness and the voices of Charlie and George chimed in above the grumble of traffic noise.

'What would you do in this situation?'

'What do you mean, what would I do? I'd do that.'

The tape warbled forward—

'Okay, so good news, we're alive. Bad news, we're in the wrong car. Good news, we know some quick-change artists, bad news . . . they're all in Service, you know, radar.'

'Wait. Write this number down.'

And Charlie's voice began to recite the recently memorised mobile-phone details of a man called Craig. Latham listened and thought deeply in a dark pool of calm. He had much to do, and the phone records from the houses weren't even here yet.

He was looking forward to hearing them too.

21

Early morning in Euston Buildings looks like any other time of day. A few lights glow twenty-four seven in the unprepossessing modern structure that looks, to all intents and purposelessness, like an insurance company.

Unlike the Thames-side structure, all Faraday Cages and haughty sweep, the Euston side of operations was stolidly *functional*. It was all squares and rectangles. The height and density of the office buildings also rendered a savage micro-climate around adjoining streets, skirling crisp packets and dust into inconsiderate, aggressive spirals, causing eyes to narrow and rippling overcoats in the wind.

It also kept curious eyes down, and so far as scrutiny goes, fewer eyes mean fewer questions.

Only the video cameras and discreet but fulsome police presence around the grid of pavements surrounding the place would tip a paranoid pedestrian off as to the real activities bustling inside. This was, of course, not the main headquarters of the Service, not by a long shot. But many operational details and many departments were located here in the past, and despite the move to the Thames in the Eighties, many had stayed.

Floor D was, with classic Service logic, located at street

level. Below here, underground, in floors E through Z, in amongst the high-security database nexus and sealed communications conference nodes, men and women number-crunched and people-crunched and altogether worked their Marks & Spencer's socks off. Above, on floors C to A, and 7 to 1, more earthy matters, the coordination of several categories of field agent, source, informer and contact. Narrow corridors bisected each other with brown doors and ugly carpeting. Nicotine-stained walls offered unopened windows with waxy views of gasworks. In the winter the boiler shut down for so long that many workers brought their own convector heaters to work. In the summer the radiators never flinched from their duties and pumped enervating waves of scalding air into every crevice of the building. Half of the toilets flushed; the other half spat things back at you. Spies who came in from the cold to this usually went straight back out again.

Neil Mackay was grateful he worked elsewhere. Even Embassy duties, with their damp basements and the lullabies of static surveillance feeds, were better than what amounted, in Neil's mind, to ritualised environmental torture.

Floor G housed the personnel files. Neil's clearance allowed him in here under normal office hours only, and so he felt obliged to nurse a caffe latte in the Coffee Republic across the road before following his twitchy nose for research. Time passed slowly. When the seconds were finally out, he flashed his cyan and white-striped lobby pass with impatience and half-trotted to the lifts.

The mechanism was dodgy at the best of times, and, despite the areas of high security above and below, the technology of lifts had not been exported to this Security

Service building – not, at any rate, to those lifts used by the worker bees.

Thus it was that despite pressing 'G', the system had already decided that it had someone to collect on Floor X.

Neil sighed and waited. He had visited Floor X once before. The place had only just been built. His reason for going was for a high-level surveillance operation that required a clearance far above his own, but special dispensation had come down from his boss. Anywhere below W there were no more smiles and good mornings. Down there it was stern looks and a quickly presented ID or special dispensation document, or you were frogmarched back to the lobby with five strong fingermark indentations in your shoulder.

The lift wobbled slightly as it arrived; the doors opened to reveal a stark and empty corridor stretching to a small security desk and one-way mirror some fifty feet ahead. A man in a yellow striped shirt and blue tie shambled in and avoided eye contact. Neil pressed 'G' again, this time with great force. The man in yellow leaned across and pressed the button for the parking level. Neil willed the lift to stop at his floor and, amazingly, it did.

Floor G, by contrast, had the smell of new paint and Magic Trees. It reminded Neil of the children's ward in a hospital. *Someone should paint a smiling sun on one of the walls*, he thought to himself as he exited the lift. *Or a ring of bloody roses*.

Neil punched his personal ID into the cryptolocked door of Filing 2/55 and found a small workstation cubbyhole near a defunct shredder. He swiped his encryption keyfob and typed today's password with one hand.

Over the next twenty minutes his brow began to furrow in

exactly the same way as it did the day he turned over his Higher Physics prelim paper.

Despite Charlie's name appearing on the personnel database – well, the gate security department's checklist, at any rate – Charlie's actual personnel file was missing. More disturbing still was the new coding that Neil could read in the bottom left-hand corner of the file. Specifically, the letters 'NFC'.

Not For Circulation.

Whatever Charlie had been up to, thought Neil, someone was keen that no-one could easily read up about it. The file was effectively deleted on the database system. At least for anyone with his security clearance. The only remaining information would be paper-based.

When Neil left the building, he took care to avoid the main corridors. He didn't want to bump into anyone he knew. Not at this hour. Not with these thoughts.

22

I t was hard to make out who they were in the dark. A small group of figures of average height and build were loitering outside the communal entrance to Charlie's block of flats. Two hundred yards down the street, a car with emergency hazard lights blinked on, off, on, off. Two more beside All Night Wine, known to both Charlie and George as a popular listening post – several rat-run rooms below, soundproofed communications area, a holding centre with a cold basement cell with easy access outside to a man-sized skip that could be emptied in minutes by a phone call. No questions asked.

'What did I tell you?' whispered George, hands itching to get back on the wheel.

'We don't know who they are,' said Charlie.

'I'm prepared to guess. But why don't you just walk over there and ask them?'

Charlie nodded, silently answering the question he'd posed himself inside his head. He leaned forward and placed his chin on the wheel, sighing at a place he would never see again.

'My Orbital albums . . .' he murmured.

George made a grunt of condolence. There was no doubt in his mind what was happening here. The question of who, however, remained open. As, he might have added, did the question of What Now?

'We should be on a motorway.'

'I just wanted to see it one more time.'

Charlie looked at his watch as a thought flashed in front of him. George shifted uncomfortably in his seat because he'd seen that look before and it usually meant something involving risk. He was right.

Thirty minutes later the car pulled up outside Liverpool Street mainline station. George stared at Charlie for what was not the first time and rested his forearms on the top of the wheel. He looked a little like he was praying.

'Say that again.'

'I said, George, give me the keys. Please.'

'Why?'

'So I know you won't drive off again.'

'You don't trust me.'

'George, you'll forgive me for saying this, but after recent incidents in my life I have decided that it's probably better that I don't trust anybody. For now. So . . .'

George handed him the keys.

'Fair enough,' he said.

The parking nazis wouldn't be on patrol for another twenty minutes. Charlie vowed to return before then. In fact he knew he would probably be a lot quicker than that.

The commuters were swarming. Charlie descended the escalators and hid behind a bank of telephones. Checking the arrivals board, the 0734 from Bishop's Stortford was due in one minute. Charlie triangulated his best position and vantage point and settled on a space on the stairwell leading to the cafés and shops on the upper level of the station.

By the time he'd walked there and turned around, the train was in. Now Charlie's mind began to race. This was certainly a risk. But George had been right. He had told the guy. He needed to know. And here was the safest place to ask him a question.

True to form he was one of the first to sweep out of the platform. Bill Skelton was balding, sweaty, a man suited to a lifetime manning a formalwear hire department perhaps, or demonstrating laser printers in Birmingham NEC. His trousers were an inch too short, revealing ill-fitting socks and – living the fully realised sartorial stereotype – grey shoes. His stocky frame allowed the absurd Harris tweed jacket he mistook for fashion very little room for manoeuvre amongst the City Boys and Girls. Charlie used this to his advantage, sidling in close to him just as he hit the halfway mark of the concourse. Bill kept pace with a medium scuttle, arcing around a slow hand-holding first-job couple, his eyes fixed firmly on the entrance to the Tube.

Charlie fell into step with him and Bill registered him out of the corner of his eye without losing focus on the crowd ahead.

'Charlie. How are you.'

It seemed more a statement than a question. Despite his evident hurry, he was professionally offhand when he spoke. It was almost a drawl.

'Tell you the truth, Bill, I could do with a chat.'

'Well, come in later, would you? Love to hear how it's all going but right now I've got a departmental powwow I'm likely to miss unless I get on the Central Line in the next forty-eight seconds and counting.'

Charlie studied his expression.

'All right,' said Charlie.

Bill Skelton nodded as a punctuation mark to their exchange and walked off, licking his lips as he went. Charlie watched him go and a thought blazed across his mind.

He's lying.

He licked his lips and he's lying.

Charlie only took a few seconds to catch up. By this stage they were in the ticket hall of the Underground. 'Actually, Bill, it's not really something that can wait until then, I'm afraid,' said Charlie. 'I might even hazard a guess you know exactly what it is I'm talking about.'

'Not a clue, not a clue,' sighed Bill, irritated, suddenly feeling for his coat pocket. Charlie, now on edge, scanned his jacket for signs of a weapon but from what he could see Bill was not armed. A gold travelcard appeared moments later.

Charlie bit his lip and spoke. 'Do you know anything about a recent Frame Thirteen order?'

Bill stepped aside to allow another stream of Tube-bound commuters to flow past them. 'Honestly,' said one man who passed at speed. 'He's a bastard, innit?' said another, talking on a mobile phone.

A seemingly sincere wave of professional boredom swept Bill Skelton's face. 'Look. I can't be expected to keep on top of every single order despatched to every single cover station and field agent at all times. I'd have to look in your file. You've been submerged for about a month. I just organise you, remember. I'm not privy to how your contracted services slot into other departments. You're not exclusive to me and I'm not exclusive to you. I have other haddocks in the grill at the moment. Dreadful hostage exchange in the Caucasus, lives very much at risk, and something I am currently rushing to discuss – so if you don't mind, Charlie—'

'Are you hanging me out to dry?'

'Am I whatting you out to what?'

'Is the department actively engaged in eliminating me?'

'You're eliminating yourself, you berk. You've tendered your resignation.'

'I mean on a more permanent basis.'

Bill glared at Charlie and pulled him aside in a confidential whisper. 'The Service frowns very heavily on drinking on the job, all right? It frowns even *more* heavily on drinking and then letting the beer do the talking and then being *found out*. So if that's the reason for this lunacy, take a piece of advice from me and hook up an intravenous cappuccino drip for the rest of the day. You're not supposed to be even talking to me now, you blithering idiot, you're officially on mission. What the hell's got into you?'

Charlie just stared at him with hard eyes. Bill was still the only person he knew who used the phrase 'blithering idiot'.

'And if you're concerned enough to track me down like this, come in, and we can talk. Call Phil and make an appointment. But right now I have to get to this meeting or you will be talking to another supervisor instead of me, as I'll be on the streets and destitute and my loving yet periodically unfaithful wife will have to find another means of supporting her golf habit.'

'Are you still okay about me leaving?'

Bill Skelton pinched his nose so tightly Charlie wondered whether he was trying to stop it falling off. He did it for quite a long time.

'Bill?' asked Charlie eventually.

Bill expelled a pneumatic sigh with great force and pain.

'For God's sake! We've been through this a thousand times! It's a shame to lose you, Charlie, it really is, but you've had a trial by fire and even though I don't like it, I fully understand. These things take time and sometimes all the time in the world is not enough.'

Bill's eyes played the innocent Cub Scout but Charlie knew how deviously clever they were and invested no relief in their sympathetic gaze. 'The only real concern I have is why one of my field agents is hanging around major transportation nodes and not his contracted cover station, wherever that is at the moment – Wimbledon, is it?'

'Oxford Circus.'

Bill's face flashed curious for a second. 'Well, wherever it is, go back there, for all our sakes.'

A voice over the Tannoy proclaimed – a little smugly, Charlie thought – that all Underground services were running normally. Charlie nodded and watched Bill as he turned to go. Before turning to take the escalators, he watched him remove his mobile phone and begin to make a call.

Charlie turned and ran.

He was back at the car in twenty seconds.

A wave of relief swept over him when he saw that George was still there. He was humming to himself and tapping his foot.

'I drive,' Charlie shouted through the window.

George thought of something to rejoinder but instead focused on hefting himself into the passenger seat. Charlie dug the keys from his pocket. A parking attendant began writing down their details as he pulled away.

'We need a friendly face,' said Charlie. 'And we need one now.'

'I know someone.'

'So do I and that's where we're going.'

'Well so do I,' said George, with equal conviction. 'So maybe we should go there instead.'

Charlie turned to him. 'How friendly is yours?'

'Pretty friendly.'

'Who is it?'

'That material's classified.'

A motorcycle courier roared past and Charlie's stomach churned to think what that phone call had been about.

'Fine. So we'll try mine first. My idea. I get first dibs.'

Charlie weaved carefully through the morning traffic. George was rummaging in his pocket as a sign to the M11 flashed past. 'Heads or tails?' Queen Elizabeth again. Charlie drove quickly out of London.

Four storeys turned to three storeys, three storeys to two; terraced houses lining the lanes, half-boarded, soot-drenched. Trees stopped dying of lead poisoning and began looking green. Clumps of high-rises clung together in fours. Industrial spaces, railway tracks, overhead power lines and a cool grey wind.

'I think we're in real trouble,' said Charlie, finally.

'You don't say.'

'I mean it.'

'So. What did he say?'

'He told me not to worry.'

George's ears seemed to flick back like a dog's. 'Shit.'

'He didn't flinch.'

George shook his head. 'Maybe he's telling the truth. I know that's pretty unlikely but . . . unexpected as it sounds, that might just be on the level.'

'You've not been hallucinating what's been going on.

Neither have I. Unless you fancy turning up in reception waving a white flag I think we'll be safer at the friendly face. Friendly face will sort all this out. They make the contact, not us.'

George didn't speak for a few minutes. When he did, his voice was softer. Reflective:

'Perhaps this is all part of *you* finishing the job,' he said, looking innocently out of the window as the terraces showed glimpses of green. 'Taking me to a remote farmhouse and shooting me in the eye with an ice dart through the slats in the window like the duplicitous countess in *Frost on the Manor* by T. Ellingsham.'

'It isn't,' said Charlie.

'How do I know that for certain? I don't.'

'How do we know anything for certain, George?'

George elected not to venture into that question.

Not just yet anyway.

George knew from the roads Charlie was taking that they were headed southeast and saw fit not to comment. Both men had realised their limits and the badinage between them was losing its freshness, ushering in a quite different odour.

George knew more than Charlie about the state of affairs, of course – much more. His years in the job had given him at times unprecedented access to the way the New Improved Service was operating. As things evolved in the here and now, he realised he might even be forced to continue alone. But inside track or not, their predicaments were now the same. If the Service officially wished them dead, they were surely on stolen time. If their problem stemmed from a freelance source . . . well, then they had a chance. The problem was, running to someone they knew had risks too.

People they knew had contacts that led right back to Euston and Thames-side. Which made them no less vulnerable. Because anyone attempting the scale of terror against them would need, at the very least, access to the kind of infra-structure only the Service could provide.

George's head began to hurt. His paranoia was sending him around in spirals.

Vulnerable or not, George also knew that the friendly face was the best chance for now. His brain got to work and downloaded pertinent names and addresses. Worryingly thin. He'd memorised lists of yes, no and maybes all his life. People he could be certain about, people he knew to embrace as true enemies, and people who enjoyed flirting with the centre of the fence at all times. As the years rolled by these classifications had begun to change, to circle each other in a mental gavotte, before plunging, each and every one, into George's mental waste-paper basket. The old adage was true. When it comes to true reliance, true dependability, it only ever really comes down to one person. Yourself.

He glanced up from his morbid reverie and tensed. All this thinking had taken his eye off Charlie's driving. George had let himself be carried. He had taken his hands off the handlebars. He chastised himself silently in the passenger seat. And again, seconds later, when he glanced at the speedometer reading 110.

Charlie slowed a little and made a right turn. The road filtered into another that joined a dual carriageway.

A few seconds later, a police motorcycle emerged from a hidden slip-road and fell in behind them. It seemed to pause momentarily, letting a safe distance expand between the two vehicles. But almost as quickly it came to its senses, closing the gap with a sudden burst of acceleration. First came the lights, flashing blue and red. Moments later, the siren.

'Any thoughts?' said Charlie as the siren increased in volume and traffic began to pull over to let the bike pass.

'Yes,' said George. 'You shouldn't drive so fucking fast.'

Charlie had also been thinking about their options. He had concluded that despite the shock their sudden arrival might engender, this friendly face might indeed prove to be useful. He had become excited. His blood began to pump happily as his mind churned over the possibility that they might be finally able to stop moving and get a true handle on all this. In his enthusiasm to drive to this state of affairs as quickly as possible, he had been careless. He reasoned that a chase at this stage, in this car, was pointless. The policeman was on a motorbike and Charlie didn't like motorbikes much any more. He stopped the car on the hard shoulder.

'What are you doing?' asked George.

'Pulling over. Unless you have any other ideas?'

George did not.

On a normal day, of course, one glance at their Service-coded driving licences would send the policeman cheerily on his way with the compounded message: 'Don't ask'. But the way things had been going, there was no assurance. For whatever reason, they were *personae non gratae* and Charlie knew from experience how heavily you can make trouble for someone if you really want to.

Charlie wound down the window as the policeman approached.

'I'm sorry, officer, but the thing is that my father's dying, he's in hospital—'

'Planning to kill a few more fathers on the way? Or even fathers-to-be, sir?'

Charlie sighed – there was no way out of situations like this unless you're in a movie. There, a quick car-chase and everything would be fine. He knew these roads and a car chase, especially in this vehicle, would spell the end. He handed over his licence and kept his foot hovering on the accelerator. Just in case.

George kept quiet, fingers poised on the clasps of the attaché case. Charlie noticed this small but subtle movement and had a thought.

'Apologies,' said the policeman, handing Charlie back his licence.

'No problem. Just doing your job, I know.'

Charlie pulled away and back into traffic – realising with creeping horror that someone had broken wind very recently. And it wasn't him. Charlie gritted his teeth and, keeping the speedo just below 72, opened the window wide.

'Maybe not the motorway,' said George after a minute or so. 'Too much . . . you know. Scrutiny.'

23

Craig was thrilled. More than thrilled – he was ecstatic. He was coming, right now, in his pants. He'd won a car. A fucking car. Coming in his pants, right now, look. Fuck me. The lady had called him up about it. Right after him having to sell the Daishitsu and all. Un. Be. Fucking. Lievable.

He'd bragged about this down the pub at opening time. The pub, in turn, had taken the piss out of him for being the kind of man who enters competitions. But he had an answer for that too –

'I'm not.'

To which the pub asked, 'So how did you enter?'

'I didn't. Or at least, I don't remember me entering.'

'No, Craig, that's what your last girlfriend said.'

The pub was still sceptical about Craig's prowess with anything but Craig vowed to show them all and drive up in his brand-new Mini Cooper and moon them from the back window. 'Your arse', chuckled the pub as he left, 'wouldn't fit in a Mini.'

He took the Tube to the offices of the Prime Movers Transport Giveaway. They were in a strange part of town for a competition HQ, but then again how was he to know what an HQ's supposed to look like. Someone at the pub had mentioned an episode of that TV show where the fat Mafia bloke gave his friend a ticket on a cruise to get him out of town so he could blow up his restaurant. Someone had said to be careful. Craig hadn't really listened. He didn't even own a restaurant.

Craig rang the bell. It didn't work. He rang it again and the door buzzed without fanfare. Inside was damp-smelling and about as un-Prime as you can get. As the stairs creaked ominously under his feet, he wondered if it had been a chocolate bar. You had competitions in chocolate wrappers. No purchase necessary, he remembered. He might have won this from a chocolate bar he hadn't even eaten. How cool was that?

He opened the door of the third-floor office and found himself in a bare room staring at a person in police uniform, who Craig immediately and mistakenly presumed to be an actual police officer.

'What's your name?' asked the uniform.

Craig explained that he was called Craig.

'You're in a lot of trouble, Craig.'

24

The road opened up like the warm embrace of a long-lost friend. A palpable sense of relief flooded both men and intensified with every new mile of tarmacadam between Charlie, George, and the phonebooth. They were headed through Kent, but Charlie was taking the long way round. They passed schools, hospitals, shops and houses. People falling in and out of love, lonely and together, empowered or at a loss. At a traffic light, Charlie was fiddling with the radio and George looked up to see a small patch of green. A small care-home had a picture window and all residents – some young, some old – were staring at a television. George tried not to stare and focused instead on the sign. Soon they were heading north again, battling to stay off the M25. Essex whizzed and wound by, grids of trees and signs to Stansted and Bishop's Stortford, and as the road unfurled, the sky grew in scale and stature. The motorway would have been quicker, but the twists and turns of the road ahead felt satisfying and safe.

'Nice road,' said George, for want of something else to say.

'Isn't it,' said Charlie. 'Know why I like it?' George gestured that he didn't. 'It goes that way,' said Charlie, pointing to the horizon, 'and not that way,' pointing behind.

George looked through the near window just to make sure he was right.

'So it does,' he said, as the bend in the hedgerow offered a glimpse of a straight that took them to the far horizon.

A moment of peaceful contemplation passed between them. Then another. Finally:

'A man is found dead in a cellar, locked from the inside by a deadbolt—' began George.

'Why do you like those so much?' asked Charlie, hoping it would stop him. It did.

'I find them very satisfying.'

'What's wrong with proper books?'

'They are proper books.'

'No they're not, they're stupid. They're like crosswords.'

'At least they involve a bit of thought. I've stopped reading novels now.'

'Why the hell have you done that?'

'Look, I used to read them a lot. Thrillers, mostly. Maclean, Deighton, Follett, le Carré of course, Higgins. Ludlum. I like a good maze, you see. A puzzle with people. But they're all lazy now, the new writers. Lazy writing. Lazy plotting. What do I care that a Doomsday Device just got stolen from Monte Carlo. Nothing thrilling about them at all, in fact.'

'Not true.'

'Well, there's some good ones, I suppose, but not many. At least in locked-room mysteries there's a challenge. It's the same every time. Someone's dead. And they're—'

'In a locked room?'

'It's actually very hard,' snapped George, 'to think of plausible ways out of impossible situations.'

Charlie drove on in silence for a minute.

'Isn't it just,' he said.

In the distance, the sky grew grey and then black, ragged dark clouds rippled ominously and the very fabric of the air itself seemed to be sucked into a single hilltop, everything draining towards a vanishing point of colour and light, like some earthbound black hole. George reached over and switched on the radio. A local station was playing Groove Armada's 'Suntoucher'. George listened for a sarcastic second and fiddled with the dial. Charlie harrumphed.

'Wait, I like that song—'

'Don't see how,' said George, slowly pressing station presets before laboriously tuning the radio. 'Anyone who sings about a tofu sandwich needs medical attention as far as I'm concerned.' He flipped to a Classic Rock destination. '*This* is what roads like this were built for.'

He upped the volume. The singer was explaining that here he was going, on a repeated occasion, on his own.

'No,' said Charlie, gripping the wheel.

'How can you not like that?'

'Like this.'

And Charlie turned it off. George reached in to turn it on again. Charlie, very calmly, turned it off.

'Well we can't just have silence.'

'Maybe it'd be a good idea,' said Charlie, 'if we did.'

George glared at him. 'I hate silence.'

'I've noticed.'

'Local news?'

'Fine.'

And George quickly found a farming report. Neither man passed comment and so the station stayed.

'This friendly face,' George began. But before Charlie could interrupt there came a sound like a mortar being fired.

25

Craig's buttocks were starting to hurt. The officer kept asking him questions. He was stuck in an orange plastic chair and he was suddenly regretting his earlier enthusiasm.

He was relaxed, however, as the questions all seemed to be about the recent sale of his car and not at all about the small-time drug deal he'd been trying to land. For a while he'd suspected that the screws in his bathroom mirror were being used as miniature surveillance cameras by Special Branch, but he guessed they would have used this up-front as evidence.

Craig suddenly tensed again when he remembered that it was his mum's car, not his. But the way the conversation was going, there didn't seem to be a line of questioning that was setting him up.

Bursting with relief, Craig agreed to help in any way he could. He'd always heard about people who were taken somewhere to help the police with their enquiries. So now he knew. A bit weird, to be honest, a little unexpectedly rank in the refreshments department, but nonetheless quite professional.

They asked about the people who had bought the car. Craig explained everything he knew about them. He described their garments, or what he could remember from the brief encounter with the one lad. He described his mum's – sorry, *his* – car in copious detail. He felt quite proud, in fact, to be able to talk with such assurance on the matter. He felt quite important, as if what he was saying actually mattered to the person he was talking to. He watched them write everything down on a pad. They wrote softly, with one of those retractable pencils that seem to float above the paper.

He wished he could write with such beauty and grace. His mum could hardly write her own name. She wrote in capital letters all the time because she always maintained she'd missed the day at school when they taught lower case. He saw himself briefly, from the corner of the room, being important. For a heartbeat or two he even considered a career in the police, but quickly erased that as his mouth continued on with facts and details of his day.

He also tried to talk about the young kid who'd been working for them, but by that stage he was bleeding from a small wound in the centre-left of his chest that would, in a few minutes, kill him.

26

The noise came from the engine. It had been protesting around the tighter bends but this was different. Charlie realised too late the steering was becoming erratic. The lack of responsiveness came at a bad time, however, as the straight road was now lending itself to a tight bend up ahead.

'What's that smell?' asked George.

Charlie sniffed hard and immediately wished he hadn't. The lower registers of his nose had already picked up the acrid-smelling atmosphere in the car but a full lung of it sent him into a coughing fit. The retching caused his right hand to shade downwards. The car strayed erratically into the wrong lane as a black Mercedes screamed around the corner – swerving onto the grass verge and back on track, narrowly missing the Daihatsu. Charlie struggled to regain control, the car now on a beeline for a low stone wall at the edge of a farm. Another swerve sent him back onto the tarmac but by now the cab was filling with smoke and stench from the boot area.

George held his hands in front of his mouth. 'Stop the bloody car!'

'I'm trying!'

Charlie touched the brake. Nothing. He tried again.

A little give, nothing more. It felt like the brake pads had been replaced by bath sponges.

He tried to open a window to let out the now billowing smoke from the back seat and boot. The handle broke off in his hand and instead of attempting to re-affix it he shouted at George to open his side. This he succeeded in doing, but it was too late to clear enough of the cloud to give Charlie any chance at all to see he had now left the road and was about to plough straight through a hedge and into a farmer's stile.

The field, by a miracle, was overgrow and muddy enough to slow the car's path a little so that by the time Charlie's forehead hit the wheel, and George's neck snapped back and then forward into the only airbag that deployed, the results were only painful, not fatal.

The two clambered out and sat in stunned silence on the wet grass. Smoke continued to billow out of the gap between the boot and the bodywork. George helped Charlie up and pushed him towards the fencing.

'Just in case,' he said, a little slurred, as he willed the two of them away from the car. There was no explosion. Only the slow dissolution of the noxious cloud into the clean rural air.

They were a hundred metres away when George turned around and trotted back to the car. Charlie, still dazed, rubbed his head robotically as he watched George yank open the warped door of the Daihatsu. He grabbed the holdall from the back seat and dashed back to Charlie.

'We can't leave it here,' said George when he returned.

'Why not?'

George sighed, rubbed his eye with the base of his palm. 'I presume you've never read *Eye of the Needle*.'

'Pardon?'

'*Eye of the Needle* by Ken Follett. A man on the run never

leaves his car in the open. Or indeed behind a blackberry bush unless I'm mistaken.'

Thus is was that, still aching and adrenalised by the crash, Charlie found himself pushing a Daihatsu towards a small clump of trees and shrubs fifty feet from the stile. Mercifully, it was downhill all the way. Once the car was camouflaged to George's satisfaction, they began to walk.

Several miles later, a small country track gave rise to some farm outbuildings. The sky had grown dark again and a light rain began to fall. The track ended far up ahead in what appeared to be a farmhouse. No cars visible. George looked at Charlie and an unvocalised decision was made. With a final sprint that nearly killed George outright, the two men found a cattle shed. Empty, for now. Some plastic sheeting in the corner offered sanctuary. A conversation of water debated itself onto the corrugated iron roof.

The two men dropped to the ground in the shadows and for several minutes caught their breath, watching the ground outside begin to churn in the onslaught of the stair-rod rain. Charlie thought it sounded beautiful.

'My wife grew up on a farm,' said George suddenly.

'You never mention her,' said Charlie.

George kept his eyes on the rain, a twinge of sadness behind them. 'That's cos I don't like her very much,' he explained.

'Sorry to hear that.'

'Marriage changes people,' said George. 'Why d'you think they call it the *altar*?'

Charlie nodded till his head hurt. He lay back and listened to the drips of wet from his hair plop onto the plastic sheeting underneath him. 'I was married, once,' he said.

'What happened?'

'Oh . . .' sighed Charlie. 'You know.'

'Sorry to hear it.' George's voice took Charlie aback with the level of its sincerity.

Charlie shrugged. 'It was the job.'

'Tell you what,' muttered George, 'let's not talk about the *job*.'

And the rain gathered weight in the darkening sky.

He was back in the Canary Islands, snorkelling with Becky. Her legs entwined in his, an underwater kiss in the company of kissing fish. They spiralled together in the bubbles, holding the moment, and each other, tight.

They surfaced, laughing, gazing in wonder at the colourful scene only inches below the surface. Iridescent fish of all sizes and shapes teemed around them in the warm translucent waters, a vision of purples and yellows, oranges and emeralds. A flick of her fins and she was away, and Charlie beside her, making for the crescent of beach on the other side of the bay. But Becky was a strong swimmer with a head start, and Charlie felt himself falling behind. Try as he might, he wasn't moving. He kicked again but a steady numbness held his legs. A dull throb pulled his temples together. Becky was halfway to the shore now, oblivious to his difficulty, and the water began to close around him, growing colder by the second, cramping his limbs, wrapping around him like a mercury shroud. He was in trouble. He tried to cry out but the water shot down his snorkel, squirting into his lungs. He grabbed at the mouthpiece but he was weak, immobile . . . paralysed by the cold. He was a dead weight . . . drowning . . . dying . . .

Charlie woke with a start to find George standing over him. Just how long he'd been unconscious he wasn't sure.

But judging from the darkness outside and the cold, stiff feeling in his lower back, Charlie estimated at least a couple of hours. His eyes, accustomed now to the darkness around him, sought out George's face. In his half-sleep, for a moment he had dreamed that George had abandoned him. He roused himself to his feet. A wave of nausea hit Charlie square in the throat and he began to realise he might have hurt himself in the crash.

George held out his hand and yanked him up – a finger to his lips. Charlie heard why. A diesel engine was churning outside. Distant, but approaching. Green and purple spots floated around Charlie's eyes. He shook them off as the two men crept to the darkest edge of the opening. They heard the wheels sloshing in pools of water that filled the deep channels of tractor-track and mud. The engine purred to a halt. A car door slammed. And a single pair of footsteps squelched up to the wall just outside the doorway. The footsteps paused, then walked back around the building, surveying the three sides of the cattle shed. George edged to a better angle as the footsteps began to emerge to his left. The most almighty headache began to crack a straight and pounding path through the front of Charlie's sinus cavity. The green spots returned, on their own this time, sparkling like the northern lights, and Charlie struggled to stay on his feet.

George stayed utterly still. The footsteps, Charlie realised, now faint and distant.

'Female,' whispered George, eyes unblinking.

'Pardon?' said Charlie.

George merely beckoned him to look.

Charlie looked. A young woman in a bright cagoule was walking past.

An intense feeling of injustice jabbed Charlie in the ribs as he watched her. He had done nothing to deserve this treatment. Neither, so far as he could ascertain, had George. They were simply leaving their jobs. For different reasons, but then people left jobs every day. There was no call for this. The emotion was dulled, of course, a distant light in a thick fog. But he saw it, he recognised it, and it made him think about revenge.

The ache in Charlie's head only worsened with the passing minutes and he knew that if he wasn't lying down again very soon, his body would make sure he adopted that position – will or no will.

'I'll go and have a word,' offered Charlie.

'Wait—' said George, and stepped back.

A couple trudged past, following the same route taken by the woman. They may have been in her vehicle, thought George. But from the delay they would have had serious problems with their seatbelts for that to be entirely true.

No, chances are they've walked. He took another look at them: sturdy boots and windcheaters. Walkers they were. What were they doing on a farm?

Charlie had migrated to another side of the shed and was peering through a small hole in the corrugated iron. A small shaft of sunlight was now spilling warmth onto the sodden ground. And through the tiny viewhole, Charlie was able to make out three of the most welcoming words a cold, wet, starving spy can hear after his employer decides to kill him.

Bed and Breakfast.

The main building was solid and grey, not particularly welcoming as such, but clearly a sturdy structure used to broad farmers and their broad partners. The Norfolk Broads, after all, were not too far away. The door knocker was sturdy and brass.

A pretty girl in her mid-twenties poked her head out of the door. She had a strong jaw and a bright-eyed intelligence about her. To George and Charlie she seemed a little too slim to be a farmer's daughter – for no other reason than neither man had ever met one before and they had resorted to type.

She led them through a modest stone-flagged hallway. Dried flowers in a large vase. The smell of tea and toast wafting in from a beamed kitchen visible near the end of the hall.

'My parents run the place, normally,' she was saying as they passed by a small table. She handed them a form and a small glossy leaflet outlining a number of local farming-related attractions.

'Just the one room, is it?' she smiled. There was a little glimmer of mischief there, well-suppressed but little did she know the character analysts she was talking to.

'We'll need two,' Charlie smiled back. 'If you've room.'

'I think we can stretch,' she said.

All the will to resist in Charlie was draining fast. Training told you to keep on the move, to stay out of scrutiny. And here, as their host – 'Call me Emma!' – led them through the kitchen, there was plenty of it. The other residents had gathered to warm themselves on the Aga and sip great brown mugs of tea.

Charlie and George smiled politely but kept their eyes away – at least directly – from the others in the room. Their peripheral vision, however, picked them out perfectly.

Two couples and a solitary man. The couples were old, old, young, young. Red, red, blonde, blonde. The young blondes still had their brightly coloured waterproofs on. They were grinning the most in welcome, so George inferred they weren't English. Charlie felt their gaze very strongly on his face.

The rooms had an adjoining door and low ceilings. Emma left the men 'to it' and hinted that the tea wouldn't last long downstairs.

Charlie winced as he sat on the bed.

George shrugged and passed through to the adjoining room, carrying the holdall. Charlie eyed it with suspicion but the pain in his side soon caused him to lay back. When he opened his eyes again George was standing over him, freshly showered.

'Get your face cleaned up,' he said. 'It's shepherd's pie.'

The farmhouse table groaned under the combined weight of elbows and a large brown dish full to the brim with mashed potato. Plates clanked and a fire spat and fizzed in the grate.

Conversation only really began when Olli, the Finnish man, uncorked the first of what became a multitude of bottles of wine.

After-dinner chat ranged from local walks to international politics. With each passing hour, however, and each meandering anecdote from Olli and Riika (his girlfriend, Charlie presumed, despite her strange looks in his direction), the conversation grew more ribald and more dangerous. Questions were being asked of George and Charlie and there is nothing a spy likes less than a set of questions after alcohol. No matter how efficient their liver is. George had enough and headed for bed. Charlie looked for an opportunity to do the same when, ten minutes later, Olli fell asleep in an armchair by the fire. Charlie and Riika were left with the glowing embers.

Knowing people as Charlie did, it became obvious to him that Riika had taken a shine to him and for a moment Charlie felt human again in the warm glow of such appealing female attention. But he was too tired, too bewildered and on edge to enjoy it.

Charlie could stand no more and when Riika went to the bathroom, trod heavily up to bed. Lying on the mattress, focusing on the ceiling as the room fell gently away underneath him, there was nothing he could do about it this time. There would be no sleep tonight.

It is a truism to say that every spy has a coping mechanism for what becomes, psychologically, a deep schism centred at the solar plexus of their identity. Charlie had discovered this, and in order to truly do his job to his full ability he found he had to separate the necessary betrayals and lies from the person he believed inside was good, kind, generous, fun at parties, remembered birthdays. A person who knew hate was a strong word. Who understood that when he said, 'I love you', it was something that was meant, it really was forever.

Of course, such distinction of Work Charlie from Life Charlie had developed, over time, into a separation anxiety. There was a growing distance between them now, two friends on different hilltops, waving. Unsure if in welcome, or farewell. It was one of the reasons he'd decided to leave. One of the many, many reasons.

The sleep of the just, of the innocent, or just of the tired working man, could only come to Charlie if he placed the work version of himself on the bedside table when he turned out the light, like a watch or a pair of false teeth. But with the increasing knowledge in himself that the two had merged completely had led, in the months since Becky left, to a difficult road to slumber. The only way he could guarantee quality unconsciousness was to drink himself there.

Next door, George couldn't sleep either. There were some paperback novels by the bed. Judging by their thickness and fractured spines they were thrillers of some sort. Against his better judgement he extracted one from the shelf behind him. *FULL FATHOM FIVE*, proclaimed the cover; the blurb continued below in equally excited lettering, '*from the files of Deep Sea Delta*'. George turned idly to a page. A man was crossing a gantry of some description. There may or may not have been a nuclear weapon involved. He tossed the book aside as its acres of text felt like homework. He picked up another. It was called *THE COPENHAGEN GAMBIT*. It looked a little more promising as it showed a man in shadow running on the cover. The first chapter opened – oddly, George thought, considering the title – in Zürich. The book had short sentences. The second chapter jumped to Bangkok. George flipped ahead several chapters but couldn't see any mention of Copenhagen at all. He wondered whether that was the ploy. In these sorts of thrillers there seemed to be a common idea that whatever the world-shattering array of problems, there was always a way through.

How refreshingly optimistic, George mused, as compared to the way his life was going.

He yearned to live in a world where things worked out. He yearned to turn ahead a few pages and see.

He turned back and looked again for Copenhagen.

It didn't take him long to fall asleep.

In the adjoining room, Charlie heard the book drop to the floor and waited until George's breathing became deep and regular. He estimated George would be in slow-wave sleep en route to REM and would thus not be woken by exterior noise.

As he pulled on his shoes, Charlie hoped to God – or at least, as he was technically an atheist, hoped very, very hard – that the floorboards were not as creaky as they looked.

They weren't.

He crept along the corridor and felt the chill night air on his face. He waited until he was a hundred yards from the front door before breaking into a run.

The car was still there. Charlie produced his trusty Maglite from his keychain and flipped it on as he lifted the bonnet. He cradled it in his fist so as to focus the light away from the house. The beam shone cranberry red through his fingers and played over the grubby engine. He was looking for something.

Specifically, sabotage.

He was crazy, of course. A crazy man with a flashlight in the wee small hours of the morning. A spot of witching-hour mechanics. But Charlie wasn't crazy, he assured himself. He was just being careful. The airbag had only deployed on the passenger side. The car had been in perfect working order when Craig had been driving it.

The fact that it had packed in when it had was enough to put Charlie on edge. Over the past few days his paranoia had been pretty bloody spot-on.

Charlie was not a man who had done anything wrong. Even within the hulking bureaucracy of the Service he had managed to steer a nondisruptive course, stay out of petty infighting, swear allegiance to no-one but himself. Duly diligent as he was, he nevertheless downloaded every relationship he could remember. There was no crossover.

No conceivable link to George. Or to anything that might suggest he had blocked, irritated, angered or disappointed anyone.

Nevertheless, they were trying to kill him.

The inner child, the one Charlie was still recklessly in touch with, wanted simply to turn up in the lobby and stamp his feet until he had enough attention. And shout at the top of his lungs, 'Why me?!'

Shouting was preferable because when extreme measures were taken there was generally no more time for being reasonable.

Then there was that night. There had been that.

Ever since that night, perhaps, he had lost his sense of poise. It was understandable. Perhaps it was as simple as that. In the spy game it was often reason enough.

Aside from his concerns about his previous employers, Charlie refocused his paranoia on his concerns about George.

The light-beam found nothing. Charlie found nothing. When George had done his mechanics, he really had been doing his mechanics. Of course he had.

Charlie closed the bonnet silently and trudged back to the farmhouse.

George. The bag, George. If you would only show me what's in the case I might finally trust you.

'Trust me?' said George to Charlie's subconscious. 'How can I trust you if you check up on everything that I do? It's a two-way street, my lad, a two-way street . . . trust means never having to see the evidence.'

Charlie crept back into the farmhouse, up the stairs. He made a vow to try and be less suspicious in the future. He tiptoed into his room, shut the door, and stopped.

There was someone under the sheets.

He glanced around and realised this was indeed his room. This was no mistake. There was someone *here*.

'Olli was snoring,' whispered Riika.

Charlie could hear that George was doing the same thing in the next room. He walked towards the bed so his voice wouldn't carry.

'What are you doing here?' he managed.

She pulled a small amount of cover back to reveal what could either have been a low-cut nightgown, or, as Charlie suspected, her fleshy nakedness.

'I didn't mean to shock you. I always forget. British men are easily shocked.'

Riika explained that Olli was her friend, not her lover, and that they shared a bed for cost-cutting purposes. She was quite drunk, Charlie could see that. And very forward. Both of these things put him on edge. But she was young and desiring of him. In the cruel universe that had spat and shat on him in the past days, weeks, months, it seemed a gift from God. A truffle for a dying man. A small consideration.

But Charlie was an atheist. And yet . . .

He moved towards her. She smiled and pulled the covers over herself – suddenly bashful.

'You must think I'm terrible.'

'Not really.'

'I don't do this very often, you know.' And she kissed him lightly, sweetly. 'At all, in fact. I just like to be honest.'

And you are, Charlie thought.

He moved his face to hers and she cradled his head and kissed him again.

'When was the last time,' she asked, 'that you kissed someone so sweetly?'

Charlie winced a little. *A few days ago, actually. But she was shot in the face soon afterwards.*

He decided not to share this with her. She kissed him again. The kiss lingered deliciously as her hands ruffled his hair. And with the touching lips flooded the memory, sudden and painful, that here, once again, was NotBecky. The very present tense of femaleness. The very absence of the woman he loved. A tear exploded from his eye. She tasted it and pulled back, briefly mistaking it for one of joy.

'You should go,' he blurted. He tried to smile. He couldn't, even with the years of training, he couldn't. The disappointment and hurt in her face suddenly so painful to Charlie too.

'What's wrong?'

'I'm very flattered, but I just think you should go.'

And he walked over to the door and opened it for her. It didn't take her long to get there. She flashed him an embarrassed look. He tried to return one along the lines of *You really have no idea how much I'd like to but the timing is way off*. But that's a hard amount of sentiment to convey through the face. So he simply shrugged and looked sad. She nodded in accord, touched his arm, and left.

The empty room, and George's snores, beckoned. The bed was warmed by her body, quickly fading. *Should try and look at the case*, thought Charlie. *George will have it with him. I should look inside. While I still have a chance.*

But his eyes closed all options for him and Becky was back, beckoning him to cycle faster up the hill.

Charlie awoke to paralysis once again, and as he struggled and failed to move his legs the regret crashed down that he'd spurned Riika in the middle of the night. Everyone thought spies always got a lot of women throwing themselves at them. It was nonsense, of course. But suddenly here was Charlie, living the stereotype, getting a whole bunch of attention and there was nothing he could do about it.

The noise of the car outside focused his thoughts.

He'd only been asleep for a few hours.

A red and blue light flashed through the window and projected itself onto the wall. Charlie told his legs to get him out of bed. His legs ignored him. He turned his neck, one of the few muscles still in operation, to face the window. It was first light and the windows were wet with condensation. The door to the adjoining room opened and George crept in. He was dressed and gripped the holdall tight, jaw marbling slightly with tension.

'We have to go.'

Charlie tried to speak but could not. He implored George with his eyes.

'We have to go,' George repeated.

Charlie managed a noise, half-sigh, half-groan –

'Now, Charlie.'

'I can't move. My muscles . . .'

Charlie tried to breathe in. It seemed to help. A small tingling in his fingers. He tried to move his legs again. Nothing.

Footsteps now, on the gravel outside. Steady steps. One person. George peered out of the window.

'There's no way—'

'Charlie—' said George.

'I told you,' cried Charlie. 'My legs. My fucking legs.'

Charlie heaved air into his lungs. He turned his head back to the window, but George had already moved to the other side. Charlie heard George's fingers tapping gently on a metallic surface. And then he heard a click.

George was opening the case.

Charlie gritted his teeth and turned to see George removing a handgun from the attaché case and closing it with a *snap*. George tucked it into the back of his trousers. He hadn't noticed Charlie watching him.

Charlie moaned again and George ran over to the bed. He began massaging Charlie's calves. Then pounding them. Soon he was practically beating Charlie up in bed.

A knock on the door downstairs. The edge of a fist, not the knuckles. A softer impact. It was regular, unhurried, respectfully official. It echoed off the flagstones, amplifying the noise in the entrance hall.

George dragged Charlie's legs around and onto the floor. Tendrils of cold reached up through the soles of his feet until he could feel, for a moment, his knees. His thighs were still jelly, however. George frantically dressed him – trying not to look as he pulled Charlie's trousers over his boxers. Once dressed, he yanked him to a standing position. Charlie steadied himself. Held George's shoulder. And somehow, slowly, made it to the door.

As Emma sleepily answered queries about an abandoned car on a neighbour's farmland, of which she knew nothing, George and Charlie slipped quietly out of the back of the farmhouse, through the low mist of first light.

'A signature,' said George suddenly, his breath a jet-stream of vapour behind him.

Charlie kept walking. He left it to George to fill in the gaps. George obliged.

'Someone signed those Frame Thirteen orders.'

'So—'

'So there are ways of finding that sort of information out. Such as. Reading the signature.'

George eyed Charlie's reaction carefully. He sensed no resistance. And took that as a yes.

'They'll find the car,' said Charlie, eventually.

'No doubt.'

'Maybe we should head back into London.'

'We've only just left—'

'Exactly. So if we head north, they'll be expecting it.'

'Apart from one thing.'

'What's that?'

'They'll also know we'll be expecting them to expect it. I mean, we do work in intelligence you know.'

'. . . So?'

'So in our current situation my call would be: don't second-guess. Because they're already doing that to us.'

'So we triple-guess. Which is basically—'

'The last thing they'll be expecting will be for us to behave like a completely normal person.'

They heard the dual carriageway long before they saw it, and with the help of some luck and a fifty-pound note they had soon hitched a ride on a lorry bound for Cambridge. Charlie explained that would be a convenient stopping-off point, considering that was exactly where they were going.

'What's in the case, George?' asked Charlie innocently as they climbed into the smoke-filled cab.

'Tell you when we get there,' said George.

Charlie smiled back. 'I'll look forward to it.'

27

Rose enjoyed early mornings because the phone didn't ring. She liked early mornings because it also meant that she experienced a very real sense of being a woman who was ahead of the game; a woman who could tell her colleagues, in no uncertain terms, what time she had been in the office this morning.

Her colleagues, of course, knew she was compensating for everything that had happened, with her husband and all, and ignored her inducements to join her in the cafeteria at five a.m.

Rose was a woman who also enjoyed the hunt, which, as luck would have it, used to be played out and enjoyed in early mornings when she was growing up. Her early girlhood was a patchwork of memories – of warm Cotswold stone, of boiling kettles on the Aga, and of La Chasse – crisp mornings resplendent in pinks, the periodic appearance of a bearded father, the smell of wet sod, clouds of beagle breath. Cheltenham Ladies' College followed: hockey, academia, bullying. She had been bullied most of all by her brother of course, who picked on her constantly at half-terms and holiday times. He kept calling her 'jolly hockey sticks', something she simply did not understand. She comprehended what the words were meant to convey, of course, but not the inherent logic. How a sport so utterly violent could have been rebranded as so very Home Counties, so very tame and feminine, was beyond her. *Rugger's tougher*, her brother would taunt her, *there's tackling*. Hockey doesn't need tackling, she would counter. Hockey already has *weaponry*. Hockey, if played correctly, was aikido with a ball.

As a riposte he had slammed a door on her fingers, one by one. She had not cried out, of course. That would have been unseemly. Family life was all about brutality for Rose, and fingers in the door was nothing to complain about. It was only pain, after all.

Oh, but how she missed the hunt. Not so much the rationale, or indeed the social component, but more the sheer tradition of it all. The beauty of the Chasse, my Lady Leads, Full Cry, the pursuit's many stages and calls. Foxes were wily, the hounds less so but they made up for it in fury and enthusiasm. As a girl, Ruth early on surmised that the world itself, the people in it, was divided into foxes and hounds. As she grew older, Ruth discovered that she was a rarity – she was both. She had all these qualities – temper, energy, brains and brutality – in abundance.

Her confidante, Latham, of course, was even more committed to such pursuits but this was no surprise. Rose cried at the blooding; Latham would gaze enthralled. As the only other person to know about the way the Section really worked, or at least Rose's part of the Section, Latham had taken to some peculiarly Lathamist behaviour. He was a force of nature. One from the ice age, mused Rose. He had a sense of loathing for the underclass of fuckups that the Service liked to jettison. He enjoyed their chaotic psyches as they bubbled like an undersea vent next to the glacial calm of his own mental landscape.

He had long considered himself an intellectual buccaneer and eschewed the suburban trappings of his contemporaries – spouse, children, herbaceous borders – for an altogether more lean and hungry attitude to life.

And, of course, he had Rose to thank for all of it.

She settled back with this comforting thought and placed Charlie Millar's personnel file back into her floor safe.

Playing back the phone manifest from George Shaw's house, she heard a voice unfamiliar to her until she had meticulously searched the security voiceprints on both the Thames-side and Euston Buildings computers. A wave of calm broke over her as she reminded herself that, as yet, no-one had made enquiries about the two Frame 13 operations she had finessed through the Special Planning department. There were no enquiries, presumably, because in order to do that they would have to know exactly where these two files were located. And only two people, Rose and Latham, were privy to that sort of high-precision information.

She stirred her tea and continued her search for that voiceprint. The tea had turned cold when the Thames-side computers came up trumps.

As the sun came up, Neil Mackay was surprised to find that he had been promoted.

28

S t Crispin's College, Charlie remembered, was a well-located place. One hundred and fifty yards from the Baron of Beef, two hundred to the Maypole – both first rate pubs – a short stagger from Nadia's, an insanely debauched sandwich shop. It stood proudly and to many eyes arrogantly near the front of King's Parade, where from the gothic promontories of the south gate a freshman might gaze down on all Cambridge and feel more or less assuredly that she owned the entire place.

The best thing about Crispin's from Paul Steadman's perspective was that it gave him a second chance. Dr Steadman was an eighteenth-century specialist, an economic historian who had, over time, begun to realise that economies only exist in terms of the people who inhabit them, and that people were a hell of a lot more interesting than Gross Domestic Products. Economic indicators rarely had sex, killed each other, or got hanged for it. Thus he had crossed the academic rubicon into social history and even, it was muttered in the dark corners of the SCR, some arcane form of historical sociology. He didn't care. It meant he was suddenly, after thirty years in the business, a bit of a bloody star.

He liked the eighteenth century because it had a sense of churning possibility about it, the age of reason but an age of friction, of revolution, where the murky worlds of Tyburn Gate and low-life crime were lit from above by the likes of Locke, Voltaire, Rousseau, Kant, and Hegel. Professor Sørensen of Harvard thought the eighteenth century was a veritable *Skagerrak* of potentiality. Steadman thought it was a little like the Cambridge University Library. Surrounded by all this knowledge and silence, you felt simultaneously a sense of profound enlightenment and an overwhelming urge to fuck someone.

Steadman's increasing interest in the lower forms of British eighteenth-century life had bled into his daily work. His lectures were sprinkled with whispers of murders and mayhem, of perversions and hints of the occult, of untoward happenings in dark corners and of guts spilling from the hanging gardens of Newgate. Thus seasoned, his lectures were often standing room only.

Today Steadman's didactic chores were over, and after a deeply unsatisfying scone in the Sidgwick Buttery he made his way over to the University Library. A friend had tipped him off about a recent acquisition, which he suspected might just be a reprint, of some of the early Newgate Calendars: 'Being the Lives and Histories of the Most Notorious Highwaymen, Post-Pads, Shop-Lifts and Cheats.' He thought there might be a cool and groovy front-plate that he could borrow for his notice board. Something with gibbets, he thought, might cause a stir in young minds.

It was always poignant, he had felt, that his true academic leanings had been towards the liars and cheats of the old world. Because his second career, his parallel life, indeed the means by which he secured his continued comfort in this grand old College, was as a recruiter of liars. Since he left the Service in disgrace and returned dewy-eyed to academe, his own sorry hide had been bought through his promise to recruit the brightest and most nimble minds for his betters – nay, his saviours – in their secret castle on the Thames. His early days had been profitable. Some raw and rising stars of espionage had been tipped the wink over a Michaelmas brandy. He'd lost the passion for it now, of course. He'd been recruited in the same way and realised this was not the life he imagined himself leading. And now here he was sending other young bucks and bunnies to a life of subterfuge and personal-life meltdown. They might be his saviours, but he despised them with a passion.

Formal Hall passed slowly but deliciously. A pea and prosciutto soup, near-perfect lamb jardinière with galettes of a celeriac disposition, an indulgent jam roly-poly with near-perfect custard. Spoiled only by overboiled coffee and a rambling monologue from Professor Stoll on Quantum Field Theory.

Clumping his tired legs up the narrow spiral staircase that led to his rooms, Dr Steadman thanked God once again for His gift of cancer. If Professor Leventhal hadn't got it in the prostate he'd still be in that grotty terraced house in Paradise Street. So full of gratefulness, was Steadman, to the creator of Heaven & Earth that in the darkness he missed the figure standing in utter silence three steps past his narrow landing. He'd already turned the key and pushed open the sporting oak before he heard the voice.

'Hello Paul.'

Steadman whipped round to find Charlie – Millar, he seemed to remember vaguely, yes, that was the surname – Charlie Millar, smiling warmly, invading his personal space.

'It's Charlie,' continued Charlie helpfully. Steadman's face flushed with greetings, even though his heart was still hammering from the surprise and the effort of the stairs.

Steadman had always found Charles Millar's intelligence a little *feral*. The intervening years had done nothing to this opinion and here, in the semi-dark, those eyes were not in the least bit settling. Charlie stood aside and waited for Steadman to do something.

'How are things?' mumbled Steadman as he finished unlocking the main door.

'Tell you in a minute. May I come in?'

'It's a little late.'

'I didn't want to disturb you in Hall.'

'I wish you had.'

Steadman pushed the door wide open and was a little relieved to find he'd left a light on. Charlie followed him inside, without invitation. George was already there, standing in the middle of his living room. Steadman was about to voice a challenge when Charlie's finger leaped to his lips.

Charlie and George checked the windows and swept methodically, albeit manually, for bugs as Steadman poured himself a large calvados from a crystal decanter and drank it. He refilled his own immediately, plus two others. The man in the room had to be expected with these sorts of people. Steadman hoped this wouldn't take too long. Despite those dangerous eyes, Steadman had always enjoyed Charlie's supervisions. A slight unwillingness to toe the accepted line had made him cautious about recommending the boy to the Thames House Piracy Collective. But he had done so, nevertheless. Talent is such a terrible thing to waste.

Steadman did not, however, enjoy catch-ups. He enjoyed youth in the bubble of University. Once gone, their repeated appeals for a pint to catch up were really invitations to listen to their success stories. Something Steadman could do without, thank you very much. Much rather smell the flowers when they're in first blossom. Much rather listen to the fanciful career projections of an ambitious twenty-year-old scholar, even more so in the dark winter night, her ivory skin resting warm against his wolf-like chest, post-coitally grateful and secret and oh so very naughty . . .

'Someone's trying to kill me,' said Charlie.

'Sorry to hear that.'

'Thanks.'

'And me,' said George. He sounded rather plaintive.

Steadman sipped a large finger's-worth of alcohol. 'Anyone I know?' he asked.

'That,' said Charlie, 'is why I'm here.'

Until that point the day had been a spotlight of bright sun and scrutiny, yet both Charlie and George had remained in the shadows, trailing this loping academic from appointment to supervision to library hide, to ensure his behaviour was not unpredictable. It had confirmed itself to be exactly as they had envisaged. Steadman's day was a Swiss timepiece, powered by the pedals of his silver mountain bike.

In the intervening time, Charlie and George had been talking. Rather, George had been talking, and Charlie had been doing an awful lot of listening.

'I'm leaving,' George had said as soon as it was quiet.

'I remember. So am I.'

'You never asked me why.'

'Let me guess,' said Charlie. 'You don't like it very much.'

George's reason was a variation on that theme, and he laid it out with a passion that lit up his eyes with bitterness. The

185

Service was rotten. 'Not to the core, nothing so dramatic,' he explained. 'But there are worms within.'

As he said these words, George unlocked the case and handed it to Charlie.

Inside, in addition to a self-defensive firearm, a couple of old legend passports and two thousand US dollars in cash, was a CD-ROM, or more accurately a CD-R. On the silver disc, explained George, was a locked copy of a Microsoft Word document with the title: 'M'.

'Middlemarch?' asked Charlie.

'Memoirs,' said George. 'Discursive, extensive, and very detailed. It's important that you know. My reasons, I mean.'

Innocent people had died, explained George, as they filled up on tea and toast at a blustery street-side café near the bookshop where Steadman was taking his time browsing. 'And after a while, when you're standing around watching this happen, week after week, month after month, things start happening inside you . . . I mean, naturally, you fight it. But then there's only so much compartmentalising you can do, isn't there? Without a degree in librarianship.'

'You're making a stand?' asked Charlie.

'I'm taking my leave and blowing them a kiss,' said George.

'By writing a document and burning a CD?'

'By telling the truth about what is done in the name of this country. And what happens to the people who do it. I used to be a good person, Charlie, I did. I used to be happily married, like music, enjoy Sundays with a cafetiere and the Sunday papers. I liked people and I wanted things to be okay with the world. I look around me now and wonder what the hell happened. I'm alone. I lie. I betray. I witness injustice and wrongdoing and do nothing. The one thing I have left, and there's scratch marks on it, believe me, is my peace of mind. And I tell you right now. They are not having it.'

Charlie eyed him carefully. 'Is that blowing a kiss?' he asked. 'Or blowing a whistle?'

'That depends,' said George.

'On what?'

'On what you're holding in your hand.'

Silence descended between them on an icy, skittish wind. Their professional radars never once leaving their quarry, two men quite casually sitting in peaceful café quietude together, warming up with a mug of hot char. From twenty yards away, they were two friends catching up, familiar enough with each other to sit on the same side of the table and watch the world go by.

'Tricky,' said Charlie eventually.

'It's not your fault. I don't expect you've been in the job long enough to really appreciate what's happening,' said George. 'It's like a cult. You only start to see how deeply fucked it is after it's too late.'

Charlie shook his head and sighed. 'They'll never let you do it. They've never let anyone do it.'

'Publish, you mean?'

'You'll be damned before you do. Or killed. Either way.'

'Where, exactly,' said George, 'will they be doing the damning?'

George raised his eyebrows for effect but Charlie had noticed Steadman leaving with his heavily laden plastic bag protruding sharp edges of square objects.

'You see, this,' said George, pointing to the CD, 'came from this,' and he pointed to his head. 'They want the capacity – *my* capacity – to talk about this over and done with. That's how all this bloody business has come about. Mark my words.'

'What have I done to get caught up in all this?'

'I guess you're not telling me everything.'

'There's nothing to tell. I promise. One day I'm at work, next day I'm sitting here with you, trying to avoid getting a rocket-propelled grenade up my backside.'

'There's always something to tell,' said George. 'There's always something.'

They stood up and moved off, keeping a conservative distance between themselves and the errant lecturer as he turned into St John's Street and, as streetlights flickered on around him, finally headed for home.

Steadman's pace slowed. The light was beautiful, a Cambridge mist descending from the ether, St Mary's doors hiding golden lights in greeting to the Senate House.

George became wistful. 'I used to think I worked for all this. I was an architect, Charlie. A creator of clever designs to sustain the world. I thought I was an information broker. And I believed in my power to change things because knowledge is power, that's what you're told, knowledge is bloody-well power. But I know the truth now. Knowledge, information, intelligence . . . it's not power. It's opinion. We're not intelligence officers. We're sewage workers, Charlie; we trawl the gutters for gossip and try to get out of the game before the smell gets into our bones for good.'

'Not true,' retorted Charlie, knowing in his heart that this strange man had just touched the only nerve he had left.

'Oh really?' George was facing him now. 'When was the last time,' he continued, 'that you had a pleasant thought?'

Charlie snorted with laughter, causing a passing girl on a bike to glance up, cheeks red and raw as her bike clattered over the cobbles. And then Charlie stopped as Steadman continued his world-weary course against the wind. Pausing to answer the question had made him realise a terrible truth.

'I don't know.'

Steadman cut across King's Parade and entered a newsagent's. George and Charlie slowed down and adopted a holding pattern some thirty yards behind.

'We're spies, you idiot. Our jobs, Charlie, okay, even our lives, depend on thinking ahead. Forbes had it right. What kind of outcome is least likely? What are the options, and what should we anticipate?'

'I remember, George . . .'

Steadman emerged with a packet of cigarillos and a lighter. George was working up a sweat now as they resumed their tail, their voices loud enough to be heard, soft enough not to draw attention. 'And what that means is that our actions are rarely anything that affects our situation. Because our situation is, by definition, beyond our control. And yet it's something we prepare for every second we're awake. The twist in the road ahead. The spanner in the works. What's bad about this situation? What's wrong with this picture?'

'George—'

'That's no way to look at life,' he went on, his voice rising, cracking in places with passion and effort, 'that's no way to look at *anything*, for God's sake. How can people like us hope for the best when everything in our lives points a flaming finger to the fact that nothing good *ever lasts*?'

Charlie rubbed his head as they walked. 'All this university's gone to your head, George. I'm serious.'

But he knew George was right. Even now, Charlie realised, he was doing mental somersaults, scanning the intersections, the escape routes, subconscious preparations for a sudden change of direction by Steadman, what he'd do if he suddenly turned this way, got in a car, climbed on a bike, met an old friend, pulled a gun . . . it was all laid out ahead of time. All had been anticipated. What good is the good news when all you're waiting for is the bad?

'I can't look at anything *nice*, Charlie, not on its own. All I see are the downsides. I can't even smile. I want to look forward to the future, you know, but I can't. And what's that? It's losing hope, mate. And once you lose hope, you have to ask, what's the point of tomorrow?'

'Stop it, George—'

'So I've learned to live in the cracks, you know. In the waiting, that's where you can stay sane. Some people worry themselves into a tumour for things that never happen. Some people live for the day and then get cut down by a rotary cultivator crossing the bloody road—'

'George, for fuck's sake—'

And he stopped, mid-flow, panting for breath.

Charlie looked at him there, silhouetted in the street light, suddenly more human, more truly real, than Charlie had ever appreciated before. Just a man, a man called George, forty-something, lover of the Village People and sometime intelligence officer, adrift, standing stock still on a cold pavement. Fifty years ago he didn't exist. Fifty years hence, the same would be true. Here they were together, standing in the cracks.

Charlie grabbed the sleeve of his fleece. It was moist with the fog and their pursuit.

'Sorry – Charlie, I'm sorry—'

'He's gone inside.'

*   *   *

Three hours and five courses later, Steadman had plodded up the staircase and felt the steady, patient gaze of Charles Millar drilling into his back.

Charlie finished a brief precis of their predicament in the warm glow of Steadman's emberous grate. Steadman listened with professionally scrunched eyebrows, nodding at appropriate junctures, looking away and lending his ear, sipping his drink and eventually sitting down, knees pulled high, hands clasped in academic prayer.

'What do you want me to do,' he said finally.

'Someone somewhere ordered this,' said Charlie, approaching him with small, precise steps. 'Someone higher up knows exactly what is going on.'

'I suppose I could make a few calls—'

'You're still recruiting. You practically recruited the whole of the seventh floor in my building. There have to be reasons behind all this.' Charlie paused, the alcohol suddenly affecting him. 'There have to be.'

Throughout Charlie's expository opening and Steadman's analysis, George had stayed stock-still and unblinking. He finally spoke. Never once did he look at Steadman:

'Tell him we need names,' he said to Charlie.

'I think he probably heard you,' Charlie replied.

'Tell him we need to know names, departments, and the numbers involved. Someone somewhere authorised the Frame Thirteens. Someone tasked Logistics. Someone passed it by Special Planning. Someone signed off on the couriers. Someone got on a bloody motorbike and pulled the trigger. There's a sewer of paperwork underneath this and it will lead directly to who is running this and who is trying to bury us both. Tell him to find these things out and tell us what speed we should be perambulating towards the exit.'

George was clearly not going to address the man to his face.

'I'll see what I can do,' said Steadman. 'As subtly as I can, I'll do it. Jesus, Charlie, what the hell have you done?'

'As far as I know, Paul, nothing. That's why I came to you.'

'All right,' said Steadman. 'I'll make the calls tomorrow. But you shouldn't come here again.' He shot a worried glance up at George. He still hadn't blinked once.

'I understand,' said Charlie.

George cleared his throat and finally locked eyes with Steadman. 'What's your measure of the situation?' he asked.

'I said I'd make the calls, didn't I?'

'And I said, "What's your measure of the situation"?'

'Look, as it stands . . . come on, it's obvious. There's either a benign reason for all this or a malignant one. These things don't just happen by chance.'

'In your experience with the Service, has there ever been a benign reason for anything?'

'The Service doesn't exist. The Service is a group noun signifying thousands of individuals. And grammatical terms do not try to kill people. People do that.'

'Individuals make policy. And policy gets implemented. That's how group nouns kill people, Dr Steadman.'

'I'd be surprised if this was a policy decision,' said Steadman after a long pause for thought. 'I really would.'

'Terrible business,' he added as he moved the men to his sported oak, the thick outer door to his Fellow's set. He felt the chill of the stairwell seeping in from the other side and shivered slightly. 'Where can I contact you?'

'Fulham?' said Charlie.

Steadman thought for a moment and then nodded – a glimmer of recognition passing before his eyes. George presumed he had understood what Charlie had meant. Which was a relief to him, as he had no idea whatsoever. He was certainly not going anywhere near SW6. Or any postcode of London for that matter. Not for a very long while.

George and Charlie exited onto King's Parade to find the edge had gone from the cold. They walked across the market square, closed and bolted. Over the Town Hall the street-lights were weak. The market stalls were empty, their skeletons shrouded in ghostly grey tarpaulins. The over-whelming impression was metallic. A metal square under a metal sky. Even the edges of a vast Fenland storm front loomed silver on the horizon.

Once, Charlie's eyes had seen a similar cloud. He had seen it through torrential tears and a dark, winding road.

Once, Charlie's eyes had seen a lot of things they wished they hadn't.

George, in his venting, in his stupid spot-on analysis of their situation, was unlocking parts of Charlie's mind he had been trying very hard to keep shut.

Ever since.

'Fulham?' asked George.

'He used to make me practise dead-letter drops in the library. When he was trying to recruit me. It's just a code. Nothing that scales the cryptographic heights of 1–2–3–4, but . . .'

'You said he was a friendly face.'

'He is.'

'You just left him alone in a room. With a telephone.'

'He's on side,' said Charlie, 'I promise.'

George nodded quietly, not believing this for one moment. 'So what now,' he said finally.

'We wait until it's clear to proceed.'

They spent the night in a club called 'Shenanigans', close to the railway station. In a corner booth of waxy blue banquettes they quietly watched a succession of men with short hair and bright shirts stand in groups, drink bottles of American beer, nod their heads to the music in a strangely proprietorial way, attempt to talk to the two girls dancing together, and leave. That was the extent of the shenanigans at Shenanigans and they were both grateful for it.

At around two forty-five the club began to close its doors and George and Charlie wandered the streets for half an hour before finding a park bench in the shadow of a grave-yard yew. George fell asleep and Charlie struggled against his falling eyelids.

The night was as cold and as sharp to him as when he had answered a call from a Duty Controller of Operations, leaving Becky curled up and half-awake under the duvet, mumbling to him from her dream to come back to bed. '*A last-minute change of plan,*' the voice had said. '*Meet contact in Biarritz, and await further orders.*' He had been planning on a short jaunt to Nice but Logistics probably knew what they were doing.

She had looked so peaceful, lying there in his old sweat-shirt, knees to her chest, clutching a pillow to her in lieu of him. She always slept like that. He would often find her on the sofa waiting for him if he was forced to work the late shift. She roused quietly when he sat back onto the bed and when he told her of the extended mission she merely whimpered in protest and they clung on to each other so tightly it seemed as though their lives depended on it.

'*Just a couple more days,*' he told her.

'*Okay,*' she had said.

'*Not okay*,' he corrected her.

She had kissed the back of his neck and plumped up the pillow. '*Correct*,' she had whispered. '*But what can you do.*'

Charlie had nodded back, aching for sleep and aching for her. Little knowing this would be the last time.

What can you do.

At four a.m. the cold won its fight for the bench and the two men stood and moved off once again. Yellow streetlight washed the tarmac. They located, after some considerable effort, an all-night petrol station that served coffee. An hour later, in the midst of the deserted streets, a miracle – a kebab house still open. George and Charlie sat in the chill of a frosty bus shelter, picking the fat off the scraps of steaming meat.

'I arrived early once for a supervision with Steadman,' said Charlie without prompting. 'The door was open so I went in and found him getting it on with my friend Jenny. I promised not to say anything. That's how I got recruited. He decided I was good with secrets.'

'I don't think that's a particularly strong case for trust,' said George.

'Her dad's high up in Special Branch. At the time, Steadman could have been framed on so many trumped-up charges he'd have been found guilty of inciting the decline of the Roman Empire. He'd have eaten prison food the rest of his life. So that's what he owes me. His life. If you ask me, I think we'll be just fine.'

'I didn't. But thank you for the unsolicited information.'

Charlie dumped their kebab detritus in the bin and explained that Steadman would leave word of his investigations in a copy of his first book. The only copy still in print could be found in the University Library. Charlie knew that this would never be consulted. It was a deeply boring tome that appeared nowhere on any reading lists. A signal would tell them if a message was waiting.

The sun rose and milk vans hummed into traffic. The day passed with meticulous precision. At nineteen minutes past every hour, Charlie would walk up St John's Street and glance casually up at a third-floor window. When he saw nothing of significance to him, he would pass on and meet George at the end of the road, innocently perusing the window of a bookshop. On the fifth or sixth circuit, George began to get nervous.

'It's a waste of time,' he explained. 'I don't care what you've got on him, this is too much exposure.'

'He'll come through,' said Charlie.

'The point of forward planning,' continued George, 'is to anticipate. We're putting our lives in the hands of a man who feels blackmailed by you. I don't call that a very secure calculation of risk.'

'Sure. I mean, we could always call them ourselves. But quite frankly I don't think they'll be particularly forthcoming when they recognise our bloody voices—'

Charlie stopped his diatribe and gestured for George to be quiet. He glanced up again at the window. Instead of dirty glass framing the back view of a Chesterfield, the curtains were now drawn. On the ledge, previously devoid of life, sat a sinewy yucca palm, its thin leaves casting shadows on the curtain lining in the weak afternoon light.

A look between them was all it took to communicate: *it's on*. They strode quickly through Senate House Passage and across the river to the looming Stalinist façade of Cambridge University Library.

'*The Electric Man*,' muttered George as they approached. 'Detective Sexton Blake investigates the disappearance of a murdered man from a locked library.'

'What was the twist?' asked Charlie, happy to keep his mind on something apart from how long he still had to live.

'Turns out there was a secret exit.'

'That's not a twist, George, that's a slipknot.'

'It's not my favourite, I will admit.'

Avoiding students and lecturers on incoming bicycles, the two men passed by the grand stone steps in their first security loop of the building. George kept himself alert despite his growing exhaustion. No police, no suspicious vehicles, he mused. Nothing that suggested this was a bad idea.

But then, he reminded himself, nothing ever does. At least Charlie seemed to be thinking ahead. He'd been right to trust him.

'Fulham?' said George, eyes already scanning the gates on either side of the parking lot.

'The dead drop's in a book stack. South Wing Six.'

George's face clouded. 'I've always had problems with that word.'

'Which word?'

'Dead. I don't like that word at all.'

George watched Charlie disappear up the wide entrance steps and slowly but firmly crossed his fingers.

The queue for admission was thankfully small and that odd-looking woman with the glasses was, amazingly, still the main security cordon. She still looked like she belonged in Middle Earth rather than on any mortal dimension. His card had nearly expired, but the graduate card lasted five years and Charlie's appearance wasn't too different to the image on the plastic.

Heart pounding, Charlie arced up the main left staircase to the foyer and search stands, where students crowded the library search engines. Charlie decided he would approach by the South Wing lifts and cross the entire building, allowing him to sweep for unfriendlies as he went. Steadman could have tipped any number of people off about this. The thought sent Charlie into a sweat.

The lift was small, coffin-like, and as Charlie approached it he became aware he was being watched. The librarian with the bald pate had been staring – with hawk-like intensity – from his book-stamping corral ever since Charlie rounded the stairs.

He tried not to look back as he pressed 'up' and waited.

For what seemed a ridiculously long time the crude engineering clunked and whirred. Eventually what amounted to little more than a souped-up dumb waiter juddered to a standstill in front of Charlie.

Once on the sixth floor, Charlie hauled open the cage and stepped out. He was at the end of a narrow corridor stretched in the distance. Book stacks to the left passed Charlie with increasing speed as he walked. A long bench to his right qualified as a study table with a view; small groups of students hunched over journals and notepads in regular intervals, every once in a while looking up at him and trying to catch his eye out of boredom.

The classifications descended and Charlie's heart-rate quickened:

220.c.98.1000–1419 . . .
220.c.98.533–999 . . .
220.c.98.200–532 . . .

Charlie finally found the one he was looking for. He checked quickly behind him and turned the corner.

The good news was, the coast was clear.

The bad news was, so was the shelf.

Not just the shelf, in fact, but the entire section of the book stack. Charlie looked helplessly at the sign and back to the shelf a few times but it was clearly not going to help.

He spied a library assistant pushing a squeaky cart – tracked him down to the other side of the book stack. Seeing his face, the assistant sighed mournfully and pointed to a small notice that hung on the end of the shelf section. It said: '*All 220.c.98 classifications now in Reading Room.*'

'Are they all in the Reading Room, then?' asked Charlie. The assistant merely sighed, glanced with ironic complicity at some invisible accomplice and pointed back at the notice. Charlie cleared his throat and tried again.

'How long have they been there? Please?'

The assistant clenched her jaw. 'We only moved them this morning.' She did not appear to blink.

Outside, the wind whipped George's hair. His unruly strands were encouraged into exotic angles. Students flowing upstream and down on their bikes noticed him and chuckled to themselves. Several hours later, in college bars around the town, George's hair would be the topic of great mirth and anecdote. George was unaware of any of this because he was so deep in thought that even his own peripheral acuity was taking a break.

It was conceivable, he was thinking, that Charlie could find a note from Steadman and be gone. There might be employee exits to this place, he realised, tradesmen's entrances. A cafeteria, perhaps. A basement. The note might explain exactly who issued the Frame 13. It might warn they were both in great danger. It might, for all George knew, be another Frame 13 with his picture on it. Charlie had a head start, therefore, on whatever future outcome lay ahead. George started to compute the probability that Charlie could simply take off and leave him.

He realised that in order to do that, he had to have the measure of Charlie. And he wasn't sure he had that. Yet.

George was a man of good intentions. He knew this to be true and everything in his career had drawn from that place inside him. There were times to be brutal, of course. There were times when self-preservation compelled a person to do whatever it took.

He finally caught a glimpse of the mirthful stares and patted his cowlick down. He wished, as he often did, that he carried with him the book of his life. In the thrillers he had read and enjoyed, skipping ahead was often not required. When he felt anxious or concerned for the safety of the characters, he would need to do no more than feel the weight of the pages in his right hand. Halfway through a book, for example, he would know not to worry too much – the volume of pages were a reminder that there was still time to rectify matters. Reading a story meant knowing with physical certainty that *these things were far from over*. As the left side gained weight, there was more reason to get worried.

George wondered where they were in his own story.

He liked Charlie. He wanted to help Charlie, and for Charlie to help him. He hoped very much that Charlie wouldn't leave him.

They still had so much to do.

He looked at his watch and realised it was still probably too early to call Tate.

*   *   *

The U.L. Reading Room was warm, vaulted and dark, lit by low yellow lights and alive with the hushed sound of breath and page turns, the light tapping of laptops, vibrating mobile phones and whispered flirtations for tea at four. Two hundred eyes glanced up at Charlie as he strode in at speed, until the eyes decided he wasn't worth following after all and landed instead on a handsome young linguist in a Selwyn College rowing top.

Charlie presumed that even if the book had been moved, he and George had seen the signal and Steadman would have made sure the message would be ready to be received. Move or not move. Kill or be killed.

An overwhelming sense of isolation swept Charlie for an instant and he felt the sudden urge to be sick.

Charlie approached the main desk and filled in a small yellow slip with a small yellow pencil. 'Steadman, P.M.,' he wrote, '*Welsh Land Law and the Econometrics of Reformation England*'. He had to press quite hard. The weird-looking male student in front of him shot him a sarcastic look as he poured his own pile of slips into the box before Charlie.

The librarian took the slips and placed them in another box, which was promptly removed by another man pushing another cart and transported through a small portico to a lift that led, legendarily, remembered Charlie, to both the bowels of the library collection and the mythical tower. On the top floor lay the most extensive collection of pornography outside of Peter Stringfellow's bedside table. Or so you learned in your first week.

The weird boy was still staring at Charlie over stern and studious glasses. There was an arrogant mien to him, a sharp leading edge that suggested he was calculating how much better he had done at his exams than the person he was looking at. Whatever the reason, the scrutiny made Charlie nervous and he turned away, developing a sudden and intense fascination with the book next to his shoulder: Bristow, Philip, *Through the Belgian Canals* (Lymington, Nautical Pub. Co., 1972). He nodded sagely, leafing through the index of black and white plates. They featured, mostly, canals. Looking up, Charlie saw no sign of the book cart so turned instead to *Proceedings of the Third International Colloquium on the Ecology and Taxonomy of Small African Mammals* (Antwerp, 1981). The fountain of Brabo flashed briefly into his head. He thought of Becky's cold-flushed smile framed by the Flemish arches – their first holiday in a while, they had run off on a 'citybreak' in the early hours of the morning. She wasn't a fan of coffee but arriving for breakfast that day she decided, for once, she needed the hit. He hadn't stopped laughing at her manic energy all day. The vision and smile faded as a microscopic squeak filtered in – it was coming from the centre of the reading room.

The book trolley was here.

Charlie set off immediately and noticed the weird kid was in step with him from the other side of the Reading Room. The librarian was yawning as the two men hit the book cart at the same time. Charlie knew the volume by its cover and reached for it – but his wrist was held in a limpet grip.

'Mine,' whispered the weird kid. 'Sorry.'

Charlie smiled. 'Actually, I think you'll find it's mine,' he whispered back. 'Sorry.'

The librarian glanced up at them both over his varifocals.

Charlie looked down at the slip and saw it was signed by 'M. Potts'. The limpet grip held firm and Charlie also noticed that Potts was piling the other five books on the cart with his free hand. All were labelled with similar writing. Things were not looking good. Charlie looked to the librarian for help. He needn't have bothered.

'You asked for the same book,' he said. 'This gentleman was first.'

'What gentleman?' Charlie blurted, in all honesty. He'd been a little loud. Two hundred faces stared up at what was becoming a small tug of war.

'Let go of the book please,' whispered Potts.

'I really need to just have a quick look at it,' smiled Charlie. 'Would that be okay with you?'

'No,' said Potts. 'It would not.'

Charlie released his grip on the book and watched M. Potts return to a corner seat where he had already surrounded himself with a veritable Berlin Wall of historiography.

Unsure of what to do next, Charlie spotted an empty chair next to him. He filled it. Potts shifted uncomfortably on his seat.

'Look,' said Charlie in his most reasonable whisper.

'You know as well as I do what's going on here,' said Potts suddenly, not looking at Charlie at all. Charlie's nerves flipped to alert. 'Steadman's setting Paper Thirty this year and we both want to quote him back at himself. I know your game and you know mine. Well, that's just tough, mate, cos I got here first and I'm taking this out till June.'

Charlie sighed. He could try and sneak a look at it, of course, but the overly ambitious Potts was not going to make it easy, having barricaded the book safely up on his section of the desk between *The English Economy from Bede to the Reformation* and *An Agrarian History of Wales*.

Charlie pretended, at least for a moment, to let it go. He waited for the curious stares to dissipate, and moved instead to the book stacks behind him. Removing a similarly thick and portentous volume from the shelves, he signed it out and made his way outside.

George was stamping his feet to keep warm as Charlie ran down the main stairs.

'What the hell kept you?' said George, who looked like a lost sales executive with his attaché case and windblown hair.

'Sssh,' said Charlie.

Martin Potts ambled down the stairs ten minutes later, his books in a plastic U.L. carrier bag. He was going to cycle quickly, to hit Hall before they closed the cafeteria. With these reading materials, and an extra serving of nut cutlet, a first was a given.

He placed the bag in the basket of his bike. He bent down to unlock the chain. When he looked up again, the bag was on the wall. He blinked a couple of times and decided to stop drinking U.L. coffee as it made him dizzy.

Back in his college room, Martin found he was the proud owner of a book on Belgian canals. Around the same moment as Martin was kicking the leg of his desk, The Maypole Public House was full of student boat-club members on a Viking-themed pub crawl. Plastic helmets with horns, red faces, and black ties. Charlie and George sat with the locals in the lounge bar, quietly making comments on the youth of today. Charlie finished his pint and opened the book. They had taken a while to warm up.

On page twenty-one, a phrase in pencil in the header. *Contact Zero can help. 10 a.m. Picture House. 2561.*

'I always thought that was a myth,' said George.

'Oh ye of little faith,' said Charlie.

204

29

'There will be times,' said Forbes, 'when the loneliness is too much to bear. Times feeling that there must surely be a way out, a backstop, an escape route. Well, I am here to tell you that those times will number more than you care to imagine. But there will be people' – he was glowering out at them now, sniffling under the weight of a head cold – 'who will try and tell you that an escape pod exists. Contact Zero, they'll call it. I know, you've all heard the rumours already. Some benevolent field agents got together, you've been told, and decided to make a plan. Should every possible kind of shit hit the fan, you can make some discreet enquiries. And Contact Zero will come to your aid. Contact Zero will save you. Contact Zero is where all sins will be forgiven. A place known to only a small number of individuals in the world. Not just any old safe house. A run-aground haven, you hear, a place where if you are in the know and willing to get there, at any cost, you are guaranteed peace and an untainted sleep. This is because mistrustful and paranoid Service officers have created the place for themselves, from scratch, its location moved every month so as to avoid suspicious minds, jealous hearts, or wagging tongues.

'I am not a religious man. But I understand the need for Contact Zero to exist in the same way that I understand the need for an overarching deity to exist in the world of human endeavours. Both of these concepts, I am sorry to report to you, are false at the best of times; dangerous at the worst. Particularly when the belief in them is vehemently strong in defiance of all evidence to the contrary.

'Your only recourse in the field is yourself. If you have the resources yourself, by all means create your own "bolthole". A pied-à-terre on the coast of Normandy has been mooted as a popular destination for the well-heeled spy on the run. Ditto Porto, the Dalmatian Riviera. Even South Africa for the adventurous or the lover of fine seafood.

'But for those of us without a private income, obliged to live de facto at Her Majesty's Displeasure, courtesy of your Intelligence salaries, there is no total solution to our problems. There will be no helping hand if you get into trouble. There will be no-one there to pick up after you. It is important you understand that before you head out there. It is important you know the truth.

'To truly rely on yourself, you have to be fully alone. I am here to tell you that. Only then can you take care of what is most important to this Service – yourselves.'

30

Neil thought the office looked like some Victorian tart's parlour. But then he wasn't going to say that. Neil thought a lot of things he didn't say. Some people had a sluice from mind to mouth. Neil, despite his outward chattiness, had in fact been installed with a deeply insubordinate network of antiquated Victorian plumbing. It took a while for the words to make it down at the best of times. There were occasions when no evidence of a thought even played out across his face. That's why he was good at his job.

He'd mitigated his surprise at his sudden promotion with the assurance that Rose Willetts was one of the more trusted older managers in the Service, an administrator of long-standing who kept clear of the internecine boys' club and the one-upmanship in the main buildings Thames-side. His boss had agreed to his transfer like a bolt of lightning. But Neil wasn't too impressed with his boss and he presumed the feeling was mutual. Perhaps he'd been the one hinting to her that Neil should make the leap. Neil didn't really care. He was twelve hundred pounds a year richer, and nothing else really mattered at the moment.

Liz had been ecstatic when he'd told her. Jake was two now and with another one on the way there was the immediate need for a projected gradient of money, a reassuring graph over time that suggested that all would be well three years from now when Sprog Number Two was crawling around and Jake was tying up his shoelaces for his first day of school. And an added plus would be he'd stop lurking around cold, damp basements, something he never spoke about but Liz divined quite easily from the bouts of chest infection, the musty smell of his shoes and those bloody cold feet in bed. He'd used to be her hot-water bottle, she'd explained to him only the week before. Recently he'd been as cold as airline cutlery.

He thought of Liz as he walked in the next morning, and Rose had smiled, looked him up and down and lilted, 'Finally, a man who knows where to buy his ties.'

In any other circumstance this might have been some weird form of sexual harassment but as Rose's entire demeanour was one of welcome and a vague disconnection to the social norm, Neil felt flattered and vindicated. He would have to tell Liz her instinct had been right.

Rose had fast-tracked the promotion and bullied Bill, she explained, because of a pressing research project. She gestured to a grey PC workstation in another room, visible through a Perspex wall that was nicked and scratched and streaked by years of neglect.

'We're not exactly the CIA Ops Center,' she said to him as they both turned to take in the cubicle, 'but one does one's best with the money available. Now, more important matters. Would you like a cup of tea?'

Neil decided that he would. And, half an hour later, he was settling into the small black office chair, opening the heavy brown drawers of his desk and picking the old masking tape from the corner of the keyboard. Rose had delivered his tea herself, in a red tartan mug, a gift from Edinburgh Woollen Mill that made Neil smile. He suspected that her only experience of the Highlands was driving around it in order to kill its wildlife. And here she was, attempting, in her own way, to make a Scotsman feel at home.

Rose explained his promotion further as he nibbled on a plain digestive biscuit. The project, she said, was the perfect match for him. His analytical skills had been noticed. They would come in vital in cross-referencing mission plans with logistics dispensations. In English, to see what had gone where, to whom and why.

She admitted it wasn't the most exciting of tasks for someone so clearly also suited to a life entirely in the field, but this was a position from where he could truly use his brain. All manner of Service promotions could easily be reached by such work – indeed, no high office had ever been attained without it – and in Rose he had, she took pains to explain, something of a secret fan.

He took the information on board and with hardly a pause to make notes, began to tap away. Rose marvelled at the nimble beauty of young minds and retired to her own office. She gazed out at the urban blight below her window – as well as the reflection of the boy Neil working diligently away through the glass.

Rose worked out in this moment that there were a limited number of Service-related options open to two ex-Servicemen on the run in East Anglia. Well, technically she knew they were not as yet retired. But it was, she felt, a moot point.

The car's description and registration details had, thanks to a verbally haemorrhagic previous owner, been quick and easy to track down. It hadn't taken that long either to trace it to the farmhouse, thanks to a local constabulary who laboured under the misapprehension that there may have been a missing dog within the vehicle and that time was of the essence as the night temperatures plunged. Rose always found local police forces were more motivated by vehicle searches when they knew a small defenceless creature was in jeopardy. And she certainly didn't want anything so grand and attention-grabbing as a vehicle theft springing up on police radios. At least for the time being, she required things smooth and silent, a conger eel amongst the rushes.

The tracks behind the farmhouse had also come as a pleasantly speedy surprise – courtesy of the same two constables who proudly reported the discovery of the Daihatsu. 'Perhaps the animal was abducted from the vehicle by the missing guests,' they reported back like terriers, eager to please but not sure how. Rose had thanked them for their professional application to the job in hand, reported the dog as recovered, apologised for wasting their time, then sat back and mused to herself over a cup of Lady Grey. The colvert, a hide in hunting language, had been cleared. When a fox leaves the earth they are given time by the hounds to reach open ground. There, the hunt is faster, easier, more direct to the kill.

Thus, in this East Anglian case, there were a limited number of options for even the most intrepid fox. Humans very rarely go to ground for very long. They are, in most cases, wound up in constant flight or constant pursuit – fleeing fear, commitment, responsibility; chasing money, fame, skirt, scrote. For Rose, it made second-guessing most people a simple task. Since the tracks led to a dual carriageway, her quarry had two basic options from their colvert-of-choice. A return to London, or fleeing to the Fens.

An ordinary individual would flee northeast, of course. Away from the troubles of the past. But these were clever men, inculcated by Forbes Mackinnon after all. They would anticipate what ordinary men would do and do the opposite. Lay a trail in one direction, double back and flee in the other. So London it was. Unless –

Unless they were *very* clever men. Very clever men would factor in the people who were chasing them. And in that moment Rose remembered something her father had once said to her: *When a fox goes to ground, they always choose a lair with two exits*. At least, the cleverest ones do.

With this thought sparking a smile on her lips, Rose recalled the conversation she had overheard in the cafeteria and decided that Latham would have to make some enquiries Fenward.

The boy Neil tap-tap-tapped away in the next room and brought a great sense of peace to Rose's lonely heart. She knew, more or less, that whether or not she lost the trail, she had a trace of the scent here, in her office. If he was as conscientious as she thought he was, this would all be over in a few days. The paperwork, then the people. The people, then the paperwork. Both of these were missing and both would be found, eventually.

And then all would be well with the world.

That night, Steadman's phone rang and rang. He knew who it might be and he cursed himself for even trying to make a few calls without the benefit of Dutch courage. His voice, unless commanding the confidence of a lecture script, sounded tremulous on the phone. And any sign of weakness was the beginning of the end. One does not casually call up your Service colleagues to 'see how it's all going'.

The details were as clear as mud to Steadman, but it never

mattered what you knew. Of course there was a bloody signature on the Frame 13 orders. It probably wasn't the signature of the person who ordered it. The way the Service worked was like anything else in the corporate world. No-one ever takes responsibility for something unless it's starting to be a success. Operations developed their own centres of gravity very quickly once the word of their excellence emerged. His cack-handed personal politics were never enough veneer to hid his fear. The fact that you knew anything at all was usually enough to get you into trouble. The general advice for people like Charlie and George was usually to 'keep under the radar'. Never mind the fact that most planes that did that generally ended up crashing into a mountainside.

He let the phone fall silent.

It began to ring again.

A chill blasted through Steadman and he reached a tremulous hand for his bottle of Scotch.

31

The pub had long since chucked them out, but Charlie and George were following a tip from Malone, their new-found friend-in-beer, about a legendary lock-in on Mill Road. The first train was in a few hours and it made sense to keep out of the cold in any case. As Malone swayed and sashayed his way slowly ahead, George brought it up again.

'It's a trap,' he said.

'Why would it be?' said Charlie.

'Because if you or I were trying to lure someone back into our radar we would do exactly the same thing. He's sold us a myth, Charlie. He wanted nothing to do with us. You could see it in his eyes. There's no more a Contact Zero out there than there is a Santa Claus.'

Malone appeared to pause, ahead. Perhaps he'd over-heard. Perhaps he'd never been told the truth about Christmas.

'It's there, George.' Charlie waved the library book at him from the holdall with the strap that squeaked over his shoulder. 'And it's waiting for us in the Picture House.'

By Picture House, Charlie was referring to the National Portrait Gallery, a well-known and popular destination for covert meetings, brush-pasts, and other espionage behaviours of an undercover order. Spycraft there was almost too easy. It's important to have a public place to conduct your business, but the problem with public places is generally the 'public' part. It means people. People like to look and people get nosey. But in the 'Picture House', a spy has crowds with focus, crowds who are looking elsewhere. A portrait reference number and a time is all that's required to ensure that a contact is where you want them, and when.

'You and I don't know Contact Zero. It's a field-agent secret. No-one in the upper echelons knows—'

'No-one apart from Forbes Mackinnon—'

'They talk about it, George, but they think it's a joke.'

'It *is* a joke. It doesn't exist. Beer, however, does. So I think it's time you paid your way.'

'With your money, George? It will be my pleasure.'

George smiled and chuckled to himself as Charlie fished out some money from his pocket. Malone had stopped outside a large window that had been blacked out by a sheet of dark cloth. He rapped on the front door. A knock came back on the window. Malone beckoned the men around to the back of the bar by the bins. The door slid open and a large woman with short red hair ushered them inside.

George took the bag and found a seat in the corner by the toilets. Charlie offered to buy Malone a drink. As he made his way to the bar, he caught the eyes of several young men in short-sleeve shirts in the classic three-two-three formation, excluding the world and marking their territory very clearly. Charlie, acknowledging their dominance, simply excused himself and walked around them to the bar. Malone followed him in a drunken lurch.

As he did, one of the men, shaven-headed and mid-anecdote, gestured drunkenly with his arm. It hit Malone on the shoulder and spilt a small amount of the man's drink.

Another man pushed Malone back and he fell to the floor. Charlie glared at them and picked Malone up.

He knew he was a stranger here and despite Malone's protests, guided him to the other side of the bar, away from trouble.

But trouble decided to follow.

Malone's attacker arrived just as the man was in Charlie's face.

'—the fuck was that?'

'Just an accident. You want a drink?'

'We all want a drink.'

'Whatever you want – what you having?'

The man swayed quietly on his feet and stared. This wasn't going correctly. He wanted something back from his investment, but the offer was too good to turn down.

'Five bottles of Grolsch.'

'No problem.'

'And me,' said Malone. Charlie ignored him and ordered the drinks. George, seeing the situation, arrived a few seconds later.

'You thinking what I'm thinking?' he whispered.

'Bail,' said Charlie.

And when the drinks were paid for, the two men made for the door.

The cold slap of air outside was a welcome change from the Chernobyl-like atmosphere of the lounge bar. Charlie and George were walking calmly away from the bins when they heard a burst of music and a slam of the door.

They didn't need to turn around to know who had followed them.

'We didn't say you could leave.'

The voice was behind them, but again, they simply kept walking.

'You hear what I said?' came the shout.

'Oi!'

And George was first to turn. It was a great throw. The bottle was a virtual missile, nearly full and headed straight for Charlie's head.

So George did an extraordinary thing.

He turned around, looked the four men in the eye, and dived in front of Charlie.

He slightly misjudged the speed of the projectile, and the bottle hit him on the side of the head.

He fell hard, cold, on the tarmac.

Charlie stared at the unconscious George at his feet. He stared at the boys as they stared back. A moment passed, of surreal calm. There was something deep in Charlie's eyes that reminded the boys in the parking lot of a large tank slowly but surely turning its turret to point right between your eyes.

The shaven-headed man felt himself take a small step back towards the door. Behind, his friends were bored and barred his way.

George woke up coughing and was surprised to find himself in motion. He was sitting up, and as his eyes focused ahead of him he saw lines flitting past. Lights blinded him briefly and were gone.

He reasoned he was in a car. Outside, it was dark.

He turned his head to his right and it hurt. He turned it a little more to find Charlie at the wheel. Charlie glanced over at him grimly and returned his eyes to the road. The car was grunting with the effort of transporting the two men to the top of a slight incline. It was unclear how much longer the whole thing would stay together.

Charlie was thinking the same thing and was relieved to see George's breathing grow deeper. Lit by the vaguely green luminescence of the car's control panel, George was reminded of the long car-journeys his mother would make with himself and his brother. Two sleeping children in the back of the Rover. A more blissful peace and sense of possibility he could not remember. He leaned back in search of the headrest. It hurt. Still tender. Like the night.

'What happened?' asked George.

'They didn't like us very much,' said Charlie.

'I noticed. So where are they?'

Charlie cleared his throat as he kept his eyes on the road. 'In a skip.'

George's eyes flashed –

'Alive,' added Charlie. He seemed rather detached. George reasoned he'd have to be.

'Whose car is this?' murmured George.

'Theirs, I think. We'll dump it in a sec. How's your head?'

George became aware of the throbbing feeling at the back of his neck. 'Fine. A little sore.'

'I couldn't see much blood. No glass in your skin. You'll be fine.' Charlie shook the cramps away and began to realise just what George had done for him.

'I can't believe you did that,' said Charlie.

'Not a problem.'

'Thank you.'

Charlie kept his eyes on the road for several minutes before he spoke again. When he did so, his eyes were wet with memory – and an overwhelming surge of warmth for the man in the passenger seat. It suddenly became important to Charlie that George knew the truth.

'My wife died,' said Charlie.

George stared ahead and nodded in silent sympathy.

'I told you she left. I lied. She died.'

Charlie was getting the words out slowly, precisely, as if he were driving a mountain road and careful of every movement.

'In a car crash,' he said. 'She died in a car crash.'

George sat in silence for a moment and gave the words the respect they deserved. Charlie was faintly aware that George's teeth were grinding.

'That's terrible,' was all George could say.

'Yes,' said Charlie. 'It was. It is.'

The trees whizzing by at the sides of the car had grey and spindly branches that pointed somehow to the road ahead.

'I left on a job,' Charlie continued. 'Last-minute thing. I was delayed. A second order kept me there an extra day. I came back to hear she'd been run off the road. Hit a bridge and died instantly. If I hadn't been away so long . . . she hated driving. I always drove her everywhere.'

He shook his head and contemplated the frosty tarmac on the hard shoulder. 'Once she was gone, there was no way the job could hold me. Not the way it did. I killed her, in a way. Together with the job. We were accomplices in that crime. I don't know why I'm telling you this now,' said Charlie. 'No idea at all.'

It took another minute or so for someone to speak again.

'What was her name?' asked George.

'Becky,' said Charlie, tensing his stomach as the name came out. 'Her name was Becky.'

The vehicle seemed to accelerate slightly as an engine

roared behind them and a pair of car headlights skyrocketed over the crest of the hill. It was gaining fast. Charlie saw the tension in George's hands as he pulled the attaché case onto his lap.

The car behind them pulled to within twelve inches of the vehicle's rear bumper before roaring out into the other lane and streaking past them. The car was a Mercedes and was full of teenagers.

As the red lights disappeared into the distance the trees were giving way to a patchwork of fields and moonlight.

'I'm so sorry about your wife,' said George.

32

Steadman was fast asleep when the keys turned in the lock. It was fascistically early, in fact, and if he wasn't so bloody waylaid by the half-bottle of Macallan still brawling with his liver he'd be having words with that bloody bed-maker.

He sat upright and bleary when he heard the key turn a second time. This confused him momentarily until he reasoned that this time it had come from the *inside*. An unlocking, and then a locking. He began to realise just how early it was. It must still be the middle of the night. No bedmaker, no matter how psychotic, would attempt to clean the place at this hour. He wondered in a cold and half-dreamed sweat if Tracey Yip still had her key.

'Hello?' said Steadman.

There was no response from the gloom of the living area. Somewhere outside, the college clock chimed four. He swung his bare feet into bedside slippers and rose as quietly as he could. He noticed with a small amount of pride that he had an early morning erection. Perhaps he'd imagined it, he thought.

Perhaps this was the whisky talking.

He felt it, though, a change in the air. A sense of certainty.

He was good at this sort of thing. There was someone in here.

'Look,' said Steadman, feeling faintly ridiculous as his dressing gown failed to cover the still-protruding hard-on, 'I'm picking up the phone and calling the porters. Do you understand?'

He peered into the darkness. Spots swam in front of his eyes. Turning on the bedside light he picked up the phone by the window and found that he could not hear a dial tone.

The pain at the back of his neck lasted only a moment but he remembered feeling relieved that his window seat had soft cushions as his forehead impacted with its leading edge.

Latham surveyed the room half an hour later and pulled at the fingers of his gloves individually to loosen them. His palms were hot and sweaty with effort. With light arriving soon the work was nearly done. He had made the bed neatly and ensured that any signs of a struggle – not that there had been anything but a slight impact on a cushioned surface of wood – had been removed.

Steadman, meanwhile, was quietly taking a bath. Life was leaving him in pints, however, as his wrists had been opened with tremendous care and precision, and the warm water had long since clouded solid with the colour of beetroot. The overall effect was shocking but not one that would fool any half-qualified detective and that was exactly as Latham wanted it.

Latham checked his watch and slowly removed the plastic food-bag from his coat pocket. Inside were a small number of hairs and dead-skin cells that Latham had retrieved from the bathrooms of 35b Portnall Gardens and 73 Stendall Road. He re-trod the steps of the fictitious struggle he was resetting before him, sprinkling the genetic evidence like cayenne pepper on an omelette. He had been particularly sadistic in his choice of wounds, it was true, but he was keen to cause a stir and he was also irked. Irked that after all the planning and training for what was, after all, the stock-in-trade, the realm of the unexpected and the unforeseen – and even after applying his in-depth knowledge of Future Outcomes to this covert war – after all of that, the thing that precipitated this admittedly extreme exit strategy was a chain of unexpected consequence. Unexpected! In the world of a spy there cannot be such a thing as coincidence. Experience had taught Latham that it is only in life that we allow the world to take the blame. In the world of spycraft, the only fault is your own.

Latham tread softly in his plastic shoe-coverings and relocked the door with the domestic staff's stolen keys. He cursed the night air that took him past the front gates of the college, whose porters were more intent on the alarm that had recently tripped off at the far end of the Chapel building, and, after a brief spot of window shopping, Latham slipped into his well-concealed car and drove off to the sound of the BBC Farming Report.

33

Charlie stared at the numberplate and realised that, apart from each other, this sorry assortment in front of them was about all they had. The car, themselves, and a library book.

In his bedsit, Charlie had felt alone. But there he'd still had his music. His CDs, his beloved leather jacket. That was all gone now. That was life BG, Before George, and standing here Charlie felt not just disconnected, but *untethered*. He felt that unless he was particularly careful, before too long he might just float right up out of his shoes and disappear They'd find him centuries later, fossilised in orbit, frozen on the side of a long-forgotten weather balloon.

They had parked on a secluded river bank. Charlie avoided the stinging nettles as his shoes darkened in the early morning dew. Charlie opened the front door and released the handbrake. A gentle shove and soon the only sign of the car was the melancholy bubbles that rose to the surface amongst the weeds.

The walk to the station was only a mile on the country roads, but George wanted to take the public footpaths and double back on themselves. Another standard drycleaning manoeuvre but for Charlie — cold, hungry, desperate for some peace in his life – it seemed like an eternity. He kept his irritation to himself. George had jumped in front of the bottle. He'd taken a hit for him. He hoped one day to return the favour. Just not any time soon.

The train limped in from the gloom and Charlie and George were surprised to find this small commuter station suddenly clogged with bleary-eyed office workers in grey suits and overcoats. They clearly timed their treasured last five minutes of sleep to perfection. Charlie boarded first and acquired a corner seat. A heater by the window piped foul-smelling but mercifully warm air onto their feet. George sat next to Charlie and avoided the eyes of everyone else.

'That street outside the Picture House,' whispered George when the train had moved off, 'it's a sniper's paradise. There are crowds to melt into, rooftops to lie on. The Jackal's mum could blow your head off with a bow and arrow. Or they could just as easily do it close quarters. A busy London weekday. Everyone's got to get somewhere. In and out with a stiletto, a poison flick-knife, a silenced weapon. No-one's going to notice.'

'Try and keep your voice down,' said Charlie, noticing a man reading last night's paper was staring at them.

George nodded in apology. Lowering his voice, he continued. 'They did that study, you know. A journalist fell over in the street on a busy Monday morning. It took half an hour for anyone to stop and ask her if she was all right.'

'No-one's going to fall over,' said Charlie.

'And what happens when we get in? I don't know the layout, do you? Two minutes after that we could get sprung by the Gainsboroughs. Once we're in, we're on our own. We can't bring a weapon through security. Outside, inside, it's stupid, it's dangerous.'

'So don't come.'

'I told you, Charlie, we're getting to the bottom of this.'

George watched frosty hedgerows scream by. Weak light crept over a small rise in the land and began to trickle gently into the fields. Where was Gainsborough when you needed him? The carriage was heating up now. It felt good to let someone else drive.

'We'll be in Liverpool Street by seven thirty,' said Charlie. 'Get some breakfast in the City. Start a drycleaning circuit at nine and move into position at nine forty-five.'

George finally shrugged. He was too exhausted to argue any more. And the breakfast sounded too good to turn down. 'All right,' he said. 'We go. We case it. But any sign of trouble and that will be that—'

The train arrived on time and no-one was more surprised than the driver.

George and Charlie ducked into a 24-hour café across the road from the station and hid behind a *Daily Express* in a corner booth. The smell of cigarette smoke and stale morning-breath hung in the air. The two men talked in low voices under the cover of the noisy Gaggia machine.

They saw the staring eyes of a couple of men in overcoats who looked too much like Special Branch to help any kind of digestion. Charlie's leg began to tingle and he knew he'd have to get up and leave soon or that leg would be useless in five minutes.

A surprisingly handsome waiter brought them both full English breakfasts. Charlie abruptly got up and left. George, sensing unwelcome attention, followed him out.

'What was that?'

'Just keep walking, all right?'

Against the flow of morning pedestrians, they turned into

a road that led to the old Fruit and Wool Exchange, now home to high-tech firms hanging on to their first-round funding in the desperate hope of any upturn.

'I didn't like them.'

'Neither did I, but that's no reason to— Okay, we've got a friend.'

They were being followed. Not by the overcoats. There were two uniforms in a car. Two minutes before they had passed slowly behind. Now the car had swung around and 'bumped into' their path several hundred metres ahead.

And George and Charlie knew the only time you bumped into the uniforms was when they were looking to bump into you. A man from the café was running behind them now, shouting. Faces were turning. He was a hundred yards away. Charlie was gripped by a thought.

'Did you pay—?'

'No – did you?'

'Fuck it.'

And they had no option now. Staying to explain would be too risky. Charlie dropped a ten-pound note on the ground and ran. George was already way ahead of him.

The covered market was preparing for that weekend's five-a-side football tournament. Large rolls of netting blocked the footpath. Charlie and George took the long way around the by-line and ducked behind a Vietnamese food stall that seemed to be preparing to feed the entire population of London from a large vat of lunchtime noodles. In the corner of the market was a chain pub with greasy windows. Reflected and mottled through a half-open door, George could see two suited men in overcoats approaching from the entrance to the market.

They gazed around curiously for a few moments, then

departed. Charlie and George looked at each other and walked calmly in the opposite direction.

The lack of sleep, the need to move, to scan ahead, behind, above, below, to listen, worry, suspect . . . perhaps this was all smoke and mirrors. Perhaps these were all figments of two paranoid imaginations.

They agreed not to stick around to find out.

They weaved through Jack the Ripper's old territory in Whitechapel, avoiding the main roads, the bus stops, the taxi ranks and Tube stations. They were drycleaning any remaining tails they had accumulated – both real and imagined – and both knew that public transport was now almost certainly a no-go zone.

So they marched on. From Whitechapel through the City, as a frozen breeze assaulted them in the narrow alleys where the north meets the east. Into Fitzrovia then down, cutting through the parks and service roads, until, turning a corner, Charlie caught a glance of a clock.

Nine forty-five. Even at their nimble pace they were falling behind. George saw it too and a look between them was all it took for them to both break into a run. *That was the thing about professional paranoia*, thought Charlie. *It eats up the clock.*

When they arrived at Trafalgar Square the clock read nine fifty-five. It would take them three minutes to get to the gallery. Another two to gain access and arrive at the rendezvous. They could still do it. The sun was bright and the sky clear as Charlie dragged George towards the north side of the Square, avoiding the malevolent traffic on Charing Cross Road. Despite the time, they instinctively headed to the back of the building, cutting down Orange Street and then south towards the beginnings of Pall Mall. George kept his eyes on the tops of the buildings. Charlie kept his eyes on George.

The layout of the intersection afforded many separate and fatal angles. The Adelaide Street buildings had a corner window. A straight line from there, across the covered market of St Martin's-in-the-Field, across the fruit baskets and Prince William postcards, and a kill was assured. The same for the Chandos, the pub with a small bell tower and a model of Samuel Smith. Pub workers lived in the flats above. It wouldn't take a professional more than two minutes to find their way to the communal staircase and into the high promontory.

The Edith Cavell needle seemed to loom down portentously at George. On four sides, carved and illuminated in stone, it stood like a sentinel, a beacon of warning.

SACRIFICE, yelled the carved letters on the north side.

HUMANITY, screamed the east.

George paced carefully back to St Martin's Place and on the roof he glimpsed the outline of a man.

He tugged back on Charlie's insistent grip like a dog who'd found a compelling smell. Charlie glared at him but saw the fear in his eyes. He followed George's gaze to the top of the cathedral across the road from the Gallery. Behind a stone façade, a figure was crouched. A glint of light. A scope? Charlie pulled George flush against the dirty window of a newsagent's.

'Now do you believe me?'

Charlie stared at the man for a moment longer. The figure stood up straight and gestured to another man, who joined him.

'Snipers don't socialise,' said Charlie.

The window cleaners began to assemble an apparatus that would allow them to be lowered down the façade of the building and George found himself dragged off once again.

The foyer of the National Portrait Gallery was empty.

Now free of charge to culturally minded citizens, the glass doors opened automatically. It felt a little like the lobby of a trendy hotel.

The meeting point.

One minute.

Right.

A guard sat in a corner peering at a small CCTV feed. She regarded the two men through bottle-thick glasses. Charlie approached in his most polite-schoolboy tones. *'Could you direct us to the Tudor Gallery please?'* The woman nodded in the direction of the vaulted entrance hall. The only conceivable route to take was the three-floor-high escalator that clanked in ominous repetition up the blank east wall.

As they ascended, eyes scanning the peripheries, the Tudor Gallery was hushed with contemplation. A short distance away a small group of Italian art students were looking closely at a small label that read: *NPG 1. On display, the Chandos portrait of Shakespeare.*

A few feet behind them stood Neil Mackay, staring at NPG 2561, or what has become known as the Ditchley portrait of Queen Elizabeth I.

Neil knew this painting well. Her feet firmly on Oxfordshire, behind her groovy regal collar the sun seemed to peek through the storm clouds in the firmament, a clear message, it was argued by the inscription, of redemption, hope, and above all, forgiveness. Neil thought it apt that forgiveness should be the opening theme of the Last Chance Saloon. Which is what Contact Zero was, if you really thought about it.

Neil checked his watch again. Two minutes past. Rules were rules. Whoever these poor buggers were, they'd played this hand badly. No second chances with the Contact Zero network. He wished them luck, edged past the group portrait of the treaty of Somerset House and slipped quickly and anonymously down the stairs to the back exit.

His work as a field officer had brought Neil into contact with the 'Samaritans', as they were known, a few times in the past. The Samaritans were the go-betweens, helpful souls to aid the agent-at-sea to safe harbour at Contact Zero. Not a person, of course, but a place. A very, very safe place. He only knew a small portion of the address, naturally. Getting to Contact Zero was like hopping across a river with stepping stones. All you had to do is find out where to meet the next stone in the chain. But the trick was: you could only find out once you were in midair. Still, that was enough to give hope and hope is what Contact Zero was all about. Even if they met him now, whoever they were, even if they collared him in the street, by the time he'd explained how to get to the new link in the chain, that person would also have absconded. Blind trust is never easy, he mused, as the hard wind hit him from Orange Street.

As Neil turned up his collar to the breeze, Charlie and George turned the corner and arrived in the Tudor galley. They stood in front of the portrait for a few seconds. Both knew at that moment. And said nothing.

Bellissima, said an Italian student behind them.

One minute later, Horatio and the lions gazed down in concern as George and Charlie faced some facts in Trafalgar Square.

'Can't we go back?'

'To Steadman?' Charlie's nose was running. He sniffed sharply. 'What good would that do?'

'They could change the rendezvous. Do it again.'

'We had one shot. That was it.'

'Then we need to dig in. Discuss our options.'

'What options?'

'We'll think of some when we dig in, won't we?'

'Where?'

'Well, not *here*, Charlie. Not bloody *Trafalgar Square*.'

Charlie scanned the skies. Some clouds had formed there, grey wisps, unsure of themselves. Some kids were playing football around the fountain. He smacked his forehead. It had taken him this long to think of it.

Neil came back from his Samaritan duties to find that Rose had stepped out as well.

Neil had decided not to refer the absence of Charlie's personnel file to Rose. He felt . . . not uncomfortable, but rather conflicted about calling something like this in. It implied a lack of efficiency on behalf of a colleague and if there was one thing Neil had learned in his early days at the Service, it was to avoid reporting the shortcomings of others.

It did not, however, preclude him having a nose around elsewhere. Since he was free of supervision, he turned his mind back to his old schoolfriend. He did a keyboard search on Charlie's name across all department projects over the last year. If he could get a paper trail together, Neil could locate the file – languishing perhaps in a project folder, overlooked and forgotten. It had happened before. No reason why it couldn't happen again. Every computer file had a paper equivalent – somewhere. Even when files were deleted, the paper remained.

The Service had evolved in the past few years. Levels of redundancy had been cut away – tasks that had been triplicated were flagged by successive administrations and management-directorate working taskforces in innumerable meetings on efficiency and productivity. Men in braces had leaned back in leather chairs and glowered at PowerPoints, whiteboards and photocopied factsheets and concluded that a new Service, a modern Service, a shiny and accountable Service should rid itself of fat, of chaff, of overcapacity. It should slim down and jettison redundant tasks. Overlapping intelligence reporting and analysis was simply the third leg that was not needed.

So, triplicates became duplicates, and duplicates had all but disappeared. In place, a simple requirement – every job had the coverage of one individual. A culture of responsibility. *A trust in our employees*, said the men in braces, *a display of confidence in our human-resources assets*, as they pointed their HB pencils towards their laminated workflow diagrams.

Problem was, people made mistakes.

And when people made mistakes even the most efficient administrative system can start to look like the British Rail Lost Property Department circa 1974.

Neil sometimes played shin-shattering five-a-side football with some lads from Logistics. He had a longstanding housekeeping appointment with them that day and decided to use the opportunity to take their temperature reading of this. They always enjoyed a spot of intrigue between bouts of dragging their knuckles on the carpet.

He called them to confirm the appointment. The phone was answered by Derek, the goggle-eyed Glaswegian in Logistics who never ironed his shirts.

'So I'll be down in about ten minutes,' said Neil.

'Why's that?' said Derek.

'Look in your diary,' smiled Neil. There was a short pause on the line and the sound of paper being shuffled.

'Nope.'

Neil looked at his personal organiser. It was there, in sharp, neat Neilscript.

'Um, it's here in mine—'

'Nothing till same time next week,' said Derek. 'I think you've got the date wrong.'

Neil knew he didn't have the date wrong. One week from today he'd be in a small country-house hotel with Liz; their anniversary.

'It's today, Derek. Make time.'

Logistics, he sighed, and stretched his back till it clicked. Neil wandered down after pouring himself a coffee to go, strolling and sipping his way past the media department. Their remit was monitoring, but this also had a beneficial sideline. They had the local papers. And sometimes that was the only way to find out how Caledonian Thistle were playing. Or at least what Cally Thistle had become these days. Inverness something. He didn't know why he'd started supporting them at school. He presumed it was because they were so clearly the underdogs in a world of Old Firm Derbies and whatnot.

He found Alan, who he liked enormously for his spectacular rudeness, arranging that day's early editions on a display stand.

'This is new,' chirped Neil.

'My fucking idea,' said Alan.

Neil scanned the stack for anything from North of the Border. But halfway there he stopped. And the paper was in his hand before his coffee had hit the ground.

He covered well, something about a hangover, a story that Alan seemed to have great empathy with. Neil excused himself and stood in the corridor. The strip-lights bored into him. The floor became shaky. A visit to the bathroom cleared his stomach of his lunch, but his mind still churned and burned with the news. He placed a covert photocopy of the paper in his briefcase and tried his best to keep his head down for the rest of the day. Rose showed her head only once, to offer him a shortbread wheel. He declined but remained sunny, cheery, blithe and unworried. He could have been an extra in *The Sound of Music*.

By the time he got home his shirt was soaked in sweat, his heart tight and painful in his chest. He walked a good half-stride ahead of the rest of the commuters in this area of Northwest London, walking past streetlamps that mysteriously failed to light until much later in the evening. Charlie was definitely classified as OAB, a slang Service abbreviation (out and about) for the more official nomenclature of 'field operations current/live'. Slang or official, it meant that Charlie was still, as far as the Service was concerned, a fully paid-up member of its team out of doors. Quite what he had got himself mixed up in, however, was an issue for an entirely new kind of ulcer.

He opened the door and was greeted by the same two noises he always was these days. His wife's voice on the phone and his son practising his karate chop on the prized French Regency bureau.

'Hello Grasshopper,' he said as he cuddled wee Jake to his chest and swung his feet onto the sofa. He was trying to lead with a positive foot forward, trying to keep his subconscious mind busy and nimble on the hellish situations unfurling deep below the surface.

The toilet flushed and Liz came in, still chatting on the portable. Neil shook his head. 'Pregnant mother hotline,' she explained with her hand over the speaker, 'they don't care if they hear me pee.' Jake laughed at the word and kissed Daddy on the cheek before whacking him gleefully on the head with the flat of his hand. Liz hung up and kissed Neil on the lips. They still loved to kiss more than anything.

'He's been looking forward to beating you up all day,' she said. She smiled the smile that had the power to melt him.

'Now's his chance,' smiled Neil.

'What's wrong?' she asked. She knew. She always did. Even with the training, she could root it out of him in a New Malden Minute.

Neil was trying to come up with a reasonably authentic story of stress at work when he cocked his ear to the hallway. The radio was on and he could hear it from the kitchen.

'. . . *last believed to be on a cycling tour of Kent, please get in touch with Ward Sixteen, Princess Margaret Rose Hospital, Edinburgh. It is about his mother, Jane, who is dangerously ill.*'

Neil waited for the message to repeat but he had been positive he'd heard it the first time round. He took Liz by the arm. 'Did she just say Charles Millar?'

'Did who just say?'

'The radio—'

'Was that the door?' said Liz, suddenly.

Neil became aware of a noise from the hallway. He placed Jake back down on the floor and nimbly avoided the caterpillar toys strewn around the child gate at the bottom of the stairs.

The door wasn't ringing. But it was definitely knocking.

Neil checked his watch. Eight p.m. It better not be the deliverymen. He yanked the door open, forgetting momentarily that Liz had always told him to use the chain.

A couple of tramps stood on his doorstep, wavering slightly on their feet. It took Neil a few seconds to realise one of them was saying his name.

'Neil, it's me. Charlie.'

34

Latham had been waiting to speak to Rose all day. But his need to do this had been secondary to Rose's need to work. They had exchanged messages at lunch, and again during the afternoon, but when one wanted to talk to the other, the other was invariably busy.

Thus, by the time the two of them finally managed to have words in Latham's BMW, it was approaching supper-time. And both of them, needless to say, were tired, irritable, and wanted to eat.

Latham was explaining that it was a risk.

'I'm aware of that,' said Rose.

Latham wondered if this was a genie that could be placed back into a bottle now that the local media were involved.

'It's not about control any more,' explained Rose. 'We are almost clear of the problem. And it's a local paper, for God's sake, not the *International Herald Tribune*.'

The problem, Latham mused, might increase through the efforts invested in removing it.

'And that's your thinking, is it?' Rose was tight-lipped. 'As far as I remember, I *think* things and you *do* things; I believe that is what has become the norm.'

Latham explained that it was his thinking. Normally, he

continued, he was all for aggression. The Moscow Police, so he understood, had for years covertly guaranteed that their own methods would outweigh those of the criminals they sought to track down. If a hostage-taker threatened to kill a politician, the police would simply and methodically track down the hostage-taker's entire family and threaten *them* with a more brutal fate. Latham admired the Russians very much. When you had the resources, you could double up and face down any threat. A concentration of massive, vicious force to achieve the desired result.

Such as here. Such as now.

But there was just something unwieldy about the sledge-hammer breaking this nut.

'These nuts,' she reminded him.

Latham said he understood.

'We need to draw them from the colvert,' she said, 'and it's only a matter of time before they're driven out and into the open field.'

Latham asked Rose to ease up a little on the hunting metaphors

'They don't have anywhere to go,' snapped Rose, pining now for a cup of tea. 'Full cry is exactly where we're headed and you well know it. And as long as we understand each other and the scent is properly picked up I believe that that will be the end of it.'

Latham asked her about the paperwork. He had concerns.

Rose had to control her temper. 'The paperwork,' she explained, 'is down to me. Do you know how difficult it is to manage something of this scale? For so long? The Project has been going for years. Very well, I might add. And now suddenly I have to dismantle it – with a smile on my face. You have no idea. None. I have no-one I can talk to about this. No-one I can turn to. I've been alone, you know. Since they took him away. This is all I've ever had.'

Latham apologised. He did not enjoy seeing Rose upset. These two men were the last carriers of the truth about their Project. One of them, because he was once part of it. The other through sheer unadulterated bad luck.

A piece of paper can change a person's life. In this case, a letter. The letter was at the centre of this. They both knew that. It linked them all.

If only they could find it.

35

Neil wasn't the sort of person to ask questions, thought Charlie. Even when old friends turned up unwashed on his doorstep. George was in the shower, while Charlie himself was already out, mussed hair drying flat in the warmth, feeling one thousand per cent better, munching on Neil's own carrot cake and swigging tea the colour of teak from a Postman Pat mug.

Liz was smiling from the other end of the farmhouse table in the kitchen. The stove was bubbling with soup, the grill smelled of toast; the boiler was blasting heat and happiness into every pore of Charlie's body.

'I can't tell you how grateful I am,' said Charlie, again.

Neil stared at him accusingly. 'Why not?' He broke into a smile and held up his hand before Charlie could speak. 'Any time,' said Neil, waving the issue away. 'And you don't have to tell me anything you don't want to.'

Charlie smiled but the words dug in a little deep, like a friendly scratch from an otherwise benevolent cat.

'I'll tell you everything, Neil, if you want.'

'Up to you,' smiled Neil.

George's feet on the stairs told everyone the bathroom was free.

'I'll give Jake his bath now, I think,' said Liz. 'You watch that soup.'

'Can't take my eyes off it,' said Charlie. Liz took Jake away from the small musical train that chugged ever decreasing circles around his feet. As she moved off, Neil moved forward.

'Charlie, I know all about it.'

Charlie froze mid-bite as George came in, still dressed in his dirty clothes but smelling like a lavender garden.

'What do you mean?'

'I mean, I know.'

George smiled, aware of the sudden atmosphere, and made for the teapot. Neil neither got up nor offered to show him the cups. This made Charlie even more nervous. George located them on his first cupboard inspection.

'I'm going to ask you a question, Charlie. Is that okay with you?'

Charlie noticed Neil had turned his head so that both he and George were in his peripheral vision.

'Sure,' said Charlie.

'Have you ever wondered what I do for a living?'

Charlie had not been expecting this.

'You run a sandwich shop.'

'Did you ever pause and think about why an intelligent kid from your school would be content to run a sandwich shop for the rest of his life?'

'To tell you the truth, Neil,' said Charlie, 'it never really occurred to me.'

George stirred milk and sugar into his tea and sat down on the bench next to Charlie.

'Well it should have. And it's a bloody good thing I'm a nice guy. Because you just made the worst tradecraft fuck-up I've seen in a month of Sundays.'

And Neil reached for something under the table that made George and Charlie snap alert like birds caught in a cat-flap.

The newspaper headline stared back at them from the kitchen table. It was that night's edition of the *Cambridge Evening News*. The headline was simple and to the point. 'MURDER IN COLLEGE, TWO MEN SOUGHT.' And beneath the headline, two headshots of George and Charlie.

'I work for the Service, Charlie. Just like you.'

Charlie tried to say something but the sound was unrecognisable as a proper word.

'You know why Steadman approached you? Cos I told him to. I wrote a memo. Your last year at college, was it? My first in the business. You were earmarked by me. Cos I thought you could do the job brilliantly. Never heard about you again so I figured you never cut it. Then guess what. You called me up at six in the morning to ask me to run through Future Outcomes Analysis, for God's sake.'

'You called him up?' asked George. 'When?'

'Your house,' managed Charlie.

George's foot lashed out at the table leg. 'You idiot!'

Neil kept staring at Charlie. 'So that's the story, sunshine. I know you guys are in trouble. So why don't you give me the professional courtesy I deserve and just let me know if I should be really worried? You don't have to give me too many gory details. But I think I know Charlie Millar well enough to realise you would not knowingly get caught doing something like this.'

Neil stood up and away from the table, backing into a corner by the bread knives. Charlie wondered what he would do if Neil ever came at him with a blade. Charlie decided he'd be too overcome. Too many playground football memories would slow him down. He wouldn't stand a chance.

241

Neil was pacing now as George launched into accusations. 'They'll find out you've spoken together – you're schoolfriends I take it? Then they'll make sure they watch this place. If not now then soon enough.'

Charlie rose from his seat and grabbed Neil's arm. 'We were on a cover. Both of us. The order came through. Thirteenth frame. We were the targets, Neil, someone wants us dead.'

'In the Service? Who?'

'Why d'you think we're here! We needed somewhere to work this all out – you think this was us?' He brandished the headline at Neil, spilling his tea, not that he noticed. 'That was my friendly face . . .'

'Why didn't you try for Contact Zero?'

'Not you as well,' said George.

'It exists,' said Charlie.

Neil said nothing and looked down at the picture of Steadman. He realised now who he'd missed earlier but it was too late – no point in making things even worse.

'I'm presuming this was nothing to do with you?'

'We only spoke to him, Neil. We had nowhere else to go.'

Neil decided this was not the best time to layer more bad news on their already unravelling situation.

And then the doorbell rang.

Charlie and George surveyed the windows in the kitchen. Two walls open to the outside. Neil leaped up and pulled down the blinds. Hearing Liz's steps on the stairs he ran out ot the hallway – a figure through the glass next to the front door. Liz moved towards the door but Neil's whisper was a laser of sound—

['*no no no—*']

And she stopped dead. A look between them. *What?* His eyes told her this was real, it was serious, darling, it really was, and in all the years of knowing you you've always known that one day I would ask you to do something for me, something that I would have to communicate to you in a look, but a look that you would understand because you know and love me and here it is, sweetheart, please God I hope you understand it like you understand me –

Liz understood.

She stopped dead and silently back-pedalled up the stairs, anticipating Jake's cries at any moment. The doorbell moved to banging. The doorframe shuddered. In the doorframe between the kitchen and the hallway, Charlie, George and Neil waited in silence as the banging stopped.

'So what have you done to deserve all this?' Neil whispered when he judged the danger had passed.

'If we knew that,' said Charlie, 'we wouldn't be here.'

Neil's eyes disappeared into a deep and worried thought. Charlie noticed them move up and to the right, which suggested he was picturing something in his mind. He was right.

'You should leave the country,' said Neil.

There was a chilling matter-of-factness in his voice that suggested to both men that there would be no negotiation.

'Yes,' said George.

'Leave the country and I'll see what I can do.'

Charlie sighed. 'How are we going to do that?'

Neil was trying to work out how he could get the other half of Contact Zero to work for these poor buggers. But it was too late now, there was too much pressure. This newspaper would change everything – presuming, as he had done, that whoever instigated the frame-up would have primed every force in the country on a nondisclosure file. A net, cast far and wide, with no idea why it was so bloody important. That was the great thing about the Terrorism Act. In troubled times like these, most forces just did as they were told without asking the awkward questions.

'The ports will be crawling,' hissed George. 'The airports, well, we can just forget about that. We could try and make it across the Channel ourselves, but I don't fancy risking the shipping lanes in a beautiful pea-green boat.'

Charlie moved to the kitchen table for another look at the article. As he did so, his foot hit Jake's toy. It whirred and clicked and the train went round and round. Life was talking to Charlie, and it took him a few moments to realise it.

'I know how we do it,' he said, staring down at the engine as it chuffchuffchuffed around his ankles.

A noise distracted them.

The letterbox was opening.

A pink slip of paper passed through and landed on the doormat. The three men looked at each other.

Neil was the first to move. Slowly, he approached the hallway area, deftly avoiding the sightlines from outside through the bay window.

Charlie and George joined him as Neil unfolded the offending object. There was writing on it.

It was an invitation to a political fundraiser.

Neil crumpled it up with one hand.

Charlie and George, who until this moment had come to expect the worst, waited for the door to be kicked down.

For once, no bad news was coming their way. And the door remained intact.

Neil drove his mother-in-law's car as fast as it could go, which seeing as it was a turbo-charged Subaru was extremely blinking fast indeed. Neon London gave way to residential streets and at each moment Charlie and George felt a police siren was sure to strike up in harmony with the squealing tyres and roaring engine.

'The big key opens the lockup. The one with the black marking's the van.'

The car eased itself around the residential streets and soon the roads became roundabouts. An industrial park of some sort looming in the distance. George and Charlie sat in the back, heads down, hanging on to each other through the turns.

The car stopped and Neil yanked the handbrake.

'Wait here,' he said. 'Keep your heads down.'

A sudden and panicked thought swept Charlie's mind. *He could have taken us here for another reason. One call from Liz, and it might all soon be over—*

Charlie gasped in fright as the back door swung open. Cold air needled the two men's faces as Neil lent his hand to them both. They were outside a small line of lockup garages.

'Okay, you're clear to go. I'll stay until you open the door, then you're on your own. Get rid of the keys, I'll change the locks tomorrow.'

Charlie looked at his friend.

'It's crazy . . .' he began.

'Answers on a postcard,' said Neil, embracing him. And with a warm but nervous smile he got back into his car. George was already halfway to the garage. Charlie trotted after him. By the time he'd caught up, the door was open and Neil's tail-lights were all that were left for Charlie to see.

Inside the lockup, a small van that proclaimed its sandwiches were the 'munchiest in town'. Inside Neil's car, a thought. Too late now, of course, but the thought arrived all

245

the same. *The radio*, it said. *Dammit, that bloody message on the radio.*

The van started first time. The tank was full and here, both men agreed, was truly the friendliest face they had found.

Charlie knew the direction they needed to take. But George had a request first. Charlie asked him how to get there. George told him.

'Good,' said Charlie, 'it's not too far out of our way.'

To ease the nervous silence between them, Charlie turned on the radio. A news programme was finishing. But before the weather, the announcer's voice became solemn.

'And now an SOS message for a Mr Charles Millar of London. Will Mr Charles Millar of London, last believed to be on a cycling tour of Kent, please get in touch with Ward Sixteen, Princess Margaret Rose Hospital, Edinburgh. It is about his mother, Jane, who is dangerously ill.'

George glanced at Charlie, whose hands remained relaxed on the wheel. A comedy programme was starting on the radio now, another scheduling coup, and Charlie quietly leaned forward and shut it off. They were approaching a red light and it was touch and go whether they would stop—

'Charlie!'

The rubber left a mark on the road, but the van stopped in time.

'Charlie,' said George. 'It can't be real. I'm sure of it . . .'

'The bastards,' Charlie was clenching and unclenching his jaw, 'the bastards . . .'

'It could be another Charles Millar . . .'

'My mum's name, it's my mum's name . . .'

'Could be another Jane, another Charles and another Jane

. . . I don't even know if they do them any more. Do they do them any more?'

'It's her local fucking hospital, George. And my guess is, if you contact local police, you can get them to do just about anything.'

Charlie saw the sign as they approached the roundabout. It said 'North'. With tears welling in his eyes he swung the van across three lanes and onto the slip road.

'Don't be an idiot,' said George.

'You've got something you need to do,' growled Charlie, 'well fuck you so have I.'

He lasted until the first set of services. They pulled in and sat in a corner of the parking lot where the overhead lights had stopped working.

'You could call,' said George. 'To make sure.'

'What if it's her?' said Charlie.

'Then, you have more resources at your disposal on which to base a decision.'

'I'm scared, George.'

George was rocked a little by the admission. He'd been feeling the same way but had never believed he'd share it. Even with the person sitting next to him now. He had problems sharing, he knew that. He was glad that Charlie did not.

'Do you want a cup of coffee?'

'We can't,' sighed Charlie. 'Not now.'

Almost on cue, a police car whined its way past on the carriageway nearby. A hot pursuit.

'Then we get this over with. Come on.'

He got out of the van and opened the driver's side. Charlie sat for a moment, staring at the dashboard, then swung his legs out and followed him to the payphone that stood like a lead singer in a single car-park spotlight.

'They'll trace the call.'

'You just need the information. You can be anyone you want.'

Charlie nodded. As he memorised the number from directory enquiries, he did something he had never done before. He crossed his fingers. 'I don't know,' said Charlie.

'Give it here,' said George.

'Princess Margaret Rose—'

George's voice was suddenly Scottish. 'Yes, can I—'

'Can you hold, please?'

Music cut in. It was Sinatra. At least, thought George, it wasn't 'My Way'.

'Sorry to keep you on hold. Princess Margaret Rose, how can I help you?'

'I'm calling from the BBC, we're researching the hoax callers we occasionally get from our SOS messages.'

'Oh yes, uh-huh, you mean Mrs Millar . . .'

George closed his eyes . . . he looked at Charlie whose face began to fall in tandem with George's heart.

'Do you have any idea of how many people have called in?'

'There's only been yourself so far,' she said.

'Well that's nice to know.'

George was about to hang up, but the woman kept talking.

'And the son, of course.'

'The son?'

Charlie stared at him.

'Yes,' continued the receptionist, 'here we go, yes . . .' the sound of ruffling papers in the background for a moment '. . . the son called us pretty much straight away, he was very upset. Shame. She's not so well. Ninety-six, mind, it's not bad when you think about it. I didn't think they did them any more but apparently the police—'

248

'Ninety-six you say?'

Tension sluiced off Charlie's face like a waterfall.

'Aye, it's not really a shame at that age, is it? We'd be so lucky to see that . . .'

'Thanks a million,' said George, and hung up.

In an hour, as per George's instructions, they were on a country road in Kent. George had souped up their car radio in order to scan local police frequencies. More often than they thought possible came calls relating to two fugitive males, matching their descriptions. It was not known which area of the country they were in, but forces were cautioned to be on the lookout for cars with odd markings, stolen, rented or otherwise, out of county.

The van they were driving mentioned South London and it made both men flinch every time a headlight flared up in the rear-view. Charlie was grateful when they stopped at traffic lights and George indicated that he should park around the corner.

George sat there for a few moments and Charlie wondered if he should say anything. He decided against it. He noticed that George was trembling slightly.

'Are you all right?'

'Just let me do this, okay?'

He turned his head away again and then Charlie realised why he was doing it. He followed George's gaze out of the window, across the road to a small patch of green. There, set back from the lawn, the bright picture-window of a care home. The room was empty, bar a few men and women in wheelchairs. One young girl was sitting closest to the window, staring at the TV. She had red hair and, despite her stare, the wisest eyes in the world. An auxiliary nurse in a yellow uniform walked over to her briefly and exchanged a pleasant word. The girl was either unwilling to respond or incapable of it. When Charlie glanced back at George he saw that he was crying.

'I sometimes think they're on display. Someone could go window-shopping and buy her up.'

Charlie shifted in his seat.

'I never knew you had a daughter.'

George said nothing.

'Do you want to get out—'

George shook his head. 'She doesn't really know who I am.' A sigh . . . 'I said I wanted to see her, that's all.'

'You're not even going to get out . . .?'

George turned his face to Charlie. 'This is how I'm going to do it, okay?' He turned back. Charlie stared at the floor. He knew when to shut up. Crying is something that is easy to put on. But spies can spot crocodile tears a mile away. The secret is not in the eyes, or even the liquid running from the ducts. The key difference between weeping, which is usually genuine, and crying, which can easily be not, is in the jaw. The jaw folds in when humans weep. It's a tiny movement but one that produces a strange and distinctly unattractive overbite. True grief cannot easily be mimicked. The nostrils flare involuntarily with the pressure on the sinuses. George's overbite practically hid his chin from view. His struggle to keep it in was all-consuming for at least a minute. It finally abated to silence.

'Can we go now, please,' said George.

The gears ground noisily under Charlie's trembling hand and for a moment he thought he saw George wave.

36

Neil arrived for work in the morning and tried not to look at anyone. Not through the lobby security, not in the lift, not even in the admin pool where he would normally wave and stop and shoot the shit as he strode into his new office. People genuinely liked Neil because Neil genuinely liked people. As a result, people wanted to share with him, they wanted to tell him things. It was effortless, a natural truth drug. The night they'd met, Liz and Neil hadn't stopped talking for ten hours. Life was good around Neil because nothing was too much of a problem, nothing was that serious, even the things that were. He just made things better.

Liz had asked him about the two men that night, asked him what had upset him so much when his friends had come around. To her it was another annual orbit of the paranoia comet. He hadn't had the heart to tell her the truth. Hadn't even tried to explain why he'd not been able to sleep. He'd been up in the night and swept the place for bugs at least three times in the hours between midnight and six a.m.

On the bus into work, Neil began to speculate possible theories. Of course, both men could be on some form of public discreditation list. Someone might be giving them an extreme make-under as washouts and undesirables. Thus marginalised, they might be turned into lures for foreign-national counterintelligence agencies. But this was very Cold war, very old school. Generally, any plan with ideological foundations failed at some point or other. It was pretty much understood that the only motivator that stood the test of time was money. Penury or greed could drive anyone to anything.

Neil managed to chat up the personnel and pay supervisor, Lynne, before her lunch-break. She managed to confirm what Neil had already suspected: neither George nor Charlie were on any form of Spendthrift Watch. They had neither maxed out their credit cards nor hoarded their money. Their bank balances still languished with the rest of the Service somewhere between primary-school teacher and telephone-sales team supervisor. They were fine.

He wondered for a moment where they were.

Neil survived the afternoon on coffee and shortbread. Rose sensed his exhaustion and discomfort and was politely offhand throughout the rest of the day.

In his attempt to prove to Rose that he was doing his day job, he began to trawl through a stack of interdepartmental memos. They were generally designed to obfuscate or otherwise conceal any information of any use whatsoever. They created high-tension headaches in almost anyone who came into contact with them.

Neil felt a blinder build between his eyes when he read:

S34/NFC – LOGISTICS REQUISITION
MEMORANDUM
(INTERDEPARTMENTAL)
R. Manningtree ext. 55243

The requisition-form code, NFC, was what brought the real pain to the fore. It wasn't such a random occurrence on a personnel file like Charlie's. But here, on a Logistics requisition, it was a different matter. This was, after all, a receipt, not a State Secret. The operation it referenced was also bizarre. Who reclassified an operation in retrospect? Neil supposed some operations *did* develop in importance over time. But for something to have additions made to the actual paperwork? It was like relabelling your birthday photos as 'Christmas '98'. It just didn't make any bloody sense. Unless your birthday was December 25th.

Neil was enough of an administrator to know that the only way to get to the bottom of the problem was to access every single piece of paper that dovetailed to or from this one. It was a laborious process. The references and cross-references made his head spin.

He marvelled at the breadth of cover stations. The bolt-holes and muckrake mansions where field agents were forced to spend their days. Instant coffee and ginger snaps. Some lucky buggers got shop jobs, high-end consultancy. Some even ended up as liveried servants of Her Majesty the Queen. No Ginger Snaps there. Not many, at any rate.

The mild grin that crept into his eyes soon faded as he turned another page.

He was looking, effectively, at a spaghetti junction of paper. More a dual carriageway, perhaps, the to-ing and fro-ing of resources as the build-up to an operation reached its crescendo.

One segment stood out, however.

Like a horse on the motorway.

Despite the need for two cover stations, in this particular case only one of them appeared to have ever been operational. The other, although theoretically active, had not been reported in from for the entire time the operation had been live. Which tended to suggest that it hadn't been used at all.

The coding for the agent in charge of the station was familiar to Neil – it's why he spotted it when workaday clerks on probation had probably missed it.

The agent on this cover station had been Charlie.

The overland train dropped Neil off at Wimbledon some forty minutes late. He'd already ensured a frosty reception at home by issuing the 'it's a work thing' text message. He hated texting Liz but sometimes there was no head-space left to explain. Liz usually understood. It didn't mean she liked it.

Station W330 was, according to Debs, his friend from Location Management, 'a tidy wee place' not too far from the Tube station. Neil avoided the eye contact of the work parties out on the piss as he counted down the streets. He passed the Prince of Wales at Hartfield Road and made his way anonymously through the crowds. Turning the corner, he could see she'd been half-right.

It was certainly wee.

A small photo station. The front door was misted glass.

From the looks of the pile of post that Neil could see through the door and security cage, the place had never been occupied. Not for a month at least.

Charlie and George were never supposed to meet.

The thought buzzed around his mind as he strode back to the train. Thanks to Service bureaucracy, Charlie was given the wrong cover station. Which allowed him to meet George. Which . . .

Saved both their lives.

Liz gave him the cold shoulder in bed that night. He deserved it, he'd expected it, but he also hardly noticed. His mind was turning over too fast for sleep.

37

Charlie and George had woken in the van. Once the plan was agreed they had both insisted on a standard twenty-four-hour stake-out. A mobile recce, involving drivepasts, walkpasts, anything to ensure the routine was in their memories for well and for good. Anything else would just have been suicidal.

An hour of sleep to sharpen the reflexes and they were on the move again. As Charlie drove, George had taken note of security features, weak points in the structure and frequency of patrols, and compared them to their previous data. There was no great deviation.

They would do it tonight.

As the light began to fade, Charlie disposed of the van on a defunct slip road near a construction site abutting the M20. The approach to the terminal would have to be quick, surgical, with no dress rehearsal and no room for error.

But security was generally concerned about the people coming off the train – and into the country – rather than the people getting on. Illegal immigrants had used the Eurostar over the years to slip into the country unnoticed. It was Charlie's hope, he explained to George, that the two of them could achieve the same effect. Except in reverse.

The wind, if anything, was soothing on their faces as they approached the drainage ditch separating the road from the rails. From their prone positions in the grass they could make out the International Terminal and there, some eighty metres across open ground, the fence they would have to breach in order to gain access to the track, and, perhaps, the train. They couldn't risk breaching the security cordon anywhere near the scope of the Ashford International closed-circuit cameras. The key would be gaining access to the track area some two hundred yards shy of the station.

The cameras were placed at uncomfortably small intervals along the perimeter. Beyond them, past the line of sight of the final camera, a length of fencing ended.

Although the rails were electrified, there was a gap between the fencing and the fatal area beyond. Charlie spied it first. George followed at a trot.

As they moved down the bank to the edge of the wire, the sound of a helicopter above—

'Charlie—'

'Keep your head down and follow me.'

Near the edge of the wire now, they stared down the line both ways. As far as they could see, the way was clear. The only light in the far horizon was a streetlamp glowing distant on a roadbridge.

The track ran some three hundred metres towards the platforms, where the gap between the fence and the rails widened.

Charlie looked at George.

'The cameras,' he said, indicating George should look where he was pointing.

George noticed their arcs would almost certainly catch anyone attempting to violate the track area near the platforms.

'There's only one way round that, I'm afraid.'

George nodded. He was already way ahead.

They scrambled around the end post and crouched down. Almost immediately, Charlie checked down the track.

That roadbridge was getting closer.

Soon. They would need to move soon.

The Eurostar showed itself around the corner. If they timed their run well enough, they could avoid both detection and a messy death.

They would soon see.

They were running sooner than they thought – this train was taking a speedy run into the terminal. George looked for a sure foothold to push off but the gravel was loose and slick in the night air. The noise became deafening as the engine passed them, hissing and spitting fury at the intruders it could see to its right.

The two men kept themselves in a hunched position, legs straining with effort. Charlie beckoned George to keep close and, as the train came to a near-halt, they were parallel with the final carriage.

Charlie ducked underneath. George following. A narrow fit but mercifully short as the two men appeared on the other side – now safely shadowed by the hulking carriage.

George turned when he heard the approaching commuter train's horn. Grabbing Charlie, they had only a moment to decide.

The space between the train and the larger Eurostar meant they had a clear choice – hit the deck or die. They flattened themselves to the gravel just as the nonstopping service powered through with an unearthly whine, sparks spitting from the wheels as the ground trembled under their bellies. Charlie hauled George to his feet and sprinted further alongside the Eurostar, now idling and disgorging fluid from its underside.

They ran on their tiptoes, trying hard to leave no firm treadmarks on the pebbled ground. Charlie indicated the recess beneath one of the carriages, a void in the infrastructure beneath the train, part of the actual chassis. The door easily prised up and open by George's penknife and no small amount of muscle.

Rain began to fall as Charlie hauled himself inside. George joined him with a grunt and they pulled the panel back tight behind them. Silence in the dark, bar the sound of their shuddering lungs. Above, in the first-class cabins, the sound of distant footsteps; conversation. Champagne would be flowing, thought Charlie, and someone, somewhere, was tucking into a pain au chocolat. Down here, grit. The overpowering smell of oil and dirt. George tugged at Charlie's sleeve but Charlie shushed as quietly as he could. He moved close to George's ear.

'Not until we move.'

'My leg's cramping.'

'George—'

'Look after this a second.'

George removed the gun from his jacket pocket and gingerly passed it to Charlie. He stared at it, marvelling at its weight, and tucked it neatly behind his jeans. George began to perform a stretching exercise for his hamstrings.

For what seemed an age, the train turned over and stopped, turned over and stopped. It could have been a lawnmower in a previous life. Charlie was about to say something encouraging when the train began to ease itself forward. Gaining speed, the glow of light through the gap in the recess panel dissipated into the night.

George slumped down against the wall, absent-mindedly rubbing his stomach. Charlie watched him for a second.

The sound of brakes made them jump.

As Charlie's eyes adjusted to the gloom, he could see George curled up against the far wall of the void space, foetal on his side, eyes trained on him, unblinking and accusatory.

The brakes squealed louder and the train stopped completely.

In the darkness, time can trick. Charlie avoided the temptation of pressing the groovy blue light on his watch and instead estimated only a minute had passed. A signal. Of course. Nothing to worry about. The sound of wind through the gaps in the opening. Eerie and portentous, it drowned out something else.

The sound of voices. Outside. English, two or three individuals with the footsteps to back it up. Gravel crunching and – finally – the beam of a strong flashlight.

'Which one?' said one voice.

'—ggered if I know,' mumbled a second.

Charlie's ears strained. He moved a little closer to the panel. George glared accusingly – Charlie's movements rendered a slight but audible *creak* in the structure. It was built to hold equipment, not the sizeable mass of two men.

The footsteps were approaching from the head of the train. By Charlie's estimation they were half a carriage away. There were three recesses between them and discovery.

George wondered whether they could pose as journalists and explain their presence away as some form of illegal immigration exposé. Looking up at Charlie he was shocked to see the gun was back in his hand. George shook his head – bad idea – Charlie merely ignored him. The gun was pointed at the panel. There was no argument to be had – and unless George fancied tussling with Charlie in here, and probably alerting the officials outside, he was forced to sit tight and sweat it. He watched Charlie's thumb hover over the safety. Both of them, he knew, were experts with those things. If he was thinking about using it here, there would be no stopping him. *Dammit, Charlie, we're so close* . . .

George's stomach twinged.

The panel next door swung open. In their own space the beams of the flashlight glowed around Charlie's head like a halo. The panel slammed shut again and the feet walked past their hiding place . . . and continued.

Before turning and stopping right outside.

Noise from the hinges covered Charlie's thumb on the safety.

The panel door opened an inch before a voice called out: 'Not that one, it's here.'

The panel dropped, and from outside came the sound of a wrench fastening the closure tight.

Charlie lowered the gun as the footsteps receded once again and the sound of maintenance began to filter in from a few panels down. *A leak*, they were saying. *Better safe than sorry. What about the Arsenal last week.* Relief flooded from Charlie and he flipped the safety back on.

The men worked for ten minutes and before long the sound of wheels turning restarted George's heart.

As the noise of the tracks invaded, Charlie responded to George's accusing stare with one of his own.

'We've come this far,' said Charlie. 'They weren't about to spoil it.'

'Spoil it?' hissed George. 'If they'd opened up the panel, what then? You'd have shot all three of them? In cold blood?'

'I would have threatened them and made good our escape.'

'"Made good"? I don't think so. "Made good."' He couldn't look at Charlie now. 'I don't think so.' George folded his arms and glared at the ground, a little unsettled by the movement of the train as it accelerated. This would be one hell of a ride.

'Okay,' he volunteered. 'Give me the gun.'

'I've got it,' said Charlie. 'It's all right.'

The train picked up speed and it wasn't very long before all conversation was impossible. The darkness filled with momentary bursts of light as they passed stations, houses, signals and, at one point, another Eurostar that nearly blew the panel away with pressure.

They were soon in the tunnel. Security lights strobed by through the crack in the opening. Half a mile above them, the chill grey waters of the English Channel quickly became La Manche.

When the train erupted into French air, the rain had worsened.

38

Since he wasn't sleeping, Neil decided to head back into work. The security guys were used to him being around at all hours, thanks to the odd and anti-social reporting procedures Bill Skelton had demanded of him during his Embassy days. He was on to other things now, old Bill, the little tweed whirlwind, but he was the kind of clockwork manager who you could guarantee being away from his desk from the hours of 5.01 p.m. to 8.59 a.m. if he could possibly help it.

The corridor on Floor G was empty when the lift disgorged Neil onto the carpeting.

Neil remembered going to a funfair on the Meadows when he'd been a kid. He saw his first gypsy caravan then, petted the horses. His mum had said something about their manes, or good looks, or something – he couldn't quite recall it. Whatever it was, the sentiment had been echoed by another gypsy, who promptly spat on the ground.

He'd never forgotten that. When something is good, it's time to spit. You take the curse off it. And Neil wondered what the opposite sentiment was – as he'd just found something that warranted it.

Neil knew that to get to any kind of real information about

263

Charlie and George's predicament, he would have to venture back into the realm of paper. All records were computerised, of course. But most operations were also authorised on paper. Even here in the twenty-first century the need for a rubber stamp and ink was palpable.

All of these papers were taken down to Floor X and below. And all were, because of their combined sensitivities, categorised 'Secret'.

Neil reasoned the only remaining records that pertained to Charlie or George now hid somewhere on that floor. Someone had taken pains to delete the electronic versions of these men. The only footprints they still left in the Service were on paper, locked and secure down on Floor X.

The last time Floor X had opened its doors to Neil, Bill Skelton had given him what was, in effect, a permission letter. Neil looked at his watch and decided he would just have to give him another one.

Neil followed his nose back to his old boss's corridor, austere prints of windmills framed in pine on the walls. This time of night, only the shift Operations posse would be here, in case of Embassy emergency or other listening-post disaster.

As he walked, Neil was searching his mental filing-cabinet for a word. He knew it lay somewhere inside his brain as he'd spent enough time with the man to know the kind of word or phrase his password would be.

Generally, the gatekeeper to the world of desktop access in the Service was now the encrypted keyfob. But Bill had conscientiously objected to high security on his departmental computers simply because it meant he could leave work and get a minion to do the odd job if his wife was on the golf course. Which, generally, she was. Of course, anything high priority or with a clearance of cyan or higher was passed on to the can-do techie children, who talked Bill through the access procedures and patriotically looked away when the product came on screen. In other circumstances, as Neil had discovered, he would simply write a letter and send someone down to fetch whatever it was he needed.

Neil was now hoping things had not changed too much since he'd left. The décor certainly hadn't.

He reached the door at the end of the corridor without seeing or hearing another soul. He put his hand on the door and pushed. It was open.

'Mackay!'

Neil turned as casually as he could to find Rude Alan from logistics, on his nightly round of executive summaries.

'Evening, Alan.'

This was what Neil was expecting next:

'He's not in, in case you're wondering.'

'Is he not?'

'Well ensconced in Essex by now.'

'I guess I'll be off, then.'

But this is what he got:

'Change that fucking cologne, for all our sakes.'

And he disappeared around the corner. Not a single glance in Neil's direction.

Two minor heart attacks later, Neil took a deep breath and pushed open the door. The place was in darkness but lit from the corridor lights and the waxy yellow glow from the streets outside.

The screensaver showed the 15th hole at the Old Course in St. Andrew's, and Neil was touched. Bill didn't really enjoy golf, but he'd taken it up because his wife loved it so much. And he didn't like the idea of her hanging out with the weasels at the 19th hole all weekend.

He hit a key and the picture faded. Neil sighed in relief that the technology budget had not spread to the 486 computers that still hummed on these floors. They saved the flat-screens and plasma monitors for the groovy gang over in the Anti-Terror Section.

A prompt asked for username and password. Knowing Bill's penchant for directness, he typed '*billskelton*'.

Now the password. He had three chances, he knew that. When Bill had asked him to do this last time, he'd confided, Neil now remembered, that he cycled his passwords on a monthly basis.

Neil typed '*rosie*' with great care and attention. He thought his wife's name might be a good idea.

[x]USERNAME OR PASSWORD ERROR[x]

Neil took a deep breath and tried again.

'*19thhole*'

He pressed as softly as he could but still the sound echoed, in Neil's mind, all the way down the corridor, down the lift shaft and into the very lughole of the security guards in the lobby.

The same error message. A door swung open from outside. No denying it now. He had to get this one right. A memory struck him and he smiled. He was even tempted to spit.

'*Blitheringidiot*'

Neil hit enter. A humming sound and he was in.

Three minutes later, a perfectly polite and reasonable-sounding request for temporary security clearance was sitting on the printer station, its coding identifying the user as

William Skelton, and the recipient of so high an honour, one Neil Thomas Mackay.

The lift deposited Neil on Floor X with a *clunk*. The doors swung open and the corridor beckoned like a septic tank. Neil's stomach started churning but he knew this was for his friend, this was the real test.

His shoes clacked on the flooring. Ahead, no doors, only a single security station, manned tonight by a delightfully morose gentleman by the name of Brendan.

Brendan glared at Neil's cyan security pass and looked at the temp clearance form in his hand.

'I'll have to pass this upstairs.'

'He's gone home,' said Neil. 'I've got the number some-where—'

A chill ripped through Brendan at the thought of con-fronting the admin class on their home turf, tired, hungover, and petty to a man jack of them.

'On you go,' said Brendan.

Neil nodded and only on the other side of the door, away from the security camera, did he exhale.

The Floor X files were arranged in a circle, a little homage to the old British Library Reading Room. Cubicles fanned out from the central filing column, which moved up and down as the automated retrieval system hummed and hahed before delivering requested papers to the appropriate desk.

A hostage exchange was being mooted in the Caucasus. A degree of interdepartmental badinage was ongoing over whose fault it was that those telecom workers had been nabbed in the first place. As a result, Neil had a few cohabitees tonight, all of whom seemed utterly engrossed in their own worlds. It was still no surprise to Neil that he and Charlie had never met. Even if they'd wanted to meet, Neil mused, they'd have had a job finding each other.

Neil made himself comfortable and typed 'CHARLES MILLAR' into the central intranet search-engine. As files popped up in monthly date-succession, Neil calmly asked the filing computer to 'select all'.

Over the next thirty minutes, the delivery system began to fill Neil's inbox with pages and pages of the activities of his best friend from school.

Charlie had joined five years ago. He'd been posted domestically following his probation, a few trips to Berlin, the jammy bastard, a few others in liaison with SIS to Moscow. Then he'd got stuck into several small-to-medium-profile operations in the British Isles.

Next was a four-page report on Rebecca Helen Gallagher, Charlie's fiancée. Neil chuckled quietly to himself at the thought of Charlie resisting the rigmarole of Service relationship paperwork. Her vetting was positive, as were the file photos, Neil noticed with a smile.

His smile faded when he saw what had happened to her. Both news of the crash and the other (drunk) driver's death hushed up from local media. A staff therapist despatched to doorstep him with the news at Heathrow airport.

Big on touchy-feely human resources here, no kidding.
Poor Charlie.
Poor bloody Charlie. He'd never mentioned it.

Next came a short spell of leave, a variety of desk jobs, and then came Charlie, clearly bouncing back, devouring work and wanting to lose himself.

A few months after that, the tender of resignation.

And here, to the final job.

Neil wasn't surprised. These things generally took themselves eighteen months to truly impact. It was like any plate tectonics. The tsunami only hits long after the earth has stopped moving.

He was about to go when curiosity got the better of him. He typed in 'GEORGE SHAW' and waited. A full forty minutes later, a tower of files dwarfed the others on his desk. Not wishing to draw too much attention to himself, he skim-read the early years: Moscow, Paris, Berlin, Prague. Old school. The man had had some fun. Then Canada, strangely, some liaison work with the CSS and some American agencies, and a variety of classified fieldwork back in Blighty. Here, no operational details were available, only boring stuff: logistics references, location codes, and so on.

There might have been something about Neil's personality that made him do what he did next. He was certainly teased at school for using his ruler to underline every word. Whatever the reason, he looked again at the location codes for George's recent operations.

One of them caught his eye. LM1544. A pub, if Neil's memory served him well, in Warren Street.

The reason for Neil's attention was simple. According to the records, at the same pub, and on the same day, Charlie had been on an operation called TwelveStep. Neil knew the two men had doubled up at the photolab.

But this was six months before *that*.

And as far as Neil could make out, neither man appeared to be aware that the other was even there.

39

The rain was merciless. Sheets of it, slugs of it, cleaving the ground before it in twain, showering shards of mud and grit. The channel of sludge at the base of the TGV track rippled and shimmered and finally ran for its life as the Eurostar powered past, carried on a shrieking whine of the rails.

Here, in the wider expanses of the French rail system, the speeds were beginning to climb. The train was gearing up to trace the distance between Calais and Paris in the same time it took to perambulate through Kent.

Inside a small crawl space, ten inches from electrified rails, sat George and Charlie. Fear now a rictus grin on both their faces. Fists clenched in the realisation that here, finally, was what they had been reduced to. Utter insanity.

George wished he'd been part of those spy novels he'd read in the farmhouse. There, people switched countries, even crossed the Atlantic, in what amounted to a click of the fingers. Being on the run was never that much fun, he thought. Being on the run really means losing everything you've ever known in the blink of a bloodshot eye. He cried a secret tear in the darkness and turned a colder part of his mind to his plans for the future.

The darkness of the night permeated Charlie's mind. It had taken its time, but the constant pressure was finally unpicking the edges of Charlie. It was ripping the stitches from his sense of self, memories long gone now rushing forth like a deluge down a storm drain. Once they began to run there would be no stopping them here in the cacophonous dark. They would hit him broadsides and there would be nothing he could do.

The rain on the panel was to Charlie the rain on the roof of a long-abandoned car. Once, Charlie's eyes had seen such rain through the frantic fendings of windscreen wipers. He had seen it through torrential tears and a dark, winding road. His headlights probing the hedgerows on the turns.

Once, he had arrived back from a business trip. Although to call it such would be to classify a funeral as an administration exercise. The trip involved a mortally responsible operation abroad. This was a trip where Charlie had been ordered, in no uncertain terms, to say something to another man. This man, he knew, without any flicker of a doubt, would then call on another man. That second man would order someone to be killed that night.

Once, the order to proceed had been given to him, as was often the case, in the middle of the night. He had said farewell to Becky. He had done the job proud. He had done what was expected of him.

In its aftermath, Charlie had been on a plane. As those thoughts had begun swimming in front of his eyes he had realised he was having trouble breathing. He had done these things and come home, and now, in seat 25A, there was nowhere to run. He felt his chest collapsing in that window seat, in that sodding Boeing 737-400, as all passengers stood up, seatbelts clicking off despite the dire warnings from the cabin crew, mothers with babies and uberpaunched businessmen standing and crowding him in, imprisoned with his memories, bustling and grabbing for baggage and coats, leaning on seat backs and muttering impatiently for the doors to go bloody manual. And the only thing that stopped Charlie from choking, literally choking to death with horror and regret at what kind of human being he had finally become was the thought that his wife, his wise and beautiful and loving wife, would be waiting for him on the other side of the arrivals terminal. He powered on in his mind through that door, along the grey and green flecked carpet, the low-ceilinged fluorescent parallel lines of the travelator, around and around the carousel into escape velocity and out, out, onto the ramp and the sea of eyes and the one pair he knew, and that knew him.

Once, he had passed through all of this but in the mass of faces, those eyes were not there.

In their place, two others. He knew them too.

Once, Charlie's eyes had seen the rain. The road had taken him into the countryside as the air sighed in expectation of a thunderous deluge to come, the murmur of an audience all too aware of the excitement ahead. As the breeze rose on the heavy air, the car drove on and tears became rain as the heavens pummelled the windscreen.

He had driven south, north, somewhere *else*, and found the hills, a lonely expanse of air and grass and stone. He had thrown open the car door and walked out into the wind as it grabbed the handle and slammed it shut behind him in a brutal, random rage. Charlie had not heard, his footsteps sinking deep in the sodden grass and mud.

The face he knew. The face he did not want to see.

Hearing her words echoing in his spine, 'Bad news, Charlie, bad news . . .'

It had taken him his life thus far to open up to anyone. *And now . . .?*

Once, he had screamed at the sky like some Shakespearean king, knowing the biggest fool was him, knowing he delayed, he stayed away one more day, and one day was all it took for Fate to conjure up the car accident that took her away for good.

And here flashed his memory again; in the middle of this moment of exquisite hatred at this casually brutal universe came the cloud, and from the cloud came the spark, and there, on the high ridge, alone, came a bolt.

Even here, even now.

The bad news ready to bite.

The charge, travelling at over fifty thousand miles an hour, was seeking out the ground, and nothing was getting in its way. As the voltage passed around his skin and found solace in the turf, his wedding ring, the only item of metal on his person, was superheated and burned his flesh in a permanent loop of red.

The hospital staff couldn't believe it.

Neither could the Service psychologists who knocked themselves out with ever-more-elaborate theories about his behaviour. At least they'd enjoyed themselves, Charlie had thought, picking over his mental remnants like they were some hastily abandoned meal.

On Charlie's mind was not the tragedy. He was too numb for that, succumbing even now to a form of emotional hypothermia. Instead, at that moment, Charlie developed a newfound respect for the unexpected, the way the future dances ahead of you, elusive and ungrasped, the soap in the shower. To lose your wife to the mundanity of a car wreck was one thing. To lose her and be struck by lightning in the same day was the road to a whole new level of consciousness. In hospital it had become plain to Charlie that life was, at best, an enormous cosmic limerick that proceeded in an orderly fashion to the last line which, instead of rhyming neatly, reached out from the pages of the book and punched you in the face with the final full stop.

His scar would always be there. The ones on the outside, at least, were easy to see. George, watchful George, could never see the scar on Charlie's mind.

The train's wheels sparked on the rails.

A hydraulic hissss shook Charlie back into the present. Something, he realised, had come loose that day on the hill. More than the scar on his finger, more than the knowledge he was truly alone in the world, there was something inside him that had disconnected from his fellow man. People usually found out in the end. He wondered if George had worked it out yet.

He stared at him. He speculated for a moment how they would look if the train was invisible. Two men lying down and travelling at two hundred kilometres per hour, one foot away from an electrified rail. He wondered how fast the trains in Japan travelled.

He wondered if he might have to kill George after all.

'Do you believe in God?' Charlie suddenly heard himself say.

George looked startled. He managed an irritated look by way of return. Finally, above the sudden clamorous keening of metal, he shouted back, struggling to be heard:

'How the hell are we going to get off this thing?'

And with that, the floor gave way.

40

Neil ran back to his desk. He caught the security guys on shift-change and no-one actually seemed to notice or care that he was leaving. He was still amazed at how security *out* was never as tight as security *in*.

Arriving back at his desk, Neil proceeded to spread the papers he'd smuggled from Floor X out in a large fan across the grey plastic, like a deck of yellowing, officious cards. All were uncopiable, of course – light green or light pink and specially treated to come up black when placed on a Xerox machine.

The heat was oppressive. The radiators had come on in time for the majority of staff leaving and the windows, despite Neil's attempts, did not budge. The air draped like a twelve-tog duvet around him and he cursed the heating engineers as he got to work.

Before him were all the paper references to Charles Millar's and George Shaw's careers in espionage he could get his hands on.

There were recruitment questionnaires, progress reports, psyche assessments and recommendations for field-mission promotion. There were also curious crossovers. Both had manned the same cover station, that was known. That had been a genuine mistake. He'd cleared that with Logistics. A coffee spill had stuck their assignment forms together. It was mistakes like this that had cost missions before. Because it was the only kind of thing that can go wrong. Human error's human error. No matter how mundane.

He went over it again, his brow now at dewpoint, baubles of sweat appearing in the crinkles. Six months ago, Charlie had used Location 1544 on an operation. Location 1544, a small series of computer-key taps confirmed for Neil, was a grotty little pub in Warren Street.

Not for Circulation.

There were Logistics requisitions on that date, camera sign-outs, all the bureaucratic paraphernalia of a working agent in the field. There was no doubt that Charlie had been there, on that operation, at that time, on a highly routine but eminently visible mission.

Not For Circulation.

Which was deeply confusing to Neil because as far as he could see, George had been in exactly the same place.

At exactly the same time.

TwelveStep, Charlie's operation, had been a product of long-range planning and patience. The publican of the Pig and Whistle on Warren Street had long been suspected of underground activities with organised crime. In the Service's new broadband remit, Charlie had been despatched there to befriend and analyse his character. Charlie's reports, Neil read, showed he thought the man a braggart and a hardcore drinker. His memos outlined his feeling that this man might start dropping more information to a man he trusted. He only trusted people he liked. And he generally only liked people who spent money.

Thus TwelveStep was born – Charlie, a reformed alcoholic, falling off the wagon in front of the landlord's eyes. His favourite kind of customer, Charlie presumed. And he was right. On the night that TwelveStep's operations took a new direction, Charlie decided to record what the man was saying.

Charlie was the only operative engaged.

Yet there was George. George was there.

For George, there was no operation. At least, nothing with official documents supporting it. But Logistics had, in its wisdom, issued arms, equipment and monies to one George Shaw for precisely the same location on precisely the same evening, six months previously.

The only difference was, *no mention of it anywhere*. A double-check on the computer confirmed for Neil that these records had been reclassified *after the event* on the system. The only evidence that remained was here, in paper, in front of him now. And Charlie and George had both said they had never met each other before their posting to the photolab. There was no reason to disbelieve them.

Neil wiped the sweat away and sighed.

'Progress?' said Rose.

Whether she had walked in without Neil noticing, or whether perhaps she had been here all along . . . it was hard to say. Particularly for Neil. When Neil started concentrating he often had trouble remembering to breathe.

'Actually,' he managed, 'not that bad, thanks.'

She cast her eye slowly and methodically over the entire range of documents. It was like she was filming it with her eyes for posterity.

'Smuggling, are we?'

Neil held his breath. He needed an ally, it was true.

Without someone's help on the inside, he might not get to the truth. He was normally a good judge of people. And Rose, for her nosiness, was clearly someone who cared about details.

He cleared his throat – but decided against it for now. She looked stressed. She looked – he had to say it – sweaty. Even more so than him. For the moment, this could pass off as *work for her*.

'Using my initiative,' he smiled. 'These are pretty useless, but there's some interesting stuff down there they wouldn't let me nick.'

'Flash them a smile, my boy, that usually does the trick.' Neil tied up his papers and placed them in his work safe. 'Didn't mean to surprise you, I was suddenly in great need of placing a secure call.'

Neil smiled, and wondered as he left when he'd be forced to risk a bit of trust.

As soon as he'd left the office, Rose was on the phone again with Special Branch. The van found in the lay-by in Kent had been traced to a Mrs Margaret Wilson. Mrs. Wilson had a daughter, Elizabeth. Elizabeth had married a man called Neil Mackay. The proximity of Ashford was too much for Rose to bear and she called up the face-matching software she'd been trawling over the past few days – airports, seaports, Waterloo International.

As she clicked and double-clicked, searching desperately through the data with her bottom lip firmly bitten, she yearned for John. The removal of her husband from her life had been sudden and unexpected and, yes, unfair, dammit. The product of a bureaucratic error not here, not in the corridors of power, but in a hospital.

A dirty, inefficient, inner-London hospital.

A misplaced ultrasound. A tired junior doctor. An impenetrable signature and a nurse who'd been told he was a different person altogether.

No individual's fault. Simply the end product of committees. They had been pleasant, of course. Even in diagnosis, they had been smiling and inclusive. John's work fascinated them. He had sat in that ward for days, endless streams of nurses perched on the bed. 'Special effects, you say? Pinewood? How exciting.'

Smoke and mirrors to distract you from the truth. That everyone was missing the obvious. Inside of him, his body was eating itself; life was ending, all of it was ending, and with him, Rose too.

That day was, for Rose, the end of doing what committees judged to be correct. The committee of medics who claimed such intellectual high ground hadn't seen the shadows on his pancreas. Hadn't even felt the need to act when he presented to them. She could see the trails of inefficiency that led to his demise just as clearly as those that resulted in misappropriations of equipment, fax paper, telephones, flick knives, burst-transmission bugs.

Or cover stations.

Committees enjoyed safe words. They enjoyed the status quo. They required consensus and rejected hunches. Her Project had grown from this loss and her Project had been a success. The War on Terror meant that any request with enough weight and gravitas was generally approved – not from any sense of due diligence, but from a sense of patriotism. *If it's coming from on high, then bugger it, it's eyes alpha and then some. And well, then that's good enough for us.* Her new way of doing things had bypassed the bureaucrats and got results. And wouldn't you know it.

Bureaucracy got its own back. A bureaucratic failing may well have spelled the Project's demise.

Well, bureaucracy and that bloody letter.

There was still a chance. She knew there was. Together with Latham. Yes, together even with Boy Neil, even though he was not aware of it. Together, the three of them would see this through and quietly but firmly shut up shop. John would have loved to see it. Rose trembled slightly as her fingers tapped the mouse once more and more faces appeared.

The faces that had flashed briefly on the Ashford security cameras appeared suddenly and clandestinely onto her screen, on the understanding on both sides that this was the War on Terror, this required discretion, this was not for circulation.

41

C harlie's hands shot out in two directions at once. The first, to the small crevices near the top of the void space, allowed his fingernails, at least, some sense of security.

His other hand stretched out to George, whose knees were suddenly and of necessity splayed across both sides of the compartment floor to their very edges – because in the middle, the panel was gone. George's crotch dangling ominously over the abyss.

Just below him, the blur of a track that would dice human flesh like a food processor. In the small space now a roar so murderous and malevolent, George's screams of terror made not a dent. Of course, Charlie couldn't hear him. In any case he was already shouting back.

George finally saw the hand as his legs began to tremble. He was in a strange and awkward half-prayer, balanced on the remaining structure on his side of the void. Lost for anywhere to secure himself, he had placed his knuckles in the far corners of his side of the compartment. Swallowing hard, he moved forward.

He grabbed hold of Charlie and the physical connection helped unfreeze his mind. He realised now that he would have to stay like this. He would have to remain in this position for the remainder of the journey or he would risk bringing down the entire floor.

He met Charlie's eyes and it was clear to him that, despite his strange behaviour, they had been right to stick together, right to tough it out between them. Together they would get through this.

It may have been a minute, it may have been an hour, but eventually both men felt the train begin to slow. The noise abating, George mustered up the words he'd been meaning to say all journey.

'Thank you,' he said.

Charlie nodded. And with that, the train slowed to a complete stop.

A track halt.

A pause.

A window of decision. They could drop now and move. George racked his memory for some semblance of time. They might be hundreds of miles outside Paris; they might be right outside the Gare du Nord. It was impossible to tell. He glanced sidelong, attempting to peer through the crack in the void's opening. But there was nothing there but darkness and a distant pinprick of light.

'Now?' said George. It was clear there was not a lot of juice left in his arm muscles. Charlie had to agree. He nodded.

The time came and they let go.

George dropped down first. His legs compressed like pistons and he landed heavily onto the track into a crouch.

A thought gripped Charlie: *That track's electrified.*

Too late to warn.

George clambered gingerly over the rails and dived onto the central gravel reservation. He heard Charlie drop down just as he noticed the *banlieue* of Paris in the distance, and the red signal turn to green.

He turned back to Charlie who was now crouched underneath the carriage as the wheels began to move. Charlie, unused to gymnastics, suddenly found a focus and leaped for a gap between the wheels.

George was there to stop his fall.

And, slowly, the two men stood up.

The lights of a city beckoned. And unless Bruxelles had copied the Eiffel Tower any time in the last year, it was almost certainly Paris. Crossing quickly to the fences past the swift-departing Eurostar, they clambered up the weed-infested incline to a footpath.

What can you do?

This. You can do this.

George unfolded his Euro clip and one dark and gloomy bus ride later, the two sought refuge in a café on the corner of *Place de la Nation*. Neil had tipped them off that his long-term contact would be waiting for them. They had a few hours to go before the meet. The contact, Neil had assured them, would have a good way of getting them settled, sorted, secure—

'We're not staying here,' said George.

Traffic was manic around the four-lane roundabout that ran rings around Dalou's *Le Triomphe de la Republique*, the sculpture that forms the centrepiece of the *Place*. A light rain began to fall and Charlie was tired. He stared at George long and hard but could summon no bad feeling except an irritated sigh. 'Why not?'

'I have another idea.'

'Which is what?'

George was looking at him strangely. Charlie's eyes hurt from exhaustion and trauma.

'Canada.'

Charlie cleared his throat politely. 'And how is that an idea, exactly?'

'Your friend Neil knows we're here. Correct?'

'Yes – and I trust him with my life—'

'One problem. My life is also here. Which means – sorry, Neil – but that's as far as it goes. Your trust extends to him. Mine does not. No matter what the truth is, right now I would rather proceed on what I know. Rather than what I don't. So I'm leaving. And I want you to come with me.'

'*Canada?*'

'Name me the country you associate with the world of international espionage. Russia, yes. Germany, of course. Europe in general. Our lot have ties all over the continent. Where can you go these days without bumping into every single world intelligence agency? I'll save you the effort. It's Canada. It's far away. It's English speaking. It's big enough to hide in. And from your reaction there you really weren't expecting it.' He sighed.

'There's something else going on here,' said Charlie.

'No.'

'Or . . . someone else?'

George blushed. Charlie knew him better than he realised. He nodded. 'I have a good friend there who can help us. My publishing contact. That's where I've been planning to launch my book. I didn't think I'd be getting over there so quickly, but what the hell. Needs must.' George shrugged. 'I mean, you don't have to come, of course. And he's my contact, and you'd be completely within your rights to tell me what I just told you. But after all you've been through, and how you've helped me . . . I thought you might appreciate the gesture. That's all. Trust me, Charlie. It's safer than staying here.'

George's face had fallen and Charlie thought he might cry. A life alone on the run in Paris flashed before Charlie's eyes but he quickly dismissed the notion. George was right. Once the security cameras at Ashford had ID'd them . . . he shivered as the thought froze his spinal fluid. There were no more friendly faces in this town.

'How do we get there?'

George flashed the wad of Euros and winked.

They left a large tip and walked against the run of traffic. The architecture calmed them both. Gracious avenues, straight lines. Order.

George stared ahead as he laid out his idea.

'Last year there were fourteen baggage handlers arrested at European airports for taking bribes. Mostly cargo planes. Illegal foodstuffs, some drugs. Animals too from time to time.'

'You're suggesting we pack ourselves up in a crate?'

'I covered the court cases. I'm suggesting we pay a visit to the fifteenth man. The one who only got off because I got him off. He's been my gatekeeper into the French side of things ever since. If you were scared about airport security before, I suggest you look away until this is all over.'

Charlie's face was sceptical. But for once, he was prepared to go along with it. Despite their mishaps, they'd got this far . . . They were a team now. No. More than that.

This man was his friend.

'Just promise me one thing,' said George. 'If we get there.'

'Anything,' said Charlie.

George was momentarily taken aback.

'Really?'

'Yep,' said Charlie.

'You actually need to say it. To promise.'

'Okay. I promise.'

'If something happens to me, you'll find a way to look after my daughter.'

'Look after her?'

'See her right. You know.'

Charlie nodded. 'Of course.' A thought struck him. He picked at his nails, trying to work out if it had been his fault he'd never asked these questions before. 'What's her name?'

'Katie. Katie Shaw. You remember where she is, don't you?'

George's heart soared as Charlie said yes. The two were getting out of here. They were headed somewhere the tendrils couldn't catch them.

They were going upcountry.

By the time two faces on the watch list had been cross-referenced to the ones on closed-circuit cameras at Charles de Gaulle; once phones had been dialled and Interpol Ops Rooms had been paged; once the labyrinthine baton-passing of international security had reached the sweaty hands of Rose Willetts in Euston Buildings, Charlie and George were long gone and a solitary cargo worker was considerably richer.

Bureaucracy, hissed Rose, to the empty office.

42

Silver cataracts fizzed down narrow channels in the ultrafolded rock. Gossamer tufts of dandelion weed floated in the air like a recent sneeze. Even the breeze was fertile. And all around, the quiet. The determined quiet. The kind of silence that magnifies. Everything here, it seemed, wanted to mate or kill. Or both. Renewal was in process and it brought sunshine into Charlie's soul. If, he reasoned, he had one.

This was upcountry all right.

It was nearing springtime in British Columbia and things were changing.

A plane had taken them as far as Calgary. A couple of smaller twin props had flown them northwest, first into central BC, then finally bouncing down onto a grassy airstrip near a place called Fraser Lake.

George was on a high. His assessment of Charlie had been correct – so far. And despite the fatigue and the cold, the sun was strong for the time of year. This would not be as much of a problem as he'd anticipated.

They slept in a roadside B & B that resembled a toy log cabin Charlie used to play with as a kid. They started early the next day. By the time they began to trudge into the forest on a rocky tourist trail, the sun was peeking over a far ridge of mountains, a cool wind blowing when it disappeared behind.

They followed a trail parallel to a river, where green water still meandered over boulders closer to the centre, holding salmon steady in flight. George had ditched the attaché case and gun at the airport, choosing to distribute the money evenly between them. The CD stayed with him.

Charlie could see George was elsewhere in his head. The way he smiled now was reassuring. He was clearly used to the wide expanse of sky.

Charlie was less comfortable. And his mind began, slowly, to unspool.

A last minute change of plan, the voice had said.

Just a couple more days.

Not okay.

What can you do.

He'd left her that night, framed in the doorway, shivering but trying to hide it, trying to make him relaxed about having to leave, trying to make it easier. Always, trying to make life easier.

'*They've extended the conference again . . . a day or so,*' he lied to her, on the phone from the hotel. She knew the lie and sighed a lie back in return. '*I'm sorry,*' he'd added. This at least was true, true, true.

'*How long?*' She knew not to place any emotion in her voice. No matter how upset she would get. A simple need to get the facts straight.

'*Just a day, I'll be back by the weekend.*'

How he hated the calls. Email would be so much easier, but even with that . . . eyes were watching, watching . . .

They paused for lunch and George noticed Charlie's anxiety. He wondered if his own expressions were getting as easy to read as Charlie's.

'You're nervous,' said George.

'Just tired,' said Charlie. 'Tired and cautious.'

An audible *tscchhhh* issued from George's mouth as if he'd just recalled he'd left the iron on. It was full of warmth, though. Like news of a surprise birthday party. 'There's something else I need to tell you,' he continued.

Charlie nodded as a signal that he was ready to receive the information. But George seemed reluctant.

'What is it?'

'I'll give you a clue,' said George, with no hint of humour on his face. 'It makes the world go round.'

Any self-respecting spy has what is known in polite circles as fuck-you money. The pressures and insecurities of the job lead many to set aside what they can in a pot for a rainy day. Still more come into contact with so much hard cash in their daily grind – cash destined for other people, other wallets – that the temptation begins to set aside some for yourself.

'What if I told you,' said George, 'that my book isn't the only reason I've been trying to get over here.'

'I wouldn't be surprised,' sighed Charlie, 'because I don't think anything surprises me any more. No offence.'

'None taken,' said George, and began to explain. One of his first placements in the service had been to Canada. While there, he had been forced into contact with unsavoury individuals. 'Prehistoric times, far as you're concerned.' He'd been tight with the CSS, the Canadian Secret Service, 'back in the day.' During those years, the only real problems the Canadian border had to deal with were immigration and draft dodging. In return for a blind eye or a cold shoulder, their targets were allowed to move around more or less freely – so long as they paid cash and paid well.

'Protection money,' murmured Charlie, not entirely sure why he disapproved.

'We sort of got the idea from *Marathon Man*. Everyone wants an even break. At the time, it all seemed very innocent, I promise you. Long as we knew we wouldn't need to act *now*, we let them pay. We still kept tabs on them. They knew it, we knew it. It all worked out fine. Hell of a lot more honourable than other schemes I've heard of. False agents? Double-entry book-keeping? Sod that.'

'So you have money here?'

'I have money here. Correct.'

'In a bank?'

'Swiss bankers? No thanks. My cash, my friend, is all *frozen assets*. In this part of the world, the time from autumn until spring gets a tinge of permafrost in the soil, some fifty feet deep in places. This makes the entire topsoil impermeable to harm. If you plan ahead enough, you can bury anything for safekeeping. And no-one's going to know about it till spring comes around.'

From the way George was describing it, all over the north of British Columbia were metal boxes conveniently submerged in welcoming turf.

'Why are you telling me this?' said Charlie, squinting in a sudden burst of sunlight.

'Because I like you, you idiot. Because if we get there, and find it, it's ours.'

'Where is it?'

'It's in the grounds of a property up past Strenton. My old contact sorted it all out for me, but he died a few years ago and I've been meaning to get back here to dig it up ever since. The mortal termination of my employment seemed as good a time as any. No-one else knows it's there. Well, apart from the new owners of the house.'

'Who are they?'

'They're problematic, Charlie. They're underworld entrepreneurs, shall we say.'

'Drugs?'

'And guns. And anything else besides.'

'How much is there?'

'Enough to get us anywhere we like.'

'Such as?'

'Who knows . . . Panama, perhaps . . .'

Charlie shot him a quizzical grin. George merely shrugged.

'I like canals. I like hats. It seems the perfect place.'

'What about your book?'

'One thing,' said George, 'at a time.' He looked at his watch. A strange look came over his face for a second. George's face left Charlie's and watched the ground as he marched off again. Charlie stared at the crude map that George had drawn. The money was buried in the garden. It was really that simple.

'No,' said Charlie.

George nodded and watched him get up and walk away. He let him trudge fifty yards or so before he trotted after him.

The two walked in silence for a few minutes.

'It's not that I don't want to help,' said Charlie. 'I just can't face it any more.'

'Money?'

'Violence.'

'There won't be any. Not if we work together. Not if we persuade them.'

Charlie shook his head. George realised he was going to have to be more brutal. The boy needed to know. It had to happen now.

'What would Becky want you to do?'

Charlie glared at him. 'Please don't bring her up.'

'What would she want, Charlie?'

'She'd want me to be happy, George. What else?'

George suddenly looked old. He began to slow down. 'We've come this far together. I think it's time you knew the truth.'

Charlie heard George sniffling. He wondered what the hell was coming.

It was a verbal punch to the solar plexus:

'Your wife was killed, Charlie.'

Charlie thought he'd misheard and didn't speak. But George repeated himself and Charlie found enough nervous energy to make some form of noise.

'No, she was in a car crash . . .'

'Said who, Charlie?'

'Said everyone, said the report, said the mortuary, said my own eyes who saw her body, George – what the hell are you trying to do to me?'

His teeth were grinding hard.

'Look. I saw the paperwork. Her name was Becky. You said it was, in the car. I was hoping it wasn't her, but . . . I've been thinking about it ever since. And, oh God, Charlie, I'm sorry, but she was killed all right. She was murdered.'

Charlie had always wondered. Somewhere, deep down, the paranoia had stayed bubbling. That Becky had no points on her licence, that the weekend had been dry, that the man who had run her car off the bridge had been killed himself before the trial . . . there were murmurings even now, late at night, before sleep, if sleep ever came to him . . . *Where are the coroner's reports, Becky? Why did I accept this as gospel truth?*

As any truth?

'Who . . .?'

George held Charlie by the shoulders. Firm hands and the eyes of a true friend. 'We can get them back with this, Charlie. We can screw them to the wall. With the book, with the money. The two of us. We can live like kings and drink Daiquiris as we watch them all strung up. I promise.'

Charlie closed his eyes for a moment and when they opened again they were on fire. He had quietly vowed an end to violence when they left the country for good. A fresh start. A new leaf. He had thought himself past it. But the flames were back. Revenge was never something cold for Charlie. Revenge was an emotional *fajita*. Something that sizzled and stung the eyes.

That night they camped rough. Charlie trembled as he slept. Bad dreams. He woke to find George had placed his own jacket on him. We're a team, dozed Charlie through the tears. And together, we can get this thing done.

43

Neil had a special smile, Liz had often commented, for truly good news; one that flashed his eye teeth, one that crinkled his eyes so much they almost disappeared. The day she said 'I do.' The day she surprised him at lunch to tell him she was pregnant. The news of friends' victories over hardships, bosses, bad feelings and illnesses.

He smiled that smile now.

The postcard was blank. It showed a picture of an Air Canada 737–200. It told Neil all he needed to know. Neil was bemused for a few seconds before the glimmer of recognition lit up his face. And the smile arrived soon after.

He'd skipped into work on the knowledge that his friend was okay. The perfect bolthole. And enough time for Neil to get to the bottom of whatever vessel they were swimming around in.

There was no sign of Rose when he arrived. He'd been a little lax, falling behind in the delivery of reports to her admittedly gruelling schedule.

In fact, Rose was in the communications centre, several floors below. She was on a secure line to Interpol again, hearing that there was no data in any flight manifest that suggested either Charles Millar or George Shaw, or anyone matching their descriptions, were on any commercial flights out of Paris on the day their faces were seen by the cameras.

Which led her to two paths of escape. Either they had gone to the airport knowing their faces would cause a stir; or, they'd skipped out on a cargo flight.

Her hand trembled with her mug of tea as she realised that the latter was by far the most likely.

It seemed she'd have to use the boy Neil after all.

Neil left his desk a few minutes later in search of caffeine. Like many new schemes in the building they had relocated the free coffee from a small grey area near the lifts into a large grey machine that forced you to pay money for it.

It lived halfway down a particularly over-lit and unfriendly corridor. He felt the zap of static as he pressed the button for extra sugar.

As the machinery clanked and whirred, Neil became aware of a small insistent finger tapping on his shoulder. Wheeling around revealed a small man in a tweed jacket. Bill Skelton rocked gently backwards and forwards on his heels, a curious smile on his face.

'Got a sec, Mackay?' said Bill. 'Having some problems with my password.'

44

An area of high fencing was broken only at one point, a small and brightly coloured sign promising great scoops of fun. But there would be no fun this winter. The park had been abandoned mid-construction when the money ran out. Splash World was not going to be making any kind of splash any time soon.

The idea seemed reasonably sane. A water park near a campsite near the northwest coast of British Columbia. The fenced land seemed to be near the area's only summer vacation zone, and presumably the optimistic soul behind the project had cobbled together some local seed money to try and finance it. But here in the cold, despite the spring sunshine, the place was unutterably depressing.

Charlie thought these things to himself as he followed George through a gap in the security fence. His legs had recovered some strength since the news of Becky. His dreams, of course, had been full of pain and torment. But as the sun began to probe rays through the circle of firs around the compound, the light brought unplumbed reserves of strength back to his body.

George began a security circuit of the place. Charlie followed. Segments of pipes, flumes, disassembled plastic palm trees, all were scattered around a small horseshoe of fake beach and an empty concrete basin, half-painted in aquamarine. The wind whipped up a small sandstorm that strafed the steel supports of the main waterslide, the only construction that seemed to have been completed. There was a large model of a clown on the top, in Bermuda shorts.

'Super place,' said Charlie.

'Great,' mused George. He'd mentioned his contact would arrange to meet them somewhere 'unexpected'. Charlie had to agree that, so far, at least he was pretty consistent. George began to get worried. He began to talk in order to reassure himself.

'He's a bit volcanic in the mornings,' said George. 'Let me do the talking.'

'Does he usually turn up on time?'

George looked up at the waterslide again and saw the man step out from behind the clown. He bit his lip and tried to hide his fear. 'On the button,' he said.

Charlie began to follow George towards the steps that wound up the side of the structure. George turned half-back, firing a whisper from the side of his mouth.

'Look, it's probably best I make the first contact. Stay here and look after this.'

Charlie caught the silver Frisbee coming towards him and realised it was George's CD. He pretended to stop and tie his lace and slid it expertly into his back pocket.

George climbed slowly, heaving himself up with the handrail. The entire slide wobbled slightly with the effort. It wasn't really designed for men like George. The man at the top was medium build, medium height, brown hair – your average ID parade nightmare. Charlie presumed the two of them had been associates during George's first tenure here. From what he knew they were a friendly lot.

Mind you, thought Charlie, *he couldn't have chosen a more unfriendly place to meet if he'd tried.*

Charlie could lip-read, but at this distance the going was tough. He could only see George's mouth. A greeting. A handshake. And then – no more. Their heads obscured, perhaps they were laughing. The wind whipped their discussion away from Charlie's ears, not that this distance would afford him anything but a whisper.

George gestured back to Charlie and the man gazed at him. This seemed to change things for the worse.

George's body language became defensive. He seemed to be asking the man what the problem was. The man was gesticulating, shouting, but Charlie still could not work out what was being said.

He didn't need any lip-reading to work out what happened next.

The man had pulled a gun.

Charlie, fumbling in his mind, tried to remember who had the firearm until he remembered . . . George had ditched it before buying passage on the cargo plane.

The men grappled and fell on the top of the slide.

And then Charlie heard the gunshot. Single, and at that distance, fatal.

Charlie's legs began to tingle as he watched George's hands move to his stomach. A blooming stain of red and black told the worst. George tried to get up but the man kicked him. He toppled over and now George was on the slide.

It was slow-going with no water, and the red streak behind George painted out only half of the descent. His body stopped at the crest of the first half of the slope, and Charlie shouted at his legs to start moving. But the tingling was getting worse and the numbness was creeping past his knees.

The gunman began to run towards him.

Another shot rang out and the ground near Charlie erupted in a terrifying divot. What the hell was he using? Snub nose?

George was not moving.

The blood was real.

This news was bad.

Very bad.

A third shot released Charlie from his paralysis. He burst through the fencing like a sprinter from the blocks and zigzagged into a maze of brush and woodland at the edge of the clearing.

Another shot sang through the tree trunks. His fists punched the empty air, branches and ferns scraping at his face, his eyes. The footsteps behind him were strong, fit, fast. Charlie crashed on through the undergrowth and hit a slope that sent him tumbling over, head, heels, knees, elbows, a painful descent stopped short by the trunk of a fallen birch. A manic rushing in his head would not stop and, despite the pain, Charlie leaped to his feet and over the other side of the trunk, out of sight.

Then came the footsteps. Pausing at the top of the slope, the killer. Charlie made sure he memorised his face, his gait, his clothes. He would meet him again. One day. He was sure of it.

The man did not see him. As if hearing another noise, he took off along the edge of the gulley and disappeared from view.

Charlie slid down the side of the log, thin branches caressing his cheek. He held his knees and rocked quietly to himself.

Okay. Okay.

He waited for ten minutes then took the long way back

towards the clearing. He proceeded in concentric circles, checking behind, in front, until he was sure he was alone.

George's body had gone.

Charlie wasn't surprised. He may have been moved. Or removed completely. It was never good policy to leave your corpses where they fell. Carrie Watson and friend had been the rare exception. It was true.

They had been betrayed. But Charlie had one up. He felt for the CD in his pocket. He felt for the knowledge his friend George had given to him before he died. Even now, a plan forming in his ever-sharpening mind.

He would show them. He would show them all.

He turned around and ran.

Thirty minutes later, chest heaving, he hit the highway. An empty black artery through the green and grey. He fought back nausea when a car slowed down in response to his thumb. Seeing him in his current state, it accelerated right back up again.

A tourist shuttle finally took pity on him. No tourists were onboard. The driver's name was Jim. Jim told Charlie that *only the other week there* he'd had to stop the van in the middle of the highway because of the caribou. They got worse later on, in summer when they were rutting, he said. Charlie focused on this information rather than the previous hour of his life in a vain attempt to keep his thoughts fresh.

The van powered on past what Charlie first took to be a cloud forest but on closer inspection revealed itself to be a concrete factory. The chimney smoke hung low in the air. When Jim asked where Charlie was headed it took a while for the answer to come. But eventually, it did.

He knew exactly where he was going.

45

Neil revisited Floor X several times that week and by the time Friday was coming around the mountain he had developed a considerable collection of papers on his desk. He'd been sleeping in the office, too, a couple of hours at a time. Rose found him both mornings, slumped and snoring and whimpering for Liz.

She had noticed this trend.

Neil noticed her noticing.

He had also identified an increasingly strident sound to her voice on the phone. Part of the reason for his new work schedule was to keep a very close eye on what came into, and out of, this very office. Her repeated calls to Interpol and points European, for example. Her need to promote a perfectly good field-agent without consulting the Human Resources department.

Not that she was aware of any of this scrutiny. Neil didn't want to worry her. She was far too busy.

Her feverished work changed tone that day. It might have been his honest face, his charming way, it wasn't clear. But as Neil staggered back to his desk with his fifth coffee of the day, he saw the tears descend in silent rivulets down her cheek. Her sobs were audible. Her sobs were meant, in fact, to be heard.

Neil put down his coffee and approached her, awkward, dry-shaven, bleary:

'You all right?'

Rose nodded. 'Oh, fine.' She attempted a smile. Still the tears, the public display of difficulty that demanded a response.

'Some problems on an operation, that's all,' she said. 'Nothing for you to worry about.'

'Oh – sorry to hear—' said Neil.

'A couple of agents. Out in the field. I don't know where they are.'

Neil shook his head in empathy.

'No idea at all?'

'No. Not really. France, perhaps. But I can't be sure. There's not a lot of certainty about at the moment.'

'Well – put out a bulletin, Europol, Interpol—'

'What do you think I've been doing?' she snapped. And then calmed herself, the old Rose who'd brought shortcake was back. 'It's not that simple.'

Neil wondered how she would respond to a curt 'Well, good luck with everything!' He let the thought pass. Instead, he pulled up a chair and offered her his most concerned and interested face. 'I'll get you some tea.'

Tea. The Great British Placebo, he thought as he headed for the machines. When he returned, he half-expected to find her in the death scene from *Camille*. But she was still there, picking at her nails, eyes and nose red from crying.

'Someone is trying to hunt them down.' She leaned forward and whispered, 'Someone in this building.'

'Who?'

'I can't say for sure. But if I don't get to them first . . .'

She staved off another sob and breathed deep.

'Well who is it? Can I help?' Neil sat on the desk now, arms folded. A man of action.

'You won't know them. Apart from making calls—'

'You never know. Who is it?'

Rose sighed a fatalistic sigh. Perhaps, the sigh said, perhaps it doesn't matter any more. The gloves are off. She walked casually to the corridor and checked the level of activity. Most other officers were deeply occupied in paperwork. She walked back quickly and bent down to the floor. A small latch pulled up to reveal her personal safe and in one swift movement she removed two large dossiers. The smaller one, Neil could read upside down, was Charlie's personnel file. The larger one was George's. She pushed them over to him.

'I know him,' said Neil, pointing at Charlie. 'He went to my school.'

'You're not serious.'

'Never more serious, Rose. What's he done?'

'He's done nothing, that's the thing.'

'So how do you know he's in danger?'

'I can't reveal my sources, Neil. Not yet. But he's out there. Both of them are. He doesn't trust his handlers and I think he's right to do so. So they've gone feral. My guess is, when your professional network lets you down, you revert to your personal contacts. I've been monitoring his family, his friends. He's not been in touch with anyone.'

'Really? Is that right? Really?'

'Has he been in contact with you at all?'

Neil thought of the aeroplane postcard, pinned up on the notice board in his study. He thought of the football they'd played, the in-jokes and the bonds of friendship.

'Yes,' said Neil, 'he has.'

And he showed her everything. Took her through it all. His concern had been piqued after Charlie's phone call, he explained. After that, no contact at all. He explained the paper trail. He talked Rose through the bungled cover station. The Frame 13. Whoever had sanctioned the Frame 13 operation hadn't counted on Logistics screwing up their station.

Then there was the pub. The two operations, one official mission for Charlie, TwelveStep; and yet George seemed to be there too. Another Möbius strip that Neil had yet to unravel.

Finally, there was the letter.

He'd only just found that.

In a 'Not For Circulation' file, Neil had found a typed and vitriolic document that had been addressed to all heads of department in the Service. Marked 'IMPORTANT', it was signed by Mrs Rebecca Millar. Neil told Rose this was Charlie's wife. Rose nodded, as if learning this for the first time. Rose looked at the letter and asked Neil if that was the only copy.

Neil shook his head. He'd taken the original home. She thought in silence for a few moments. Opened a tin of shortbread and began to nibble on a small piece.

'We need to meet tonight. Not here. Bring everything you have. Originals, copies, everything. We need to go through all this together. We'll go off-site.' A couple of case workers ambled by her door and she lowered her voice. 'Tell no-one.'

'What about my wife?' Neil waved Becky's letter in Rose's direction.

'Not even your wife.'

46

It has come to my attention—

No, wait, that would be ridiculous.

She was juggling three things at once, as usual. She double-locked the door and swapped her bag to her right hand to compensate for the bag of recycling in the other. Inside her head, in addition to a swift computation of the change left in her purse for the bus, she was recomposing a letter.

She was not in a good mood.

Dear Sir/Madam—

Again, a little bit like a complaint about the quality of weave on a bathroom carpet. Something a little stronger this time. The first letter had been strong enough as it was. That had been an expiation, a cathartic eruption of anger.

Her mind flicked back to it as she strode along the pavement. She wondered who was reading it. If anyone.

To Whom It May Concern

Now that was the way to get attention.

I believe in the Service. I believe in what you do and I believe that the pressures and strains you are consistently under are astonishing. I feel for you and I feel for the people working for you. I know this because I am married to one of them.

I will not tell you his name.

No, sod it, excuse my French, I will. His name is Charlie. Charles Millar. And this is what happened to me last night.

Mrs O'Toole had another cat, Becky noticed as she passed by the corner house with the hedge. A giant overfed tabby was sitting imperiously on a gatepost and watched her as she walked.

I was at work and my husband rang me. He would be late, he explained. It was work. Now, I understand what this means more than anyone. And I know a lot better than to ask him any details. But as it turns out this would have been a very good idea.

The man fixing the manhole was staring at her again; she knew he was and she felt sorry for him. Charlie would be back tomorrow. Late, of course. But he'd be back. And this man, perhaps, sensed it. This might be his last chance to wolf whistle in comfort.

But time was short and so I left work and went for a drink with a colleague. And this is what happened then.

A stab of pain shot up her arm and Becky wondered if it was a heart attack. As the car pulled up and her vision blurred she felt warm and fuzzy, like a fleece.

This is what happened then.

Her subconscious, unaware that her conscious mind was in serious distress, kept going. But without the reins it began to wander.

Dear Sir and Madam, We would like information about your school. We are new to the area and keen to meet all prospective headteachers.

Her heart began to flutter and despite the solid medical training in the person at whose feet she now lay, it began to slow down and stop.

Dear Charlie . . .

Darling, I'm dying. I don't really know why but I think it's actually happening. I love you. I won't be able to collect you from the airport.

The car turned sedately onto the main road. Minutes later, at seventy miles an hour, Becky Millar was catapulted face first through the windscreen of her Vauxhall Astra and collided with a concrete breeze-block half-embedded in the muddy riverbed below.

47

The forest was breathing. Deep, endless, formless, it took in the air with silent, shuddering gulps, sighing it out to the lakes and the turbulent skies for miles and miles around. A giant lung, it clung to the hillsides, the crags, the angry protrusions of granite and sandstone and moss.

The forest was also wild. It danced and whispered around Charlie, his every step uncovered in new pools of light and shade. Rotten shavings and dead leaves crunched underfoot and twigs lodged themselves into the grooves of his Reeboks. Polyurethane hoofprints on the mossy ground. Above, slate-grey skies ambushed him with occasional halogen beams of warmth, only to disappear on a breath of wind.

When Charlie had been ten or so, he had walked calmly out of the back door, through the side gate, and onto the road. Once there he had taken the long road up by the bypass and up into the Pentland Hills. His mum had been apoplectic. His dad couldn't have cared less, but by that stage it was clear to him that his dad was an enemy to be defied and that, perhaps, was why he wandered off.

In his meanderings, through a gorse-riddled golf course and up the slopes near Hillend Ski Slope, he had met a young couple called Callum and Moira. They had asked where his mum and dad were, and he had, quite on the spot, come up with an elongated and totally fabricated story about a lost penny.

He had walked on, spurred by this amazing revelation on life. *You can say things*, said the thoughts racing in his brain, *and if you say them right, people believe you*.

He had wanted to make it to the top of the ridge, to the seat he could see if he squinted enough. When, several hours later, he had flopped onto the weather-beaten bench by the makeshift cairn, when he surveyed the shimmering Firth of Forth, the homes and crescents and gasworks and offices of Edinburgh spread before him, young Charlie had known that somewhere, somehow, his bright and shining life would have a noble purpose. How could it not, given all this?

Charlie never knew that feeling again until this moment.

Here, on the run through an endless forest.

The man who had saved Charlie's life. The man who had shared his knowledge, his money, his friendship.

The man called George was dead.

And now he was alone.

There had been theoretical practice, of course, in the kind of isolation he had felt in his five years of service in espionage. The biting loneliness he felt just knowing that there were things, important things, trivial things, that he simply could not share with anyone. But the problems with those modes of speculation were always visceral. Experiential. There was no way to experience the true meaning of being alone without doing it *hardcore* – eschewing any means of contact and staying utterly reliant on himself.

He'd never been sure he'd cope with that.

Well, now's your chance to find out.

He knew to keep moving.

The van had taken him towards the edge of the national park. Jim told him good luck and Charlie returned the sentiment. Promises made, promises kept. He set off in a northernly direction. Half an hour later he had lost his way – the small drawing by George his only guide now – and when a tiny residential strip appeared again, next to a tarmacked road, he vowed to take advantage of it. He was shaking with cold and needed some human warmth. Of any kind.

Despite his hardships, though, inside he felt like a new man. He was starting to get the feeling that he had a purpose. He had something in his life worth living for.

He had a girl to look after.

A friendly building promised coffee. Even out here, they knew about civilisation. The place was tiny inside but welcoming, plastic chairs and wooden benches. The people were younger than Charlie was expecting. A guy in the corner, curly hair cropped short to his head, nodded in greeting as Charlie walked in. He fumbled for change and took his coffee to a small corner. There was no escape from scrutiny here. But Charlie didn't care. Not right now.

Half an hour and two coffees later, he heard the grumble of a 4 × 4 and two sets of feet approach. Two girls entered – they were early twenties and wrapped up against the chill. The taller one had indigo hair down to her waist, plaited and tucked into a bright orange hat. The other girl was in a parka, frizz untamed by a retro Russian soldier's ear warmer. They both walked over to the man with the curls and kissed him on the lips.

Charlie tried not to watch but his world had been ruptured lately and human affection was something of a rarity to him.

He returned his gaze to his coffee before they noticed his

stare. He was on the point of ruminating again when the girl in the parka slid in next to him, one leg hooked up behind her.

'What happened?' she said as Charlie blinked.

Charlie checked behind him. He was certainly alone. She was talking to him. She took his silence for bemusement and tried again after lighting up a cigarette.

'I mean, you look upset. You all right?'

'I'm fine.'

'Are you here for the party?'

'I'm just walking.'

'Right. Out here. Just walking.' She stubbed her cigarette out and thrust out an elegant hand in greeting. 'My name's Angie. You should come over to our place. You look wasted.'

Her voice seemed so reasonable, and Charlie's feet so cold, that he thought he'd better do what she said.

He joined the small group, all smiles. Angie's friends were Dean and Kai. They were also keen on the idea of a lonely traveller finding warmth and soup. Although Charlie's professional radar signalled danger when any goodwill came his way, he made a decision there and then to embrace this particular good news with all he had.

'Let's go,' he smiled. And a minute later he was in the front seat of a GMC Yukon.

They coasted down a trail towards a lakeside property, past a large boat with twin Yamaha outboards. A number of wetsuits and snowboards were scattered outside a small and ramshackle log cabin. There were dead cobwebs in the windows and a professionally planted vegetable patch. Along the side of a porch were, in Charlie's estimation, nearly four hundred and sixty wine and beer bottles, all empty.

The living room was roasting hot, and Charlie's cheeks

began to sting. The place was dominated by a satellite television. The empty bottle theme continued here, snaking up and around a giant mound of forgotten dishes stacked next to the sink. A man was lying splayed across one of the sofas, a blanket half-covering his chest and entirely uncovering his genitals. A half-naked female torso poked out of the same chaos and Charlie's nostrils were filled with hash-heavy air.

'That's Matt and Rachel, don't mind them.'

A hand waved in greeting from the blanket. Charlie nodded back, a little embarrassed.

Over a bowl of soup, in the kitchen, Angie came over and chatted.

'I do a lot of travelling,' she said. 'Sometimes you're lucky, sometimes you're not. The people you meet, I mean. I guess you just got lucky.'

'. . . Yes,' managed Charlie.

'You looked upset, is all.'

Charlie looked at her.

And for the first time in his career he told a half-truth. Normally, the fictions a spy creates are parallel ones, stories that contain themes of the reality underneath but have no true connection to the raw material. Charlie told them about a friend called George. Who had recently died. In doing so, he broke his own personal rule. But by now, he didn't care. He felt himself opening, reaching out. What the hell, it was springtime. He was starting to blossom.

Dean came out and hugged Angie as she sat listening. They watched Charlie cry for a while, in a strangely detached way, as if they were watching him on television. Dean explained apropos of nothing that he was a parascender. Charlie didn't know what it meant, so Dean told him.

'You just jump off cliffs?' he asked.

'Mostly,' smiled Dean. 'Or get towed behind boats. You should try it.'

'I have enough excitement in my life,' smiled Charlie. He downed the remainder of his soup and got up to stretch. 'Any of you have a map?' He tried to sound as offhand as he could.

'Where you headed?' asked Dean.

'Strenton.'

'I don't like going near there much.'

'Why?'

'I dunno. This place gets a little tribal at times. You be careful up there.'

Charlie saw the dope buds on the windowsill and drew his own conclusions.

Dean shrugged as Angie sloped off towards the bedroom with a wave. Charlie realised that they were all going to bed now. They'd been up all night. He smiled to himself and wondered what he'd been doing with *his* youth recently. Telling lies and killing people. He wondered if they knew how it felt. Dean finally found a map under a pile of twelve-inch singles and slid it over with a smile. Charlie memorised it in a minute and passed it back. Dean hugged him over-zealously and disappeared into the bedroom.

Soon the cabin was silent and the water lapping on the shore the only noise bar the soft, tender kissing from the sofa.

Charlie quietly purloined a thin, serrated steak knife from the kitchen drawer and closed the front door quietly behind him.

48

Charlie walked all day, keeping to the thinner areas of forest around the main highway. At one point he strayed too far, and worried he would be found a week later, gnawed to the bone with his socks still around his ankles. Dean had warned him earlier that there were things alive in this part of the world that looked at you as nothing more than human sashimi. He kept his ears open and his eyes wide and before too long wound back onto the tarmac.

There was no traffic on the two-lane road when he found it again. He walked for several miles before the driver of a logging truck took pity on him and carried him for a couple of hours through lazy curves and weak shafts of afternoon sunlight. Where the road forked east–west, the driver let him out.

The reason for the fork in the road was one of the most beautiful lakes Charlie had ever seen. Fringed by conifers and birch, it was almost entirely empty and utterly silent. No development or dwelling that he could see as he made his way to the rocky shoreline. The driver had told him Strenton lay a few miles further east. If he followed the shore, he'd find it.

Charlie knew that Strenton town centre wasn't his final

destination. But it gave him enough time to work out his strategy in his own mind. George's instructions had been very simple. The money's in the garden.

If no-one's around, dig.

If there is someone there, George had said, *we'll persuade them we really need to dig.*

Charlie waited. Night fell. It took him a good hour to walk the shoreline. Charlie reasoned he would stay off the roads now. To his right, through the trees, he could make out the lights of a small strip. A gas station with a single pump. A hardware store that sold chainsaws. And that seemed to be about that for downtown Strenton.

Charlie skirted the main drag and ducked back into the woods. He continued on for half an hour before he saw the road again. And ten minutes after that before he saw the path.

Bright moonlight lit the small dirt track, just as George had said it would. About two hundred yards away, the trees began to thin out to nothing in what amounted to a clearing where by all rights there shouldn't be one.

And there, peeking out from the ferns and the tree trunks, a simple bungalow. Formed from local timbers, but erring more on the modern than on the rustic. It was styled like a craftsman's cottage. It had triple-glazing and a newly tiled roof.

A small generator grumbled away from somewhere on the other side of the building, presumably heating the teeming water in the large spa tub set into the decking on the western side of the property. A brave soul to get in that on a winter's night, thought Charlie. Fall asleep in the bubbles and a grizzly might mistake you for a fondue.

Charlie took care to tread lightly in bursts of five or six

steps, pausing after each to listen, check the wind, use the peripheral senses. He began to skirt round in a giant arc, encircling the property. As he did so, he noticed several large tyre tracks and a small light in a back room. The cold was beginning to bite again and Charlie knew the night would be uncomfortable. But to do this properly he would have to do the thing he knew he was best at. Watch. The chills, the pain, the hunger – all of these would no longer be a problem to a man who had a purpose.

He dug himself a hide and watched all night. No movement, no activity, no real sense that anyone alive was in the place at all. In the dark again, Charlie wondered why people without any sense of meaning in their lives find sudden focus in children. Maybe, he thought, people might have a child as continuance, as a need to see evidence that their genes will march on.

But flushed with his own sense of need now, a man so totally alone and in need of some scrap of possibility – of a future outcome in his life that was good, and right, and proper – he developed a new theory. Perhaps, he thought, we had children in order to relive our own early years through them. To thrill to their daily miracles as if they are our own – which, of course, in a way, they are. To fill their new lives with the same sense of forward momentum, the same sense of wonder that our own adult selves imagine our childhood once was. Not that we would remember, thought Charlie. Not that we'd necessarily want to.

Between his thoughts, Charlie watched, as he had been trained to do.

At five a.m., a face appeared at the window. The man was middle-aged, around fifty or so. He seemed to be making a cup of tea. He was a baby once. He may have had parents to marvel at his first words. And now, here he was, thought Charlie. In the middle of nowhere, in a cabin, drinking tea. *Heavily guarded, George?*

Charlie decided not to go on first impressions.

His current vantage point provided a perfect line of sight into the house. Leaning from his position he would see the blacktop of the highway and a small dirt track directly across from him, leading up a slope and turning right past another slew of trees.

Charlie made a move forward. But an unseen and sudden grassy incline took him by surprise – a verge hitherto disguised beneath a slick coat of leaves. Losing his balance, Charlie windmilled ungracefully, airborne for half a second, his outstretched foot hitting the edge of a wet branch at an appallingly awkward angle. His full weight in counterbalance, he felt his shin moving in the opposite direction to the leading edge of his ankle, his ligaments unable to take the strain – and for a moment the silence of the night was filled with what sounded like a WWF wrestler tearing a phone directory in half. Had Charlie's vocal cords responded to this white-hot flash of molten pain, the man drinking his tea, indeed the population of the entire bay, would have been aware of Charlie's presence. Instead, training took hold and he bit into his tongue so hard that for the next hour and a half he had to retreat into the shadows to stem the flow of blood.

The pain focused him.

Charlie waited until the pins and needles had subsided enough to test the pressure on his ankle. He could walk on it, but the tendon, if not snapped, was certainly starting to tear. He resolved to keep it slow, and soft, and steady.

There's a place in the garden, George had said. *Persuade them, and dig.*

Charlie crouched below the kitchen window. Above him, the man was washing the cup under a small hot-water spout. The light cast a short corridor of warmth along the ground that disappeared beyond the tree-line and the darkness beyond. Suddenly the light winked off, and Charlie retrieved the knife he had taken from the cabin, and felt the blade cool and comforting against the flesh of his forearm. He focused on the cold and willed it to draw the agonising heat up from his ankles.

It would have to be the knife. He never enjoyed any contact, but he never *ever* enjoyed close contact. There was a chance, of course, that he could persuade the man to take a sleeping pill. He could be drugged, if there was provision enough in the house.

Charlie was not looking forward to ending any kind of life. Not after trying so hard to prolong his own.

It was time. Charlie stood up, breathed in deeply, and knocked on the door. The light winked on again.

A voice inside: 'Who's there? Dan? That you?'

Charlie listened from his new position, tucked around the corner in the shadows. There were no other voices discernible. A few thuds and bangs and the door clicked. The man was alone, or other occupants were asleep.

The man's shadow on the dirt path outside the door.

'Dan?'

Clearly this was Dan's last chance to show himself.

'All right,' went the voice. 'Whoever you are, leave now, or die. I mean it.'

Charlie furrowed his brow. That actually sounded quite scary. *That's what you get with underworld entrepreneurs up here*. He shifted his weight but something, perhaps his toe, snagged on the ground and suddenly Charlie felt himself falling. In his effort to correct himself his toe nudged forward and knocked a wine bottle. It scraped resonantly against the concrete walls. The man was around the corner in a second.

No-one around to see. By his feet, a bottle still teetering. Charlie, from his new hiding place, heard the man's steps as he ran, but wanted him further away from the light. The footsteps stopped.

'No joking. You're dead.'

George had taken pains to explain that while the house was the property of the occupants, the money was not. Charlie had half-considered reasoning with them about this, but that kind of reasoning tended to double-back on itself very quickly.

Wire would have been better, he suddenly thought. The fear of imminent strangulation was a powerful and persuasive tool. George had told him that although several places like this had armed guards, this one would not.

The man removed an automatic pistol from his shoulder holster and clicked off the safety. Charlie heard it and cursed George softly inside his head. Speaking ill of the dead was bad manners, but now there was a problem.

Suffused with the confidence of a sidearm, the man strode out into the shadows and trees, straight past the bush where Charlie lay crouching like a wildcat.

He sprung up noiselessly, grabbing the man's gun with one arm as he elbow-locked his neck with the other. His lips close to the man's ear, his voice reasonable.

'Anyone else inside? Nod your head for yes, shake it for no. If you speak, I will end your life. I have killed twelve people in mine and I have no wish for you to be unlucky thirteen.'

The man, quivering, shook his head.

'I need something from your garden,' Charlie explained. 'I want you to help me find it.'

The man nodded.

'I'd prefer not to have to kill you. I'd prefer it if you never saw my face. I want you to tell me if you have sleeping tablets in the house.'

The man nodded vigorously.

'Good. Let's go look, then, shall we?'

As they walked, a sharp breeze began to pick up. Charlie timed his footfalls with the man's. As they approached the light of the building, he noticed the man had grey hair.

The man pushed the door open and they entered the house. It was warm and cosy, despite the chill from outside. Charlie pushed the door softly shut with his heel and kept the pressure tight across the man's neck. The gun, safety clicked off, now in his pocket.

The entrance hall led directly to a small kitchen. There were two windows on each wall and a small fitted cupboard on either side of the economy boiler.

'Bathroom?' whispered Charlie.

He let the man lead him past the kitchen and down the corridor towards a door at the far end. Out of the corner of his eye, Charlie saw two forks sitting in the draining board.

The realisation came at the same time as the suspicion, which was just as well for Charlie as his sudden movement redirected the path of the silver baseball bat into his right shoulder. The pain came yellow and flashing in front of his eyes, but the spike of adrenalin also sent him ricocheting into another door to his left. Whoever had swung that bat was behind him to his right and very strong. The man with grey hair chose that moment to slam his heel hard into the delicate bones of Charlie's injured foot, whereas Charlie chose the very same moment to retrieve the gun from his pocket, aim, and fire.

The house was plunged into darkness almost simultaneously and it was only from the lack of breath in the room that Charlie surmised his shot had hit its target. His nostrils were full of the smell of gunpowder and sweat. He dived to the floor as the door came open – but the sound of the hinges also informed Charlie that the man he had in all estimation just shot in the head was now a semi-lifeless lump blocking the doorway.

Charlie concluded this was almost certainly true and fired quickly into the door at chest height. He had been absolutely straight with these people, he had tried his best to be professional and courteous, but he had a purpose now and despite all of his best efforts to end this without bloodshed, they had made the first move. This would be the end of it, he thought to himself as he listened to the slumping sound on the other side of the wall, the gurgling and high-pitched hiss of a punctured lung, a broken rib, life ebbing away. The end of lies, the end of murderous treachery. His name was Charles Lachlan Millar, he was twenty-six years old, his mother's name was Jane and now he had a purpose.

I shall be the active uncle, he thought as he switched on the light. The grey-haired man's face was a mess. The hulking figure behind the door, wheezing and staring at the ceiling, had been shot twice in the sternum and was seconds away from oblivion. He had been trying to reach the room where, moments before, the grey-haired man had indicated they would find the bathroom.

I will watch her grow up. And teach her about the true

meaning of life. To live it richly with a view to the context, always. A life where no news is good news.

And bad news is buried, in a box, in the ground.

Charlie looked down as death came to the burly man. His mobile phone began to ring. It was peeking over the lip of a bloodsoaked pocket. Charlie leaned over and picked it up. Bizarrely, it had reception. The display also indicated the 'roaming' was 'on'.

It might be worth a shot, Charlie figured. He dialled, carefully checking the other rooms.

The bathroom was not the bathroom. The 'bathroom' was a small square place that contained what appeared to be a small army's arsenal.

Uzis, other automatic weaponry, and several slabs of deeply worrisome plastic explosive – Charlie thought it was probably C4 – arranged on a table.

Charlie found no class 'A' drugs in any other room. But he didn't feel that they were very far away. The only people who need that kind of weaponry are survivalist militia and drug traffickers.

The mobile phone accepted the call. A minute later, the familiar ring of a British phone. It rang just twice before a tired voice struggled with the receiver for a moment.

'Hmm.'

'Mum?'

'You need the doctor?'

'Mum, it's Charlie.'

Silence on the line. And he heard his mother laugh.

'Do you know,' she said, 'that is the first time I've done that in a month of Sundays. I was fast asleep. I thought that was my dad, God rest his soul. How funny. Your old mum's getting senile in her old age.'

'Nothing old about you, Mum.'

He heard the sounds of recent death now, the creaks and groans of what Charlie knew was not life leaving as much as death settling in and making itself at home. He felt himself slide softly against the wall of the hallway into a crouching position. His ankle ached but the position seemed to stop the stabbing pains in his shoulder.

'Are you all right, sweetheart? You sound tired.'

'I'm pretty tired.'

'How's work?'

She had no idea. Charlie presumed she probably thought he was on his own in the 'office' where he worked.

'Tell you the truth, Mum,' he sighed, checking the dying battery briefly, 'I'm thinking of changing jobs.'

'Are you not happy where you are?'

The blood from the burly man had made a pattern on the opposite wall that, in the darkness, appeared to Charlie to be some form of morbid Rorschach test. To Charlie it was a butterfly.

'I just don't like the people, Mum.'

'I shouldn't worry too much about other people, love,' she said. 'Just look after yourself.'

Charlie smiled ruefully, shook his head. Of course. Mothers all think the same. Perhaps that's why we all reproduce. We have no say in the matter.

'I worry about you, Mum. I had a dream where you died. I got so upset. There was only me left.'

'Well, dear, that's going to happen. One day it will. But you mustn't let that sort of thinking get in the way of what you want to do. We all face it sooner or later.' She sounded so certain that even were that to happen it would be as comforting as tea and toast. 'I just want you to be happy, darling.'

'I love you, Mum—'

But the phone itself had died.

For a second, the wind on the trees outside.

No more death.

Just a couple more days.

A thought arrived in Charlie's brain. Work Charlie had been on a distant hilltop and waving to Life Charlie. Now he was feeling ready, Life Charlie was going to turn around and walk away. Waving not in greeting, but in farewell.

Charlie imagined what Becky would say to him. He'd begun talking to her through his days of darkness. After she'd gone, it was all he could do to brush his teeth without wondering whether to end it all.

Get up, she'd probably say to him. *Get up and stop slacking. Just a couple more days.*

He got up and walked very carefully to the erstwhile 'bathroom' door. No more death.

He stared at the handle and pushed. A small sliver of light illuminated the room, the table, the silence. Surveyed, inside, the weapons of killing. The automatics. The six-shooters. The slabs of C4.

No more death.

He'd make sure of it.

Three very careful minutes later, he was outside. And digging.

49

Liz was preoccupied with Jake when he got home, so she wasn't really in the mood to talk. Neil followed her around as she picked up toys, removed small fingers from toasters, answered questions and reassured tired cries.

She was looking forward to passing the baton and having a bath. She looked tired. Neil vowed a family holiday in his head but knew this could not wait.

And he only had a few minutes to explain.

'I have to go out. Important. I'm sorry.'

'On Friday night.' Liz was quiet. It scared Neil when she was quiet.

'You know it's not up to me.'

She nodded, snapped something about responsibilities and instantly regretted it when she heard the door slam. She hadn't meant to be sharp with him. She made mental plans to apologise when he got home. Jake began throwing biscuits around, however, and she soon forgot about all of it. Working late on a Friday. It was enough to make you weep.

She'd forgotten about those bloody photos, too. She ran to the door and shouted. Neil jogged back with a quizzical look on his face. The postal shots had come back *on the wonk*, Liz explained, in Liz vernacular. *As in, completely not our pics*.

Neil loved Liz vernacular and kissed her. Trying to make good. He took the offending prints to his study where he looked at them again. It was true. They weren't Jake's birthday photos. But they made a huge amount of sense to him. He would have to run.

Luckily for Neil, Rose's house wasn't too far out of his way. Traffic was light and Neil wondered whether there was an automotive equivalent of the pathetic fallacy. Whenever his mood was strong, he seemed to have clear roads and the lights were green. When he needed to keep things together and stay calm, there was inevitable gridlock. He was grateful for the smooth ride. Strength was absolutely what he needed.

The house was immaculate, and set back from the road in a posher part of town, near to the river and full of the sense of its own importance.

Neil parked on the street and carried the holdall past a silver BMW that was parked in her small crescent of driveway. It didn't seem to be Rose's kind of car. He didn't give it another thought as he rang the bell.

Wisteria crept up the sides of the front porch. Classical music was playing as Rose ushered him in. The living room was large, inviting. A hefty real fire in the grate. A few tasteful furnishings, nothing busy. Nothing fussed. She passed him a sherry and offered him a seat by the fire.

'Thanks for coming so quickly,' said Rose

Neil nodded gravely, sipping the sherry with great care. She glanced at the large bag he'd hefted into the hallway.

'So you have it all?'

'You mean the documents? Yes. It took some doing but they're all here.'

She nodded. A calculation, visible to Neil from the sofa, clicking over in her mind.

'Any news?'

'None, I'm afraid. This really is most worrying.'

She wandered to the other side of the room. A picture of a pig hung on the wall. It looked rather strange, in close-up.

'My husband,' Rose said. Neil blinked a couple of times before she continued. 'He made that.'

'Is that right?'

'Prosthetics. He worked in Pinewood. God rest his soul.'

'I'm sorry,' said Neil, feigning ignorance. In fact he knew John Willetts's file very well by now. The poor man had an undiagnosed tumour. Very painful it must have been. And very traumatic for Rose. At least, thought Neil, he hadn't lived to see Hollywood replace him with a computer.

'Shall we get to work?' Neil was on his feet now. Rose kept gazing at the picture.

'This place is still full of his things.' Rose was mid-reverie, her voice trailing off into silence. 'Can't bear to clean them out.'

Neil stepped forward to examine the picture. A small inscription read: 'Edward Willetts, Animal Farm, '64'. Out of the corner of his eye he also took in the high-volume shredder that had been half-hidden in the corner of the room.

Behind him, Rose had already grabbed the poker from the grate and was swinging it towards the back of his neck.

Rose had decided to take care. Latham would have crushed his brain into pulp. So she had decided this was a job for Rose. This brain should not be pulped. This brain still had something inside it that was needed quite urgently.

Neil, knowing exactly what was coming, had already shifted his weight and twisted to the side, a move that Andrew Crombie had found enormous problems with twenty years previously on a small school football pitch in Edinburgh. He brought his left hand around to stop the weapon and pushed Rose back into the armchair directly behind her. She gasped, flushing red with the effort and the shock.

'You know, Rose,' smiled Neil, 'I'll let you in on a secret. I haven't got a clue what to do with you.' Headlights briefly silhouetted Neil as a car roared up into Rose's drive. 'But I know a man who does.'

Neil kept his eyes on Rose as the front-door lock was forced open and a man in tweeds scuttled triumphantly into the room. Bill Skelton's flushed face was hiding a dreadful razor burn.

Rose moved to get up.

'Stay down there, Rose, if you don't mind. This won't take very long.'

The small gun now held by Neil stopped her brief motion and she sank back into the cushions.

'Nice shredder,' said Bill. 'You weren't planning to use that at all, were you?'

'Of course not.'

'Mmmm. We're going to stay here until we audit this whole thing, Rose. So I suppose you may as well start chatting. I've brought some whisky and shortbread to make it all hospitable.'

Rose seemed lost for a moment, peering out of the corner of her eye at the two men. She seemed to collect herself, and then, with some poise, walked to the sofa and sat down. A small trestle table next to the fireplace sported a small pot of begonias.

'We understand, Rose, that you have felt marginalised. Since your breakdown. Your husband was a good man.'

Neil nodded, and pretended he really gave a fuck. Ever since Bill had dropped by and explained what this woman had been up to, he'd been hard pressed not to throttle her with every muscle fibre in his body.

She fixed Bill with a cold stare. 'The Service has been failing the very people it purports to protect. Committee-minded nonsense is getting in the way.'

'Rose, we know how much you love and respect the Service. So it's doubly unbecoming of you to embark on a personal crusade that taints its name.'

'You lot spend too long covering your own behinds. Nowhere near enough going out and stopping these people.'

Bill poured out equal measures of whisky into the glasses he retrieved from the drinks cabinet.

'I'd prefer some tea,' said Rose.

'Fine,' said Bill, after a few moments' reflection. 'Tea.'

Neil stared at Bill and realised Bill meant him to go and play tea boy. Okey-dokey. He'd rather stay out of hitting range. He walked through a small hallway full of strange and wonderful pictures. Rose wasn't lying and neither were the files. John, her husband, really had been busy up at Pinewood. Grotesque Quasimodo creations competed for space with sub-*Blake's Seven* aliens and assorted other prosthetics.

He could still hear the conversation pan out in the living room as he reached the kitchen. *A halogen hob. Very nice.*

'A catastrophe,' Bill's voice was saying.

'And all this because of a letter?'

And Neil's ears perked up again.

The letter. Becky Millar. Charlie's wife.

Neil shook his head. He hoped Charlie was safe. He couldn't wait to see him again. A Service exoneration was a rare occurrence. But he'd been right to stay away.

Back on the sofa, Rose was crying now; soft, silent tears. She'd been closing things down, she explained. There was no need for this nonsense any more. She was almost finished.

'When you finish things, Rose, people start dying. We can't be having that any more.'

As far as Bill knew, the facts were these. Rose had decided long ago that the Service did not have the efficiency that she felt was required to get the job done. So she began to construct the ways and means to do what it took to get it done. Since her husband's death, that was all there was to live for. *There was a War on Terror on, after all*.

She needed deniable personnel, of course. Cast-offs who the Service no longer regarded as useful. Or members of the current pecking order who had been classified as flakes, drop-outs, or early leavers. George, of course, had long been complaining about pay and conditions. His departure was clearly something to anticipate for even odds at least.

Inside Rose's mind she knew all this. Inside Rose's mind there were other arguments raised in protest.

But that blasted woman.

That blasted Rebecca Millar.

How was she supposed to have anticipated *that*?

Future Outcomes, Forbes? The least likely event times the least likely event times the least bloody likely event?

Becky had written a letter. She had copied it to everyone in the department. Her letter referenced the official operation in the pub.

Bill knew all about the letter. In fact, he had a copy in his pocket.

'*What do I find on an after-work drink?*' It read. '*My husband. On Service business. Pretending that I don't exist. Some of my colleagues know who he is, but not what he does.*

What was I supposed to do? This administrative snafu has driven a wedge between myself and my husband, myself and my friends.

'The problem is not that he had to ignore me. This was a dangerous operation and I would never fault him for doing his job.

'The problem is with you. You do not allow him to TELL ME ANYTHING. If he'd TOLD ME where he was GOING, I WOULD NOT HAVE GONE THERE.

'Look into this. Please. Or I will start to raise merry hell. Because I love my husband too much to let you ruin our lives.'

Rose knew full well that a letter like that might lead to another. And two letters from the same Service spouse would red tab a file. And a red-tabbed file gets looked into. Closely.

It would only have been a matter of time before they found out about the Project operation. Because George Shaw had been working in the very same place on the very same night, and if you did enough cross-referencing of resources Rose would be found out.

And she couldn't live with that.

So Rebecca Millar was removed. And Rose realised that once you cross that line, you have to follow through.

George, her ex-operative. Attempting to leave.

That would not do.

Charlie, Becky's husband. One day he would look into her death. One day, he too would find out. And ask questions.

That, also, would not do.

So much simpler, then, to let them take care of each other. Her own life was at stake, after all. These were threats to her own way of living. To the way she was doing things now. After John, this was all she had. And she would cling to it like a drowning woman.

Bill listened to her defence with an ill-diguised sneer.

'You should look at yourself in the mirror, Rose. See what the hell you've become.'

Rose stood up and walked to the grate. Bill, taken aback at this literal interpretation, stood and stared. So did Rose. She stared into the gilt-edged frame of the mirror.

And as she stared, Latham looked back at her.

He regarded Rose closely. Rose looked back at him with the same expression. Exactly the same expression. Rose was a difficult woman to work with, he thought.

He, of course, being she.

She, of course, being Rose.

'Are you all right?' said Bill.

Rose had found, in her time, that in order to carry out the worst acts of brutality it was often important to safeguard the human psyche from harm. To this end, the construction of an entirely separate cast of characters that are components of, but not central to, the person in question is vital. Latham was one of these people she employed. So much easier to get your alter ego to do the shitty stuff. Particularly one so XYY as Latham. A deeply flawed argument, Rose knew that of course. Women are capable of just as much brutality and mindless aggression as men. Anyone witnessing a mantis or a board meeting or a middle-school catfight could testify to that. But, historically, men were known as the precipitators of war, and blamed more or less by all for most crimes of violence in the world today. So a man seemed to Rose an excellent choice of sexuality for the heartless acts that needed such pressing attention. Separation of church and state, good from bad. Work Rose from Life Rose. She'd heard some case officers talking like that in the cafeteria once. That seemed to be an apt way of explaining it. You need to be a bad person to do bad things. Rose was a good person who needed to keep a good sense of decorum at the office. But increasingly her ambition required her to put bad actions into motion. And so Latham was born within her to do just that.

Neil struggled slightly with the tea tray as he walked back into the room. He pushed open the door with his foot and remembered it had stayed open when he last walked through it. He held the tray tighter and surveyed the room. To his surprise, it was empty. A pool of blood soaking into the carpet. The poker still missing from the grate.

This time it was Latham who held the weapon. And darkness came to Neil in an instant.

50

Charlie spoke to Becky as he left the smell of death. He talked to her quietly, mouthing the words, and sucked the air crisply as he stepped out of the door. He paced out fifteen steps from the door to the house and found a large paving stone lying half-hidden in the grass.

Thinking of you, he said.

Just wondering how you are.

I miss you.

The ground was semi-frozen, as George had predicted. It would not yield to a shovel. In the absence of a hydraulic hose beloved of Arctic miners, Charlie poured several kettlefuls of boiling water on the patch of earth and essayed again with the axe.

A boy and a girl, that's what we'd said, right?

You'd have been such a wonderful mother.

The first blows jarred his aching shoulders. That baseball bat had connected right on the joint. There may have been some minor fracturing, in fact, but at least the thing was still operational. He shifted the workload to the other arm and things went more smoothly.

I know what you'd say now. Use those bloody bombs inside. Blow a hole in the ground. Get the job done, and hurry back to bed. But it's C4, babe. A fingernail of that could take your arm off.

It was still like breaking through a stone wall with a plastic fork. His ankle trembling now and surely ready to give. But each new steaming pool of hot water eased the ground apart. An hour later, bathed in sweat, Charlie was a foot down and able to see the outline of a blue plastic surface.

Two hours after that, the sun was up and the surface had a hinge. A door. It edged open. Sensing the end was near, Charlie scratched and kicked and scraped the remaining earth away and pulled with all his might, releasing a sliver of brilliant light from the underside of the blue plastic rectangle.

Charlie flinched, sensing danger in this unworldly illumination, until he realised this was electrically powered, and it was merely coming from down there, under the hatch. He peered down.

All he could see was a carpeted floor.

There was enough room to fit but it was unclear whether, once in, Charlie would ever be able to get out.

This was not a time to dally. Charlie sat gingerly down on the edge of the opening and, arms trembling with fatigue, lowered himself in. He heard a generator and as he realised what this place was he chuckled to himself.

It was a recreational vehicle. Someone had driven this thing into the ground, quite literally. Buried in twelve feet of earth, it was fed air by the hardworking generator Charlie had heard in the basement of the house.

The place was a storage facility and bank in one.

In amongst the production-line bags of cocaine, a number of shoeboxes, crates and plastic bags. Closer inspection revealed these all contained roll upon roll of $100 bills, US. A table at the far end hosted a couple of high-end money counting machines. His brief estimate totalled some half a million bucks.

Charlie got to work.

A table underneath the blue hatch – a sunroof – allowed a quick and easy exit when he needed it. Charlie grabbed an empty garbage bag and shook off the dirt. Half an hour was all it took him to fill half of it.

By noon, two bags were filled and Charlie scrambled back up to the roof, and the surface.

He hunkered down over them and recounted the money in the sunlight. There would be more than enough in here to fund both their lives. *You see, sweetheart? We'll have a daughter after all. In a way. You'd like that. We'll all be fine now. Work Charlie's finished. Old Charlie can come back and live life till we see each other again.*

As Charlie tied the second bag he heard a noise in the brush behind him. He had vowed no more killing and that was the way it was going to be. He had a gun, of course. But he knew that using that was now no longer an option.

For anyone.

He breathed deep and tried to turn. But he felt his body finally resist. He lost his balance and fell, in slow motion it seemed to him, until his eyes stared upwards at the churning sky.

Slowly, the footsteps approached. He quietly said farewell and looked forward to seeing Becky's face again.

The figure cast a shadow across his face.

Blinking hard, Charlie gazed up and slowly focused on the man standing over him. He had a slightly round-shouldered look to him. Chunky, even. As Charlie's eyes got used to the light he could make out that the man was also wearing a fleece.

'Okay now,' said George. 'Don't be angry.'

51

Charlie would have kicked but his ankle was hanging by a thread. He would have shoulder-charged him but his favourite side was his right and that was semi-shattered by the evening's occupational violence.

I should have known.

All over Charlie's body his rage and upset tremored and clenched, aching to strike out but aching for peace, for calm, for an end to the pain and confusion and heartache.

Should have known!

He pounded the side of the house and yelled his lungs out. George waited patiently for the tantrum to dwindle. He'd been expecting it, of course. But there had been no other way to do this.

'I need you, Charlie, please understand.'

'You got shot—'

'Listen to me.'

'You got *bloody shot*—'

Charlie knew an explanation would come. He knew it would appear reasonable. But Charlie had decided not to be reasonable any more.

'A bit Harry Lime, I know. A disappearing act. But you

had to believe I was gone. Otherwise, you wouldn't have stepped up to this.'

'Too right I wouldn't have!'

Charlie hobbled away. He was not going to listen to this. He made for the house. The bathroom was still open. The gun still in his pocket.

No more death.

He stopped and turned. And tried to understand.

The exhaustion hit him once again and he crumpled onto the step like a concertina. Head in his hands, he sucked in air. George, understanding the impact his reappearance would have, gave him time. He knew what he must have gone through. He had been thinking about this all night. He would have given him all the time in the world.

'Look,' said George. 'You remember my house. Same principle. They would have tooled up and shot us both within half a mile of this place. They're bad people, Charlie. Their lives are about territory, patches, routes, safe areas. The wrong person turns up on their radar, that's that. I would have been the wrong person and you would have been collateral damage. The fact that they didn't know you gave you the leeway to get close.'

'And if they'd caught me, what then?'

'Why d'you think I had to go through that ridiculous charade? The gun? The crude mechanicals? If I'd been straight with you and they'd caught you . . . you don't mess with these people. They would have got it out of you. Somehow, they would have. And soon as they heard my name, you would have been killed. I promise.'

Charlie lifted his head and drilled a stare into the back of George's skull. George stepped back and the weight of the last few days began to make his lip tremble. He willed himself to keep it together. They were almost home free. Come on, Charlie, stay with me on this.

'I'm sorry I used you,' he whispered. 'And you'd be right to go. The money's yours. It is, I promise. If you want it.' An engine rose above the trees. A car on the road. People would be seeking lunch.

'Look, there'll be plenty of time to talk later—' A saw, perhaps, he reflected. Not a car. A quad bike.

'Anything else in there?' he glanced over at the house.

'Besides the dead human beings, George? Besides the people I just killed?'

George shook his head and mouthed 'sorry'.

Charlie looked back at the house. Shook his head. Slowly removed the gun he'd fired off hours before.

'So let's go,' said Charlie. He looked down at the gun as if seeing it for the first time.

George nodded sagely.

'Okay. Let's move.'

And Charlie put the gun back in his pocket.

52

The range had only recently been installed, Neil noticed. What was known as a 'catering grade' oven and hob. Halogen, instantly hot to the touch, energy efficient, with a safety light.

Catalytic liners.

Self-cleaning grill.

All in all, a great centrepiece to the family kitchen.

Neil noticed these things as he was being dragged by his hair along the kitchen floor, streaking blood on the smooth, cold, tile effect from the widening gash in the back of his neck.

He saw the reflection of the hob surface in the brushed silver heat extractor. His brain, slowly returning to a relatively excruciating state of agony, suddenly flashed him a vision of his own kitchen with this unit. It pleased him. Liz would like that. The double grill was quick-acting. A bit big, perhaps, for them. Right now of course. They'd move eventually. Once Jake was older and–

Wait. Pain.

Neil winced, forced his brain back to his present. He was vaguely aware of something cooking.

It didn't smell very nice.

Soon he was tied to a small iron kitchen chair. Plastic packing material around his wrists held him fast. Neil blinked through the slow-congealing blood around his eyes to view Rose in all her glory.

Her face had changed. She had the air of utter calm, a stronger jaw, perhaps, or a curl of the lip. Whatever it was, the change made him more scared than the thudding pain behind his eyes.

Rose walked calmly to the pot and dipped what appeared to be a paintbrush inside. She stirred for a second, and, content with what she saw there, fixed her eyes back on his.

'Now then,' she said. He heard the sound of a shredder working overtime in the other room.

'Rose—' he began. But she shook her head. Only now did he notice the small pool of blood in the corner, and a tweed-enclosed leg protruding from behind the centre worktop.

'You know Charles Millar,' she stated bluntly, and began to apply the boiling-hot latex mixture to Neil's face.

'Um—' said Neil, 'sorry, yes, I do. I told you.'

'I remember.' She'd already covered his cheek. It felt quite pleasant, in fact. Like a warm hug on a cold day.

'You said you'd been contacted by him,' she continued. The other cheek now, feeling just like the first one. He noticed the stuff was setting quickly. She ladled the stuff heavy and glutinous on the brush, dripping like syrup and smelling like shit.

'Yep.' Neil tried to smile, tried to think of a way out of this bizarre situation. Rose had killed Bill Skelton, Cluedo-like, with the bloody poker. She was shredding the documents in the living room. She knew what she wanted now, of course. And he reasoned, based on all previous experience with her,

341

that whether she got the answer from him or not, this was the end of his life.

'Where is he?' she asked. She could have been asking for the location of the local greengrocer.

'I don't know,' said Neil. 'I don't know where George Shaw is either, in case you're interested.'

'I am. But I believe the two of them are together. They were when you dropped them off at Ashford, I understand.'

Neil closed his eyes and Rose took the opportunity of brushing them shut. The goop was starting to set fast over his brow, his cheeks, his chin. It would not set solid, of course, this was prosthetics technology. Neil wondered if it would tear.

He hoped it would. Very much.

'Yes, you're right, I did that. But I didn't know you wanted to find them, did I?'

Rose sighed, and filled his left nostril. It bubbled a little but the consistency was getting thicker now, and as hard as Neil tried to blow, the stuff was blocking his air flow. He started to inhale through his mouth. It made his head dizzy.

'So you were in contact.'

'I was, sure. But I don't know where they went, I promise.'

Rose stared hard at him and filled his right nostril. Neil's heart thudded in his mouth. This was it. Even with the truth, this was it.

'Acts of kindness do not escape a thank-you card.'

'I don't know, I swear—'

For Rose, the question was irrelevant. In any case, Latham would have to take over now. He walked over to the pot and lifted it, hot and shiny, from the orange glowing hob. Neil felt the steps approach and knew if there was one place he was not going to fucking die it was in a 'Shaker-style' bloody kitchen. Liz would never live it down.

Latham, for and on behalf of Rose, poured the remainder of the hot prosthetics mixture into Neil's screaming mouth. Almost at the same instant, Neil's legs snapped free from their plastic bindings below and wrapped themselves around what Neil correctly assumed to be Rose Willetts's neck.

Because Latham was acting on her behalf, it took Rose a second to realise she could not separate her thoughts from her actions all she wanted. At the end of the day, those actions were executed by a fifty-two-year-old woman and Neil's legs were half her age.

Neil twisted himself to the ground, Rose's neck and head clenched between his thighs, jerking his hips with such violence and anger that even through the latex and the pain he could hear her neck vertebrae *snap*.

Of course, this was only half of the problem.

He was suffocating.

The human body can survive approximately four to five minutes without oxygen. The perversity of dying like this, unless being strangled of course, is the strange sense of well-being this asphyxia engenders. Neil began to feel euphoric, even as the carbon dioxide that he would normally expel began to build up in his system.

So here he was, blind, suffocating to death, and feeling great. With his euphoria came a sense of can-do. Sure, all he'd have to do is find a phone, dial 999, and keep alive somehow till the ambulance got here.

Neil shook himself free of the pride he was feeling for being so bloody smart and began to move. He had seen a phone. Where, where, where?

The hallway. He dragged the iron chair behind him, still lashed to the thing, heavy and metal and awkward, and here

343

he was, Neil Mackay, who'd have thought it, walking blindly through his new boss's house in search of a lifeline.

He located the phone on a small table. Backing up, he flipped the receiver off and felt with his fingers . . . nine . . . nine . . . nine . . .

He heard it. Dammit all to hell, he heard it.

Which service do you require?

He knew they'd come now. They always came. Didn't they? No time for ruminating. I am suffocating to death.

He dragged himself back to the kitchen but the chair was heavy and his entire body flooding with lactic acid. The will to live turned grim and iron-red in his mind. It was a sharp blade to grasp at but there was no other option he could rationalise. Blundering in the dark of his mind he backed into the kitchen again, feeling for the smooth features of the centre island. He found the fridge instead, warm under his hands, buzzing with life. His fingers scattered something to the floor, a magnet, perhaps. Neil searched the white spots of spacial memory, short-term placing of things fading now, and turned, sweating, grimacing with panic.

It would look great in our new place. Great for breakfasts, great for dinner parties. The children would love it . . .

Concentrate.

His fingers found the smooth surface of the hob.

Irrelevancies filtered in now, memories, random thoughts, distracting him as the build-up of deadly toxins dropkicked his faculties, his ability to perform even the most simple of tasks reduced to a trembling pile of goo with its hands tied behind its back and its life ebbing ever more quickly away.

Necessity now a shriek in a dying man's head as Neil bit his tongue and slowly, not from fear but from a desire to get things absolutely correct, lowered his head down – because this would do it, it's chemistry, sure it is – to the memory of red. Blind to the fierce luminosity of the halogen hob, vaguely aware of the magmatic heat now blazing away at his latex-covered cheek, consciousness draining; and memories of school, Ratface for Science, the trick with the bunsen burner, football at break, Charlie Millar spinning to the floor, Andrew Crombie's leg stuck out in mid-tackle as the grey rain descended, and the cold wind on the Royal Mile, and Jake's and Liz's smiling faces as he kissed them and the baby inside her and the heat inside him becoming blue in his eyes and the pain overwhelming as he mercifully passed out.

53

Expect the unexpected, that's what Charlie's mind was telling him. When life presents you with a random pattern, roll with it. Life gives us the unexpected turns. Life gives us the windows to see the possible futures for us all.

The forks in the road.

The good news, and the bad.

So don't sweat the small stuff, that's what Mum always said. Her husband worked the rigs, drank too much and gave them both a hard-enough time as it was.

So don't sweat it, Charlie. Even when the world seems upside down.

No more death.

Charlie's mind danced around these notions as he walked with George, curious George, the man of fleeces and so many surprises. There was never just good news with this man. Or an easy life. That was plain.

But despite it all, he trusted him.

Because he was right. He was right about the house. He was right about the cargo plane. He was right about the future getting brighter.

The hike to the lake was a winner. Better than the Pentlands in spring, Charlie judged. A different kind of beauty to Sutherland, Torridon, the craggy wilderness up north; here it sat more serene on the land. You felt it wanted to shake your hand, not break your legs.

The green of the trees hugged the very rim of the lake. Like every body of water in this part of the world, it was black as tar and a mile to the bottom. Glassy, perfect, surrounded by trees and silence.

George was explaining something to him, but his mind was elsewhere. Perhaps this was how life worked. Even with the surprises, the biggest twist that things can spring is that there is no final hairpin.

Things being what they were, Charlie was prepared to accept that as a home win and be done with it.

George kept talking. 'Over there, other side . . .' Paul, that was the name he'd mentioned. Paul Tate. The contact. The point man in all this.

He wondered what he looked like.

The glint of sun on the water made Charlie squint and George was looking at him in a way that suggested he was waiting for Charlie to say something.

'Come again?' he managed.

'Which is it?' George asked again. 'We can cut across here in the boat, or hike around.'

Charlie looked at the boat. It was a small, functional human-propelled vessel. No outboard for security. Two crude wooden benches and a reassuring lack of bilge. Together with Becky he had circumnavigated the Serpentine in London on a similar vessel. He wasn't sure how it would fare in the wilds of British Columbia. George could see Charlie's cogitation and shrugged.

'Look, it's also a beautiful hike. I came over that way.

Come on, it's a little longer, I'm sure he'll still be there by the time we work our way around—'

Charlie listened to his ankle and made limpingly for the boat, tapping his pocket quietly to check the gun was still there.

54

Patricia was on her second week of nights on the trot. Her eyes were bleary and nothing, not even an industrial-strength brew, could open them. The pages of *OK* magazine were passing in and out of focus as they always did this far into the night. Now one of the patients was acting up and it was up to her to calm her down, clean her up, make everything all right as per usual.

Poor thing, though, she thought as she entered the downstairs corridor, backtracking guiltily over her bad mood in an effort to leave no trace. I shouldn't be so miserable. I don't know how lucky I am. She passed through the day room and looked down the grassy verge to the road. The traffic lights were blinking yellow. She wondered whether it was a sign of some sort. Her horoscope had said to look out for the colour as an important element of her week.

It was Helen again, the call had said. Poor Helen, thought Patricia.

She opened the bedroom door and smiled at the girl with red hair and the wisest eyes in the world. The smell of urine in the air; she had wet the bed while crying. The crying was continuing, low and constant moans that resonated through the mattress.

'What's the matter, sweetheart?'

The night-duty supervisor was in there with her already.

'She's talking about her daddy again.'

'Oh, Helen.'

'When's he coming when's he coming?' wailed Helen, full name Helen Peters, twenty-one years old and in need of constant full-time care. 'When's Daddy coming?'

Patricia gently lifted Helen up as she stripped the bed and prepared a new plastic undersheet. 'I told her, Sister, Daddy's already been to her last week.'

Helen cried again as she felt a sponge cleaning her. 'Come on now,' cooed Patricia, 'soon be back in bed.'

'I want to see my Daddy now,' screamed the girl with the wise eyes. 'Pleeeease?'

Patricia was sweating a little now with the effort and keen to help Helen down from the mental ledge she was on.

'Look, Helen, see? Here he is. You can see him in this picture.'

She grabbed one of several framed photographs from the chest of drawers by the wall, and held it up for Helen to see.

'I know it's not the same at all,' continued Patricia, 'but he was here a few days ago, wasn't he? And he'll be here tomorrow night. And once his leg's better you can go back and live with him and Mummy!'

Helen nodded, sniffling slightly, and returned her gaze to the picture in the frame. It was a happy family scene, a birthday group in front of daffodils, and there was Helen smiling next to a man.

A man who didn't resemble George in almost every single way.

55

The boat rocked a little as George pushed off but righted itself by the time he'd pulled the oars back and propelled them across the glassy surface.

Charlie placed the bags of money on the exoskeleton of the boat beneath them, and balanced his firearm between them. He felt it was a little like putting it to bed. The hope burned bright within him that it would stay asleep forever.

Charlie gazed at the scene across the waters. He filled his lungs with the cut-glass air. As his whole life was now a mere reflection of his life with Becky, the moment dissolved the grief inside him.

George kept his eyes on Charlie, rowing slowly but strongly into the centre of the lake.

'You know what the most upsetting thing was, after all, George?'

George grunted no.

'The Service sent someone to the airport,' continued Charlie. 'A therapist. When they knew. She turned up to tell me, you know. At the gate. Planning ahead, caring, sharing and all that. And what do you think she did?'

'She told you?' asked George.

'She got dressed up. I mean, she put on make up, really quite a lot of make up. Putting on her face, as Becky used to say. Now, she wasn't to know this, I mean who would, and you'd think you couldn't make things any worse than the way they were at that moment, but even as she sat me down, George, even as she told me these things, she told me to take a deep breath and I did and blow me down if she wasn't wearing the *same perfume as her!*'

Charlie kept his eyes on the horizon, on the comforting ribbon of green. George shook his head.

'Charlie—'

'"Welcome back to Britain," she was saying. "Oh and by the way, your wife died in a car crash. Here's what she smelled like. See you."'

Charlie lifted his head to the sky, gazed at the canopy of cobalt blue above. A glorious day to finish the grieving. A glorious day to begin again. He was in touch with Life Charlie again. The one Becky had known. The one she had trusted in, the one she had married. And the one who'd been lost on the day she had died.

Charlie was smiling. He'd nearly forgotten how. 'I want to thank you, George,' he said, squinting into a ray of sudden sunlight. 'For everything.'

George did not reply. Charlie turned back to the bags. The gun had gone. He looked up at George.

For some inexplicable reason, George was pointing the gun at Charlie's chest.

'Don't do that,' said Charlie.

George was not smiling.

'Actually, Charlie,' he sighed, 'talking of bad news – I have some for you.'

The sun glistened on the black water.
George had stopped rowing.
Charlie, for now, had stopped breathing.

56

The pub was very ordinary. It stood in a dirty end of a grotty street. Built of brick and London timber, Formica, spit and sawdust, it had originally been called The Axe. Several other public houses had come and gone on the same site. Several murders in the upper rooms in the Thirties, but the upper storeys were destroyed by bombs in the war.

The building as it now stood was 130 years old and very proud of it. But with this age had not come wisdom. This was a selfish building, an out-and-out villain if truth be known. Because it was here that all manner of chaos had been created for a man called Charlie and a man called George.

But no-one ever blames a building. Not for anything. They don't get arrested and they rarely stand trial. Yet they are often the accessories to unprecedented sadness.

In Charlie's case, the building harboured two levels of unexpected outcomes. The product of these was what had led to meeting George; the death of his wife; the end of the life he had known.

When Rose Willetts decided to begin her feudal reign in the Service, a separate accounting process was required. And it worked. The jobs were few and far between. The

Service provided the support. But the paperwork, its culture of secrecy and its pure, glorious inefficiency helped her keep the thing from view for many years.

Anyone who happened to fall into the net and cause problems was dealt with by her alter ego Latham with brutality and efficiency. Like dolphins in tuna nets, they were simply in the wrong place at the wrong time.

She had anticipated problems, of course. Even when forced to shut the whole thing down, in this final loving act of closure, she had foreseen how her colleagues might behave. This was why their end had to come before the network's. Even Latham would be finished. It was just a matter of planning ahead.

But the pub, the pub. How could she have anticipated that? An official operation using Charles Millar, a high-tension and sensitive meet, a mission of high importance; and yet one where his wife managed to drop by with friends from work.

Why she chose that pub it is impossible to say.

Why that day, that time?

In a city of nine million, it was likely precisely because of its unlikelihood. Charlie, of course, on this important mission, was unable to acknowledge her presence.

Blanking your wife does not come without recrimination. How were they to know that on that very same night, Rose had employed George Shaw to rid the Service of another individual in the gents toilets? How was she to know that this woman would write a letter? To *Whom It May Concern*? Circulate it into orbits close enough to draw attention to that pub? To that night? And to the bloody ubiquitous paperwork that would start a blame-filled travelator leading straight back to her?

It was the only thing she could do.

Getting rid of them all. The only thing.

It was only right, in retrospect, that a bureaucratic error saved their lives. The bad news came in buckets. The good news in a thimble. And that was life, and you cannot blame life for what life can do.

So we must blame the pub for what happened.

As well as for what happened next.

57

The boat undulated like a cradle in the silence. It was perfectly calm, perfectly peaceful. And so much going unsaid, as one friend pointed a gun at another.

'I know who killed your wife, Charlie. I know who killed her. The bad news is, it was me.'

The wind sighed. A solitary cloud appeared over the ridge behind George's head. A bird was circling high above. Charlie took it all in, awareness all around, calculating what could come next.

'I was only doing my job.'

Charlie shook his head.

George shifted on the bench, pulled an oar to correct the gentle drift. 'Come on, you've done it too. You do what you're told. In the field, you just *do it*. How was I to know who she was? How was I to know I'd end up with you? What are the chances of that? How the hell do these kinds of things wind up happening to nice people? Come on. Try and look at this from my perspective.'

Charlie said nothing.

'Are you trying?' George asked. He sighed. 'I don't really think you're trying.' He pinched off a headache and adjusted his balance.

The water lapped the sides. The black bags rustled slightly in a gentle breeze.

'If you hadn't said her name, we wouldn't be here.'

'It's my fault, you mean.'

'Yes. In a way. Yes.'

Charlie wondered how easy it would be to drown them both.

'Look. Until you told me her name I was with you all the way. Once I knew, I had to make the decision. I had to. You forced me into this position. I've been weighing it up all this time. We'd both get the money and part our ways. But I knew deep down that wouldn't work.'

'You could let me go.'

'I could. Yes.'

'Do you really have a daughter?'

George stared at him for a moment. Charlie reasoned he could have disarmed him then, a short snap of the leg would send the gun into the water and Charlie fancied himself hand-to-hand with the man, now he knew about the double-joint.

But he didn't want to do that. Not just yet.

'No,' said George. 'I just made that up to make you like me.'

'I'd never find you. You could disappear forever.'

'But here's why I can't. Because there's no guarantee that you won't, at some point, want to end my life. Or hire someone to do so. Or even turn against your nature, you know, and want some of my money.'

Charlie looked like he was listening, so George continued. 'You might get a drug habit, an alcohol habit. You might meet a girl and want to buy her things. Go on a vacation with her. Have a child and provide for their future. And you would start to resent this pleasant, sunburned man who you know without any hint of uncertainty removed your life partner from this planet . . . We both know that there's always something more, always. Even when the chances are low. We've always strived for certainty, Charlie. And that's what I'll be sure of when I shoot you and you die and sink to the bottom of the lake. I'll know, with total certainty, that you won't turn up in my house in the middle of the night and wish me harm. I'm sorry, I am genuinely, truly sorry about all this. I'm just a bad judge of people, I guess. Including myself. I never thought I would go through with this, not after all that you've done for me. But I've been alone so long I don't know how it could possibly work any other way.'

Charlie remembered the face again. George's mask.

The Mercedes full of teenagers.

His eyes had kept hard ahead.

'I'm so sorry about your wife,' he'd said.

George hadn't been empathising.

He'd been *apologising*.

Charlie looked around him in the boat. The sun blazed down now. Summer was on its way. Half a mile to one bank. Half a mile to another. And two miles straight down into the inky embrace of the glacial water.

'So you're going to shoot me.'

There was a look in George's eyes, a measure of sympathy, a measure of the tragically inevitable and a twist of sarcasm, a visual cocktail known simply as *YES*. Loneliness does things to people. Secrets that create that isolation are generally innocent. There is no blame. The standing wave of loneliness in George had created a cocoon. Inside there, George lived, for and of himself. Because there could be no-one else, you lived for no-one else. The pure and almost beautiful levels of selfishness that you attained were also self-preserving. His solitary harmonics were as pure as the music of the spheres. A tone perfectly minor, perfectly singular, perfectly bowed across the lonely people of the world who all knew that note, as it was the soundtrack to their lives.

'Think of it like this,' said George. 'If I pull the trigger, most likely the bullet in this gun will hit you in the heart and kill you.' His voice was level, even calming. 'Now, most people, hit in the heart with a bullet, would most likely die. But it's not *entirely certain*, is it? Not one hundred, you know, per cent.'

Charlie was edging towards the side of the boat as George expounded on this theme further:

'Most people would die but you might *not*. You might be the first, Charlie. You might just be the very first to cheat death like this. Think about that. We prepare for the least likely future outcome and, let's be honest, under these circumstances, that's almost certainly *on the button* of it right there.'

Charlie *was* thinking. But it wasn't in reaction to George's words. He was thinking in and around a memory, a clear but distant one, a scrap of advice his dad once gave him. It was the only thing his father had told him sober that seemed to have stayed with him. Bizarrely enough Forbes Mackinnon had echoed him many years later. The advice was this: *never get into a fight you can't win.*

Charlie was now at the edge of the boat.

'What are you doing, Charlie?'

'I'm about to jump in the water.'

'By which you mean to say, you're not.'

'By which I mean, I am.'

And Charlie launched himself over the side.

Had you been watching from the bank you would have seen a man dive frantically into the inky liquid collected in this ancient valley, later labelled by modern civilisation as a 'lake'. Had you been a fish looking up at Charlie as he entered the water, there would have been something else to see there . . . had you possessed the capacity to see it. An expression of doubt. Of concern. Of something more than evasion and flight. The wonder of possibility. The last shreds of hope and anguish dancing at the edge of his life.

Charlie started swimming under the boat.

He half-thought of capsizing George but knew that the effort would require at least one breath. And his current injuries meant that there was no margin for error at all. As well as that, Charlie was hoping for some distance between himself and the boat before George pulled that trigger.

George sighed, knowing this was the fruitless act of a dead man. And then he was struck by a thought. And checked the clip. Nope – the bullet was still there.

George waited patiently for Charlie to finally surface. The boat was rocking with the ripples from his plunge. George kept his knees slightly bent, absorbing the shocks, keeping the thing as level as he could. Scanning the surface for signs of life.

It didn't take long to find it. Some thirty feet away, a trail of bubbles announced themselves on the surface. Charlie's head followed soon after. George took aim. George was a crack shot. At this range he couldn't miss.

He wept a tear for his lost friend.

Then he steadied his hand.

And pulled the trigger.

58

The good news was, the hammer hit the pin.

59

The bad news—
    Well, it depended on what you were holding.

Because the hammer, in hitting the pin, also hit the fingernail-sized wedge of C4 plastic explosive which Charlie had placed there. In the bathroom, in the solitude, it seemed the logical end to no more death.

Whether he used it, or someone else used it, Charlie wanted the outcome to be the same. Like so much nitro-glycerin for the fishmonger's hammer.

They found Charlie's clothes on the southeastern shore. Someone had recently opened a café there and had complained bitterly about Fate.

Of George there was no sign. Simply the broken pieces of an otherwise innocent boat.

There had been two witnesses. Of sorts.

The first had been a man called Paul Tate. He had worked with George over the years and found him to be a pointless bore who nevertheless knew the location of a large amount of money. He'd welcomed his calls in the previous week, once from a payphone in London, the other from Cambridge, and had been planning to kill him once he got to the rendezvous. But after hearing the explosion he looked on the bright side and saved the money on a bullet. The man had already cost him four through the business in the theme park.

The only witness who could have helped the Mounties with their enquiries happened to be 1500 foot above the lake at the time of the explosion. Dean wasn't the type of guy to help the authorities with any kind of enquiries whatsoever, as enquiries often lead to house searches and people writing numberplates down and that kind of behaviour can some-times cause all kinds of problems down the line for a young man in a hurry.

Instead, he nodded, smiled, and said nothing other than the fact that he heard a loud bang but was focused pretty much on not crashing into a mountain.

The only hint of something awry as far as the local Canadian press was concerned was the mysterious appear-ance of several thousand dollars in the stomach of a prize brown trout that was hooked in the lake two days later. The locals gave it not another thought.

Except one. He'd been a bit baked, for sure, but Dean was pretty convinced about what he'd seen up there.

And what he hadn't told the cops.

Ten seconds or so after leaping from the cliff he'd caught a large thermal that he'd taken gladly, one that had arced him in a lazy spiral right up and over the lake.

When the bang resounded off the pines, he'd looked down. A ripple on the black waters. Some insane individuals occasionally tried to swim the width of the lake but normally waited till summer. And usually didn't explode, either.

He'd banked left and tried to swoop back around but a thermal only took him higher. By the time he'd arced back round, the ripple had gone.

But on his way back across the lake his attention had been drawn to another area of sand. He'd looked closer. He wasn't entirely sure, but he thought he saw a one-armed man limping into the trees.

60

The man's brogues clicked on the hard linoleum. He *clicked* past reception, *clacked* up the stairs, presuming as he always did that news of his arrival had preceded him. Normally, his eyes would twinkle with mischief. Today – indeed, for the last few weeks – there had been a certain lack of sparkle and he was not best pleased to be inside a hospital. He rather distrusted the things. The news today had cheered him, however. It would be good to see the laddie.

'Gentlemen,' he said, as he passed a couple of bemused nurses. '*Ladies*,' he added, to the small gaggle of junior doctors at the entrance to the long-stay burns unit.

The news had taken a while to percolate back from Canada. A week or two after that, a CSS notice arrived at Central Service Despatch. And soon the corridors of Euston Buildings began to buzz with gossip and sadness at the deaths of Charlie and George. Charlie, the innocent caught up in the confluence of Rose Willetts's treachery. George, the good man gone bad, and made deadly by simply doing what he was told.

Forbes was the messenger, now, to the hero of the hour. He hoped he would stay decorous.

Neil heard the news and wept hot tears that stung the

burns on his cheek. Forbes sat on the low orange chair, ankle hair tufting over the lips of his socks.

'Rose herself is also gone,' he explained. 'Her desk is now yours. When you're ready.' A broken neck, Forbes elaborated, and a textbook move if he may say so. There would be no charges but bravery. Neil was unmoved and sorry for everything. He asked Forbes about Bill Skelton's funeral. Forbes reported that everyone was hoping Neil would feel well enough to attend. Neil said he would try his best.

Forbes smiled in support and slid several brown envelopes onto the bedside table. 'Your post,' he explained, and without another word turned on his leather soles and left. Neil waited for the clicks to recede before closing his eyes.

Liz and the kids came to visit him later that day and Liz was strangely numb, Neil thought. She was delighted to see him as ever, the baby was well and happy and kicking inside her, Jake was full of beans but not too full, not so much of a handful as to bring on the migraines, not like before.

But still, Neil was unsure.

The doctors had assured him his constitution had saved him. Perhaps even his positive attitude. He always tried to see the good things in life. He'd passed out twice, once from a blow, the second time from hypoxia. His brain wasn't supposed to work properly after that.

Only he could tell for sure. And he wasn't sure.

Liz *was* feeling odd. She didn't want to tell him but she simply couldn't work out how to frame it. For reasons she couldn't actually explain a large sum of money had turned up in their bank account without warning.

Jake hit Daddy on the top of the head but Daddy just smiled back at him and blew him a kiss. He was adamant that he was the one to open the envelopes on the bedside table and Neil had no energy to argue. As he placed each envelope and notelet carefully on the blankets, Neil noticed a small postcard sitting amongst the official stationery.

He asked Jake if he wouldn't mind passing him the card with the palm tree on it. Jake was only too pleased to help. Neil looked at the back. The postmark and stamp were from Panama. The date put it at six days ago.

Apart from his address, a single word on the postcard made Neil grin. It was Charlie's writing. One solitary word. It said simply:

'ANSWERS.'

There they were, on a postcard.

Neil kept laughing even when it started to hurt.

61

Karl was twenty-three but still felt seventeen. This was partly because his emotional intelligence hadn't really progressed past that stage. But the new employee in New Mexico's Premier Photo Shop seemed pretty pleased to be alive. This was in stark contrast to most of Karl's world view and it irked him so badly that he had begun to carve the word 'WHY?' into his area of countertop. A small improvement, he felt, on his last effort, which had been the word 'BRYAN'. He didn't know why he'd carved that. He didn't even know anyone called Bryan. Life posed so many mysteries and inconsistencies for Karl that he usually preferred to get stoned and forget all about them.

This new guy was sort of fun but talked weird stuff. He was local, for sure, from his accent – Karl knew people, at least. But his school must have been the booger-nosed private one out of town, because no-one really knows that much about stuff in this town and gets away with it. The weirdest thing of all was that he seemed cool and all, but the fact that nothing ever happened in this county never seemed to rattle his cage one bit. In fact, the dude sort of seemed to kind of like it.

'So what's going on?' asked Charlie.

Karl shrugged.

Charlie had made his way up here with more or less full legality. Large amounts of money could buy you things in the United States, that was certain. Money could not buy you happiness, it was true, but it could underwrite a large amount of sadness and that suited Charlie just fine. He wondered if Neil ever got his postcard.

'It's about time to clean the infernal machine,' grumbled Karl.

'Whose turn is it?' asked Charlie.

'Let me consult the oracle of doom.'

Karl pulled out a paper calendar that depicted Monster Trucks. May's selection was the Bigfoot 15 chassis with the #34 Firestone/Tonka Team Big Foot bodywork. Today's date revealed the letter 'K' and the news, from Karl's position at least, was not good.

'Dammit to hell and back again,' he said.

'I'll do it if you like,' said Charlie.

'You can't do that,' said Karl.

'Why not?'

Karl tried to think of a reason but failed. Somehow all he could think of were Kimberly Mason's breasts. She was hot and tasty all right, like a tamale.

'I really don't mind,' smiled Charlie.

'I don't know.'

'Tell you what,' said Charlie, liberating a quarter from the tip jar. 'We'll flip a coin for it.' Karl shrugged and walked away.

The coin flipped in the air, catching as it did so a ray of late afternoon sun. A song came on the radio. Charlie had heard it only once before. He had been seventeen and had wondered if the book of his life would be as blank and full of possibility as that song.

And as he listened, he realised.

The coin was still in the air.

It just stayed there, spinning and spinning. Charlie was laughing now, wide-eyed and astounded. No-one could believe that outcome, no-one would ever believe it. It was here, just for him, just this once. Just this life.

And for the first time in a very long while, Charlie found himself looking forward to the future.

Heads, tails.

Heads, tails.

Heads, tails.

Acknowledgements

Thank you, thank you, thank you. To Jonny Geller for persuading me that novels are a lot of fun. To Ben Hall, who told me Jonny was probably telling the truth. To Nick Sayers and everyone at Hodder for knocking me off my chair by believing in those words, and patiently waiting while those words were put into a much better order. To Mari Evans for her momentous foresight and taste. To Annie Dudek for her love, encouragement, support. To Tess Cuming, Ben Stoll, Mark Evans and the Mirren Clan for all their help and advice. To Mike Baker for ballistics tips. To all my unlucky friends who endured the process vicariously through me. To my luckier friends who wondered where the hell I got to. Sorry, I was writing this. To my parents and my brother and his family for love and understanding that constantly shocks and awes. To Harry Quinn, for inspiring. To Josh and Christine, for putting up with the constant tapping sound. To Gandalf for invaluable phreaking research. To Stephen Garrett, Jane Featherstone and the rest of Kudos for your friendship and encouragement throughout my career. And to you, the reader. Novels *are* a lot of fun, I've learned. To read.